THE
LAST
LUNAR
WITCH

S.F. HENNE

Originally published September, 2023 as The Witch of the Lunar Order by Tara Davis

First Paperback Edition May 2024

ISBN 978-1-964791-00-5 (Paperback Edition)

Published by Ink & Magic Books

Cover Designed by Trif Book Design

Developmental Editing by Hart Bound Editing

Formatted in Atticus

ALSO BY S.F. HENNE

<u>The Lunar Order Chronicles</u>

The Last Lunar Witch

Forged in Moonlight

Sworn in Twilight

Eclipsed in Darkness - *coming soon*

<u>From the Academy: Cursed Curriculums and Lessons in Lore Anthology</u>

Shield by Duty

<u>Pronunciation</u>

Nyssa Thornheart – niss-ah thawn-haat

Tobin – tOH-bihn

Voren – vaw-ren

Zola – zOH-lah

Beylin – BAY-lin

Indra Terral – IN-druh t-uh-r-EH-l

Rynac Terral – RYE-nak t-uh-r-EH-l

Carmen – kaar-muhn

Danika – DAN-ick-ah

Kaelan Renatus – KAY-lan Reh-NAH-t-us

Nathaniel Einheri – nuh-thAEN-yuhl in-HAIR-yee

Astrid – AST-rid

Thaddeus Flamebury - thAE-dee-uhs flaym-buh-ree

Selene – suh-leen

Aelia – eye-lee-uh

Terrarum – teh-ruh-rum

Trutina – tru-Tee-nah

Arkirith – Ah-k-ear-ith

Dedicated to me

Because without me this book never would have been written.
I mean I did all the hard work . . .
And no one ever reads these.

Chapter One

My alchemy professor always told me, "Success is built on commitment and unwavering resolve." And though I might be committed, my resolve to break into the restricted section was wavering. Not to mention, if security discovered me, I'd be expelled from the Alchemy Guild.

Shafts of golden morning light filtered through the stained glass windows, illuminating the dust motes dancing in the air, and leaving me few spots to hide. The towering shelves stood sentinel, burdened with rows of tomes, their spines cracked and faded with age.

Wedged between shelves, I shifted to find a comfortable position. Near impossible as books dug into my back.

The silence pressed against me, broken only by the soft rustle of pages, the creak of ancient wood, and the shuffling steps of Pyter.

The wizened librarian was a fount of knowledge when it came to his books, but age dulled the shifter's senses and he lost track of his surroundings.

I tamped down my guilt at the thought of exploiting him. After all, the Alchemy Guild's library in Arkirith stored a wealth of knowledge from across the land, and hidden somewhere downstairs was the information I needed.

The formula for a potion that would save me.

I huddled deeper into my black hoodie, pulling the hood's strings tighter to further conceal the coral pink hair that marked me as a witch. My fingers rubbed over the smooth stone of my necklace to settle my nerves, and I sent up a silent thank you to Aelia that they hadn't installed security cameras yet.

Stealing at night might seem preferable, but I'd have more security measures to bypass.

After all, I was an alchemist, not a professional thief.

Low-ranking members of the Guild like me didn't have access to the restricted section, so I'd volunteered to help in the library to scope out the place. Climbing the ranks took too much time. It was a miracle I'd survived this long.

The air felt heavier in this section, charged with an aura of power and knowledge that prickled against my skin. But I wasn't here for any of that. What I needed was locked below in the masters-only section; they kept the best books there, sealed away from prying eyes.

I'd stalked these shelves for the past month, searching for any leads, hunting for a glimmer of hope that I could save my magic. Each day chipped away at my resolve as my stomach coiled into a tighter knot. Down those twisting stairs was the only place left to search.

And what if it's not there? What if you hit another dead end?

I scowled. That traitorous voice. It liked to whisper in the quiet moments. I ignored it, because if I failed, if I didn't find a way to fix myself . . .

No. I swiped those thoughts away. I couldn't waver. Not now.

Other races might accept their declining magic, but not witches. Was it too much to ask for my kind to accept me at last?

Most of all, I hated fearing that I might hurt those I cared for.

Again.

Determination swelled within me as my fingers brushed over the cold metal of the keys I had "borrowed".

It was too late to turn back.

The echo of Pyter's footsteps receded, followed by the click of a lock as the librarian returned to his desk.

I crawled out of my hiding spot, my pulse thundering.

Glancing at the time on my phone, I had fifteen minutes before shift change, and Pyter noticed his keys were missing.

I inched toward the thick metal bars, lusting after the forbidden knowledge locked below. This close to the gate, the air thrummed with latent magic, warded to protect the knowledge within.

On instinct, I reached into my pocket and gripped my conduit—an essential tool for any witch. Like most witches, I opted for the traditional wand-style conduit to aid in directing spells and the flow of magic.

If I'd been a skilled full spectrum witch, I might have been able to craft a spell to break in. But sometimes the mundane option worked just as well.

I slid the key into the lock; the metallic clink was deafening in the quiet, and my breath caught as I stepped inside.

Orbs of light hung in the air, glowing brighter as I neared the bottom of the staircase, which descended into the heart of the space.

My steps faltered at the sight.

I found myself surrounded by towering shelves, their curved forms creating a mesmerizing spiral that stretched into the shadows. Each one laden with ancient tomes and scrolls, their secrets bound within weathered covers.

My sense of trepidation mingled with awe.

The sheer magnitude of the collection was staggering. What hidden knowledge was trapped down here? What secrets waited to be discovered?

My heart skipped a beat, but not with fear.

Focus, Nyssa. Time was against me.

During my shifts, I'd rifled through the card catalog for this section and jotted down a few titles of interest. But the sheer volume of books suggested many were unlisted or stricken from the catalog.

Just what kind of dangerous secrets did the Guild hide down here? And why didn't they have better security?

A musty scent wrapped around me; a mixture of aged parchment infused with the faint tang of magic.

Twisting around the next shelf, I spotted the first book on my list and flicked through until I found the section devoted to magical binding.

These were dangerous potions; in the wrong hands they could cause great harm. But the only person's magic I wanted to bind was my own. I'd be doing the realm a favor.

Worthless.

My lip curled as I snapped the book shut and shoved it back. I'd found that formula in the witch archives. It was hardly dangerous enough for the master-only section. I'd experimented with these potions, and each had failed.

The next book had a few formulations I copied out. None provided long-term solutions, but they might buy me some extra time.

Frustration gnawed at me as I scoured the last book on my list, but I was almost out of time and luck.

What if fixing me was impossible? Was I being foolish, searching for a way to suppress my volatile powers rather than have my connection to magic severed?

No!

A witch without magic . . . that was a fate worse than death.

Heat flushed through me, and my heart hammered as if it could outrun my fear.

I fumbled for the talisman in my pocket to suppress my magic. The cold, heavy device was a reassuring weight in my palms as my fingers trailed over the smooth amethyst at the center.

Taking slow, deliberate breaths, I calmed my mind, casting out the anxious thoughts. The magic within me smoldered for a moment before winking out.

My shoulders drooped as I inspected the talisman. Its original purpose was to control imprisoned witches and nullify their powers.

My brother had acquired it for me through not-so-legal means, and it was my last line of defense against myself. The gem absorbed the magic of the user when touching their skin. As long as the stone had no cracks, it would continue to function.

Squeezing my eyes shut, I shook my head. I needed a permanent solution. It was only a matter of time before my powers grew beyond anyone's control.

A shiver of magic whispered through the air, and I stilled.

Had I triggered an alarm? Or had someone realized the keys were missing?

I needed to move. Fast.

Pocketing the talisman, I shoved my gloves on, cursing myself for forgetting to wear them. Crafted from a flame-resistant fabric, they would protect anything I was holding, at least for a short while. And here I was, surrounded by priceless—and flammable—tomes, and I hadn't taken the most basic precaution.

A blue glow darted between the shelves, and I froze midstep.

A pair of bright sapphire eyes peered around the corner at me. Pointed ears twitched in interest as the cobalt vulpine padded over to me, their bushy tail swishing in excitement.

"How did you get in here?" I hissed. "Little fox, you need to stop following me."

It was my fault for offering them part of my breakfast last week. The fox had followed me all the way home, but I'd shooed them away before they entered my apartment building.

Since then, I kept seeing blue out of the corner of my eye and knew the fox was stalking me. But why would it follow me here?

My phone vibrated in my pocket, an alarm for the shift change.

Shit. I needed to get out of here. I hurried toward the staircase, but the fox darted between my feet and I almost tripped.

"What are you doing?" I whispered. Was I really talking to a fox? "I need to leave before I'm caught."

The fox blinked up at me with far too much intelligence behind their eyes, before racing away. They paused, looking back as if waiting for me to follow.

"I don't have time for this," I said, starting off again.

The fox yipped. My heart missed a beat.

"Could you *not*?"

The fox spun in a circle and then darted down another row. I hesitated, debating with myself. They were no ordinary fox. Vulpines had a touch of magic, but that didn't mean I should trust them.

A heavy thump made me flinch, and I rushed toward the sound, fearing the fox had been injured.

An ancient tome lay sprawled on the ground. The little fox appeared unharmed as they sniffed the book.

Swearing under my breath, I scooped up the tome and tucked it back into its spot on the shelf. I was ready to escape when the fox yipped again.

"What?" I hissed.

As if the tome had a mind of its own, it slid from its place and tumbled to the ground.

What in all the hells?

I picked it up again, but when I turned back, there was no open space on the shelf. I checked the shelves below, but they were all full.

A tremor of magic vibrated against my hand.

Great, I've awoken a magical tome in the restricted section.

My gloved fingers trailed over the letters on the cover, but the words were in an unfamiliar language.

Magic pulsed in response to my touch, the sensation almost familiar. A deep longing welled up within me, my breath catching. Could this be just what I'd been hoping for?

Power stirred in my chest.

Shit.

I jerked back, trying to fling the book away, but it refused to leave my hand. The magic within the tome stilled, and my powers responded in kind.

My heart hammered, a frantic beat against my ribs.

Whatever magic this book contained, it called to my own. Which terrified me even more.

But what if it holds the answers?

Voices echoed down the stairwell.

Oh Goddess, they're coming.

Footsteps thundered down the stairs, and I pressed myself against the shelves.

How was I going to get out? Why was I such a useless witch?

Fear ignited in my chest, snapping me out of my spiraling thoughts. Heat blazed through me, faster than last time. The tome tumbled from my grip as I scrambled for the talisman.

No, no, no.

Heat scorched my lungs as flames licked my skin. Power built in my chest until it ached. Visions of a wall of fire pressing in filled my mind.

No! Not now!

Stumbling away from the flammable shelves, I wrapped my arms around my body and dropped to the ground.

The talisman bit into my skin as I squeezed hard, willing it to smother the wild magic that burned through my veins and seared my throat. I shoved at the magic, trying to push it back down, but it ignored my command.

Why can't I control it? Why do I always fail?

Something cracked. Then the heat ebbed, the talisman ice-cold in my grip as my body shuddered. The last flicker of magic faded, leaving an empty hollowness in my chest. I squeezed my eyes shut as if that could stop the tears.

Why couldn't I be normal? Why was my magic—the supposed divine blessing of Aelia—so broken?

And here I thought I was improving. I hadn't had a flare up in months. But I'd become too complacent, enjoying my new life in the city and living as if I were a regular magical being.

Of course, my magic had decided to put me in my place, latching onto my wild emotions.

Useless.

A wet nose pressed against my cheek, pulling me back to reality. The mournful eyes of the fox watched me.

"I'm okay," I whispered. But as I sat up, fear gripped me.

The grains of the shattered gemstone fell through my fingers; the talisman destroyed.

A soft pulse of magic emanated from the tome, a soothing vibration that washed over me. It didn't appear to be damaged, and I hugged it against my chest. I was out of options. The talisman had been my last line of protection.

The fox's ears perked up, flicking around. Right, I wasn't alone down here.

Not the best time for a breakdown, Nyssa.

Tucking away the spent talisman, I peered around the corner.

A burly guard stood at the base of the staircase, blocking my only escape route, and the radio clipped to their uniform meant backup was only a call away.

The guard's sharp, angular features and onyx-black skin marked them as an oread, a nymph of stone and mountains.

I chewed on my lip.

I'd never make it past them—no one ever picked a fight with an oread, not unless they enjoyed broken bones.

Something brushed against my leg, and I found the fox staring up at me. Whatever the vulpine was trying to convey was lost on me.

It darted out into the open, and I almost yelled after it.

Guess it was abandoning me to my fate.

"Stop right there," the guard yelled. I froze. "Hey!"

Heavy feet pounded closer, and I braced, ready to be discovered.

"Get that fox!" another voice called out.

The footsteps echoed off the towering bookshelves, growing more distant with each second. I peeked around the corner.

The guard was gone.

Had the fox done that for me?

I raced for the stairs, trying to keep my steps light. I fumbled for the keys, unlocking the gate with so much noise that I half expected the rest of the security team to rush in.

As the gate clicked shut, the shouts from below let me know they still hadn't caught my cheeky little friend.

I rushed away from the restricted area as murmuring voices came from the front of the library.

Slipping through the next gate, I hid away in the back corner and paused to catch my breath.

Horror spiked through me.

I'd just stolen a book. Breaking in was one thing, but stealing?

Even if it's for a good cause?

The tome thrummed in my grip. Would they believe me if I explained the tome had wanted to be stolen?

I rolled my eyes. That would go down just as well as my other explanation.

I couldn't deny I wanted to read it. And what if this book could help me control my wild magic? Then I wouldn't need the binding potion . . . if a formula strong enough even existed.

Since I was already halfway there, I decided to become a full-fledged thief before getting caught. But first, I needed to ditch the keys.

I found a librarian's cart loaded with books. Making sure no one was around, I slipped the keys under the pile at the bottom and scampered away.

I pulled off my hoodie and wrapped it around the stolen tome, walking along as if it were any other day and I was just a normal person. I swallowed hard as I slipped behind the counter and into the staff room.

"Finished studying for today?" the paper-thin voice of Pyter asked.

Only staff members were allowed in the small locker room, but as an occasional worker, I kept my belongings here. I plastered on a smile as I turned to face him. He was searching through his coat pockets and offered me a kind smile.

"I have to run to an appointment," I said, clutching the hidden tome tighter. "Are you alright?"

"Just misplaced my keys," he said, waving me away.

Guilt sank like a stone in my gut. I was a terrible person.

I rushed to my locker and stuffed the book and hoodie inside my bag. Clutching the strap, I hurried back out but paused at the door.

"Did you check your cart?" I asked Pyter.

"Good thinking."

He shuffled off as I darted for the exit. Rushing through the massive stone archway, my steps echoed off the polished tiled floor as loud as my pounding heart.

Crisp spring air greeted me as I hurried out of the Alchemy Guild and spilled onto the bustling city street. No shouts or racing security guards followed, but the tome was a heavy weight at my side. It had better be worth the risk.

I wiped away the sweat that threatened to drip into my eyes and prayed that this time I'd found the answers I needed.

That I'd found a way to change my fate.

Chapter Two

With a glance over my shoulder for pursuers, I ducked down a side street. Even though I was several blocks from the Guild, my heart still bounced off my ribcage. Nor could I escape the sense of impending doom that nipped at my heels.

Then again, that could've just been guilt from stealing.

The spring sun streamed through the tree branches, but did little to diminish the scorching temperatures. Witches relished the heat. The Goddess of the sun was our patron, after all.

The air buzzed with laughter and conversation, overlaid by the faint hum of traffic, as people strolled along. Life under the embrace of the sweltering sun.

Such a far cry from my home city. In Arkirith, many different races went about their business and lived as one community. None of them cast me a second glance.

I knew I should head back to my apartment—to hide the tome—but all that waited for me was silence and my thoughts . . . and the terrifying reality of what I'd just done.

My stomach twisted with dread, but I shoved the thoughts away and turned down the next street. Out here, I was just another citizen going about my day. Catching glimpses of the shops, I wondered if I'd ever enjoy such independence.

I'd moved to the city, not to steal books, but for the opportunity. The Alchemy Guild was a wealth of knowledge, and I hoped to open an alchemy shop of my own. But I needed to fix my magic first. And if I wanted to stay here, I required a new plan before I was homeless. Guild contracts were lacking, both in quantity and pay. What I needed was regular clients, but I still had no idea how to find them.

A shiver of magic skittered over my skin. My breath rushed out as I scrambled toward an alley. Had they found me?

With my head low, I pushed through the crowd, muttering weak apologies until I broke through. I pressed my back against the brick wall; my hands shook as I tried to figure out what to do next. Run or hide?

The energy pulsed again, only softer. A poster hung on the opposite wall, and I wouldn't have noticed it except for the faint aura of enchantment. I swiped a hand across my face and huffed. A magical poster had almost scared me to death.

Definitely not cut out for a life of crime.

I brushed my fingers over the poster. "Help Wanted: Full-Time Barista Needed." Magic surged beneath my touch and within my bag, and I jerked away. If this tome kept it up, they'd catch me soon enough.

Time to go home before I had a heart attack.

I hurried down the alley and nearly jumped out of my skin when my phone rang. With a groan, I answered. He always had the best timing.

"Hello Tobin."

"Little sister," he replied, never one to pass up an opportunity to remind me. "Have you booked your flight home yet?"

"Why? Do you miss me that much?" I said with acidic sweetness.

"Haven't you grown weary of the noise and all those people?"

For the last twenty-one years, I'd lived in Myrite. But the largest witch city paled in comparison to Arkirith. After my first day here, it was clear I'd been sheltered. Unlike the other magical races, witches kept themselves isolated. We were the last race that still had broad access to magic, and the fear that our powers were declining put our leadership on edge.

"It hasn't even been two months," I said, ignoring the little voice that whispered, *And you're already running out of money.* "You had a year off after graduation."

"Yes, but I traveled across the continent, visiting all the major hubs, meeting new people and having new experiences."

I rolled my eyes. He'd spent his year partying and dating new women in each city. But he had that luxury. Tobin was a full spectrum witch with his pick of any career path. He didn't risk punishment for one slip of control.

Witches had access to six branches of magic, but in every generation, fewer full spectrum witches were born.

And then there was me.

My parents had endlessly tried to "fix" me, hunting for a way to tame my wild magic. But the volatile power that ran through my veins resisted.

Over the years, I'd learned to stabilize it by using a spell array. Otherwise, I kept it tucked away, repressed that part of me, and channeled everything into my alchemy. But I needed a long-term solution.

"It's safer for me here. This is the only chance I'll get to . . . sort out my problem. I can make a life here."

"Nyssa," he growled.

Great, I'd activated big brother mode.

"You need to be careful."

You mean like not stealing a book from the restricted section?

"I know," I muttered.

I always had to be extra cautious, ever since that night just after my thirteenth birthday. That night I glimpsed a vision of my future, an all-consuming fire raging around me, intent on destroying me. My own magic turned against me.

I'd confided in Tobin all those years ago. He'd protected me from myself and had later helped to convince our parents to let me move away. They still believed it was just for alchemy.

"This is my one chance, Tobin."

"You'll have opportunities later—"

"No, I won't," I snapped, and then a weary sigh escaped me. "I made a deal with Mum and Dad. I can live here for a year to pursue alchemy. If I establish my business and prove that I can survive on my own with no 'accidents', they'll allow me to remain. Otherwise, I'll have to go back."

Despite being an adult, I was burdened by the weight of my family name that stifled my freedom. Not to mention my parents' high-ranking positions and the scrutiny that came with that.

Only away from the politics and the witch population could I shed those restrictions and live how I wanted.

"Would it be so bad to come home?"

I gnawed on the corner of my lip as I veered into a small park, following the gravel path that twisted between the trees.

A heavy, earthy scent clung to the air. A rainstorm was brewing.

"The council was already breathing down my neck. And that last brush with the Inquisitors . . ."

I swallowed hard around the lump in my throat. It had been far too close. I still had nightmares about that night.

"I can't live with that constant fear. Here in Arkirith, I feel like I can actually breathe for the first time. I'm not under constant scrutiny."

Volatile magic was dangerous. I mean, it's right there in the name. Inquisitors were specialized witches with the authority to hunt those with volatile or dark magic. To capture and strip them of their powers.

After my vision, I could understand why, but that didn't mean I'd accept it as my fate.

Last time the Inquisitors had detected one of my unstable spells, Tobin had shielded me. He'd cast a powerful spell to conceal the aftereffects of mine, taking the blame for the surge and risking his own reputation.

Returning home would mean risking my magic every minute of every day. I knew my parents wanted me to turn myself in willingly, believing that would protect me. But surrendering my magic would take away my one passion, the only thing that had kept me sane over the years. My alchemy.

"You can't protect me forever," I whispered.

Even if he tried, I couldn't let him. He had his own life to live, his own legacy to build. It wasn't fair to ask so much of him. We both deserved freedom.

Tobin was silent for a long time. "How are you doing with money?"

I winced. My parents and I had argued too many times to count. I'd refused their money to fund this trip, thinking I was taking some moral high ground. More likely, it was stubbornness and stupidity. I'd never lived on my own and failed to understand how much it cost.

I made a noncommittal noise when my eyes snagged on the same poster fluttering on a lamppost. I traced my fingers over it again, but there was no surge of magic. "Help Wanted: Full/Part Time Barista/Baker Needed." I squinted. Did the other poster say that?

"Have you found any information at the Alchemy Guild?" Tobin asked.

"Not yet."

I might love my brother, but I wouldn't admit what I'd done. He wouldn't believe me anyway. I always did what I was told and never broke the rules.

"You know I love you, Nyssa. I'm just trying to look out for you. I thought you'd take this year to enjoy yourself. Get this dream of alchemy out of your system. In the end, you knew it was a long shot. Come home where we can protect you. I know you'll find something else to devote yourself to."

Annoyance sharpened within me, its edges hardening in my chest. Of course, he didn't understand. He excelled at anything he put his mind to. Magic was second nature to him.

Alchemy was all I had. All I wanted.

"I don't want any of that," I shot back. "I'm sick of doing whatever Mum and Dad want so they can hide their broken daughter. Can't you let me have this one year to live my life? Before . . ."

The rest of the words died on my lips. I couldn't even utter it, fearing it would become a reality.

Tobin sighed. "I want you to succeed and find a way. But I'm worried about you. Maybe you should come home."

My patience snapped like a brittle twig. "You're supposed to be on my side, supporting me!"

"I am on your side. But I'm also a realist. Your magic is dangerous and we're not there to intervene. In a big city with minimal warding, how many people could you hurt?"

I flinched, hating the truth of his words as my frustration boiled, hot and violent inside me. "This is my passion, my calling. I won't give it up without a fight."

No matter how hard my family tried, they could never understand my situation.

I lowered my voice so no one would overhear. "How would you like to forfeit all your magic?"

"I don't want to be the bad guy, but you need to be honest with yourself. Maybe it's for the best."

"For the best?" I repeated, failing to keep the hurt from my voice. How could he say that?

A buzzing filled my ears, drowning out the rest of his words. My own flesh and blood didn't believe in me anymore.

I jabbed the button to hang up. Why couldn't he understand how much this meant? Was it unreasonable to expect support from my family? A chance to save my magic?

The first fat raindrops splattered on the ground and stole away the warmth of the day. I rushed down the street, but the storm refused to wait; a deluge of rain cascaded over the city. I ducked into a bus shelter to avoid being drenched.

Tobin's words echoed in my mind, bringing an undercurrent of doubt that I couldn't shake. Did he believe I was destined to fail? Was I just a fool chasing an impossible dream, while those around me were simply trying to shield me from the inevitable disappointment?

Rain hammered the shelter's roof as the wind whipped through the air as if it had a personal vendetta against umbrellas.

A poster flapped on the wall, the tape doing a valiant job to keep the paper in place. "Help Wanted: Full/Part Time Barista/Baker Needed $20/hr."

My gaze snagged on the starting pay. Perhaps working part-time during the day would allow me to support myself until I could afford to open my alchemy business.

I worried my lip between my teeth. Working at a coffee shop did have potential. It wouldn't cut into my alchemy time, as I brewed at night, but I didn't have a clue what being a barista entailed. I was a Thornheart. My family deemed summer jobs beneath us.

My phone vibrated with a notification from my bank. Fearing I'd overdrawn, I clicked on it.

Tobin had transferred money into my account.

Anger bubbled through my veins. Was this his way of apologizing? Throwing money at the problem until it went away? I hated that I needed it, but I refused to touch it. I'd do this on my own.

For the best.

The words reverberated in my mind like the drums of war, mirrored in the rumble of thunder above. Was it for the best to be stripped of my magic? To have all my hard work and dedication to alchemy thrown away? For the best to never craft potions again?

Why couldn't he understand my desire to be a normal witch? Was that too much to ask?

Magic churned deep in my chest as if a storm brewed within me, thrumming in time with the tome in my bag. Yet I didn't fear it.

I snatched the help wanted poster and plugged the address into my phone. I would prove them all wrong.

Fueled by determination, I stepped into the pouring rain, shooting a fierce glare at the dark clouds. It appeared the world conspired against me today.

My apprehension and anxieties took a backseat to my unwavering conviction. I trudged forward; the rain seeping through my shoes and squelching with every step. *Damn spring storms.* At least the tome was safe in my enchanted bag, which protected the contents from water, fire, and impact.

In defiance of the rain pelting my face, I halted and stared in wonder at the coffee shop. *"Divine Coffee"* had been hand-painted in shimmering gold letters above the entrance.

Warm light spilled out of the windows, warding off the chill of the storm. The rich wooden interior evoked a cozy ambiance, its swirling colors reminiscent of fresh espresso.

Delicate plants dangled from the ceiling, their trailing vines eager to hear the conversations of the patrons below.

An inexplicable force tugged me closer, luring me inside, but I paused a few steps from the entrance as a customer left. I almost missed the horns poking out from her jet-black hair as she dipped her head.

The heady aroma of freshly ground coffee curled out behind her. The scent conjured memories of gossiping with my friends over a mocha at our local coffee shop.

As I reached for the door handle, I winced at my reflection. My coral-colored hair was now plastered to my face after all my hard work curling it this morning. Why had I thought I needed to look my best to break and enter?

I lifted my chin and squared my shoulders, projecting an air of confidence as I gripped the handle.

I can do this.

No one was going to decide the course of my life except me. And I would do whatever it took to prove that I could control my power.

The spark of confidence fizzled as my hand shook so hard I feared the door would rattle. Worse, I was certain I was about to throw up.

I can't do this.

Though I desperately wanted to run, my legs wouldn't budge.

No, I can't back down.

I'd just broken into the masters-only section of the library. Why did *this* feel so daunting?

Do you want to give up your dream?

I didn't. I needed an income because I liked to eat, but what if I failed? What if they took one look at me and rejected me on the spot?

I looked as if I'd just been fished out of the Torrens River. I shuddered, brushing off the visualization before it could add to my anxiety.

Since I'd moved here, I'd experienced one failure after another, one step forward and two steps back. Maybe Tobin was right. At least at home, I had my family and didn't have to endure the scrutiny of strangers.

"Are you going in?"

Startled by the unexpected voice, I whirled around.

Spiky hair, a striking blend of silver and blue, complimented their androgynous face. The pearlescent sheen of their skin contrasted with their stormy gray irises, framed by azure sclera reminiscent of the ocean's depths.

A water nymph!

Excitement bubbled up within me. I'd never expected to meet one in the city, and I was gawking like an idiot. Could I be any more embarrassing?

"Sorry," I stuttered, holding the door open for them.

They cast me a curious look but nodded with gratitude before entering.

Come in, a voice beckoned, compelling me forward.

Warmth enveloped me like a grandmother's loving embrace as I crossed the threshold. The enticing aroma of cinnamon mixed with earthy scents hung in the air with comforting familiarity.

Magic shivered across my skin, and the water drenching my clothes evaporated.

I blinked. That was no minor magical feat, and I hadn't even sensed the wards activate.

Latent power coursed through every surface. The weight of the magic pressed against me, but rather than being overwhelming or suffocating, it was soothing. Even back in witch cities, this amount of power was rare, yet here it all was inside a coffee shop.

Despite my bedraggled appearance, customers had the decency not to stare as I approached the counter. The dryad barista at the register watched me, her golden irises ringed with rich earthy brown, and her deep myrtle green hair flowed around her face as if a soft breeze blew.

"How may I help you?" she asked, her voice a soft melody of wooden wind chimes.

I held up the poster as evidence. "I'm here about the job opening."

A barista peered out from behind the espresso machine. "You are?"

His vibrant red curls fell into his eyes as he looked me over. My old friend, paranoia, whispered in my ear. Was there something wrong with me?

"Fantastic, fresh meat."

"Voren," the dryad scolded. "They don't know you're joking."

"You're hired!" a voice yelled as a figure burst from the back room.

Flour dusted her apron as she flicked her pure-white braid over her shoulder. But it was her bright eyes that snagged me.

Glowing like two full moons reflecting off the shimmering waves, they called to me like—

Magic shuddered over me, and I blinked. Had I been caught in a spell?

"What?" I croaked.

"Are you a baker?" Her smile brimmed with hope.

"Alchemist."

She shrugged. "Close enough."

"Thayna, we should test her out first." A stern-looking dwarf pushed past Thayna and assessed me with his critical gaze.

I met his scrutiny with a bewildered stare.

"Remember what befell the last one?"

Well, that was ominous. What had happened? Were they devoured by a rogue sourdough starter or chopped to bits by an overzealous enchanted knife?

"Quinn hasn't shown up for her last two shifts," Thayna replied. "We need the coverage."

The dwarf grumbled. "At least ensure they can bake and handle the kitchen first."

Thayna sighed, her shoulders drooping. "Come on."

She beckoned me to follow as she disappeared into the back.

I glanced at the baristas, unsure if this was real. Voren flashed a grin and gave me a thumbs up, while the dryad took the crumpled poster and nodded with encouragement.

My palms were slick with sweat. The truth was, I didn't know how to bake. Sure, I'd whipped up box cakes, but that's not the same.

Against my will, my feet followed.

Without hesitating, Thayna pointed out the crucial items in the impeccable kitchen. I half-listened, but this place was a marvel.

Arranged to maximize efficiency, it felt as though I had stepped into a sophisticated patisserie, not a neighborhood coffee shop.

Everything was a blend of stainless steel and wood, making the space inviting rather than sterile and practical like the school kitchens.

Along one wall, shelves stood in perfect alignment, organized to ensure that every item had its designated spot. An array of bakeware, utensils, and glassware adorned the lower shelves. Higher up, dividers separated baking ingredients from front-of-house supplies.

Thayna guided me to a workbench; nestled beneath were several large bins on wheels containing a variety of flours and sugars. Above it, a shelf displayed an assortment of jars within easy reach. I would kill to have a setup like this for my alchemy workspace. Perhaps one day.

She pivoted on her heels and leaned against the bench as she studied my face, her intense gaze peering into my soul. I busied myself with the apron she handed me, hoping she couldn't read my thoughts. Was she aware of the stolen book in my bag?

When I looked up, she extended a laminated sheet toward me, releasing it when I met her gaze. The scrutiny had vanished, replaced with a somewhat sympathetic expression.

Great, just what I needed—more pity.

Who cares *if it gets you the* job?

"Just follow the recipe, and you'll do fine," she said with a half-smile.

I stared at the paper; could it be that simple?

"Oh, and watch out for the ovens. They can be a tad territorial and rather grumpy in the morning."

I spun around. "What?"

My mind raced to catch up, but she had disappeared. I eyed the ovens. Their metal doors stared back in a distinctly oven-like manner. Had that been a joke?

I reread the instructions. Everything seemed straightforward, just like alchemy. Follow the directions, and it would work out. If you messed up with baking, it didn't result in an explosion that attempted to dissolve half your dorm room.

What's the worst that could happen?

Chapter Three

"Are you creamed yet?" I peered into the mixing bowl. "What does 'creamed' even mean? Cream is a liquid. How do I turn butter and sugar into cream? This isn't logical!"

So much for simple. I suppressed my rising panic and turned the mixer on again.

Please, let this work.

I focused on preparing the hazelnuts while the mixer did mixer-like things. I'd selected a standard knife, avoiding the few that had pulsed with magic.

My hands had steadied, finding calm in the familiar rhythm of the task. The methodical work had a soothing quality that quieted my thoughts. With only the ovens watching me, I pretended I was safe and alone.

While the butter and sugar didn't resemble cream, the mixture had lightened. I tossed in the next ingredients on the list and hoped. Stress crept up my spine as if I were back at school taking my exams.

If I failed to get hired, what would I do? My rent was due, my alchemy supplies were running low, and even if I found a potion that could help me, how much would those reagents cost?

And if it didn't work? What if it bound all my magic? What if stripping my powers was my only option to prevent harming others?

A pulse of magic snapped me out of my thoughts, and I stood frozen, staring at the pulverized hazelnuts. Obliterated not by my knife, but by a whisper of my unruly magic that had slipped past my control. I shoved it back down, burying it deep within before it jeopardized my chance here. Or damaged anything I couldn't afford to replace.

Failure isn't an option, Nyssa. One step at a time.

I eyed my bag, sensing the faint thrum of magic from within. Was the tome trying to be discovered? No, the magic seemed soothing, reassuring . . . and clearly, I was losing my mind.

Mustering my determination and tucking away my tumultuous emotions, I tipped the hazelnuts into the cookie batter. This place needed me as much as I needed the job. I didn't want to let them down. I took a slow, deep breath and held it for a moment before exhaling and releasing the stress along with it.

The next step of the recipe read, "If time allows, chill for an hour" which, I assumed, referred to the cookies, not me. But time did not "allow." There was no way I would loiter in this kitchen for that long.

I straightened my shoulders and seized the cookie scoop. I'd secure this job, make this new life in Arkirith work against the odds, and most important of all, I'd find a way to control my magic.

Please let them like these. No. Not like. They will love you.

I portioned out the dough. But like the relentless tide wearing down a sandcastle, my self-doubt eroded my naïve confidence.

No, I snapped at myself. I'd worked too hard for this chance to move to the city. For Goddess's sake, I'd just broken into the library and stolen a tome! I would *not* let cookies defeat me.

You will taste irresistible, I told the batter.

I was willing to work hard and make sacrifices. I'd claim my place in this realm.

They will savor every bite and then hire me.

I would carve my own path to greatness, no matter what it took. Make my dreams a reality.

You will be the best damn cookies that they have ever eaten!

A faint tingling sensation danced across my hands as I portioned the last of the cookies.

"Hello," I said to the oven, feeling awkward. I wasn't sure of the proper way to greet a disgruntled kitchen appliance. "I prepared some lovely cookies for you. Could you please bake them to perfection?"

The oven remained silent. I hoped that was a good sign and slid my two trays in. Setting a timer, I cleaned up the considerable mess I had created. With nothing left to do, I pulled out my phone and opened my banking app. My finger hovered over the button to reject Tobin's transfer. I needed the money, but I wanted to do this myself.

As I waged an internal war, a notification popped up. I frowned down at the text from my brother, clicking it despite my better judgment.

I'm sorry. You know I only want what's best for you, and I'm just trying to protect you.

I was so sick of everyone "knowing what was best for me" and not letting me decide that for myself.

I can look after myself, and I don't want your pity, I texted back.

I denied the money transfer and silenced my phone. I'd do this on my own terms. It might have been foolish to reject it, but I needed to prove I could stand on my own two feet.

With nothing left to occupy me, I endured the most agonizing five minutes as my timer ticked down. Chewing on my lip, I paced while maintaining a respectful distance from the oven . . . which turned out to be smart, as the door flew open a full thirty seconds before my timer.

"Are they ready?" I asked.

The racks clattered with annoyance, because of course a half-sentient oven possessed better judgment. I rushed to retrieve my cookies before the oven had the audacity to eject them.

The heavenly aroma of fresh baked hazelnut and chocolate cookies wafted around me, and I hoped they would taste just as divine. A sense of satisfaction filled me as I admired my handiwork.

"They look great," Thayna chimed as she approached. "I apologize for my abrupt behavior. We're short staffed, and I'm desperate to hire someone who can cover me and handle the ovens. As I didn't introduce myself, shall we start again? I'm Thayna, the head baker."

"Nyssa," I managed before she enveloped me in an unexpected hug. "But I haven't gotten the job yet."

"Semantics." She dismissed my concerns with a wave of her hand. "If you could see the help wanted poster, you've already passed the most important test. Now, let's plate up these cookies so the customers can try them. But leave a few for us."

Trailing behind her, I strode out, plate in hand and a beaming smile, as curious gazes turned our way.

"Ready for taste testers!" Thayna announced loud enough for the whole cafe to hear. A swarm descended with eager eyes and hungry expressions.

"What did you make?" a customer asked with anticipation.

"Oh, these smell amazing," another added.

"Thank you!" Voren called with a grin as he snagged a cookie.

Surrounded by the bustling throng of baristas and customers, I stood still, clutching the plate with a mix of pride and anxiety. Just as quick, the crowd dispersed, leaving scattered crumbs in their wake.

Well, that was terrifying.

"Everyone loves free stuff," I muttered, retreating to the kitchen. I didn't want to watch as they critiqued my creation.

Despite my doubts, I couldn't resist taking a bite of one of the cookies I'd left behind.

By the Sun Goddess, they were delicious! The cookie was warm enough that the chocolate chunks were ooey-gooey, blending with the hazelnut. A match made by the Goddess herself.

Devouring the rest of mine, I regretted when there were only crumbs left.

"They're a hit," Thayna proclaimed. "Go out there and chat. I'll take this to the boss. Don't worry. If he doesn't hire you, they'll riot."

Summoning my last dregs of courage and social energy, I emerged to mingle with my potential coworkers. I hoped the delicious cookies would overshadow my less-than-ideal first impression.

"Nyssa!" Voren exclaimed as he rushed up to me.

His wide grin revealed pointed incisors. My eyes rose to his wild hair and the pair of curled horns peeking out. *An erebian?!*

"Did you only just notice them?" He scoffed, guiding me over to a seat by the espresso machine.

Should I apologize?

I'd encountered several demon-born at the Alchemy Guild, just never up close. But the signs were so obvious now, I didn't know how I'd missed it. That red tinge to his skin, the otherworldly glow in his bronze-colored eyes, and . . . I mean, horns were a giveaway. I just wasn't used to being around anyone besides witches.

My mouth opened and closed as I tried to form a suitable apology. He didn't seem to notice.

"We all loved the cookies," Voren said. "So, when do you start? Can I make you a drink? And what are you? We've been placing bets."

The words tumbled from him, and I tried to process the bombardment of questions. I hadn't been prepared for a pop quiz.

"Give her a moment, would you?" the dryad interjected. She broke her cookie in half and extended it to me. "I'm Zola, and it seems we were too excited to save you a cookie."

"Thanks, but I saved one in the back."

Voren handed me a mug, the foam adorned with a flower design. I took a sip to avoid meeting their eyes and savored the caramel latte.

"So, you're a shifter, right?" Voren asked.

Zola scoffed. "She must be a siren. Who else would have hair that color?"

The two started bickering as if I were invisible.

"Um, actually, I'm a witch."

"Oh," they said together.

Voren seemed to deflate. "Are you sure?"

"Pretty sure," I chuckled.

"Next thing you know, we'll have a nephilim waltzing in," Voren said with a grimace.

I supposed the animosity between the angel-born and demon-born was an issue the witch archives had been correct about.

"Well, no one guessed a witch, so we'll put the money toward our next bar tab."

They bet on what I was? What in the world . . .

"Oh, yes!" Zola's eyes lit up. "Nyssa, you'll have to join us."

"Of course," my mouth said despite my brain screaming *"No!"* Everything was moving too fast. I could barely keep my feet under me.

"Sorry, I sometimes forget Divine can be a bit overwhelming . . . along with their employees," Zola said with a nod to Voren.

"I'll take that as a compliment," he said.

"Thank you." A genuine smile lit my face. "I still find everything overwhelming since I'm not familiar with the city."

Thayna reappeared and waved for me to follow.

"Beylin can be gruff," she said, guiding me up the stairs to his office. "You'll get used to it."

I knocked on the door and entered, feeling a strange sense of déjà vu as if I were entering the headmaster's office after getting into trouble. Beylin hunched over a mountain of paperwork.

"Nyssa, is it?" he grumbled, setting down his pen and acknowledging me. The headmaster vibes were strong with this one.

"Yes, sir." Better to err on the side of caution. His mouth quirked at my response. Was that a good or bad thing?

"According to Thayna, you passed with flying colors. And it seems you're getting along with your coworkers."

Did he mean Zola and Voren, or the ovens? *Wait, how does he know any of that?* Were there cameras around that I hadn't noticed?

"But . . ." he continued, and I tensed.

How could there be a "but"? I'd followed all the instructions and done everything right. This couldn't be happening. Visions of school life flashed before my eyes. I'd achieve the desired results, but somehow it was never in the "right" way and they deemed my efforts a failure.

"Do you always bake with magic?"

"Do I . . . What?"

"Magic," Beylin said, drawing out the word as if his accent had caused the confusion. "I could taste the magic in the cookie."

My eyes widened. I thought I'd suppressed it fast enough, but I'd tainted the cookies. "Oh, that was an accident. It won't happen—"

"Do you think you can replicate it?"

What? "Probably." He wanted magic-infused cookies? Unintentional use of my powers always resulted in trouble, not opportunity.

"This is a magical coffee shop, after all." He stroked his beard as he scrutinized me. "Magic-infused baked goods would attract more business."

The door rattled behind me. I turned, expecting someone to enter, but the room was silent.

Beylin sighed. "And Divine seems to have decided and won't take no for an answer. Very well. Be here tomorrow morning at five for your trial shift with Thayna."

"What?" It took a moment for his words to register. "Thank you."

I beamed, excitement bubbling through me, but the disgruntled look on his face told me to suppress it lest he retract the offer.

"I'll be going then?"

The dwarf grunted, engrossed in his paperwork again, so I took my win and retreated.

I did it?

The door closed behind me. I paused a beat, waiting for someone to tell me it was all just a joke.

I actually did it!

A wide smile stretched across my face as I grabbed my bag and said bye to Zola and Voren. Was this the first step toward the future I envisioned?

Chapter Four

The thrill of finally landing a job had me taking the stairs two at a time, but I skidded to a stop when I saw my landlord waiting at my door, her scowl killing my victory lap on sight.

Despite only being five feet tall, she cut an imposing figure with her hands on hips and a menacing glare. I didn't want to tangle with her.

Internally cursing myself for not being more cautious, I pushed my bag behind me to shield the tome hidden within.

"Good afternoon," I said, hoping I sounded pleasant and not like I wanted to bolt past her.

She scowled. "Rent's due in five days."

"I get paid at the end of the week."

It was an effort to keep my smile in place. That wasn't an outright lie; I would get paid by the Guild, I just didn't know if it'd cover what I owed. The money might not even cover the cost of the reagents I'd bought to brew the dang potions.

Okay, I didn't feel as bad for stealing the tome. The Guild owed me.

My landlord just hmphed as I slunk by. Unlocking my door, I hurried inside at record speed and slumped against it.

How was I going to scrape the money together? I hadn't even asked if I'd be paid for my trial shift at Divine.

Why had I been so stupid and rejected Tobin's money? Doing it on my own would mean nothing if I were homeless.

I swiped my hand across my face. I'd figure something out.

The tome.

Excitement chased away my sour mood as I settled onto the couch.

My heart kicked up a notch, butterflies swarming in my stomach as I brushed my fingers over the weathered cover. Tracing the delicate lines of the silver letters etched into the leather that read *The Lunar Codex,* a faint tingling sensation zipped across my fingertips.

The intricate depictions of lunar phases adorned the surface and came alive under my touch. It was enchanting, but I couldn't help feeling disheartened.

Aelia, the Sun Goddess, blessed witches with her divine magic. While mine was wild, I was still a witch who used solar energy. Shifters were the children of the moon, blessed with Selene's lunar magic.

What could a lunar codex offer me?

The pages were yellowed and soft with age, covered in flowing script. My stomach sank as I flipped through it. I couldn't read a word. Didn't even know the language.

I dropped my face into my hands, not knowing whether to laugh or cry. I must have imagined the familiar magic when I'd held it.

The heavy weight of failure pressed against my chest, a feeling I was far too familiar with.

I snatched up my phone and snapped a photo to search for a translation. But they all came back as unknown.

What good was a book if I couldn't even read it? I should have guarded myself against being too optimistic.

My stomach grumbled in annoyance, reminding me I'd only eaten a cookie today. I stood, ready to hunt down some food, knowing disappointment awaited. There was only so much soup a person could eat, but it was cheap and fast.

I researched baking tips and ate my sad dinner when my Guild supervisor texted my next contract. Annoyance smothered my initial excitement. Another batch of poultices that didn't need a drop of magic to craft.

Don't get me wrong, I needed the money. I just didn't expect to make facial masks that would brighten and smooth someone's complexion, when those same ingredients could be used to craft potions that promoted healing and reduced scarring.

Fatigue gnawed at me. I typically slept during the late afternoon, waking after dusk to maximize my alchemy hours.

A child of the sun brewing at night? I know, one more quirk of my magic. While we didn't need sunlight to wield solar magic, it strengthened it. But if I tried to channel my power during the day, it was too erratic. When night fell, the magic mellowed out and obeyed my commands . . . most of the time.

Pulling my blinds closed against the sunlight, I crashed on my bed, doing my best not to feel defeated. I tossed and turned until sleep claimed me.

I jerked awake to a scratching sound. Disoriented, I squinted at my room. Had I dreamed that noise? No, there it was again.

Dragging myself out of bed, I padded to the living room. I tilted my head, listening for the noise. Blue flashed across the floor, and I froze. The cobalt vulpine twirled around my ankles, and magic prickled over my bare legs.

"What are you doing here?" I blurted as relief replaced my fear. They had escaped the library without harm. "Wait, how did you get past my wards?"

The fox darted to my couch, waiting for me to follow. Too groggy to think straight, I sat down, and the fox climbed up beside me.

"I stole this book for you," I said, waving at *The Lunar Codex* on the coffee table. "So now we're friends, huh?"

Unable to resist, I ran my hand down the fox's back, and magic crackled like static electricity. Such a beautiful creature. As a young witch, I'd dreamed of being lucky enough to have a familiar, to have that special bond with someone I could always trust. But a witch had no control if the animal didn't choose to initiate a bond.

I scratched the fox behind their ears, trying not to feel deflated when I sensed no magical connection between us.

"I hate to break it to you," I told the fox, "but this book is useless. Whatever language it's in, I can't read it."

The fox's ears perked up as if they understood what I was saying. They jumped onto the table and pressed their nose against the book.

Shrugging, I flipped through the pages. The fox sat back, their head tilted as if they were reading.

Their paw pressed against my hand as if telling me to stop. Warm magic seeped into my skin. They nudged me with their wet nose, and I blinked down at the page.

The ink had dulled, but I could decipher the elegant script. It was a recipe for a potion I'd never heard of called *magiam augere.* My gaze snagged on the details below—I had to read it twice.

"A potion to cultivate and refine one's magic?" I read the words aloud in disbelief.

The description stated it helping the user control their power and the flow of their energies. Which would allow the person to focus their magic, granting a greater command over their ability.

This couldn't be a witch recipe.

I'd scoured our archives for years, searching for such a spell. Something—anything—that would "fix" me.

The pages shook, and I realized my hands were trembling. Was this the answer I was looking for? The chance to be whole.

I was on my feet with the urge to rush upstairs to my alchemy station before I stopped myself.

No, I needed to research this first, to find cross-references and ensure it was safe. Only an ignorant fool would brew some potion they'd just stumbled upon.

Plus, I didn't have half of the reagents it required.

With a shake of my head, I shoved the budding hope back down and forced myself to sit.

The bitter taste of disappointment was too familiar. What if this potion only enhanced the wildness and I lost control? The witch council deemed magic like mine erratic and dangerous.

After living with it for eight years, I had to agree.

What if I made things worse?

"How did you know what I've been hunting for?" I asked, narrowing my gaze at the magical creature.

Had someone sent the fox to aid me? Or did they have an ulterior motive? Why else would they help me?

A spark of intelligence shone in their sapphire gaze. In one graceful bound, the fox was beside me again, their cold wet nose pressed against my hand.

"You want me to believe you did all this to aid me?" I said with a heavy hint of skepticism.

The vulpine pressed their nose under my hand, wiggling until my hand was atop their head. They blinked up at me with an innocence that made me laugh. As I stroked its head, the fox let out a soft sigh and closed its eyes.

"I guess a thank you is in order." I was unable to hide my smile. Damn them for using their cuteness on me.

To my surprise, they stayed by my side when I ventured to the rooftop to make the poultices, happy to curl up against my leg as I worked the reagents with my mortar and pestle. Lavender scented the pungent mix, likely to detract from the fact it looked like mud.

I longed to brew—the methodical process always calmed me—but it appeared no one wanted my alchemical skills but me.

I spent the rest of the night researching the reagents for the codex's potion and the other potential binding recipes I'd copied out, my hope climbing with each passing minute.

The fox trotted away when I returned to my apartment to dress for work. I wouldn't admit it aloud, but I enjoyed their company. A buzz of excitement zipped through me as I locked my door.

The research was promising, though a few reagents required further study. I needed a fuller understanding before I attempted to brew the potion.

Dawn was just a smudge on the horizon when I stepped outside. The street was empty and eerily quiet save for the echo of my footsteps. While I hated the overbearing sound of the city during the day, this silence was equally unsettling and put me on edge.

As I turned the corner, my steps faltered.

A shiver crawled up my spine as my wide eyes locked onto a disturbing sight a few paces away.

Lurking in the shadows was a creature torn from the pages of ancient legends.

Demonspawn. The word hissed through my mind. I recognized it from pictures, but how was it on this side of the veil?

It stood hunched, obsidian-black scales covering its sinewy form, so dark they absorbed any light that touched them. Elongated and twisted limbs contorted from its body. Long, jagged claws adorned its fingers, glinting with lethality.

Two gleaming eyes, like soulless pits, stared out from beneath a furrowed brow, radiating an unsettling intelligence that made me shudder.

The creature's lips curled into a sinister sneer, revealing a row of razor-sharp teeth ready to tear flesh from bone.

Tense silence hung in the air, broken only by the creature's low, guttural growl.

My heart pounded against my ribs as if it wanted to escape without me. Mind blank and body frozen, I could only stare as it straightened to almost seven feet tall.

The demonspawn's head tilted as it watched me, its nostrils flaring as it scented the air. The creature snapped its jaws, and I jerked back.

Wrong move.

It surged forward, claws scraping the ground as I grasped for my conduit.

My palms slick with sweat, I fumbled with my wand, a strangled gasp escaping my lips as sparks of uncontrolled energy erupted.

Pain sliced through my head as the spell shattered, and the backlash hit me like a physical blow.

The demonspawn lunged, its sharp talons cutting through the air. I couldn't move. I was going to die.

A force slammed into my knees, and I crashed to the ground.

Magic sizzled. Blue light flashed, searing my eyes. I raised my arms to shield myself, bracing for an attack that never came.

In the distance, footsteps pounded, growing louder. I blinked away the spots in my vision to see my little fox chasing the demonspawn down the street, magic crackling across their fur.

"Are you alright?" a voice asked.

A dark-haired woman rounded the corner and scanned the area. But the creatures were out of sight.

"That sounded like a massive dog. Whatever you did must have scared it off," she said, offering me a hand. "But it's best not to wait around for it to come back."

"Dog?" I said, eyeing her and the street behind me. My head still throbbed from my failed attempt to summon magic.

"Are you injured?" she asked.

"No."

I accepted her offered hand. It was soft and warm, my skin tingling under her grip. I met her deep crimson eyes as she pulled me upright.

"It wasn't a dog, it was a . . ."

I blinked. Black, soulless eyes and . . . my eyebrows drew together in confusion. My mind went blank.

"What was I saying?"

"It's alright," she said, a too-wide smile on her face. "You've had quite a scare."

I extracted my hand and stared past her, but there was no sign of the dog.

Yes, it had been a dog.

"I should get to work," I mumbled.

"That's a good idea," she replied, heading on her way. "Take care."

I stole one last glance over my shoulder. Empty street. No footsteps. No eyes watching.

So why wouldn't the chill in my bones fade?

I took off running; the memories spurring me forward.

The fox's magic had wrapped around me like a shield tonight. All I could do now was pray it was strong enough to shield them too.

I almost sagged with relief when the coffee shop came into view. My breath came in gasps as I doubled over, my gut churning with unease.

The pain from the magical backlash settled into a familiar dull ache as I pushed upright and peered through the window. The lights were off, chairs still stacked atop the tables, and the display case was empty.

That crawling sensation under my skin spiked from unsettling to wrong. I rushed up to the door, hoping that Thayna was inside.

I hadn't expected Arkirith to be dangerous, which was naïve of me.

Tonight I'd craft some potions I could keep on hand for protection. Even with my cheaper reagents, I could cobble something together.

The door clicked and opened a fraction as I neared. Excitement and nerves swirled in my chest.

It wasn't alchemy, but there was a comforting ambiance about this coffee shop, from the polished hardwood floors to the cozy nooks and plush couches.

The lush greenery and the bookcase that graced one wall added to the charm. Even with the subdued lighting, it exuded an inviting atmosphere. A place I could belong.

Don't get me wrong; alchemy was still my utmost passion. But an undeniable spark resonated within me when I stepped through the entrance. The door snapped shut behind me, and I flinched.

Smooth, Nyssa.

It took me a moment to soothe my heart. I wove through the tables illuminated by a light that shone from the kitchen. A faint sound of movement reached me, confirming someone was inside. I shook off my lingering doubt and cleared my throat.

"Hello," I called out, not wanting to be mistaken for an intruder. But my greeting only met silence.

Images flashed through my mind. Flat black eyes filled with hunger, saliva dripping from its jaw.

My body tensed, and I strained to listen for any sound beyond the door. My fingers rubbed the smooth grain of my conduit to settle my nerves. Not that I'd try any magic again unless I were desperate.

I crept closer, my steps deliberate, and the hardwood floors remained silent under my weight.

A small voice pleaded with me to call the police and avoid potential danger. That voice sounded like my mother, calculated and cautious.

However, my father's influence resonated in my heart, urging me forward to confront the threat. Or was it the adrenaline from earlier that influenced my actions?

Avoiding the light beaming through the window, I peered in and scanned the room. From my limited vantage point, everything appeared empty, but the quiet seemed stilted.

Be brave.

I burst into the kitchen.

With a flick of my wrist, my conduit extended into a thin stave, and I dropped into a fighting stance. I surveyed the area, but it was empty except for a workstation which was set with supplies.

I huffed. It seemed Thayna had arrived early to prepare.

Relief flooded through me, pushing the tension from my body. But my face flushed with heat as my embarrassment caught up. It seemed absurd now. Why would anything dangerous be in here?

Retracting my conduit with a snap, I stashed it out of sight before Thayna returned. She was likely in the stockroom and hadn't heard me arrive.

I hurried over to the bench as if I could forget my foolishness by keeping busy.

"Please don't tell anyone about that," I whispered to the ovens.

I didn't believe they were fully sentient, but you never knew with dwarven-made items. Both oven doors opened and closed in agreement, causing me to yelp.

Note to self: Avoid provoking sentient ovens.

I donned the supplied apron and skimmed the papers laid out on the workstation. They contained a detailed outline of opening duties, including specific times each tray should enter the oven so that the food to be ready when the store opened.

Whoever created this believed this was a military operation, not a coffee shop. But after living with my dad, I was accustomed to that.

Determined to make a good impression, I gathered the supplies for the first batch. Salted caramel brownies were today's special, which sounded delicious.

Weighing out the ingredients, I did my best to push aside my lingering embarrassment. But my brain continued to replay the memory to ensure I wouldn't forget.

I didn't know why I believed I could face a threat, especially after earlier. I blamed the adrenaline. And my dad. Ever since I was young, he'd been relentless in training me to survive without magic. It was not surprising, considering his martial arts and military background.

With a huffing laugh, I started up the mixer. I almost considered texting my dad. I knew he would be proud that his self-defense training had paid off, but then he'd worry about my safety in this new environment.

"Morning," Thayna's sweet voice rang out.

"Good morning," I called back over the hum of the mixer.

"Sorry for being late," she said, pulling off her jacket. "I was packing all night."

"But . . ." I blinked. Who had I heard earlier? Had there been a break-in?

"I'm glad that Divine helped get you started," she said, looking over my workstation.

I frowned. "But the door was unlocked . . ."

"Yes, Divine let you in," she said with a grin. "Now we won't have to rush to catch up."

"The coffee shop opened the door?" I asked, my voice rising another octave. Today had only just begun, and it was already too weird.

Thayna paused. "Did no one mention that Divine is sentient?"

"Like the building? No," I whispered. Were they listening to us now? What would happen if I made a mistake?

Thayna chuckled. "It's nothing to worry about. They're friendly—for the most part."

Pans on the shelf clattered ominously, but that only made Thayna laugh harder.

"Yes, yes. You're terrifying."

"So, they . . ." I pointed to the workbench where I had discovered everything set up.

"Divine is very fussy about their employees. They circulate help-wanted posters that are only visible to those approved by Divine. Which is why I knew you were a shoo-in."

As she entered the staff room, I returned to my brownies. But my thoughts churned.

A sentient coffee shop. The concept seemed absurd. How did a building come to life? Was it the result of dwarven magic, like how they imbued autonomy into their creations? Or was it an ancient and forbidden form of magic, in which a person's magical essence was bound to an object? Witches had once bound a fragment of their soul to their grimoire. The practice had been outlawed hundreds of years ago as they feared it would corrupt the witch and their magic.

I cleared my throat before mustering my courage.

"Thank you for giving me this opportunity," I whispered, just in case this was a prank. "I really need this job, and I promise I won't let you down."

The dry ingredient bins clacked their lids happily, bringing a smile to my face. Maybe working a second job wouldn't be as dreadful as I'd expected, even if it meant interacting with strange new people on a daily basis.

"You won't tell anyone about earlier, right?"

The glasses on the shelves chimed together, a bright, tinkling sound that absolutely counted as laughter.

"It was your fault," I muttered, half-amused, half-exasperated.

Divine only laughed harder, which was ridiculous for a building

Chapter Five

Divine opened the kitchen door for me as I strode into the coffee shop, holding the tea cake aloft like a prize, with a wide, uncontrollable smile splitting my face.

Baking, it turned out, was just science in disguise.

Science . . . with a flick of power to help it along the way.

I'd been experimenting, infusing a whisper of my magic on purpose this time, but it was still hit-or-miss.

Case in point: my second attempt at brownies had a somewhat explosive outcome when I pressed too hard, leaving me with a good portion of the batter in my hair.

I'd tested every batch myself, not just because they were tasty, but to ensure there were no harmful effects from my wild magic.

While my alchemy had never caused any harm, it was best to be cautious. Even mild side effects could damage someone's reputation. A girl in my year had crafted a fortitude brew using fresh whispberries instead of dried. Her skin turned blue for weeks.

Though my magic wasn't as strong today, I considered it a victory when Beylin deemed my baking acceptable and offered me a temporary position.

To celebrate, Thayna had taught me her gran's cherished tea cake recipe. Double the reason to smile as I made space in the display, ensuring that my cake would take a prominent position.

During breaks from baking, Voren and Zola took the opportunity to educate me on the ins and outs of working at Divine Coffee—or, as Beylin referred to it, "gossiping." One important fact was that Divine had complete authority over who they employed and even who entered the premises as a customer.

If Divine barred someone from entering, they had a good reason. Although that information was intended to reassure me, I now feared Divine might change their mind about me whenever I came to work.

"Your cake looks lovely, Nyssa," Zola said, before turning her pleasant smile on the next customers.

They were a curious-looking pair, dressed in black uniforms with body armor vests. If the clothing hadn't been a dead giveaway, then the air of disciplined professionalism and body language marked them as security or law enforcement.

"Can I have a triple mocha and a chai latte?" The woman ordered for both of them.

Strange. Her dark hair twisted into a tight braid, her eyes were a soft light blue, and by all appearances she looked non-magical, like a human.

Trying to maintain a casual demeanor as I straightened the pastries, I watched them, my curiosity piqued. I wanted to know who—and what—they were.

Humans and magicals rarely interacted. Most stayed isolated in their human-only cities due to their distrust of magic, still blaming it for the loss of their realm. Though a small number did choose to live within our cities.

There were rigorous laws to keep humans from consuming magical products, as something safe for a witch could harm a human. Anyone selling or buying magical items, such as potions, had to go through the correct channels and record transactions. My magic alone gave me enough worries, without dealing with magical laws.

Everything sold within Divine was safe for human consumption. Even the small amount of magic I'd infused within the cookies registered at a low enough level to be deemed safe. But that didn't mean I expected them to be customers here.

I stole another glance, but froze when I found a pair of steely blue eyes watching me back.

Shit.

The man assessed me with a critical gaze and a wave of self-consciousness washed over me. Did I still have batter in my hair?

"Would you like some tea cake fresh out of the oven?" I stammered, hoping to appear welcoming and not like I was awkwardly staring.

He frowned, inspecting the cake as if it had personally offended him.

"Rynac would love a piece," the woman answered with a mischievous grin.

I plated a slice, ready to retreat to the kitchen and check my appearance in the mirror when Zola intercepted me.

"These are pretty simple drinks. Care to make them?"

Crap.

And, of course, the two customers stood right next to the espresso machine as I prepared their drinks. They leaned against the counter, watching the cafe, although Rynac kept his back to me. *Ouch.*

Pouring the milk into a metal pitcher, I lifted it to the steam wand and it let out a high-pitched squeal of annoyance. Wincing, I adjusted my position, but warmth flushed my cheeks and I wanted to sink into the floor.

My first impressions were always on point. Curiosity fought my embarrassment until I couldn't resist stealing another glance.

Despite reading all the information the witch archive held on the other races, it was woefully inadequate. The internet was a valuable resource, but I found it lacking in real-world situations.

"I haven't seen you here before. Are you new?" the woman inquired. Right. Small talk.

"Yes, it's my first shift," I replied, scrambling for something else to say. Engaging in conversations with strangers was not natural to me. "Are you a regular?"

She nodded. "When we work in this neighborhood, we operate out of the East Plaza on Hastings."

"Ah," I said, not sure what else to say, as I had no idea where that was. Why was small talk so draining? I finished the drinks and was grateful for the temporary respite.

I presented their drinks with a sense of accomplishment. The milk had a perfectly smooth froth, unlike my last few attempts. But my mood deflated when Rynac accepted my drink with a scowl. The woman flashed me a smile, and too late I realized she noted my reaction to Rynac.

Can I just die of embarrassment *now?*

"Thank you. I'm Indra, by the way." She elbowed Rynac hard, but he ignored her. "And this charming fellow is my brother, Rynac."

"Nice to meet you," I said, plastering on a smile. "I'm Nyssa."

"We hope to see you around," Indra called over her shoulder.

Rynac glared daggers at his sister and retreated to the farthest table. What curious people. Hopefully, the rest of Divine's customers were as lovely as Indra.

"They seemed to like you," Zola said in her airy voice.

Her tone had lacked any judgement, but I hesitated for a moment before asking, "That's okay, right?"

"Being friendly with customers is always a good thing."

I worried my lip between my teeth. "Do you know what race they are? I'm not great at determining that."

"Oh, that's because they're altered," Zola explained. "Some people mistake them for humans and distrust them."

Altered. I had a vague recollection of the term, though the information was sparse. They were once humans but had chosen to undergo magical alterations, which placed them somewhere in the gray area between magical and mundane.

Who would choose to be ostracized from their own race? It was confusing, yet intriguing.

"There are always stigmas around different races," Zola said, as if sensing my train of thought. "I wouldn't let others' opinions skew yours. These two are quite pleasant. They serve in the MEA, the Magical Enforcers of Arkirith, our police force."

I couldn't help but smile at Zola. The dryad had been nothing but lovely. Others might have judged me for my ignorance, but she always offered an explanation.

"Here, altered act as intermediaries between different races when tensions rise. Most races see them as neutral and—to some extent—expendable."

I frowned at that, but if those two were enforcers, that meant they would be in dangerous situations. The possibilities triggered a flurry of ideas.

If I could convince them to purchase potions directly from me, it would provide a reliable source of income. I'd also be helping the police keep the city safe. Plus, it would give me an opportunity to experiment with new formulas that the average person wouldn't require.

But I dashed the rising hope. The MEA would be a lucrative client, but I was positive the Guild had already snapped them up. How could a fledgling alchemist expect to win such a contract?

Zola handed me a plate loaded with cookies, interrupting my thoughts. "It's the end of your shift. Why don't you talk to your new friends?"

I looked down at the cookies, contemplating my options. The chance to gain my first clients and promote my alchemy business was tempting. But it meant stepping out of my comfort zone and approaching strangers.

"Don't worry," Zola said. She leaned in close, as if we were conspiring. "I'll mark the cookies out as samples."

With a firm grip, she spun me around, removed my apron, and nudged me toward the altered.

My heart raced as I approached Indra and Rynac, this time without the protective barrier of the counter between us. I was halfway across the room when a wave of doubt hit me.

Why would they want to hire an alchemist who worked as a barista? Better to retreat and not embarrass myself.

Ready to making a beeline for the door and retrieving my bag later, Rynac spotted me.

Shit.

I froze like a jackalope in headlights.

Could I still make an escape? Just walk out the door with a plate of cookies. But that would create an awkward atmosphere when they came back next time. Or they wouldn't return at all. But then the shop would lose potential business.

My internal debate raged on as I stood there, unsure of what to do.

And what if they hold the key to getting my business off the ground?

Traitorous logic. My escape plans came to a halt when Indra's gaze shifted to Rynac before following it to me. As though a magnetic force pulled me closer, my feet carried me to their table against my better judgment.

"Hello again," Indra said, grinning.

"I brought cookies," I said, setting down the plate.

The weight of their stares trapped me in place.

Determined not to let the silence linger, I added, "Did you enjoy my cake?"

Rynac stilled, his gaze shifting down to his empty plate, reluctant to meet mine. I wondered if my smile was awkward, but my excitement refused to be contained.

"He did. Said it was the best he's ever had," Indra said. "Would you like to join us?"

Right, sit down.

That's what normal people do instead of lingering around the table. I perched on the seat and took a cookie, savoring the sweetness that danced on my tongue.

My mind refocused on my true goal: alchemy.

"You're altered, right?" I asked.

They both tensed.

Indra masked it with a smile, though a hint of caution remained in her eyes. "We are."

"And you're part of the police."

"Yes," Rynac said, and I jumped at the sound of his voice. "Do you need help?"

"No, not like that. I mean, I encountered a dangerous stray dog on the way to work, but that's not the reason." I brushed those thoughts away. "Can I ask you some questions?"

"What would you like to know?" he asked.

I sensed the apprehension underneath his words.

A jumble of questions filled my mind: *How do you become an altered? What does it change within you? Why did you choose to transform yourself?* But I pushed them aside. I was here for business; I could extract that information later.

"Do you use potions?" I blurted.

Great sales pitch, Nyssa.

Twin confused expressions crossed their faces, and I rushed to clarify. "Considering yours is a dangerous line of work, I assume they'd be beneficial. I'm guessing you have potions for healing and such."

Given the restrictions on the sale of alchemy products to humans, I assumed that altered, being magically enhanced, could use potions.

"We do," Indra said. "But there's a limited supply for our kind."

"How come?"

That seemed strange, considering all the applications for potions. I expected them to be as well-stocked as our witch guard.

For the first time, Indra seemed uncomfortable. "You're new to Arkirith, aren't you?"

I nodded.

"We need special formulations—" Indra began.

"Why do you want to know?" Rynac cut in, his voice carrying a hint of distrust.

His response took me aback. What had triggered such a harsh reaction?

"I'm an alchemist, and I'm looking for work. I'd need to adjust them for altered consumption, but it shouldn't be too difficult. And I have a wide range of potions that would benefit enforcers—" I pressed my lips together before I could ramble on anymore.

Both continued to stare at me, their expressions a mix of surprise and confusion, as if I had sprouted an extra head.

Potions needed to be crafted differently for each race to minimize side effects, but I enjoyed a challenge. In a pinch, a witch's brew could be administered as it was compatible with any magical race, but I doubted that was the case with altered.

"You're an alchemist?" Indra asked, caution tinging her voice.

"Yes. It was my focus at university," I replied with pride. "It's also the reason I came to the city. I'm contracted with the Guild, but they have strict limitations on what I can brew, so I don't have many contracts. That's why I also work here. However, if I can find my own clients, I'll have the freedom to brew whatever I want. No more crafting boring low-level healing tonics all night long."

Rambling again, my mind interjected, and I shoved the rest of the cookie into my mouth. Indra looked curious, but Rynac's gaze dissected me like I was a puzzle to be solved.

"You want to brew potions for enforcers? For *altered* like us?" Skepticism coloring Rynac's voice.

Obviously. I nodded as I chewed.

They exchanged glances as if silently communicating.

"I can bring your proposal to our captain and set up a meeting, if you'd like," Indra offered.

"That would be great."

"Are you free tomorrow?" She was grinning again.

"My shift finishes at one."

"I can't guarantee anything, but I'll do my best to arrange a meeting for tomorrow."

Her words filled my chest with an odd sensation, light, bubbly, and very intoxicating.

"Rynac will meet you here at one, then."

"What?" Rynac and I said at the same time.

"The captain won't be back until late afternoon," Indra explained, but the sparkle in her eyes concerned me. "To kill some time, Rynac can show you around the seaside market. It just opened, and it'd be a shame to miss it."

Before either of us could protest, Indra collected our empty plates and dashed off. My mind went blank, and the silence stretched between us.

"I apologize for my sister's behavior," Rynac said in a rush. "She's convinced that if she can set me up on a date, it will help me get over my breakup."

"Oh," I uttered, my mind scrambling.

Rynac fiddled with the hem of his shirt, looking anywhere but at me. "Not that I need her help. It's exceedingly irritating. I'm fine. Best to just ignore her."

I could relate, the constant desire of others to "fix" me and my magic.

Despite their good intentions, it often ended up hurting more than helping.

"I'm flattered," I began, hunting for an acceptable excuse that wouldn't offend him. "But you know I just act friendly because it's part of the job, right? I'm not looking for a relationship. And I don't date customers."

"I appreciate your honesty." Rynac's chuckle took me by surprise. He swiped a hand across his face, the tension in his shoulders easing. "That wasn't a roundabout way of hitting on you. I'm interested in men. No offense."

"Why would I be offended?" I said, then frowned. "Wait, why was she trying to set you up with me? Doesn't she know your preference?"

"She does, but I've rejected everyone she's suggested. She's desperate for me to go on a date with anyone, or even make new friends. As if that will somehow magically fix me. But once she gets an idea in her head, it's impossible to change her mind."

"So, we have to go on a date?" A date to earn an alchemy contract?

"No! Sorry, I shouldn't have said date. I mean . . . we could go as friends. It'd be nice hanging out with someone who isn't an enforcer."

I chewed on the inside of my cheek, debating what to do. A chance at this kind of contract was a dream come true. How could I resist?

Besides, it was a public space, and he was an enforcer—that had to count for something. And, if I were being honest, it'd be great to make more friends.

"If you agree to show me around the market," I started, hoping I wasn't making a mistake. "I'll say it's a date to get your sister off your back. Deal?"

A local showing me around would be an enormous advantage, plus helping him out might give me an edge in winning the alchemy contract.

"Really?" Rynac said, a glimmer of hope in his eyes. "Deal."

I said my goodbyes to the altered and went to grab my belongings. My mind whirled with new possibilities along with a sense of readiness to take the plunge.

Intoxicating excitement flooded through my veins as the glimmer of hope emerged, this time within my reach.

Chapter Six

Steam curled from my mug, the warmth seeping into my hands as I closed my eyes and inhaled, hunting to identify each scent.

The gentle floral melody had sweet undertones that reminded me of apples, and subtle earthy notes that grounded me. It was a cup of tranquility and calm, reminiscent of the herbal aromas that always surrounded me as I prepared ingredients for alchemy.

Despite the exhaustion from my first full shift, my sleep had been restless. Haunted by dreams of being chased, of being hunted down by some beast, but when I woke, the images faded.

Freeing my necklace, I stared down at the pendant. Delicate silver filigree wrapped around the teardrop-shaped lapis lazuli. Within the depths of the stone, golden flecks danced across the swirling blue, like distant stars scattered across the night sky.

On my sixth birthday, my parents gifted me the pendant, which was enchanted and runed to protect me.

Not a typical gift for a child, I know.

Due to my father's military position and my mother's appointment as witch ambassador to the UMC—the United Magical Council—both my brother and I had become possible targets.

I'd sworn I'd never take it off and took comfort in knowing that at least one magic was keeping me safe. Yet after today, I feared it wasn't enough. After all these years, how would I know if the protections remained?

I couldn't leave it to chance.

Tonight, I'd have to prepare some potions to keep on me at all times, or I'd never set foot outside my door again.

I longed for night to fall.

For the sun to descend, and for the moon to bathe me in its light as it rose above the horizon and watched over me.

It was odd that I felt such a connection with the moon, despite being a child of the sun. We shared many similarities. The moon was almost invisible when it shared the sky with the sun.

Near the colossal fireball that radiates light and heat, how could the moon compare?

Then night fell. As the sun faded, and people withdrew into their homes, the moon ruled her domain. Surrounded by the twinkling stars that only enhanced her beauty, but neither moon nor star detracted from one another.

In the dark sky, the moon could shine with her own light. She was in her element, even if most didn't appreciate her beauty.

With a sigh, I slumped on my couch, cursing the long spring days for stealing away my brewing hours.

After my shift at Divine, I'd made the long trek to the Alchemy Guild. I signed the forms for my next contract, then stopped by the library to research the other reagents in my special potion.

I know. Returning to the scene of the crime was risky, but they had the knowledge I needed. And there'd been no indication they'd increased security.

On my walk home, my little fox friend came to greet me, as if to reassure me they were uninjured, before rushing off.

I guess the vulpine still liked me, despite the trouble I'd put them through.

Back home, I continued my research on both the new recipes, jotting down details of every ingredient and the effect they had on other potions.

Hopeful, I flipped through *The Lunar Codex* again, but all the other pages were illegible.

When the sun retreated, I gathered my assortment of reagents and headed for the rooftop.

I'd arranged with the landlord to allow me to use the area, as I needed somewhere with direct moonlight the whole night. But if I kept cutting it close with rent, there was a good chance she'd revoke my access.

Despite my alchemy professor's many denials, the shifters of Selene had been the first to discover alchemy, and their magic became irrevocably linked to it.

I'd written a whole paper about how moonlight was an important ingredient, and how the phases of the moon correlated to the power of the brew.

To say they were unimpressed by my research was an understatement, but I stood by my work.

Animosity existed between witches and shifters; it perpetuated in each new generation, even though we didn't know the reason behind it anymore.

Then again, witches held an animosity toward nephilim as well, and disliked humans and erebians.

Nymphs were about the only race witches interacted with, though it was rare, as they were about as reclusive as my people.

The moon's soft glow embraced me as I pushed open the door to the roof, revealing the unimpeded view of the city.

Save for my small collection of alchemy tools and plants, the area was barren.

My low workbench was one-of-a-kind and had two spell arrays carved into the wood. This way I just needed to draw the required runes, not the entire array. Then, when I channeled my magic, it funneled directly into the brewing cauldron.

My setup had expanded, and hauling everything upstairs had become cumbersome.

Do you know how much a cauldron weighs? And I had two.

So I'd drawn a large array underneath to protect my belongings when I was gone. Better safe than sorry, even though I doubted anyone else came up here. Besides, I couldn't afford to buy replacements.

Anxiety knotted in my stomach. Was it meeting the enforcer captain, my friend-date with Rynac, my new job, the stolen tome, my broken magic, or that dog attack?

Goddess, why do I have so many problems?

But that's why I needed to brew tonight. Alchemy had a therapeutic effect on me, akin to yoga, but with a witch's hat and performed at night while concocting potions.

Okay, maybe not the best analogy.

I basked under the soft moonlight; allowing it to energize me after the last few turbulent days. I donned my witch's hat that was inscribed with protection runes.

Safety first, kids. Trust me, accidentally singe your eyebrows off once, and you'll never forget your hat again.

Lighting the flame beneath my cauldron, I tipped in the ingredients for my contract brew, an analgesic potion. They were easy to make and stronger than any painkillers you could buy over the counter.

I directed a smooth trickle of power into the spell array until the liquid bubbled.

Releasing my power felt like exhaling after a long day.

The magic wove the ingredients together and extracted the latent abilities within them.

While I longed to brew more tonight, my reagents were running low, and I had to pay rent before I could restock my supplies.

Instead, I would make microbrews with my cheaper ingredients. Usually, I'd brew the largest batch I could, but tonight it was the opposite as I needed to conserve reagents.

Maybe the enforcers would be interested in these brews. Non-lethal measures were always valuable.

One was a smoke-bomb brew that produced a cloud of smoke thick enough to obscure vision. Though I decided against adding any irritants—since in close quarters I might be affected too.

The other was simple but effective: a stinging nettle brew.

I know, nasty stuff.

The vial's content would cause intense discomfort and irritate the skin, but there were no long-term effects.

Stinging nettle leaves were used to manage inflammation or allergies, but when brewed with a dash of powdered gray quartz, they maintained the irritants during boiling. I always marveled at the unique properties of magical reagents.

Each plant possessed general benefits, but when a specific part like roots, leaves, or flowers was isolated, it revealed a unique quality. The way the components were stored and prepared, would alter their effects in the overall brew.

The art of alchemy unlocked a whole world of possibilities.

The Rasille leaf was a perfect example. When fresh, it encouraged blood clotting, but when dried and ground into a powder, it helped to combat blood infections.

It was fascinating, and nobody ever wanted to talk about it at parties.

I'd always be grateful that someone else had done the research, though. I didn't want to read about how they learned that roughly chopped Rasille leaves could cause excessive clotting. Throughout the body. Gruesome.

There's a reason one didn't invent new recipes without careful research and testing.

Extinguishing the flame, I ladled the brew into small vials. After corking each one, I traced a rune and allowed a small trickle of magic to flow out as I formed a seal.

A variation of an abjuration rune—the only other branch of magic I had some skill in. The rune held the cork in place unless someone intentionally pulled it out.

After finishing my other batches, I made some alterations to my bag to allow the stinging nettle and smoke-bomb vials to be within easy reach. Would these potions protect me against the threats in the city?

It had just been one dog and I doubted that it would be a common occurrence. But I wanted to be prepared in case it happened again.

I packed up my Guild batch too. When I'd texted my contact in the Guild that I'd finished, they asked if the client could pick them up. I didn't want strangers coming to my door and decided meeting them at Divine was the best option.

A heavy silence surrounded me as I headed to work.

Though I tried to project an aura of confidence, I only lasted to the end of my block before pulling out a smoke vial. The cold glass in my hand gave me a small measure of reassurance, but I jogged the entire way, scanning my surroundings.

My shoulders dropped in relief when Divine's door creaked open. Maybe I was overreacting after all.

The morning passed in a blur. Thayna and I prepared double batches of all the cookies, setting extras aside for tomorrow's shift when I opened the shop on my own.

During the first rush, I covered the register, and Zola, ever patient, fixed all my mistakes.

I don't know how she kept smiling the whole time when even saying "good morning" became a chore for me. In those few hours, I talked to more people than I had in the past month.

"Nyssa," Voren called, a few minutes into my break, and I sagged. "There's a shifter called Ruby looking for you."

"Oh." I perked up. She was here for the potions. "I'll be right out."

Ruby was easy to spot.

Even leaning against the wall, observing the coffee shop, she embodied a blend of elegance and strength that commanded attention. Her hair cascaded in waves of shimmering silver, and her eyes were a deep shade of amber, similar to a sunset's glow. But when she spotted me, she offered a shy smile that seemed contradictory to her exterior.

"Thank you for fulfilling our order so quickly," Ruby said, accepting the box of potions. "We recently lost one of our healers, and things have been strained."

"I am sorry to hear that, but it's my pleasure," I said, an idea sparking. "If your pack needs more, I'd be happy to set up a direct contract. With the Guild's approval, of course."

Everything went through them, but if I turned them into my personal client, I could cut down on the fees of going through the Guild.

"I'll mention that to the elders," Ruby said as she passed me an envelope with my payment. "They requested another batch from the Guild, but it's yet to be fulfilled."

Waving goodbye, I tucked my payment away and sent a text to my supervisor. I didn't want to poach a contract . . . okay, maybe I did, but I needed the money.

My break over, I retrieved my apron and returned to the floor. I almost groaned when Zola suggested I cover the bar. I knew I needed more practice, but it was stressful, with the customers watching my every move and spotting every mistake.

"Hello again," a familiar voice greeted.

The dark-haired woman who'd come to my aid yesterday stood across from me.

"Nyssa, is it?" she said, as her gaze flicked to my name tag. "I'm Carmen. I believe I forgot to introduce myself."

"Yes." I forced a smile as I finished making her drink. "And I didn't have a chance to thank you."

Why did I feel so unsettled by her presence?

I cleaned out my pitcher, avoiding eye contact. It had been easy to forget about what happened, to push aside the fear and sense of helplessness, but seeing my rescuer brought it all back up.

"Oh, it was nothing," she said, reaching out to touch my hand. "We magicals have to look out for each other."

While her skin was warm, her ring was cold as ice. Images flashed through my head. Black pitless eyes. Needle-sharp teeth. Claws slicing through the air.

I jerked away, my heart pounding as if it could escape.

"Sometimes we just need a nudge, right?" Carmen laughed.

I blinked, taking in the shop. Had I just blanked out? I managed a strained laugh. If she'd noticed anything, Carmen didn't show it.

"Take care, Nyssa." She waved and headed for an empty table.

I cradled my hand against my chest, trying to rub the warmth back into it.

No one else acted as if anything strange had happened. What had I just seen? Was my imagination taking over my memories, like a waking nightmare?

My hands shook as I wiped down the counter. A sense of dread slithered over my skin, seeping down into my bones.

The two potions I'd brewed were laughable against that thing. My mother had been right. I wasn't capable of handling the challenges of the outside world.

"Nyssa?" Zola's concerned voice pulled me from my dark thoughts. "Is everything okay?"

"Yes, of course." What had gotten into me?

"Good, because your enforcer is here." She nodded as Rynac walked in the door.

He'd dressed casual today in dark-washed jeans and a green t-shirt, but he still carried himself like an enforcer. Which wasn't a bad thing, but it made me question how he hadn't found a boyfriend yet.

"He's not my enforcer," I said, rolling my eyes. Not that it would stop the others from gossiping that it was a date.

"Offer him a drink on the house," Zola encouraged, ignoring my words.

With a shake of my head, I chuckled. I couldn't help but feel nervous as Rynac approached. Despite agreeing to spend today as friends, I wanted to make a good impression, so I needed to keep my oddity to a minimum.

"Hey," Rynac said. "Sorry I'm a bit early."

Judging by the tightness in his shoulders, he was as nervous as I was. It didn't help that Zola and Voren were not-so-subtly watching us and whispering to each other.

"Can I make you a drink?" I said in a rush, fearing the others might scare him off.

"Sure, surprise me."

He flashed me a sweet smile and, okay, that was pretty cute. Still didn't me I wanted to encourage the others to create something more out of this possible friendship.

I gnawed on my lip, debating what to make.

Since he'd had the chai yesterday, I picked an Earl Grey tea latte. It also happened to be my favorite. Velvety steamed milk mellowed the black tea, a hint of bergamot mixed with the light sweetness of vanilla. Perfect for a rainy day . . . or any day, really.

With a smile, I handed the cup to Rynac, but my eyes slipped past him and landed on Carmen.

She reclined on the couch, sipping her drink as she read a book. Something cold shifted inside me.

"What is it?" Rynac asked, following my gaze.

"Nothing," I blurted, before Carmen noticed. "I'll go clock out."

Chapter Seven

I had no idea where Rynac was taking me, so I did the only thing I could: follow and pretend I belonged here. That I wasn't a witch out of her depth.

Then I started thinking about my feet.

Big mistake.

One second I was walking; the next, every step felt awkward and wrong. And what did I do with my hands?

I attempted to maintain his pace, but his legs were much longer, and I had to half-jog to keep up.

Rynac must have realized I was vertically challenged compared to him and slowed down.

After walking almost three blocks—but who's counting—Rynac cleared his throat.

"I want to apologize for my behavior yesterday. We tend to be guarded when it comes to what we are. It wasn't personal."

I nodded, not really sure what to say. I wouldn't have liked a random person walking up and asking questions about witches.

"This still feels really awkward, doesn't it?" Rynac said.

A nervous laugh bubbled out of me. "I feel like I'm a teenager on my first date."

My cheeks flushed.

Oh Goddess, did I just say that?

Rynac let out a startled laugh. "That makes two of us. Why is it tougher to make friends as adults?"

"Beats me," I chuckled, the tension in my shoulders easing a fraction.

"How about we agree to no expectations or pressure? We'll be honest and see how things go."

I peered up at him, but his words were genuine. "And if we say anything too embarrassing, we can pretend we don't know each other?"

"Deal," Rynac said, a grin brightening his face.

We chatted as we walked; the conversation still somewhat stilted but a vast improvement.

The seaside market buzzed, a bustling hub of activity.

All the races mingled together with stalls crammed into every available space. A sturdy wooden deck covered the massive area before narrowing into a long pier.

The assortment of items for sale was incredible, and I stared with childlike wonder.

Almost every stall tempted me to stop and explore what they had to offer. It was like stepping into a treasure trove of unique and fascinating finds.

Despite the crowded space, once I was amidst the cacophony of voices and music, the atmosphere was charming.

A variety of aromas wafted through the air, tugging me in all directions, and it was hard to resist exploring every nook and cranny.

Rynac stayed close by to ensure we didn't lose each other in the crowd that jostled around us.

An amused grin grew on his lips as he followed me around, nodding at everything I pointed out with enthusiasm.

My excitement lasted until my feet ached, and my stomach rumbled with annoyance.

Rynac insisted on buying me lunch and guided me to the pier before disappearing into the swarm of people.

The salty air whipped at my hair, and I froze as my eyes drifted down to the waves crashing into the support beams beneath me.

A buzzing sensation pressed in on me.

I forced my legs to comply and retreated from the ocean. When I reached a place on the pier where only sand lay beneath me, I sat, trying to calm my turbulent heart.

A witch's magic was fueled by solar energies. We had an affinity to light, heat, and fire; it was only natural to shy away from our polar opposite.

I dangled my feet off the edge, focusing on the distant waves gently lapping the sandy shore. Only when someone held a tray of food in front of me did I snap back to reality.

Thanking Rynac, I dug into the meal.

"Best fish and chips around," he said, settling in beside me.

I munched away, the batter crispy while the fish was a perfect mix of buttery and flaky. "It's delicious."

"What brought you to Arkirith?" Rynac asked.

"Opportunity and curiosity," I said, devouring another chip. These were pretty damn good. "I want to open an alchemy shop. It's not something I could do back home. And I'll admit, I'm curious about races beyond mine and have limited knowledge about them. Would you tell me more about the altered?"

"We prefer 'enhanced'. Altered makes it sound like there is something wrong with us."

"Oh, I'm sorry. Thank you for correcting me. There is so much to learn here."

Rynac waved it off. "You're alright; it takes time. I appreciate that you wanting to know more about us. What questions do you have?"

"How long have you been enhanced?"

"A little under three years. It . . . it's been a turbulent time. We've only been in Arkirith for a year and a half, after we left the city we grew up in. They don't allow magicals there anymore."

I sensed there was more but didn't want to pry into personal matters. Well, maybe a bit. "Why did you pick Arkirith?"

Rynac shrugged. "Same as you. The opportunity. An enhanced population was already established here, and being a part of the enforcers gives us a purpose. A larger city means it's easier not to get singled out."

My brow creased. "Is aversion toward enhanced humans common?"

"Some places are worse than others." He shrugged. "It's best if we stick together. Humans see us as a danger, believing our magic and bodies are volatile. They fear the magic that created us, and they fear our magic could alter them . . . turning them into enhanced too.

"The magical races have mixed feelings. Most people are unsure of our place in *their* world. Some resent us, perceiving us as still human. Others see us as power-hungry, looking for any way to gain magic, and believe we are untrustworthy. The death and devastation the warlock of East Vale wrought is still fresh in people's minds."

"I heard about that."

Information had been tightly controlled, but when the UMC deployed a literal army to contain a threat, it was hard to keep quiet.

"Most witches believed warlocks were a myth until the news broke."

Though most facts about warlocks were still unknown, we knew each one signed a blood pact with one of the many demon lords who'd overthrown Terrarum, the realm of humans, nephilim and erebians.

Through the pact, the warlock gained demonic powers and could even command low-level demons.

Ice trickled down my back. Images of the demonspawn in the alley flickered through my thoughts.

No. It was a dog. The reminder of warlocks and demons was feeding my imagination.

"But you're the police force. If people didn't trust enhanced, why would they give you that authority?"

"The MEA was highly understaffed and desperate for new enforcers. Enhanced are well suited for the job, and after much debate, we were allowed to join. Safety has improved, which has helped to sway the higher-ups."

Rynac paused, gazing at the horizon.

"People don't like what they don't understand. Some accuse us of wanting to steal magic or trying to become something more. We've a great deal to offer, but it's not an easy life."

I hesitated, words poised on the tip of my tongue.

"Witches are the same," I murmured.

My throat constricted at the thought of speaking ill of my race. But I'd witnessed similar atrocities my whole life. They'd never sat well with me.

"Many treat their own blood who never manifest their magic terribly." Like how I'd been treated for my lacking magic, as if it was my own fault. "To me, we are all witches, regardless of the magic we possess. But those who shared my belief seldom voiced their opinions. And so, nothing changes."

We fell silent, consumed by our own thoughts. Something nagged at me. Unlike unmanifested witches, enhanced chose this.

"You don't have to answer," I said, picking my words with care. "But why did you choose to become enhanced?"

That was the burning question. Why would a human risk their life by consuming magic? From what I understood, the survival rate was very low after exposure to the volatile magic that altered their bodies.

Was the allure of being transformed, gaining access to magic, that compelling? But wasn't that what I hunted for too? I thought I'd made peace with never fixing my wild magic, but the new potion recipe reignited that desire.

The possibility of becoming something new—something powerful—created an enticing prospect. I'd spent my whole life trying to fit in and be someone else. If humans took that chance, their community ostracized them.

Silence lingered between us, only broken by the splash of water and the cry of a gull overhead. I feared I'd pushed too far. We were practically strangers, but my curiosity had won out.

"It wasn't a choice." His voice barely rose above the waves crashing below. "We lived in East Vale."

The blood drained from my face.

When the authorities discovered a warlock had been sacrificing humans, they tried to apprehend them, but the warlock wiped them out with a horde of demonspawn.

Then the UMC stepped in.

I'd overheard my parents discussing it—the fighting had leveled parts of the city. When they finally killed the warlock, it caused a devastating magical shockwave, unleashing wild and volatile magic that destroyed everything in its path.

Humans, magicals, buildings. Everything vaporized.

That same volatile magic coursed within me.

I wanted to change the subject, to give him an out, but determination settled over his features.

"Few humans choose the alteration. Most of us had this new life forced on us."

His gaze fixed ahead as if lost in memories.

"Indra and I were visiting our mother, trying to convince her to stay with us where it was safe." Sorrow laced his words. "When that blast went off . . . Indra and I were the only survivors recovered from that neighborhood."

Rynac swallowed hard, pain etched on his face.

"We tried to go back to our lives, tried to help the city rebuild and recover, but . . ." He shook his head.

I couldn't even comprehend his experience. The weight of that loss, the survivor's guilt that still lingered.

My heart squeezed.

"I'm sorry," I rasped. Mere words couldn't undo the pain that Rynac endured, but it was all I had in this fragile moment.

All that death and destruction. Who could blame humans for their aversion to magic?

I wrapped my hands around his much larger one, fearing he might pull away but needing him to understand. "I am so sorry. For your loss and what happened to you."

"Thank you." He squeezed my hand.

A hint of sadness lingered in his gaze, but he offered me a faint smile that warmed my chest.

"And I am sorry, that probably wasn't an appropriate topic for a first friend-date."

I mirrored his smile. "It's my fault for asking, but thank you for sharing."

"We said we would be honest."

"Yes," I agreed, a mischievous grin dancing on my lips. "Just not with your sister."

Rynac's snort of amusement lightened the atmosphere, and the spark returned to his gaze. "We should get moving if we want to hit up the remaining vendors before your meeting. Unless you want to share the worst day of your life with me."

"I'll save that for our second outing," I chuckled. "And I have some money burning a hole in my pocket."

Not that I should spend it, but didn't I deserve a bit of fun after all my hard work?

We ventured back to the market, but there was too much to see in one afternoon. As I was about to admit it was time to head out, my gaze snagged on a stall overflowing with plants.

"Oh!" was all I managed as I rushed over.

Pots of all shapes and sizes filled the area, each containing unique and vibrant plants, most of the varieties I'd never seen before. Colors ranged from mesmerizing blues to every shade of green, brilliant reds, and even some silvery hues.

The stall conjured memories of my grandmothers and our botany hikes. My heart filled with longing.

As my fingers trailed over the supple leaves, a gentle tingling sensation stirred within me.

A trickle of magic slipped from my fingertips, and knowledge rushed into my mind. I perceived the plant's vitality and health, that it would bloom in the next few days. Its fresh flowers held the essence of brightness, a quality I could harness in my potions.

I smiled down at the plant as its desire to be utilized pulsed through our connection.

At a touch, I sensed the general properties of a reagent and its qualities, which, as an alchemist, was invaluable.

"Brightness" held a multitude of possibilities, depending on how I prepared the flowers as well as what ingredients I paired them with.

All those endless combinations, all that potential just waiting to be discovered. Rather than daunting, I found it exhilarating.

A pair of captivating peridot orbs caught my eye, and I jolted with surprise when they blinked back at me.

A musical laugh filled the air as a dryad appeared, her skin silver and her hair the same color as her eyes.

"I see you're enjoying my friends here," she said, gesturing to the surrounding plants.

She flowed rather than walked. The leaves seemed to sway and follow her every move, as if she were their radiant sun, bestowing life and energy upon them.

The connection she had with the plants was unmistakable, and it filled the air with an aura of enchantment as I watched, mesmerized.

"They're wonderful. But I was wondering if you had any veridalias?"

My supervisor had agreed to transfer the contract for Ruby's pack. This batch was a potent form of pain control, and while dried veridalia leaves were acceptable, fresh were superior. If my potions stood out, the extra cost would be worth it.

"Of course," the dryad said, setting down the spiky little bush.

The leaves were lethally sharp, funny that a plant with healing properties would cause injury.

"That one's starlight tears." She nodded, and I realized I was still skimming my fingers on the plant.

The moment I stopped, a sadness filled me, but I shook it off, knowing it was just the plant's aura.

"Also called *stellarum lacrimae*, it's a wonderful addition to any garden. Its glow will encourage the other plants to grow."

"*Stellarum lacrimae*." I repeated, my mind snagging on the name.

That was an ingredient in the *magiam augere* potion. Stumbling upon it felt like a nudge from the universe.

Maybe it was all the talk of warlocks and demons, or the reminder that, unlike my family, I lacked the magic to defend myself.

I *should* be skilled enough to protect myself from these dangers.

"I'll take it," I said.

My gaze caught on a beautiful succulent, adorned with soft pink blooms and rich green leaves that turned a vibrant red at the tips.

"And that one too."

I tried to rein myself in before I spent all my cash, but that last one was for Zola. I wanted to get her a thank-you gift for training me.

The box of plants balanced in my arms as I left, and I found Rynac crouched before a little girl. A crown made of white and yellow flowers adorned her head, and additional crowns filled her basket.

With a giggle, she handed one to Rynac and skipped off.

A ghost of a smile on his lips, Rynac stood staring after her.

I laughed, startling him. "That suits you."

"I couldn't say no," he said, eyeing the twisting wreath of flowers. "I can't bring this to HQ. I'll never live it down, but I can't throw it out."

"Want to trade?" I said, nodding at the plants, while doing my best to hide my amusement at this supposed dilemma.

Before I could blink, Rynac placed the crown on my head and swept up the plants.

I chuckled, falling into step beside him as the city's vibrant ambiance embraced us.

"Thank you for today," Rynac said, a smile tugging at the corner of his mouth. "Not just for getting Indra to stop harassing me. It's been a while since I've done something for fun, and not work-related."

"Me too," I said with a genuine smile.

For the first time since moving to Arkirith, I didn't feel like an outsider. Perhaps I could find my place here, as Rynac and Indra had.

We walked toward MEA headquarters and the meeting that would decide my fate.

My heart fluttered with uncertainty—but for the first time since I got here, there was a thin, stubborn strand of hope tangled around it.

Now I just had to prove I deserved to stay.

Chapter Eight

I wiped my sweaty palms on my pants for the tenth time and tried not to fidget. Each thump of my heart echoed within the confines of the captain's office.

His stern expression paired with a close-cut haircut, screamed military. He reminded me of my dad, which threw me off even more.

Gray peppered his black hair, muscled arms strained against the fabric of his shirt, and both attributes convinced me that age was merely an annoyance to him.

When I arrived at the headquarters, the enforcers had swarmed around me like I was a new toy and devoured the cookies I'd brought.

However, when the captain approached, everyone scattered except for Indra and Rynac. The siblings had introduced me, but the captain hadn't even offered his name as he assessed me with a critical gaze.

I'd been stress-sweating ever since.

He scrutinized the list of potions I provided, his face unreadable. Was he unimpressed with what I offered?

I averted my gaze and looked around his office for a distraction.

The room was utilitarian in design, with everything serving a purpose. The desk held a stack of tidy papers, and the filing cabinets and bookshelves were in order. Not even a pen out of place.

But what stood out most was the lack of personal touches; no family photos, decorative items, or anything to hint at who the captain was outside his job.

Considering what Rynac had shared earlier, I wondered if there was indeed nothing else for him—no family to return home to after work.

What a bleak image. Perhaps I'd return to the market and pick out a suitable plant to brighten the room.

I'd narrowed it down to a succulent—as they required less care—when he set the papers aside and fixed me with his hard stare.

"Your list of potions is quite extensive," he remarked.

"Thank you," I said, unsure if that was a compliment.

His gaze seemed to strip away my flesh and reveal all my faults. "But as the majority are likely detrimental to the bulk of my enforcers, I cannot agree to a contract. We require specialized formulas and dosing, or the potions can do more harm than good."

"I understand every race is different. If you grant me time to research and learn the proper dosage for enhanced, I'm certain I can create a product that would be safe for consumption. Give me a week."

I didn't want to plead, but I sensed my chances slipping through my fingers.

"I don't want you rushing to produce results if it jeopardizes the safety of my people."

"No—of course not. I just . . ." I trailed off, trying to find the right words to express my determination and enthusiasm.

"You need the money?" he interrupted.

Ouch.

"Having an established client would allow me to expand my business." I pressed on. "And then I wouldn't need to rely on the Guild."

His brow furrowed. "It seems neither of us has a good relationship with the Guild."

The captain considered me for a moment longer, his expression now more calculating than guarded.

"Crafting potions for us will be challenging and demanding. You will need to learn new ways of formulating them for my enhanced officers."

"Witch-brewed potions are more adaptable to other races, and learning new formulas is part of the job."

"You're a witch?" Surprise flickered across his features before the stony mask slipped back into place. "I assumed you were a shifter."

A shifter who dyes their hair, maybe. I managed a polite smile. Another witch might've taken offense. "Is that a problem?"

Shifters possessed a natural talent for alchemy, and despite the adaptability of witch-brewed potions, most shunned that branch of magic.

After an excruciating pause, he said, "No. I just don't encounter many in Arkirith."

He watched me again with his unreadable expression, and I resisted the urge to break the awkward silence.

My planned speech had fallen apart, and I struggled to remember what I had written last night.

"I'm a hard worker and dedicated to my craft. All my alchemy exams received the top grade at university. I'll brew whatever you request and ensure it meets your standards." Goddess, I sounded desperate.

Oh wait, I was.

The captain made a noncommittal noise and rested his clasped hands on the desk.

His fingers flexed and relaxed as he mulled over my words.

"You realize there are risks involved in associating with the MEA. There are many who loathe our role within the city."

"I will do business with whomever I choose. My services are available to those in need, regardless of others' opinions. I relish the challenge of altering my potions to benefit all members of the MEA. Your line of work will enable me to craft a wider variety of brews than I could ever sell to the public. We share the same purpose of making a difference in this realm. And I wish to form a partnership because I believe we both serve the same cause."

I drew in a deep, shuddering breath and awaited his response.

Everything was in the open. The choice was his.

"The Council doesn't want details about our race to be common knowledge, especially among humans, so we keep it within our community. I trust you will honor our secrecy?"

"Of course, I understand and respect confidentiality. It's an important part of this profession." Though that was usually in regards to recipes and formulations.

"Have Enforcer Terral take you to our healer. You'll need to sign a confidentiality agreement, then our healer can provide you with our formulas. You can submit a batch for testing, and if you meet their standards, we can discuss a contract further."

It took me a few moments to realize he'd dismissed me. My chair scraped across the floor with a screech.

He was giving me a chance. I offered him my brightest smile, which bounced off him like a pebble against armor plating.

"Thank you for this opportunity," I said.

Emerging from the office in a daze, I spotted my new friends waiting for me.

"Who's Enforcer Terral?" I asked.

Indra snorted. "That's both of us."

"Did it go well?" Rynac asked.

"I think so," I managed, my mind still trying to catch up.

"Don't worry, I'll make sure the captain has a lasting impression of you." She winked, heading toward his office, holding the last of my cookies. "I love the crown, by the way."

Icy dread washed over me. *Oh Goddess.*

I touched my head, and I realized I'd never removed the crown. I must have looked like a complete idiot to the hardened captain.

I dropped my face into my hands. How had I forgotten?

"Are you alright?" Rynac gripped my arm as if he feared I might fall over, which was possible.

But the captain had still offered me the trial. I couldn't believe it. For once, I hadn't screwed up.

Or the captain was just that desperate.

"Where's the medical wing?" I asked.

His voice dropped low as he stepped closer. "What's wrong? Did something happen?"

"What? No, not unless you can die from embarrassment. Why didn't you mention I was still wearing this?" I scowled and pointed at the flowers.

At least Rynac had the decency to look guilty and mumble an apology. I trudged beside him and filled him in on the meeting as we headed for the infirmary.

The current healer on duty, Matti, had the disheveled appearance of an overworked employee. He perked up when I explained my purpose and was all too happy to copy out potion recipes as I read over the confidentiality agreement.

"I can manage these," I commented, leafing through the pages he'd written out.

I recognized the formulas, only minor alterations from my own. The major difference appeared to be the runes used in the spell array and the infusion levels. I couldn't understand the captain's worry.

"With lower magical input, I'll be able to produce larger batches, even with the slower infusion rate."

Matti's face lit up. "Really? Most of these are in short supply. We won't receive another shipment for at least a fortnight."

I frowned. Why wouldn't the Guild fast-track a shipment if the client required it? "Though I do need to find these reagents, but it shouldn't be hard."

"There are several herbalists along Cedar Way in the northern district who supply us with raw ingredients. Oh, though I'm sure you have Guild-sanctioned suppliers." Matti winced as if expecting a reprimand.

Yeah, and they charge a premium. "I'd be happy to work with anyone you've established a relationship with."

Leaving a less stressed Matti behind, Rynac led me out of the building and insisted on escorting me home. After all the social interaction today, I was exhausted, but I didn't mind Rynac's presence.

"If you'd like," he said as we rounded the corner onto my street, "I can take you to the suppliers to find the reagents you need."

"You're not sick of me yet?" I arched a brow at him.

He chuckled. "These potions will make a big difference for us. They're always in short supply. Plus, I enjoyed today."

"I'm just glad that I can be useful to someone," I said. Before he could reply, I yawned so wide that my jaw cracked. "Sorry, I usually sleep in the afternoon. I guess I'll have to be normal and sleep at night for once."

"I'll see you after work, then?" he asked as we stopped in front of my apartment building.

"Sounds like a plan." I waved over my shoulder as I headed inside.

By the time I dragged myself up the five flights and face-planted onto my bed, every muscle throbbed—but I couldn't wipe the smile off my face.

Today had gone sideways in all the best ways, and there was no stuffing the hope back down now.

For the first time in a long time, the future didn't feel like a problem to solve, but rather like a door cracking open to life I dreamed of.

CHAPTER NINE

A strange, invigorating energy carried me all the way through my shift at Divine . . . or was it because I slept through the night for the first time in years?

As one o'clock ticked closer, excitement bubbled up at the prospect of buying reagents and spending today with Rynac. To think that people here actually wanted to spend time with me.

But that bubble burst when my shift ended, and Rynac was no where to be seen.

"You've been eyeing that door for the last hour," Voren said as we headed to clock out. "Did he stand you up?"

"We're not dating," I insisted, not for the first time today.

It didn't matter how many times I explained that neither of us were interested in each other that way.

"Don't worry," Zola said as she swept into the room. "Voren will get enough gossip tonight to leave you alone for a few days."

"We're heading out for drinks with some of the crew," Voren added, his eyes lighting up. "You're coming, right?"

I opened my mouth to decline—my automatic reflex—but said, "Yes," before I could change my mind.

That was the old Nyssa, the one who didn't stand out or cause trouble. Since moving here, I wanted to seize these new opportunities.

"Oh, Zola, before I forget, I have a gift for you. I found this yesterday at the market," I said, picking up the potted plant and offering it to her. "Thank you for all your help and for nudging me to chat with the enforcers."

She blinked at the plant, then chuckled. "Thank you, Nyssa. That's very sweet of you."

Voren laughed, which turned into a cough at Zola's glare.

My phone chimed. I frowned as I read the message from Rynac.

"Is that your date canceling?" Voren asked.

"He's running late and wants to meet me halfway," I said. "But I don't know how to get to Wattle Park."

"That's past our apartment building," Zola said. "We'll show you."

Voren linked arms with me. "Yes, and you can tell us all about this date of yours."

"You've been grilling me all day," I laughed, letting him lead me outside. "I don't know how much more there is to tell about my *friend*."

Zola came to a sudden halt, staring down at her phone.

"What's wrong?" Voren asked.

"It's Thayna," she said. "Her sister says she hasn't arrived home yet, and she isn't answering her phone."

My stomach twisted. I might not have known her long, but I liked her and hoped she was okay.

Wringing my hands, I tried to think of something comforting to say, but my mind was blank.

"It'll be fine," Voren said, his voice low and surprisingly soothing, enough that the tension in my shoulders relaxed. He looped an arm through Zola's and pulled her along. "She might just be running late or missed her connecting flight."

The three of us wandered down the street, chatting away to distract Zola. Despite my somber mood, I realized I was still smiling after I waved goodbye. It had been the right choice to stop letting my old habits stand in the way. I knew I wouldn't regret going out with them tonight.

I regretted everything.

The Divine crew knew how to party, and I did *not* know how to hold my drink.

The night had started off tame, chatting over a cocktail and appetizers, then someone got the idea we needed to go dancing.

When we arrived at the *EtherFlow* Lounge, we were greeted with a round of shots.

Everything got a bit fuzzy after that, which should've been concerning, but at least when I was drunk, casting magic was near impossible. Without focus, magic wouldn't comply.

With a groan, I dragged myself out of bed the next morning, still wearing last night's clothes.

This new Nyssa needed to invent a hangover cure potion.

Thank the Goddess that I had today off. I would've been useless at work, unlike poor Voren had to open.

My "not-a-date" with Rynac had been fun; I'd bought all the reagents I could afford.

While the Guild vendors had a larger selection, I was more than happy to visit several shops to gather my supplies if it saved me money.

Afterwards, I'd debated canceling with Zola and Voren for about an hour and then headed out to the bar.

Despite the hangover, I had enjoyed myself and only regretted it when I moved or thought.

I wallowed in my bed until hunger drove me to track down something edible. Though I lost a night of brewing, I couldn't complain.

When was the last time I'd experienced so much freedom and fun?

Several coffees later, I dove into my research for the enhancement and binding potions. I wanted to start at least one tonight. The potions for the enforcers took priority, but I could squeeze one personal brew in. But which one?

I'd come to Arkirith to subdue my wild magic, but what if there was an alternative?

I quashed the hope rising within me.

For years I'd dreamed and even prayed for a way to fix myself, but that had resulted in nothing but heartache.

Now, I might have the chance to use my magic beyond alchemy . . . it was tempting. To have full access to magic, to not be weak, to face the challenges of my life, to become as powerful as the rest of my family.

Would I finally meet their expectations and earn their approval? Would it give me the freedom to choose my future?

That dream seemed fragile, like delicate glass ready to shatter.

I didn't think I'd be able to recover if I failed again. No, it was safer to craft the potion that would suppress my powers. I could live without fear of my wild magic being discovered. I could visit my family without fear of the council detecting it.

It was the logical choice.

So why did I hesitate?

Collecting all the reagents, I made my way to the rooftop as my turbulent thoughts swirled. Preparing the ingredients I would need for the MEA brews, my eyes kept darting to the codex. I shouldn't have brought it up here; it would only tempt me.

Something blue shimmered under the fading sunlight. The cobalt vulpine leaped across the rooftops toward me.

"Hello, my little savior," I said in greeting.

The fox sniffed at me, and I smiled as it circled around.

Such a curious creature. I tamped down my hope that it was testing me to see if I was worthy of the familiar bond. What familiar would want a witch with broken magic like me? But what if I fixed my magic? Was that what the fox was waiting for?

I shook my head to scatter those thoughts. I would've felt something by now, some sort of magical connection between us.

But a girl could dream.

The fox nudged my hand until I petted it. Magic shivered under my fingers as I stroked its fur. Images flashed through my mind.

A dark street. A hulking form blocking the path. Glistening black scales. Hungry eyes.

Demonspawn.

My heart stuttered. It hadn't been a dog. A demonspawn had attacked, and the fox scared it off. Why did I think otherwise?

More images filled my thoughts. Chasing the demonspawn. Sinister talons slashing toward me. More hulking figures. Demonspawn surrounded me before I darted between their legs and escaped.

I gasped for air as my vision cleared, and I was once again sitting on my rooftop.

What in all the heavens was that? I rubbed my eyes. Maybe last night's concoctions were more potent than I first thought.

But the fox stared up at me, as if they knew what I'd seen.

"Did you just show me that?" I asked—not that the fox could understand—but they dipped their head, holding my gaze.

What?

"Do you understand me?" Again, they nodded. "Then it was a demonspawn, not a dog, that you saved me from? How could I confuse the two?"

The fox tilted their head, as if they couldn't understand either.

"Were those your memories I saw? It's hard enough to believe there's a demonspawn running around the city. But a handful of them?"

Demonspawn were low-level beasts from Terrarum. The demon lords had waged a war against humans and nephilim for control of the realm and won. Refugees from the Great War fled to our home of Trutina, and then the veil between the realms was sealed.

The UMC had a division that monitored the veil, detected breaches, and dispatched a team to seal it and exterminate any demons who passed through. So where was that team now? And what about the enforcers? Did they know of this threat?

I doubted Rynac would've told me or any civilian about it, knowing how much panic and fear it would cause. I was sure they were handling the situation.

"How do I protect myself from demonspawn?" I asked.

My smoke-bomb and stinging nettle brew seemed laughable. The fox darted over to the codex and rested a paw on it.

I shook my head. "My magic is dangerous and unpredictable. It needs to be bound before I hurt someone. I couldn't even conjure a spell to save myself the other morning."

The fox pawed the book, then met my gaze with unwavering determination. How could I expect a creature to understand?

"No," I said, pointing to the binding potion recipe. "I need to make this one."

The fox growled and clawed at the paper with the recipe until it fell off the table, then they sat down next to the codex.

I sighed, reaching for the fallen recipe. The fox darted down to stand guard over it. They rubbed against my hand. The same images of demonspawn assaulted me.

I'd already proved I was worthless in a fight against them, but it wasn't my job to hunt them down either. I'd keep my head down and let the authorities deal with the problem.

Just like I always did.

Let those stronger and more powerful handle things. Not everyone should be on the front lines. I was much happier supporting them with my potions.

But just once, I wanted to be able to handle my own problems and know that I could protect myself.

When I walked to work early in the morning, what if I encountered more demonspawn and the fox wasn't there to chase them off?

What if the empowerment potion could give me that?

I reached out, my fingers brushing over the codex, and a tingle of magic responded. Picking up the book, I opened it to the potion and my notes.

The effects were temporary, lasting only a few hours. I could take a small portion to test its effects. Without a full moon, the power of the potion diminished.

It would need several hours to brew, but if I set it up first, it would be ready toward the end of the night, and I could craft the enforcer potions while it simmered. I wouldn't have time to brew the binding potion, though, so it would have to wait until tomorrow.

"Fine," I said to the fox. "Have it your way, I'll brew it."

But I smiled.

That small sliver of hope had lodged itself deep in my heart.

The empowerment potion proved to be a challenge, and I loved it.

How long had it been since I'd crafted a brew that tested my skills? Or a recipe where I'd needed to adapt on the spot to ensure the brew was stable?

My fox friend had curled up at my side and didn't seem to mind when I petted them.

With the hard part over, the potion needed to simmer with a slow trickle of magic to fortify it.

The longer I could maintain it, the more potent the overall potion, but since I needed to test first, I kept it at a low level.

I started with a batch of minor healing potions tailored to the exact requirements of the enhanced.

It was easy enough that my mind wandered, imagining what my magic could do if I had control over it. I didn't need access to all the branches, just a few would be enough.

It would be a massive help once my shop opened.

The second batch was an antifibrinolytic brew that helped to control bleeding after surgery or a traumatic injury.

The concoction bubbled away happily as I gave it another stir—once clockwise and twice anticlockwise, just as Matti had specified.

Extinguishing the flame beneath the cauldron, I ladled the brew into small vials.

I wanted to offer more once this batch underwent testing. I hoped that I'd be able to create a kit for enforcers to carry, stocked with potions they could keep on hand for emergencies.

During First Aid 101 in college, the instructor stressed how every minute counted.

Excitement jolted through me as I checked on the empowerment brew. A hypnotizing, iridescent white liquid swirled in my cauldron. The magic within pulsed in time with my own heartbeat.

I longed to let it gather more power, but I needed to rein it in.

This was just a test. An experiment.

I'd only crafted enough for one potion.

A few of these reagents cost the same amount I'd earn in three shifts at Divine. So I split it into two vials to be safe.

The vibrant liquid swirled as if it had a mind of its own. I sent a trickle of my magic into the vial to test the brew. It spun faster in response, as if it wanted me to drink it now.

Even at half strength, the potion brimmed with power. How strong would it be if I crafted it under the full moon?

I didn't want to wait for the binding potion.

Just a sip couldn't hurt.

No, I was being irrational. Best to have precautions in place first.

After all, I'd seen the devastation wild magic could cause, and while the rooftop was empty of all but the fox and me, I couldn't risk it.

My phone dinged, and I found a message from Rynac. I snatched the phone up and tapped on the message, but Rynac had only texted: *Busy.* Was that a question or a statement?

Just brewing, I messaged back, tamping down my disappointment.

As soon as I hit send, I wondered if I should have waited longer before responding. Did I seem too eager? Or like I stared at my phone all night?

The three dots appeared, doing their little dance.

And kept dancing.

Was he writing an essay?

Call.

I blinked at the single-word response. Why did it take him so long to type that? Did he want to say something else?

Before my self-conscious doubts could catch up, I hit call.

"Hey, Nyssa." He answered on the first ring, but his voice seemed strained.

"Hi." I'm clearly great at conversations with real people.

"Uh . . . are you home?"

I frowned and paced across the rooftop.

His words slurred together. Was he drunk?

"What's going on, Rynac? Is everything all right?"

"Not particularly. Have you started the enhanced brews?"

"Two full batches are ready, and I was about to start the third."

"Good, good," he replied, his voice raspy and uneven.

Had he called me in the early hours of the morning to talk about potions?

Don't get me wrong, I'd love it if someone called just to chat about alchemy, but I doubted that was the reason. After all, he was on duty. I froze as the realization slammed into me.

"What happened?" I blurted. Energy buzzed through my body, preparing to face the unknown danger that had my heart racing.

"Unexpected altercation."

What the hell does that mean?

"Are you hurt?" I couldn't keep the rising panic from my voice.

"Indra went to hunt down the demonspawn that fled. I could use a potion. I'm sorry to call—"

"Demonspawn." The word hissed out of me.

The fox lifted their head, watching me.

"Where are you?" I demanded, my voice sharp as I locked away my panic, even as it rattled the bars whispering that "could use a potion" translated to "I'm badly hurt." I pushed those thoughts aside as I swiped all the potions into my shirt to create a makeshift pouch.

"Third and Maple."

Gripping the fabric tight to protect my creations, I held the phone between my shoulder and ear as I raced down the stairs, the vulpine hot on my heels.

"What about an ambulance?" I asked, pushing my door open with my shoulder. Dumping the potions onto my bed, I pulled on a pair of sturdy boots—my dad had a thing about good footwear—then snatched up my bag.

"I—the thing is . . . it's not that bad," he stammered.

"But bad enough to call me?"

I rolled my eyes, though deep down, I was flattered he'd called. Enforcers seemed stoic. I imagined others would've just bled the entire way back to HQ.

"What about the other enforcers?"

"They're en route, but they might not get here in time."

Shit. I stuffed the potions into the bag and grabbed a few of my backups.

While they weren't viable for enhanced, I wanted to be prepared for anything. Plus, my enchanted bag could hold far more than it should for its size.

I picked up the empowerment potion—

No, this is foolish.

I just needed to give Rynac my potions, and then the other MEA squads could do the rest.

The fox brushed against my leg as if waiting for me. But what if there were more demonspawn? I needed to reach Rynac in time. I needed to defend myself without making things worse.

"Fuck it."

I downed the potion in one gulp. So much for caution. But my friend's life was in danger.

Tossing the vial, I ran for the door.

Chapter Ten

I thundered down the street, jingling like a rack of test tubes, the fox a streak of blue at my side. My lungs burned like the seven hells, but fear kept my legs pumping—and Dad's voice hammered in my skull: *Keep the wounded talking.*

"I'm on Maple," I puffed as I skidded around the corner.

The emptiness of the streets seemed abnormal. I hadn't seen a single car pass by.

What if those things still lingered here? The hair on the back of my neck prickled.

My fingers wrapped around my conduit, seeking comfort in its touch. I hadn't sensed any changes to my magic yet. Maybe the potion hadn't worked, but I didn't have time to be disappointed.

"Rynac?" I hissed, but the line remained quiet.

With a curse, I pushed harder.

My shoulders ached from the weight of the bag, but I didn't dare slow down. I sent a silent apology to my dad for ignoring his advice to stay active. You never know when you might need that speed and stamina, he'd say.

Halfway down the block to Third, a pungent stench hit me like a brick wall.

Gagging, I stumbled. It was as if an entire truckload of eggs had gone bad. My eyes watered, and the tang of metal coated my tongue.

Halting on the corner of Third and Maple, I squinted, searching for any sign of Rynac.

Confusion creased my brow. I almost wondered if I'd stepped onto the set of a horror movie. Gore splattered the walls and formed congealed pools on the road, yet there were no bodies.

The fox darted ahead, weaving through the battlefield and disappeared down an alley.

Sprinting after them, I stumbled through the darkness and crashed to my knees beside a body.

Rynac's phone screen provided enough light for me to see his profile. He was half propped against the wall, eyes closed, one arm wrapped around his stomach, while the other hand clutched his phone. Though he wore black tonight, it failed to conceal the slick, wet sheen of blood.

"Rynac?" I said, my voice wobbling.

The awful smell made me scrunch up my nose, but I recalled my first aid training. I pressed a shaky hand to his neck, but he didn't respond. His skin was cool to the touch, and even under the weak moonlight, he seemed pale.

But he had a pulse, and he was breathing.

"Okay. That's good." I forced the words out while I screamed internally. "Now I . . . check for injuries."

But for that, I needed to see. I tried to settle my thoughts as I summoned my magic.

Cupping my hands, I willed magic to pool within as I whispered, "*Apricum.*"

Light blazed from my fingers as bright as the sun before it spluttered. Rogue magic burned my palms. I tossed the glowing orb into the air before it melted my skin. With a hiss, I shook my singed hands.

The potion didn't work.

The bitter tang of failure coated my mouth, but I pushed my disappointment away. This wasn't the time.

The orb floated in the air like a drunken balloon; its light fading to a weak glow, but was still better than nothing. My faulty spell would only last a few minutes, so I had to work fast.

The fox sat and watched me, but I ignored it.

Removing Rynac's arm from his stomach, I tugged up his shirt and froze. I'd seen photographs of stomach wounds deep enough to see internal organs in textbooks . . . but witnessing them on a living, breathing person—a wave of dizziness crashed into me as I stared at the three long gashes.

"Nyssa?" Rynac grunted as pain rippled across his features.

I shoved all my emotions into a box, leaving only cold logic to guide me. They would only hinder what I needed to do.

"Do you have any other injuries?" My voice held a hint of command as I channeled my father.

I rifled through my bag, pulling out two of the potions I'd just brewed for the enhanced officers, along with my emergency kit.

Speed was crucial—and not just for slowing the bleeding and treating the wound. I didn't know how long I could suppress the part of my brain that was freaking out.

"A few smaller cuts and likely a couple of broken ribs." Rynac winced as he shifted. "Am I hallucinating, or is that a fox?"

"It's a friend," I mumbled, but concern creased my brow as I squeezed the vials in my hand. If something happened to him . . . because of me. "We haven't tested these potions. It could be dangerous. I don't know the side effects."

I needed him to understand the risks, but he swiped the potions without batting an eye.

"I'll take my chances. What's the worst that could happen?"

Before I could even begin rattling off the list of potential side effects—nausea, excessive bleeding, magical incompatibility rejection, forced alteration, death—he downed both vials.

Either he had a lot of faith in me, or he was that desperate. I swallowed around the lump in my throat—trying not to dwell on what my potions might do to him—and pulled out dressings for his wounds.

"You're a mini-hospital." His lips curved up in a faint smile.

"Will the demonspawn come back?" I should've asked that before running in here like an idiot.

His pause didn't inspire confidence. "Best we get moving."

Great. "And what about the other enforcers?"

With my lightest touch, I cleaned the wounds as well as I could. My shoulders sagged with relief as the bleeding slowed. But for how long?

Rynac was silent for far too long as he tapped on his phone.

"Backup's delayed." It was matter-of-fact, but I heard the underlying tension.

I didn't meet his gaze as I applied bandages, but my mind was already making calculations while ignoring *what* exactly was delaying them.

I'd need Rynac to be able to move on his own. His wounds might not be life-threatening now that the potions had worked their magic. But he still needed treatment, better care than I could provide in an alley, and someone to monitor him for any reaction to the potions.

"Where can we go for healing?" I said, trying to keep my voice steady.

Rynac winced as he shifted. "On Fifth between Olive and Grove. An on-call healer lives there."

I swallowed hard. How would I lug him that far? He was over six feet and all muscle; I was just under five foot seven.

In the end, what choice did I have? Healing spells had never been my forte, but maybe the potion just took longer to kick in and would aid me. Wishful thinking, I know.

"Brace yourself. This will hurt, but it'll make moving easier." I steeled myself, pressing my hands on either side of the wounds and attempted to steady my breath before I hissed, "*Adtractus.*"

Agonizing pain shot through my head, and my hands trembled as I wrestled with my magic. It felt like trying to force molasses through a thin tube.

Gnashing my teeth, I pushed harder. Daggers stabbed into the back of my eyes, and sweat trickled down my face.

Rynac groaned, but I didn't have a spare moment to check on him. All my focus had to be on the healing spell.

With every ounce of my will directed at the wounds, Rynac's skin started knitting itself together.

My head throbbed with each frantic beat of my heart. My vision blurred, but I couldn't stop yet.

Each breath was harder than the last, iron bands squeezing tighter around my chest with each passing second.

The fox yipped as if in warning, and I released the spell before I passed out.

I slumped to the side, as if someone had cut the tethers holding me upright. My stomach roiled, but I had no energy to vomit, and squeezed my eyes shut.

The pain in my head ebbed as soon as I stopped casting, but my hands quivered and my teeth chattered.

My eyes fluttered open when something warm pressed against my forehead and nestled against my chest.

I blinked. Rynac crouched over me, concern pinching his expression, while my fox friend curled against me. I relished the warmth that seeped from their little body.

"Gods above, Nyssa! I thought you were dead. You're cold as ice and your floating light spell failed."

"Had to . . . do something," I said, forcing each word past my lips.

"When you said it would hurt, I assumed you meant me."

I managed a weak smile, but his eyes shone with outrage. "Sorry. I'm not a very good witch."

Spells shouldn't hurt, but when a caster lacked the necessary skill or power, it exacted a toll on their body. The dire situation called for something drastic.

My one hope that the enhancement potion would work fizzled. I should've known better.

"Never do that again," he growled. His anger quickly dissipated, replaced with concern and a hint of fear. "I'm an enforcer. It's part of my job to risk my life—not yours."

Why did everything feel so heavy? I just wanted to close my eyes.

"Wasn't going to let you die," I mumbled.

Die.

That word cut through the fog in my head, jolting me back to reality. I fumbled through my bag, my fingers still not working quite right as I hunted for the potion I needed. The swirling purple concoction called to me. I pulled out the cork and downed it in one gulp.

I gasped as energy surged through my body, like five espressos kicking in at once—my version of a pick-me-up potion, although it would only last around fifteen minutes.

Since it was attuned to witches, I didn't see any reason to save it.

And if it helped me get Rynac to a healer, the reagents' cost would be worth it . . . and the hangover I'd have once it wore off.

"We need to move," I said.

I checked Rynac's stomach. The flesh was an angry red, but no more blood seeped through.

"Sorry about the scarring. How does it feel?"

"Tender, but I'll take that over gaping wounds," Rynac said.

Despite this whole situation, I snorted. Better to think about anything besides our current predicament.

I repacked my bag and climbed to my feet as the potion worked its magic. I felt like I could run to my apartment and back without breaking a sweat. But I knew to be cautious. My body might not feel the strain now, but I sure would tomorrow.

I slung Rynac's arm over my shoulders and helped him to stand. He tested his range of movement, nodding his approval.

"Don't push too hard," I warned. "This began the healing process, but the wounds can reopen."

"I—" He winced, but started moving with me. "Thank you."

I just nodded. Why was he so heavy? The pungent tang of blood still hung in the air as we shuffled past the battlefield.

Unease crawled down my spine, the prickling sense of eyes on us refusing to fade.

I shoved it down and tightened my grip on Rynac.

Getting him to safety came first.

Whatever was watching could wait its turn.

CHAPTER ELEVEN

For the first time in years, I yearned for the sun to rise. Sweat trickled down my back, while my legs protested the extra weight. My free hand clutched my conduit, even though the healing spell had sapped my magical reserves.

While I still felt a twinge of frustration at my weakness, I couldn't ignore the fact my magic had made a difference.

"Can I ask you a question?" Rynac said.

I nodded, thankful to fill the silence.

"Does it always hurt?"

"For me, yes." Some witch I was. "I can manage simple spells, although they don't always work the way I intended. But the more powerful ones? If I push too hard, it causes pain, and the spell is still weak. It's not like that for other witches, though they can strain themselves if they force too much magic out or attempt a spell far above their skill level."

"It was pretty amazing," Rynac said.

My cheeks warmed at his compliment.

"We all have our strengths and limitations. It doesn't make you any less of a witch. You came through when it mattered. I couldn't have asked for more."

I glanced up at him; sweat beaded on his forehead and his expression was strained, but I didn't sense deceit.

No witch would ever utter those words to me.

At least here I held value.

"Thank you," I said, failing to suppress a smile. "That means a lot to me. It's frustrating sometimes. I'd watch other witches effortlessly cast powerful spells while I struggled with the basics."

Rynac gave my shoulder a reassuring squeeze. "We each walk our own path, face our own challenges. Your magic might work differently, but that doesn't mean it's any less valuable. You bring your own special skills and capabilities to the table, and I have complete faith in you."

I smirked at him. "You're just saying that because I rescued you."

"That helps." He chuckled, then winced with a hand on his wound.

"What were you two doing out here?" I asked, hoping to distract him from the pain. This was supposed to be a safe neighborhood.

"We were on a routine patrol and heard reports of gang activity. Then we ended up ambushed by demonspawn."

"I can't believe they're here in the city. After East Vale, I thought the veil was being closely monitored."

The authorities feared a repeat and worried the veil's protection had weakened after standing for hundreds of years. So where were they? How had they allowed this to happen?

"I wouldn't have believed it if I hadn't seen it with my own eyes. We were caught off guard and overwhelmed by their numbers, but we killed most of them."

"Wait. How many were there?"

"Six."

"Six!" I choked on the number. That many, and all in one group? "Why isn't there a squad from the UMC?"

The first hints of a tear should've triggered a response team.

How had so many demonspawn slipped through undetected? Or had they found another way into our realm?

Rynac shrugged. "I alerted HQ. They'll send a report to the UMC. This way."

He nodded down a street. As he patrolled this area, I trusted him to guide us. I was also completely lost.

I scrutinized every shadow, searching for movement; my paranoia was slipping through, and I caught glimpses out of the corner of my eye, each one sending a shiver down my spine.

"Just one more block," Rynac murmured. Had he sensed that foreboding sensation too?

I wanted to ask how close we were to the healer, but bit my lip to keep the words in. Rynac's breathing had become more ragged. He didn't need the extra exertion.

We shuffled down the street as fast as we could, but Rynac was flagging and my body voiced its objections.

I attempted to tread with light steps, but in the silence of early morning, even the slightest sound seemed amplified.

Rynac twisted to glance behind us, and his body tensed.

Before I could look, he hastened his pace and steered us down another alley.

We hurried around the corner, Rynac urging us into a run, or at least the best he could manage given his injuries.

His weight jarred my bones with each lumbering stride, but I concentrated on keeping us moving.

My heart pounded, each breath now a ragged gasp.

I didn't spot anyone behind us, but the sensation of being watched only intensified as we ran through the dimly lit alley.

Where was the fox?

I'd been so focused on Rynac, I hadn't noticed when they'd disappeared. Hopefully, they had run to safety.

Inky darkness clung to the brick walls. The feeble light from the street behind could not reach us here. I stole another glance back, and my stomach sank.

Figures slipped into the alley behind us, cutting off any chance of escape. At least they weren't demonspawn. But where in all the hells had they come from?

"Who are they?" I hissed.

"Local gang," he grunted. "Mix of races. Rarely have magic, but they're armed."

I pushed harder, trying not to think about their weapons.

Rynac cursed under his breath, and we skidded to a stop before crashing into the chain-link fence that barred our way. He yanked on the gate with frustration, causing the padlock to rattle.

Panic gripped my throat as I scanned the area, desperate for a way out. The fence was near eight feet tall and adorned with menacing barbed wire. Neither of us stood a chance of scaling it.

I squeezed my eyes shut. My mind raced with spells and incantations as I scoured my knowledge for a solution. But I'd never cut through metal before.

"Didn't think we'd let you off that easy, eh, enforcer?" a mocking voice taunted.

Jeers echoed off the walls, and Rynac pushed me behind him.

Tension rippled off his body as he turned to confront the speaker.

We were outnumbered, but despite his weakened state, he was trying to protect me.

Trapped.

The word reverberated in my mind. A wave of fear crashed over me, scattering my thoughts like leaves in a hurricane.

I was a witch, and I couldn't conjure a spell to save us. Failure and frustration constricted my throat.

"Climb the fence," Rynac hissed under his breath.

"But you can't—"

"Climb." His voice brooked no argument.

Rynac straightened to his full height, projecting an air of strength, and pushed me toward the fence.

"I don't want trouble," he called out.

I clung to the fence; my gaze locked on the barbed wire. Could I climb over before they attacked?

My heart squeezed—no, the real question was, could I leave my friend behind?

Even injured, Rynac hadn't hesitated to defend me. But he was my friend, and I refused to sacrifice him so I could escape. How was my life any more valuable than his?

I adjusted my position to peer around Rynac's enormous frame. The figures advanced toward us, but the light behind them made it difficult to identify who or what they were.

The effects of the pick-me-up potion were fading. Time was running out. I pulled out my potions; they were all we had. They'd buy us time, but to do what?

"Left hand is a smoke-bomb," I whispered, pushing a vial into his palm. "Right hand stinging nettle."

I withdrew my conduit and glared at the enemy, who'd stopped too far away for me to see their numbers.

Could I cast a few concussive blasts? It might scare them off or force them to retreat. And Rynac had dealt with demonspawn earlier, he must have weapons hidden somewhere.

"Don't want trouble?" the thug drawled, his arrogance grating on my nerves. "That may be, but we can't just let enforcers traipse through our territory. Especially after you killed our friends."

Friends? Did he mean the demonspawn?

He inched forward, as if daring Rynac to attack. If they moved a bit closer, I could hit two with one well-placed blast.

"And you brought us a little friend."

Shit.

"She's not involved in this," Rynac snapped.

"Ah, but she is."

Rynac pushed me back as the thugs closed in, but I resisted, knowing running was pointless.

Stupid fence. I shifted my stance, ready to attack at the right moment.

"I believe you have outlived your usefulness, enforcer," the leader said, his cronies chuckling in response.

Fear coiled around my heart. My hands trembled, but I tightened my grip on my conduit, drawing strength from its familiar presence. I clenched my jaw, refusing to let them see my fear.

Rynac shifted into a fighting stance. Power radiated off him; he was ready to spring into action at any moment. I whispered a silent prayer to the Goddesses, even though I doubted they would listen.

The silence stretched, an almost tangible weight in the air. My heartbeat thundered in my ears. Desperation squeezed my chest, urging me to find a solution.

A spell, a glimmer of hope, blossomed in my mind.

I froze, a plan forming—it might work against the padlock. I spun to face the gate, hiding behind Rynac's frame. If they saw me trying to summon magic, they'd likely attack.

Sucking in a shaky breath, I called to my magic. The solar flames flickered in my chest, making my head throb as I directed them into my conduit.

"*Secare,*" I hissed.

A dull blade of energy sputtered from my conduit, slicing across the padlock.

My breath caught as the metal glowed. It hadn't been strong enough to cut through, but if I—

"Kill them," the leader ordered.

Chapter Twelve

He said it as if he were ordering a latte, not our execution. But at his command, metal flashed as his thugs moved in unison—and even in the dim light, I knew those silhouettes.

Guns.

Fear clawed at my insides, then a molten rage surged from deep within, igniting a fire that blazed through my veins.

I wouldn't let these thugs lay a finger on me, and I would never allow them to harm my friend.

Then a strange calm washed over me, reminiscent of when I'd basked in the moonlight, and all my fear and exhaustion evaporated.

Needles prickled at the nape of my neck, and time itself appeared to stretch.

Rynac tossed both of my potions; they arced through the air as if in slow motion. Glass shattered and white smoke curled through the air. Then bright flashes seared my eyes.

"No." The word was a snarl on my lips.

The command shuddered through me, and magic flowed into my hands. The air shimmered, and then the first bullet hit.

I flinched, sensing the ripple of impact, but it was not my body that it struck—rather the translucent shield I had summoned.

Time flowed again, and a cacophony assaulted my ears.

Raw power thrummed in my chest, coursing down my arms, and poured into the shield that hung in the air before me, just large enough to protect the two of us.

With each impact, the iridescent spell glowed brighter.

The hail of bullets ceased, and my gaze hardened, fixed on those foolish enough to challenge me.

The few thugs I could see through the smoke exchanged uneasy glances, uncertain whether to charge or flee.

I blinked, a weight lifting from me.

What am I doing? What spell is this? How was I even—

Fire ignited in my veins, and I stumbled as the heat surged. I swore. This magic was going to incinerate me from the inside out.

The shield faltered, and panic gripped me as I struggled to maintain the barrier.

Then the spell slipped through my grasp.

A sharp pain sliced through my mind, and another stabbed at the base of my skull as the magic violently ripped from my control.

Volatile power crackled through the air, erratic and untamed.

Rynac grabbed me as my legs wobbled, and I braced both hands on my thighs.

Panting through the drain and the stabbing pain, I had to push through.

We weren't safe yet.

At first, it was only a flicker of ethereal light.

Almost beautiful, but a heavy weight settled in the pit of my stomach. A shimmering light danced in the air, as if the fabric of reality itself shivered in response to my unpredictable magic.

An ominous humming grew louder, reverberating in my chest.

Rynac pulled me toward the fence as the smoke dissipated, but we still had nowhere to go.

The thugs paused; a few backed up, their eyes wide.

My tongue was too thick, trapping my scream inside.

This is your magic, a voice hissed through my mind, *your fault.* The words wrapped around my throat, squeezing until I couldn't breathe.

A sharp crack snapped through the air, its force knocking us back. Black lightning crashed down from where the wild magic coalesced, shaking the ground beneath me. Burning sulfur stung my nose.

The world before me warped as if I were looking through a distorted lens.

I did this.

Each word lodged like a knife in my chest.

The oppressive air quivered as tiny hairline fractures formed and then spider-webbed out.

The dark alley twisted, revealing glimpses of a burning hellscape; fissures pulsated with a sickly glow, casting eerie shadows that danced on the edge of my vision.

Dark tendrils of smoke seeped through the cracks, spilling onto the ground.

I could only watch, utterly frozen, as it whispered around the thugs' feet before coiling around their legs and body.

A few panicked, but the smoke didn't slow.

"Is that you?" Rynac hissed.

I could only shake my head. I didn't know what it was, but the magic that brushed against my awareness was oily and repulsive. A deep malevolence drove it.

The fractures shrank, the image of that other world evaporated, and I almost wondered if I'd imagined it.

The thugs cried out as smoke speared into their chests.

Their skin began to glow like a smoldering coal. Black tendrils curled beneath their skin, as if their blood had turned to tar. It crept up their necks; some fought, clawing at their chests, while others surrendered to its power.

The smoke faded, but the taint of its touch remained.

Their eyes were now wholly black, and their hands had transformed into gnarled claws.

Beneath the tattered remains of one thug's shirt, I could just make out the cracked black skin that surrounded a glowing rune.

"Thralls," Rynac whispered.

A vague memory of what that meant scratched at my mind, but thinking hurt. All I knew was we were in danger. I couldn't submit to my pain just yet.

The fractures in the air were nothing more than a smudge as the last of the wild magic faded. But I feared more smoke might appear . . . and what would happen if it touched Rynac or me.

As one, the thralls turned and set their eyes on us.

Rynac raised his gun, and I flinched at each pull of the trigger. Bullets slammed into the thralls, but did little to slow them as black liquid pooled from their wounds.

Rynac swore as he reloaded his gun.

The thralls stalked closer, flexing their clawed hands as if they could imagine tearing into us.

I had to help him—

But your magic did this. Twisted them.

No, I hissed back at that voice. *It can't be—*

Pressure built in my chest, my power demanding release. I tried to push it back down, but something within me cracked and I lost my grip on it.

Stumbling forward, magic sizzled across my hands and up my arms.

Deep in my chest, flames scorched my insides as if the sun itself burned within my ribs.

I wrestled with the fire, willing my magic to follow my command.

"Get back." My voice cracked as I strained to hold on just a bit longer.

Fire skittered across my skin, capturing the attention of every single thrall. Then I released it.

Expelling all the volatile magic from my body, I focused it down the alley, hoping that would be enough to spare Rynac.

For one moment, I was strong. Powerful. A true witch. This was the magic my people wielded, and it was finally mine.

My magic crackled and fizzed through the air. A scream ripped from my throat as it burned through my veins.

It struck the thralls; their skin hissed as wild flames poured over them. Some clawed in a vain attempt to fight off the magic. A few fell to their knees, but I couldn't stop. I tried to seize control, but my magic refused to listen.

My legs faltered, and I crashed to my knees. Magic blazed through my body and threatening to devour me too. Flames burned my throat as I screamed again, but I couldn't restrain my power. The last ounce of magic ripped from my core, and my vision wavered.

A blur of cobalt dashed toward me.

Every breath scorched my lungs as I slumped to the ground, utterly spent.

Hold on, a gentle voice whispered.

Something soft and warm nestled against my chest, but I couldn't move. My magic had sapped all the strength from my body. Searing pain consumed my mind.

A battle cry pierced the air, and a feminine figure launched herself at our attackers, slicing through them with twin blades.

I squinted—Indra?

Garbled screams and cries of pain echoed through the alley, followed by more gunfire. Shadows danced, cleaving through the enemy.

Darkness crept into my vision.

The violent tempest of my magic eased as a soothing voice whispered words I didn't understand.

I clung to that voice, clung to it as my magic stormed around me.

But I had nothing left to give, so I surrendered to the pain, allowing it to pull me into oblivion.

CHAPTER THIRTEEN

Pain dragged me from the dark depths. My skull throbbed as if I'd been on a weeklong bender.

I groaned—so, yeah, still alive it seemed.

Warmth pressed against my side. The moment I pried my eyes open, the pounding in my head spiked and my thoughts turned to sludge as I tried—and failed—to focus.

"Are you awake, Nyssa?" Indra's voice broke through my grogginess.

"Unfortunately," I grumbled.

A heartbeat later, my brain caught up. I jolted upright, on high alert and ready for danger before my head protested and my stomach roiled.

"You're safe," Indra reassured me. "We brought you to our healer's apartment. Rynac's getting patched up in another room."

I calmed my racing heart before attempting to speak, but it still came out weak. "Did . . . I harm either of you?"

"No, just yourself," Indra said.

Relief flooded me. I'd only been trying to protect Rynac, but I should've known better. I shouldn't have pushed my powers so far.

"Rest. I'll tell the healer you're awake."

I let my eyes fall shut again as Indra left. Even the weak lighting aggravated my pounding headache. My chest ached and my hands throbbed. The backlash from my spell must've damaged them, but I'd deal with the pain if it meant Rynac and Indra were unharmed.

Just what in all the hells had happened? I tried to remember, but it all seemed too surreal. And my magic . . .

I brushed the thoughts aside before they added to my headache. Right now, I needed to check on Rynac, to see with my own eyes that I hadn't hurt him. I pushed myself up, but the world spun, and I gripped the bed.

"Don't squish me," a soft voice cried in protest.

"What?" I tossed back the blanket and found the cobalt vulpine tucked against my side. They lifted their head, watching me.

"Can you hear me?" the feminine voice asked.

The fox tilted their head.

"Yes," I said with uncertainty. I pointed at the fox. "Are you talking to me?"

"You can hear me!" The fox pounced onto my chest, then rubbed her face against mine.

"Ow, too loud." I winced, easing myself back down onto the bed, my energy already flagging.

"Sorry," she whispered. *"I just can't believe you can finally hear me. I thought there was something wrong."*

"Do vulpines usually talk telepathically?"

"Of course. How else would we communicate with our kin?" The fox wedged herself between my arm and body, resting her head against my chest to stare up at me.

"And with people?"

"Only with our bonded."

"And that's me?" My mind stuttered. *I have a familiar?!*

"Did you hit your head when you fell?" She peered up at me with concern.

"I'm beginning to wonder that myself," I mumbled. "I just never expected to be chosen, not with my wild magic."

"From the first moment I saw you, I knew you were my bonded, but when you didn't respond to me, I thought I was wrong. Today proves I was right, though something was wrong with you."

"Well, I knew that already," I grumbled.

"Now that you have connected with your magic, the bond has taken hold. I can help guide you."

"Guide me? I've studied magic for years, had multiple witch tutors, but none of them made any progress. I was stupid to believe that potion would help me."

"But it did. You summoned an astral shield."

"And then lost control," I said with a frown. "Wait, astral? You know what spell I cast?"

"Of course. Though I have never witnessed it myself, my kin share their memories with me. We have long been allies of the lunar witches."

"Lunar witches? Who are they?"

I'd never heard the term.

Perhaps they were the child of a witch and a shifter?

But if a witch was in a relationship with someone of a different race, they would be ostracized from the witch community. If they bore a child, their family would renounce them and sever all ties.

No, that couldn't be right. We'd been taught such a blasphemous union could never produce offspring with a blend of magic.

"Few remember them," the fox said.

Sadness wrapped around my chest until my heart ached. I made a noise, rubbing my chest.

"Apologies. We share our emotions through our bond. I will learn to control it better." She let out a heavy sigh, and the sadness eased. *"The*

Great War wiped out almost all the lunar witches. My kin and I waited for their return, and now I've found you."

"Me? What does this have to do . . . wait, you think I'm a lunar witch?" I snorted, which only made me wince as my pain reawakened. "Both my parents are witches. Ordinary witches. Having both solar and lunar magic would be impossible."

The vulpine sniffed me, tilting her head. *"I smell both blessings upon you, but the lunar blessing calls to you even though you keep trying to reject it."*

"What are you talking about?" I rubbed my temples, but my headache throbbed harder. "I'm just a witch."

"Rest now, Nyssa," the fox said, snuggling back down. *"We can talk more later. I'm not going anywhere."*

A knock sounded, but I hesitated. A single night had turned my life upside-down. I didn't need any extra problems.

"Do you have a name?" I whispered.

I had to admit, the fact I was worthy of a familiar eased a fraction of the longing in my chest.

"Come in," I called out.

"Danika."

Indra stepped inside, giving Danika a curious look before sitting on the corner of my bed.

Rynac followed close behind, limping to the chair beside me. Someone had washed away the blood and grime, and now he just looked tired. A bandage poked out the bottom of his clean shirt, but he appeared whole.

My magic hadn't harmed him.

Rynac squeezed my hand. "You scared the hell out of me back there. Again. How are you feeling?"

"You're not afraid of me?" I asked, unable to meet their gaze.

"Why would we be? You saved my life."

"Twice," Indra added.

How could they act like nothing had happened?

"But I lost control of my power. My magic turned volatile. It—"

I scrunched my face, trying to remember what I'd seen. It had done something bad. And that sinister smoke? I banished the thoughts. I'd deal with them later.

"It's the same magic that altered both of you. How can you not fear that after what it did to you?"

"We can only transform once," Rynac said with a one-sided shrug. "At least . . . I hope."

"And you weren't trying to harm us," Indra said, gripping my hand until I looked up. "Rynac filled me in on what you did for him. We know you were trying to help."

"What about those thralls?" I asked, needing to change the subject. They were probably lying to be kind while I was recovering.

"Rynac and I took care of the rest of them before the second enforcer team arrived," Indra said.

"But what are they?" I asked. "Sinister magic twisted those people into mindless things?"

"Dark magic creates thralls from the willing," Rynac said, his voice void of emotion. "Runes are carved into their flesh, which channels demonic energies into them. It makes them stronger, faster, and more powerful, but when the contract reaches the end, they turn into those twisted creatures and obey the command of their master."

"Someone did that to them?"

"Likely the same person who controls those demonspawn," Indra added. "The warlock in East Vale had an army of thralls—humans who were willing to give up their souls for power."

"Do you think there is a warlock here?" I whispered before fear stole my voice.

The siblings stared at each other, and then Indra shook her head. "The demonspawn were too organized. Someone is controlling them."

How'd I get mixed up in all of this? I just wanted to help Rynac. I wasn't here to fight demons or warlocks. "What do we do now?"

"We leave it to the UMC squad," Indra said. "They arrived earlier to clean things up, but I brought you two here first, but you will have to meet them. I only gave a partial report before returning to check on you both. I didn't mention the fox, and I left out the part where your magic damaged everything."

Damage?

I froze, trying to remember, but it made sense that volatile magic would damage the surrounding area. "Why would you do that?"

The two shared a look.

"We thought it best to talk to you first," Indra said. "We know how harsh the UMC can be toward those with unstable magic."

"We saw firsthand what they did to those who couldn't control their transformation in East Vale," Rynac said.

Indra shot him a stern look.

"I told her about home already," he added with a shrug.

"We just met her! Why do you try to scare everyone off?"

"Nyssa's still here," Rynac said.

"That's because she is as weird as us. I mean, look at that fox."

"Her name's Danika," I interjected.

"See," Indra said, arching an eyebrow at Rynac.

"We need to get our story straight," he said, ignoring her. "I called Nyssa, the MEA alchemist, for help after being attacked by demonspawn. On our way to the healer, a gang cornered us and then became thralls."

"Do you think we can blame the magic that transformed them for the damage to the buildings?" I asked.

"It's our best bet."

"We should also leave out that I cast that shield," I said.

If Danika was correct about it being an astral shield . . . that was a spell that a witch didn't have access to. It would only place more suspicion on me.

A witch using lunar magic . . . it was preposterous. Even entertaining the thought was foolish, and yet the idea had taken root. But where did I go to find out more?

"We'll get this sorted out, Nyssa." Indra patted my hand as the healer entered.

She sent Rynac back to his room to rest before she assessed me. If she noticed Danika, she didn't say a word.

"Any pain at the moment?" the healer asked, flashing her light into my eyes.

"I've got a pretty nasty headache, but that's about it."

Which was putting it mildly, felt as if someone was trying to drive spikes into the base of my skull.

The healer ran a small disc-like object over my chest—an enchanted medical device—before offering me a potion for the pain. I almost felt guilty using it when I had my own, but after the emergency call, I think they owed me at least one.

As I downed the potion, I noticed my hands and realized they were uninjured. My rogue spell had burned my skin, had the healer repaired the damage? It was one less thing for me to worry about, at least. I didn't know how I would've explained that injury.

"All your readings are normal," the healer said. "I agree with the enforcers' assessment that you collapsed due to being overwhelmed."

Thanks for that, guys.

"I suggest you get some more rest and avoid high-stress situations for a while."

"Thank you for all your help," I said. And then I noticed the time. "Crap! I'm going to be late for work."

I scrambled out of bed, snatching up my bag. Danika made a show of yawning and stretching before she followed.

"What did I just say?" the healer muttered as I raced out the door.

Chapter Fourteen

I sprinted the entire way to Divine, my body screaming at me to slow down. Even with Danika at my side, every shifting shadow made me push harder.

And every time I looked back, the street was empty.

By the time we reached the shop, I was sweaty, breathless—and no closer to shaking the feeling that something was still right behind us.

My persistent headache refused to relent, and I squinted against the harsh glare of the lights until Divine dimmed them for me.

Every noise made me wince, and I snapped at anyone in the kitchen who talked too loud. I don't know why any of my coworkers tolerated my appalling behavior.

Beylin trudged down the stairs an hour after opening, a deep scowl on his face.

But as he looked me over, his features softened. "Are you hurt?"

I shook my head, then regretted it. "Just a terrible headache." One that pain potions couldn't relieve.

He huffed. "Why did I have to learn from the enforcer captain that one of my staff was involved in a dangerous altercation this morning?"

"I'm sorry. It won't happen again," I blurted out. Was he going to fire me?

The dwarf sighed, stepping closer. "Young one, that's not my concern. You are."

His hand, warm and rough, gripped my arm. His expression appeared almost fatherly as he stared up at me.

"Your well-being—and that of any employee—is far more important than your work duties."

"I'm sorry. I need this job, and I didn't want to disappoint you."

"While I admire your dedication, you can always come to me if you have problems or need help. You might be new here, Nyssa, but once Divine chooses you, you're part of the family."

I laughed, then winced as it aggravated my head.

"Come with me," Beylin said, leading me away. "Leave the cookies. Let's tend to that headache."

We headed up the stairs, past his office and into a cozy living room. Did Beylin live here?

An assortment of plush chairs crowded around an oak coffee table, with a smattering of books and coasters on top. Thick gray curtains shut out the bright morning sun while offering enough light to see by without adding to my headache.

Beylin waved at me to sit as he wandered to the kitchenette, which was stocked with an abundance of mugs and drink supplies.

I slumped onto the couch, resisting the temptation to lie down and cocoon myself in the throw blanket.

"Tell me about this headache," Beylin urged as porcelain and metal clinked together. "I'll make a brew to help soothe it."

"The painkiller potions the healer gave me reduce the pain, but only for about an hour. My normal headaches aren't like this; it's like my entire brain throbs, and needles are stabbing into the base of my skull. My eyes began to ache an hour ago. Harsh light aggravates them."

The dwarf frowned, handing me a delicate teacup. "Better to drink it fast. It doesn't have the most pleasant taste."

"At this point, I don't even care," I muttered.

I took a cautious sip to test the temperature and regretted my statement. The liquid, though clear, tasted like dirt—not the typical kind, but fancy dirt you buy at a garden shop.

I pinched my nose and downed the cup in three revolting gulps. My stomach threatened to rebel, and I was certain my head couldn't handle vomiting.

"I warned you," he said, not even trying to hide his amusement. "Now, let's take a look at you. What happened last night?"

He placed an oddly heavy stone ball in my hand. The dark blue exterior was smooth and shiny, but runes flickered across the surface like tiny solar flares.

I recounted the morning's adventure as best I could.

"Hmm," Beylin muttered. He took the device back and moved around me. "May I see your neck?"

I pulled my hair to the side as his fingers prodded my neck. What had that little ball told him?

"Is this a birthmark?" he asked.

"Where?"

"Right here." He pressed a finger against the nape of my neck.

"No?" My voice rose with uncertainty.

It's not like I could see the back of my neck. But if I had a mark, wouldn't someone have told me?

"What does it look like? Can you take a photo?"

I handed him my phone, and after some grumbling about human technology, he managed to snap a non-blurry photo and gave it back.

I squinted at the image. "Looks like freckles."

Only these were black, not the usual brown. Maybe I needed to show it to a doctor.

"It looks like a crescent moon," Beylin replied, brushing his finger over the offending area. He stood and walked over to the bookcase, scanning the titles.

"If I squint and hold it like this," I said, tilting my phone, "and disregard all these other freckles."

Beylin ignored me, paging through one of the books. "Aha! I knew I'd seen it before."

He flipped the book to face me, pointing at the illustration: a stylized drawing of the moon's various phases.

"Pretty, but how does this help me?"

"This one," he tapped the drawing of the waxing crescent moon. I held my phone next to it.

"I mean, maybe if it was a connect-the-dots. How is this related to my headache?"

Beylin closed the book. The deep blue cover appeared ancient, but the delicate silver letters were easy to read: *Disciples of the Moon – a collection of short stories.*

"This is a kid's book." Stating the obvious, I know. But what else could I do?

Danika's words—claiming I was a lunar witch—buzzed through my head.

And I had read from *The Lunar Codex.*

"It's an ancient tale about the moon-blessed, the guardians of the Moon Goddess Selene."

"It's a fairy tale that parents read to kids to make them go to sleep."

"All tales have a grain of truth," Beylin chided. "And it's the only legend shared by every race."

I scrubbed a hand over my face, almost wishing I'd hit my head and this was a concussion-induced hallucination. But he had a point. It was peculiar that every race would share this one tale.

"While Selene watches over the children of the moon, she also has the ability to bestow her blessing on anyone she chooses. Her moon-blessed guardians were just that. They hailed from every race. Defenders of the innocent, and powerful warriors who fought against the demon lords during the war. And they were all marked with her symbol, just like you."

Danika's words from yesterday circled through my thoughts. But how could I have both? These magics were opposites: the literal sun and moon.

"Do any of these stories mention witches specifically?"

I hated that there was a flicker of hope in my chest, but my traitorous heart wanted to believe what both of them said was true.

Beylin frowned. "Not in this collection."

"See." I dismissed that train of thought. I couldn't allow myself to get carried away, to let hope take hold. "It's just freckles!"

"We'll see," he said with confidence.

"Let's pretend for a minute that what you said is true." I resisted the urge to roll my eyes and risk getting myself fired. "What does it mean, then? Why do I have a headache?"

"I don't have the answers. Perhaps you just overexerted your magic." He shrugged. "Take the book with you, and I'll do some digging. Now head home and get some sleep. I can cover your shift tomorrow if you need more time to recover."

I nodded. Exhaustion dragged at my limbs, and it felt as if a truck had run me over several times.

Beylin excused himself, and only when the door clicked shut did I dare to pick up the book.

Moon-blessed.

I shook my head. Slipping the book back onto the shelf, my fingers trailed down the beautiful silver moons that decorated the spine before I snatched my hand away. I didn't indulge in fantasies.

And yet, I hesitated.

Cursing myself, I grabbed the book and tucked it into my bag. I headed downstairs and out the back door; the weight of last night's events lay heavy on my shoulders.

"He's right, you know," Danika said, falling into step beside me.

"Eavesdropping, were we?" I squinted down at my familiar while cursing the sun. A very unwitchy thing to do.

"The moon-blessed are guardians of the realms, replacing the lunar witches we lost."

"How am I supposed to be one if they're gone?"

"I believe you might carry both witch bloodlines," Danika said. *"Our histories state that all three Goddesses each crafted a child in their image and sent them to this realm to guide their people. Selene's descendant was Mani, who was said to lay with a witch. Their baby was born with lunar magic, but within a witch's body with access to solar magic."*

"Why haven't I heard of them before?" Although if they were eradicated over a century ago, they might have faded from memory.

I paused on the curb, checking for cars before I rushed across the street. A few pedestrians shot curious glances at Danika and me, but I was too exhausted to care.

"Solar and lunar witches were not on friendly terms. It's likely those records are restricted."

I wasn't in the mood for breaking into restricted archives again, and the witch archives had far superior wards that I wouldn't be able to bypass. "If I'm a lunar witch, why would I have a moon-blessed mark?"

"I don't know. But we could find out together."

She peered up at me, hope shining in her eyes. I gave her a small smile. I wasn't alone in this.

"The Lunar Codex *might hold more answers,*" Danika said.

I missed a step. A lunar codex for a lunar witch?

No, that was ridiculous.

"But I can't read most of it. The words were all scrambled."

"You've connected to your magic and can now communicate with me. The book might reveal more."

My thoughts battled each other as we walked in silence.

Part of me was adamant that it was nothing more than freckles, that my headache was the result of straining my magic.

But Beylin and Danika's words nagged at the back of my mind, refusing to be silent. And then there was the astral shield I'd summoned.

I still had one potion left, but I needed answers first. I desperately wanted to wield that magic again, but I'd lost control. Next time, I might hurt innocent people.

With a sigh, I trudged up the stupid number of steps to my apartment, wanting nothing more than to collapse on my bed.

Juggling my keys, I fumbled for the right one, then froze. Someone was sitting in front of my door. Asleep.

I frowned and nudged him with my toe. "Rynac?"

The enforcer jolted awake. His body tensed, but then he seemed to realize where he was.

He winced and pushed himself upright. "Guess I dozed off."

"You look how I feel," I said, gesturing for him to move. "Come in. You seem like you're about to topple over."

I headed for the kitchen as Rynac slumped onto the couch, Danika settling beside him. I popped the kettle on and hunted for some food. Since I hadn't gone to the shops, I had to make do with a half-empty cookie sleeve.

Before I could sit, Rynac accepted the tea and swiped some cookies.

"The healer cleared you, then?" I asked.

"Not exactly. They released me but wanted me to stay for observation."

"And you were sleeping on my doorstep because . . ."

He stared down at the steam curling from his tea. "I don't like hospitals."

"What about the medical ward at HQ?"

Rynac just shook his head. His shoulders hunched down. I considered objecting further, but swallowed the words. Admitting his fear was hard enough, and he appeared to be bracing for rejection.

"But they let you go?" I prompted.

"As long as I stayed with someone."

And he'd thought of me? "What about your sister?"

"She's handling the reports and is on duty tonight. I thought . . . perhaps you might want the company."

I was about to say that I had Danika, but something stopped me. Was I safe here? What if the gang came looking for us?

Even injured, I'd feel safer with an enforcer close by. "I'd like that."

"I also need to bring you to the UMC to make your report."

I groaned. I wanted to sleep and check *The Lunar Codex* for new information.

"We have a few hours to sleep," Rynac said. "The healer went to make her report and informed them we both required rest."

"I guess that's better than nothing," I grumbled. Or was that my stomach?

After finding a spare blanket and a pillow for Rynac, I slumped onto my bed with just enough energy to strip off my shoes. I fumbled through my vials for another potion to ease my pain.

My fingers brushed against a shimmering vial. It pulsed with magic, awakening that deep longing within me. I shoved it back into my drawer, under a pile of socks to keep it out of sight. I'd been foolish last night, and it had almost cost us our lives.

With everything at stake, I could *not* afford to get caught up in tales and fantasies.

Chapter Fifteen

"Why do I feel like I'm walking to my execution?" I whispered to Rynac as we turned down the next street. "And I'm not good at lying."

My headache was still a dull throb despite Beylin's dirt water, and I longed to crawl back into bed.

It also didn't help my nerves that my magic refused to settle, like a swarm of mildly annoyed bees buzzing under my skin. I worried that the tension of this meeting might set off my unbalanced magic.

"Project an air of confidence, just like when you met my captain," Rynac said. "Speak as truthfully as possible. You're not used to high-stress situations. They won't expect you to remember everything. And remind them that you're just an alchemist."

"And I'm here," Danika added. *"You're not alone, even though you won't see me."*

I smiled down at my familiar. Her presence gave me strength.

A mixture of relief and dread knotted in my stomach. The knowledge she possessed could be what I've been searching for, but I feared it all the same.

The UMC's dispatch unit controlled the area where the demonspawn and thralls had attacked. They'd cordoned off the street, which was now lined with portable offices.

How many people did the UMC need to combat the demonspawn?

Rynac introduced me to the UMC soldier at the entrance, who waved me inside.

Weaving through the temporary structures, the soldier ushered me into a small room with a table and two chairs on either side.

I sat facing the wall with a large mirror. Why was there a mirror?

It was kind of off-putting staring at myself. The dark smudges under my eyes were hard to conceal.

At least my hair looked pretty today. I'd take a good hair day, as nothing else was going right.

Someone knocked at the door, and I flinched as the sound echoed off the tight walls. The soldier pulled it open, revealing two males in black uniforms—one dark-haired and the other light.

They filled the doorway in both build and presence. A carved marble statue would've been a more suitable place for their striking features than on living, breathing people.

"We'll handle it from here," the first one said to the soldier.

His dark hair was in disarray, as if he constantly raked a hand through it. Slight stubble shadowed his jawline which I'm sure didn't meet UMC guidelines. Despite the soldier's protests, the male patted him on the shoulder, and the soldier left without complaint.

The dark-haired one smiled as his deep emerald-green gaze landed on me. They possessed an otherworldly shimmer that was unsettling. And then I spotted the wings and knew I was in trouble.

Nephilim.

"I'm Lieutenant Kaelan Renatus," the dark-haired one said. "And this is Captain Nathaniel Einheri."

He nodded at the light-haired nephilim, who gave me a hard stare. What was this, good cop, bad cop?

Kaelan sat opposite me, shuffling papers, while Nathaniel crossed his arms and leaned against the wall. His white-blond hair was long enough to fall into icy-blue eyes that narrowed as they took me in.

The graceful angles of his face were on full display as he stared down his nose at me.

Contempt oozed from him as if he couldn't stand being in my presence for a moment longer than necessary.

Right back at you, angel boy.

The room seemed too confined now. Even with their wings tucked behind them, their nephilim presence seemed to expand beyond their physical forms, and I felt crowded in this tiny box.

"That's probably their egos." Danika snickered.

It was an effort to control my face as I swallowed down my laugh.

Nephilim were the only race I'd encountered on a regular basis outside of witches.

After losing their realm and their god, they'd butted their wings into everyone else's business and were the only ones stupid enough to meddle in witch affairs.

Being angel-born held significance to humans, but in our realm, every race had a touch of the divine. Their delusions of grandeur appeared to be instilled from birth, along with their stupid good looks.

"And you are?" Kaelan prompted.

"Nyssa Thornheart," I replied, although he should've known that.

"Witch," Nathaniel sneered.

"Nephilim." I guess their god didn't bless them with a personality. *What a pity.*

"Can you explain what happened last night?" Kaelan asked.

"I received a call from Enforcer Terral around two this morning—"

"Is it common for you to receive late-night calls from males?" Nathaniel said, cutting me off.

Excuse me?

"First, Rynac is a friend and colleague. Second, he knows I spend my nights crafting potions. And third, he knew I was preparing healing potions for the enforcers last night."

"Please continue," Kaelan said. His expression was bland, but his wings twitched.

"Due to his critical condition and knowing backup was too far away, he broke protocol and called me. I'm contracted with the MEA to craft potions. It was a logical choice."

Rynac had said that his captain would reprimand him for breaking protocol, even though it'd saved his life.

"You rushed into danger because of that?"

"I'm an alchemist. It's my duty to aid those who ask for help. And when a friend who is bleeding out asks, I won't refuse despite the risk to myself."

This felt more like an interrogation rather than a witness statement.

I recounted the rest of the night's events to the best of my memory and tried to bite back the sharp retorts to Nathaniel's constant prodding. With each passing moment, the throbbing in my head made it harder to concentrate.

"So, alchemist, you're saying you didn't climb the fence to escape but hid behind the enforcer," Nathaniel said.

I bit down hard on the inside of my cheek. He was just trying to throw me off balance to see if I slipped up.

"Well, Captain," I spat back. "Thugs had trapped us in a dark alley. I was afraid. And I didn't want to leave Rynac just to save myself. He's my friend. Do you know what those are?"

"Why didn't you use any magic?" Kaelan asked, and my glare swung back to him. Mr. Cool-calm-and-collected was almost as infuriating.

"Alchemy *is* my magic," I said, which was true. I'd kept my responses as close to the truth as possible, just in case they had ways of knowing if I lied.

"And you used potions last night?"

"Yes, I gave Rynac two enhanced-grade healing potions, then we used a smoke-bomb and stinging nettle brew to defend ourselves against the thugs."

Nathaniel scoffed. My gaze narrowed on him. *This ass—*

"And was that what caused the attackers to transform into thralls?" Kaelan asked, cutting off my thought.

"My low-level brews?" I gave him my best are-you-stupid look.

But the two nephilim just waited. Guess I needed to give them a clear answer.

"No, my potions did not cause the transformation."

"Then what did?"

"A dark magical smoke appeared through cracks in the air," I said. Saying it out loud made it sound crazy. Had the others seen it?

"Where did these 'cracks' come from?"

"I don't know." Which was technically true.

"And what did this smoke do?" he prompted.

"It surrounded them."

I stared down at the table as memories flashed through my mind.

"It was sinister. Even the thugs seemed scared of it. Everything reeked of sulfur. Then it did something to them. They screamed as if they were in excruciating pain. One or two collapsed, but the others . . . their eyes turned black, and their hands were twisted and deformed into claws. I don't remember much after that."

"Do you regularly faint under stress?" Nathaniel asked.

"Are you regularly an asshole to people just released from a healer's care?" I snapped back.

Two could play at being a prick, though he seemed like a natural. Was this how the UMC officers conducted themselves? These were the people responsible for our safety?

"How were the thralls killed?" Kaelan asked, ignoring the violent tension in the air.

"I . . . I don't know. I could only guess," I stammered, hoping I appeared calm when my insides turned to lead. "Things are fuzzy, and I only remember bits and pieces."

"Because you fainted," Nathaniel said.

"Just tell us what you remember," Kaelan interjected as I glared at Nathaniel. "Even the small details could help."

"I remember their chests glowed. Even the fallen ones. Their skin charred and blackened like they were burning from the inside out. Then . . ."

I squeezed my eyes shut, wanting to block out the horrid images, not dredge them up. What else did I remember?

"Gunfire. I think from Rynac. Someone with swords coming from the other end of the alley."

I frowned. Besides Danika running toward me, that was it.

"You've done well, Nyssa," she whispered, her voice soothing me.

"And that's it?" Nathaniel said with annoyance. "Did you witness the thralls die? Or did you miss that from your vantage point on the ground?"

My features hardened. "Do you always insult witnesses, or is your judgment skewed by your personal vendetta against witches?"

I met his gaze head-on, refusing to back down. His lip curled. I wished I could throw a punch to knock it off his face.

"I thought the UMC sent its finest, not the castoffs."

In the blink of an eye, Kaelan was on his feet, his arm blocking Nathaniel from whatever he was about to do.

"Guess you just proved my point," I said, my chair screeched across the floor as I shoved to my feet.

"I think that's it for today," Kaelan said, as if we hadn't been about to tear each other's throats out. "We'll be in contact if we have further questions."

Arrogant overstuffed pigeon.

I shot Nathaniel another glare as I retrieved my bag. The nephilim turned their backs to me, their tense conversation too quiet to hear, and I couldn't get outside fast enough.

When I stepped back into the empty hallway, I paused. Which way had I come in? The soldier who'd escorted me had vanished, but I'd be damned if I asked for directions, so I turned left.

Nathaniel brushed past me. "I'll show you out."

His forced politeness grated on me. Why couldn't he just leave me the hell alone?

With no alternative, I trailed the nephilim through the maze and exited through a side door.

I paused, trying to figure out where I was. This wasn't the main road where I entered, but a side alley.

Magic vibrated through the air, and I retreated a step, but the door I'd come through refused to open.

What in the world? One moment I was standing in a normal alley, piled with garbage. The next moment, the road had cracked open, fissures spread across the walls, and every surface was charred.

I backed away from the destruction. "What is this?"

"I removed the illusion over the area," Nathaniel said, watching me with thinly veiled contempt. "*This* is the alley where you encountered the thralls, but you never mentioned the destruction."

"It is?"

I took a step closer despite myself. I knew my magic had damaged the walls, but not to this extent. It looked like a bomb had gone off.

Down at the end, the chain-link fence remained intact. Was this the effect of the potion? Had it enhanced the instability rather than allowing me to gain control?

I reached out toward one of the ruined walls. It was a miracle I hadn't injured Rynac or Indra.

My fingers hovered over the charred bricks where a faint echo of magic lingered.

I jerked my fingers away when it responded to me.

"I don't recommend touching anything," the nephilim drawled. "We haven't neutralized the magic yet."

"Did the dark magic do this?" I asked.

Maybe it hadn't been me? My magic churned in my chest, but I clamped down on it.

Not now.

"And what dark magic is that?" Nathaniel asked.

Leaning against part of the undamaged wall with his arms crossed over his chest, he was the image of casualness.

I guess grilling people about dark magic was a common occurrence.

"The one that transformed the thugs into thralls," I replied.

I should've known this was just another opportunity to pin the blame on me. Stupidly, I'd allowed myself to be isolated with him.

"How do you know it was dark magic? Have you been around it before?"

Oh, so we were back to accusing me. What a surprise.

"All witches can sense magic," I snapped. "We're trained to distinguish each type. But even without that, it's clear that it was dark magic. Nothing good would transform people into those . . . things."

"You expect me to believe that?" he said, pushing off the wall.

I opened my mouth to defend myself when magic prickled through the air. I yelped, scrambling back as the bodies of the dead thralls appeared at my feet.

The blood drained from my face. Their charred flesh was gray and flaking. White, sightless eyes bore into me. Black blood coated the ground, splattered the walls, and oozed from the bullet wounds on their bodies.

I stumbled back, tripping over myself, and landed hard on the ground. But my gaze was locked onto a head no longer attached to its body. Bile burned my throat, and I turned and retched.

"Nyssa!" Danika shouted in my mind.

"That's enough," a voice ordered.

I sensed the magic subsiding, but I couldn't move. The images of those bodies seared into my mind.

"I just wanted to ensure she was telling the truth," Nathaniel drawled, not an ounce of regret in his voice.

"She likely has a concussion, and now you've made her contaminate the crime scene," the other voice scolded. Kaelan. Bloody angel-born.

I pushed myself up on unsteady legs. I needed to get out of here, away from these psychopaths. Kaelan reached out to help me, but I jerked away as if his touch were acid.

"Piss off," I hissed.

Not my best comeback, but bile still coated my tongue, and I hated that my hands were shaking.

"Nyssa, I'm coming," Danika called out.

"I'm fine," I said as I stormed away, not knowing if she could hear me. I wanted to run, but I sensed the nephilim's gaze burning my back.

"That was out of line," Kaelan snapped.

"Something or someone tore the veil last night," Nathaniel growled back, "and I intend to stop the threat."

My blood turned to ice at his words. They thought I'd torn the veil?

I shuddered as I stepped through the illusion barrier, my mind whirling. Was that why they'd treated me like a criminal?

Rynac waited right where I'd left him. His smile faltered when he spotted me.

"What happened?" he said as he rushed over.

I shook my head. I didn't want to open my mouth, afraid of what might come out.

Danika raced around the corner, not stopping until she curled through my legs.

"Let's get something to eat," Rynac said.

Concern creased his brow, but he didn't push. I just nodded, wishing I could forget those images. If my volatile magic had torn through the veil, *had* I killed those thugs?

Bile rose in my throat, sour and hot. I'd been an idiot to think this could ever end differently.

My magic was dangerous.

Until I contained it, I wasn't a healer or an alchemist.

I was a walking disaster waiting to happen.

CHAPTER SIXTEEN

Shadows lengthened like spindly fingers reaching for me as the sun dipped below the horizon. A creeping dread shivered down my spine, fearing how many thralls might linger within them.

Fatigue gnawed at me, but I quickened my pace to match Rynac's, wanting to hurry home.

Only when I locked my door and I was secure in my apartment did my shoulders relax.

Rynac dished up the takeout he'd grabbed, and we ate in silence as the last of the daylight drained away. Out the window, the city dimmed, and I couldn't help but fear what would wake tonight in the darkness.

By the time I cleared the table, Rynac had passed out on the couch. But I wouldn't be able to rest—not until I brewed the binding potion.

My desire to fix my magic endangered lives. Next time, my luck might not hold. And if I drew the attention of the UMC, would the Inquisitors follow?

The desire to harness my magic, to be in control for once, burned bright. And for one moment, I had.

Despite the terror and the thought that I was going to die, power had coursed through me and resonated deep in my soul.

The idea of binding that magic threatened to shatter my heart. But I couldn't deny my magic was restless, constantly churning away within me since the attack.

It was too reminiscent of my early days after manifesting, when my magic would flare without warning.

The volatile magic hurt me just as much as my surroundings, but I couldn't afford a slip-up.

My brother had been right.

I'd only harm more people living in Arkirith.

My magic was growing stronger, which would only increase its volatility. It was already strong enough to damage the veil, the only defense against the demons.

What if the next hole you tear in the veil doesn't close?

My stomach sank.

Answers. I needed the binding potion and answers.

Grabbing my supplies, I snatched up Beylin's book and *The Lunar Codex* and hurried upstairs.

Reading couldn't hurt anyone, right?

The codex's magic thrummed against my chest.

I didn't want to touch it, but it had gotten me into this mess. It deserved to get me out of it.

Magic crackled between my fingertips, hot and angry.

Stop.

I commanded it, dropping the codex and squeezing my hands into fists as if I could contain my magic. It sizzled for a moment before I snuffed it out.

I hissed. The unstable magic hurt like hell. A witch's own magic shouldn't harm them, but mine did. Why was my magic acting up?

Another reminder of why I needed the potion. I hoped the channeling would drain off some of that unruly magic.

Settling my witch's hat on my head, I took a deep, calming breath, releasing all of my fear and worry, tucking all my anxiety into a box to deal with later.

As I prepared the ingredients for the binding potion, my phone chimed—an email from my Guild supervisor—and I smiled.

Ruby's pack elders had agreed to work with me, and the Guild had processed the request. They still got a cut of my earnings, but this agreement allowed me and the client extra freedom.

I shot off a quick text to Ruby, asking if there was anything they needed. Rent was due, and if I wanted to afford food, I needed to earn some cash.

"What is that?" Danika hissed as she raced across the rooftop toward me.

She sniffed at my cauldron and recoiled.

"Binding magic? What is this for?"

A tinge of fear that whispered through our bond.

"To suppress my magic," I said, refusing to look at her. "Last night proved how dangerous my magic is."

"You can't."

"Why not? I saw with my own eyes what my magic can do, how volatile it is. I won't let that happen again. This will aid in subduing my powers and keep them from erupting."

"You just need to learn control. Learning new powers is always tricky."

"You don't understand. You can't feel the magic inside me."

How could I describe the sensation? Ever since the attack, my magic had been off. I could sense it churning just beneath the surface. I'd awoken this, and it refused to slumber again.

"There isn't a way to control it."

"Lunar magic differs from your solar spells."

I knew enough about shifter magic to understand the difference. The strength of solar magic was a force to be reckoned with. While the lunar magic was enigmatic and subtle, it ebbed and flowed. It had its own deep power, affecting the world like the moon creating the tides.

"You saw what my magic did in that alley," I said. "Did that resemble lunar magic?"

"No," she murmured, as if she didn't want to answer. Her head drooped.

Guilt wrapped its fingers around my throat.

Danika didn't deserve this.

"I overheard the nephilim officers," I said, the words a whisper. "They said the veil tore last night. And . . . I think it was my magic."

All races took severe measures against those with unstable powers, and now I understood why. But wouldn't my parents have explained that to me?

Yet there was no other explanation.

It was my wild magic that damaged the veil.

My shoulders sagged. I needed answers before I did anything drastic, because despite it all, I'd felt something deep within me when I'd channeled that magic.

The thought of denying my power was like agreeing to quit alchemy.

"Will you at least allow me to work with you before you drink that?"

"This brew won't be strong enough to bind my magic completely," I admitted. "I'd need a full moon for that. In small doses, it will only subdue my power. It's a precaution. I can't draw any more attention to myself. Those UMC officers are already suspicious of me. If I lose control again and they link it to me, they'll hand me back to the witch council, and they'll strip me of my magic."

Danika hissed.

I sensed her fear; it skittered across my skin and seeped into my heart.

"Will you search the codex before you drink it?" Danika pleaded. *"You accessed your lunar magic last night. It might reveal more and offer a different solution."*

"I'm sorry that you bonded with a broken witch," I said, running my fingers down her back. "Being stripped of my magic would mean giving you up, too. And I can't bear losing you. I'll train and seek answers with you. My last resort is to suppress my magic, though I hope it will only dampen our bond. I could never forgive myself if I tore the veil and unleashed demonspawn into our realm."

"I am with you, no matter what." Danika curled up beside me.

I finished the brew in silence, portioning out the binding potion into several small vials.

There was something unsettling about this concoction. Even through the bespelled glass, I wanted to shrink away from its magic.

I started a new brew of analgesic potions for pain control.

Though I'd offer them to Ruby's pack, but I had a deep suspicion I might also need them. My headache had subsided, but having them available wouldn't hurt.

Reading a few stories from Beylin's book didn't offer any real insights, only that the moon-blessed were powerful guardians who had a tendency to sacrifice themselves to defend the realm.

While I might glean a few tidbits, they wouldn't help unless there was a story about a moon-blessed with uncontrolled magic.

I let out a deep breath as I reached for *The Lunar Codex*. Fear and hope combined within my veins until my fingers shook. Magic shivered through me as I opened the page I'd marked.

The empowerment potion's instructions were still legible, and I double-checked there wasn't any new information.

I flicked through the pages to see if it revealed anything more. But what was the point? Wouldn't it hurt more to learn about a spell I'd never get to use?

Every day at school had felt like a gut punch since I was unable to cast most spells. I watched as wonder filled the faces of my classmates when they conjured a spell, while I failed.

I almost dropped the book when my eye caught words I understood. My breath fled as I stared wide-eyed down at the writing.

"Did you find something?" Danika poked her head between my body and arm.

"Yes." My voice wobbled. I licked my lips, ignoring the tremble in my hands. "These are meditations."

While it wasn't a spell exactly, excitement surged through me. The hope I'd failed to extinguish flared in my chest.

Danika tilted her head as she studied the page.

"I can guide you through these," she said, sounding pleased. *"The Crescent Serenity meditation encourages peace and balance by aligning your inner energy to the phases of the moon. Lunar Insight taps into your magic and allows the moon energies to guide you.*

"They will allow you to connect with your magic *and offer you insight and guidance without the need to call upon your magic. With regular use, they will offer a deeper understanding of your own power."*

Unable to help myself, I leafed through the pages, searching for more.

"Lunar Attunement Ritual," I said aloud, reading the details.

Preparing rituals took time, but the slow infusion of magic supported by a spell array ensured control, even with my magic.

"Attunes the spellcaster and their magic to the phases of the moon, allowing them to harness the moon's energies to stabilize and strengthen their magic."

"That sounds promising," Danika said. She peeked up at me, and I tried to ignore the hope in her eyes.

"It does," I began, warring with my own thoughts. "But I have nowhere safe to cast this. If things went wrong, like last night . . ."

Our schools had ritual rooms, warded to contain the magic if anything went awry. I couldn't take that chance, not with so many people around.

"What if I found a suitable location?" Danika asked. *"Would you consider it?"*

"Yes," I said in a rush. "I don't know what I would do without you."

"You are my bonded," she said, as if that explained everything. *"It's my duty to guide and support you, to offer you my knowledge and strength. Our magic connects us. As it strengthens, so does our bond."*

I could hear the words she left unsaid. If I bound my magic, it would weaken our connection.

What would that do to Danika?

I knew that witches who lost their familiars suffered; it was like losing a piece of their soul, and they rarely formed a new bond. But when it was the witch that died, the familiar followed soon after.

Would drinking the potion harm Danika? Despite our bond being new, hurting her was unthinkable.

My phone chimed, snapping me out of my morbid thoughts. It was Ruby requesting more potions.

Elation washed through me. She listed quite a few; I'd receive a decent payment from them.

But my smile faltered. Why did her pack need so many healing potions and tonics? The shifters had lost a healer, but why would they need so many supplies?

I portioned out the analgesic potion and set to work on a tonic to fight infections for Ruby's pack, then pulled out my second cauldron.

The tonic required a low input of magic, so I would split my power and channel into two arrays without overexerting myself.

All day I'd been brainstorming potions I could keep on hand for protection, but I needed to research more viable formulas. I'd hunted through my grimoire and stumbled upon old recipes I'd used to play pranks on my brother.

One time, I crafted a thick ooze that stuck to anything it touched.

It wore off after an hour, but that's what my brother got for trying to read my diary.

With a few minor tweaks, I could make it harden. Slowing down my attackers might be the difference between life and death.

Danika remained silent, curled up at my side. She had retreated into herself. I sensed it through our connection and even now it ached like a hole in my chest.

"Would you guide me through a meditation tonight?" I asked.

Her ears perked up. *"Of course."*

I swore I could hear a smile in her voice.

Clearing a space for us to work, a thought occurred to me. "Do you need anything?"

"What do you mean?"

"Food, water, somewhere to sleep." Embarrassment bloomed in my chest. "I'm being a terrible bonded. What do you need?"

"I'm accustomed to caring for myself, but I would appreciate those," she said, warmth wrapping around our connection. *"I also like fish."*

Chuckling, I settled down on a cushion with my legs crossed. "I think I can manage that."

I'd buy her the best fish I could afford. With my hands resting on my knees, I nodded to Danika.

"Close your eyes and take in a slow, *deep breath,"* she began. *"Allow each breath to gather up the tension, the fear, and the anxiety from your*

body. Then release it as you exhale. Feel the soft moonlight as it washes over your skin. Allow it to penetrate your body. With each breath, draw in its glow and let it gather in your chest."

My body relaxed as I focused on her words, the outside world falling away until there was only my mind and Danika's voice.

"Imagine the moon in your mind's eye. Its bright, serene glow in the night sky. Let it bathe you in its light. Let it guide you to the answers you seek. Feel its energy, steady and unwavering, pulse through your body."

Power gathered in my chest, not burning with the same intensity as solar magic, but subtle in its influence. Soft yet strong enough to pierce through darkness.

"Lunar light, illuminate my path," I repeated after Danika. "Share your guidance and impart your understanding to me."

Something shifted deep in my chest.

The wind brushed over my skin, and I imagined a soft glowing aura wrapping around me, embracing me.

A fire flickered in my heart. I pushed it back down, clinging to the steady presence of the moon. The flames lashed out, burning through my veins with anger. Images filled my mind.

An all-consuming fire blazed around me.

Heat pressed in until I thought my skin would melt.

My arms shook as I channeled more magic.

If I stopped, the fire would reach me. The flames flickered in a myriad of colors.

My magic faltered, and the flames rushed in.

Gasping for breath, I fell forward.

Danika darted back before I crushed her. The memories faded. I was back on the rooftop.

I flinched as flames crawled over my skin, but I clamped down hard on my magic until the fire snuffed out.

"Nyssa?" Danika asked. I sensed her panic thrashing through our connection.

"I can't even meditate without making mistakes," I snapped.

I ruined everything—me and my useless magic. Anger burned through me, as if the flames I had just extinguished now tried to burn my insides.

"It was your first try. These things take time."

I opened my mouth, a retort on my tongue, but snapped it shut. She was right. It had taken me years to master alchemy, months to learn a new spell. I was just so tired of failing.

"Rest, Nyssa. You expended a large amount of magic yesterday. We can try again tomorrow."

I finished my last batch, gathered my supplies, and went downstairs despite the remaining moonlight because my energy and magical reserves were depleted.

After messaging Ruby that the first batch was ready, I reached out to Beylin to ask for a partial shift tomorrow.

Staying home all day, even with Rynac here, sounded dreadful. I needed to distract myself from my failures.

I rolled a vial of the binding potion between my fingers, yet I couldn't make myself drink it. Despite the destruction my magic had caused, drinking it didn't sit right.

My magic was worth fighting for, and I wasn't built for easy routes or clean exits.

The potion was only there for peace of mind, a last resort if it all went sideways again.

Nothing more.

Nothing less.

CHAPTER SEVENTEEN

"**W**iggle it," Voren instructed. "Then drag it across the top."

Biting my lip, I tried to follow his directions, but as I set the cup down, I frowned. "That's one ugly-looking fern,"

Voren made latte art look so easy. Kain, the other barista working today, peered over and erupted in laughter.

"You're lucky you're related to Beylin," I grumbled.

Voren chuckled. "Just takes practice."

That's what everyone kept saying, but I was over being subpar at making drinks and using magic.

"Maybe we can head to *Etherflow* to watch the bartenders in action. I'm sure a few might give you some pointers."

"Is that right? Or do you just want to go out drinking?" I arched an eyebrow.

Drinking with the Divine crew had been a blast, though I could've done without the hangover.

"Maybe," Voren said, giving me the side-eye. "I can neither confirm nor deny that a certain someone was enquiring after you. They may or may not have offered me free drinks if I convinced you to go back."

Heat flushed my face, and I'm pretty sure I turned red all the way up to my ears.

Bartenders are meant to flirt, I reminded myself. But that didn't mean I hadn't enjoyed it.

"Better than this guy," Voren scowled as Rynac entered.

I whacked him on the arm. I'd given both Voren and Zola the heavily edited version of the thrall incident. No matter how hard I tried to convince him, Voren blamed Rynac for putting me in danger.

"He's my friend," I hissed. "So play nice."

Voren grumbled and started cleaning up the mess I made as I greeted Rynac.

"What brings you here?" I asked, trying to smile even as I feared his reason for stopping by.

I'd told Rynac about my plan to complete the ritual tonight, which he had protested.

Not that I blamed him.

I wasn't thrilled about going out alone at night or attempting the lunar ritual.

We'd made a compromise; he'd agreed to accompany me as far as the park and would wait to escort me back home.

I wasn't heartless. I'd leave him at one of the local cafes that stayed open late.

"Just had my checkup," he grumbled. Guess it was bad news.

"Still not cleared for work?"

I hadn't been hopeful. Despite my magic speeding up the healing, his wounds had been deep.

But Rynac didn't take well to being sidelined. Another reason I'd caved and let him come tonight; I hoped making him feel useful would lift his mood.

"Not yet." He frowned. "But I caught up with the others. No new updates, but patrols have increased."

I nodded, understanding the hidden meaning. Rynac had poked around to see if the UMC still suspected me. If things were quiet, I hoped it meant they believed what I'd told them.

"I'll let you get back to work," Rynac said, looking over my shoulder. I turned to find Voren eyeing Rynac and aggressively cleaning the milk pitchers.

"See you at nine," I said.

"Make sure you keep her safe this time, enforcer," Voren added, jabbing a finger at Rynac.

He met the erebian's stare, his muscles bulging as he crossed his arms.

What in the realms is going on here?

"I always protect those in need and would never willingly allow any harm to come to Nyssa."

"Bye, Rynac," I interjected as I stepped between whatever this was.

Thankfully, he got the hint and headed out.

Hands on my hips, I rounded on Voren. "I thought I told you to play nice."

Voren just grumbled something about beefy enforcers, and I wasn't sure if it was an insult or not.

Shaking my head, I left him to his mutterings and went to fix the pastry case before my shift was over.

My stomach churned as my thoughts turned to Thayna.

We still had no word of her whereabouts.

Just as I was finishing up, Ruby arrived, holding the hand of a young girl with the same shimmering silver hair.

"I'm just about finished if you're okay with waiting a few minutes," I said, flashing them a smile.

The girl, who couldn't be older than ten, hid behind Ruby but peered out at me.

"That's no problem," Ruby said, trying to suppress a chuckle. "I promised Jade a treat if she behaved."

"Oh? And was she a good girl?" I asked.

"Yes," a small voice said from behind Ruby.

"Well, then she'd better pick out the best-looking treat," I said.

Ruby picked Jade up so she could get a good view of all the pastries on display. The girl's eyebrows drew together as she contemplated her choices.

"You know, Nyssa here bakes these," Ruby said.

Jade's round eyes met mine before darting away.

"And the potions to make us better," Jade mumbled.

I smiled. Jade picked a double chocolate chip cookie, and the two sat on a couch as I clocked out.

Grabbing my belongings, I bought one of my salted caramel brownies and a box of cookies before joining the shifters.

"Come sit," Ruby said. "This is my sister, Jade, if you didn't guess that already."

Jade stuck out her tongue at Ruby, who smiled back.

"It's lovely to meet you, Jade," I said.

"Hello," she replied with a mouth full of cookie.

"What did I say about talking with your mouth full?" Ruby scolded, then shook her head. "I didn't have anyone to watch her, so she had to come on errands with me."

"Maybe if she's really good for the rest of the day, you'll share this treat with her at home," I said, passing over the brownie.

Jade's eyes went as round as saucers as they followed the treat.

"Can I have a hot chocolate too?" she asked, bouncing on her seat.

Whether from excitement or the sugar, I wasn't sure.

Ruby sighed. "Sure."

"Jade, you see that barista up there?" I said, pointing to Kain. "If you ask him nicely for a hot chocolate, he'll make you a super-special one."

Her face lit up, and she raced over. Kain smiled down at the little shifter as she went up on her tiptoes to see over the counter.

"Thank you," Ruby said. Her smile seemed muted as she gazed after her sister. "It's been rough. We lost our mother in an attack a month ago. Now it's just the two of us. I try to make ends meet."

"I'm so sorry. Does the pack not help?" I didn't know much about shifters, but I always thought their packs were tight-knit.

"They do, but I want to pull my weight to look after her. We've lost too many of our pack over the last month. We're all hurting."

"That's terrible." My heart twisted for them, for all the losses they had suffered. I never expected such brutality within the city. "Have you reached out to the enforcers for help?"

"The elders are stubborn," she said, her shoulders dropping. "They want to keep pack matters within the pack. It was hard enough convincing them to agree to external alchemists. But we were in dire need of the potions."

"Speaking of which, I have them here." I pulled out the packed box and handed it over.

I chewed on the inside of my cheek, trying to hold back the words. This wasn't my place to butt in, but their pack was suffering and needed help.

And though I was new to the city, from my encounters with Rynac and Indra, as well as the other enforcers, I knew they served to protect all the people within Arkirith.

"The enforcers would offer assistance if you requested it. Especially if dangerous people are hurting your pack, they're likely a danger to everyone."

Ruby blew out a heavy breath. Her eyes fixed on her sister, who was peering over the counter, watching Kain craft her drink. "We really need help. These attacks are getting worse."

"Any idea who's behind it? I could pass the information anony-mously to the enforcers if the elders won't."

"I don't know much, as I'm not one of the pack's fighters," Ruby said. "At the start, I thought it was just a gang trying to claim more territory. But now I'm not so sure."

My heart skipped, fearing my suspicions were true.

Her eyes darted around the room before landing back on me. I nodded with encouragement as she gnawed on her lip.

"I saw the wounded fighters when they came back." The words tumbled out of her in a hushed whisper. "They had injuries that looked like a beast had attacked them, so I figured it was a rival pack. But they brought back one they had killed the other night. It wasn't normal. The elders hid the body, but I know what I saw. It looked like a person, but its hands were twisted into black claws and some sort of black substance covered its body. I don't know what twisted magic did that, but I never want to see one again."

Dread crept over my skin as a pit formed in my stomach.

"Did you see its chest?" I whispered, not wanting anyone to hear.

"You've seen them too?" Ruby said, leaning closer as her voice dropped lower. "With runes carved into their flesh."

"I think they might be thralls."

Shaking my head, I banished the images of their dead bodies. I wanted nothing more than to help Ruby and her pack, but I was not the person for that job; I'd likely make things worse.

"You have to notify the MEA or the UMC detachment. There was an attack the other day that they are investigating. Thralls are dangerous, Ruby. The enforcers fear they're linked to a warlock."

"Goddess above, protect us," she hissed.

"Please convince your pack to come forward. For Jade's sake."

Just how many thralls and demonspawn were lurking around the city at night?

While I might have my reservations about a few choice members of the UMC, I knew they would deal with the problem. But everyone would need to work together. And the MEA trusted them when it came to demonspawn.

Jade returned, holding her hot chocolate with pride. Whipped cream towered high, covered in chocolate and caramel drizzle, and sprinkled with chocolate curls.

I sat with the shifters, chatting about baking and the cafe, the rest of my worries falling away.

But as they left to finish the rest of their errands, I headed home, and the gnawing fears returned.

My smile at Jade's delight faded with each step.

Why would the thralls be targeting the shifters? Was there more behind their movements than just bloodlust?

I knew I'd have to tell Rynac.

The elders might prefer their secrets, but Jade and Ruby deserved more than whispered warnings and half-truths.

They deserved to feel safe in this city—and I was done pretending otherwise.

Chapter Eighteen

With a box of cookies tucked under my arm, I followed Danika through the dense foliage. The first stars pricked through the gray sky, but inside the forest's embrace, the night didn't scare me—not the shadows or what they might hide.

My magic twisted and churned in my chest, as if it knew something I didn't.

I'd been thankful for Rynac's company as we made our way to the park. He'd been concerned about what was happening with the shifters and said he'd make some calls while I was gone.

After buying him a mocha to say thanks—despite his insistence on coming—I left him at an all-night cafe.

"Leave the cookies here," Danika said as we stepped into a small clearing.

The treats were for the fairies who resided in the park, payment for use of their sacred space, and so they would alert us to any disturbances.

I set the box down on the flat stone in the center and flipped open the lid before retreating a few steps.

Fairies always required payment; I was thankful their sweet tooth won out over more malevolent desires.

This massive park was their home. While trails skirted the border, people only walked them during the day.

At night, one only entered with the fairies' permission . . . or if they had a death wish.

"We may enter," Danika said.

I hadn't heard a thing, but maybe they didn't wish to converse with people. I followed Danika through the silver-bark oaks, their branches overhead thick enough to block out the sky; while floating fairy lights illuminated our path.

We emerged into another clearing, this one twice the size of the last.

Despite the towering oaks, the open ring was large enough for the moon to shine down on us when it rose.

Clovers and wildflowers covered the area, except for the center where a large, flat stone rested. The fairy lights danced in the air as the soft evening breeze blew. It was utterly enchanting, and a deep longing vibrated in my chest.

I shook my head. If this was the magic of the park without the fairies meddling, I never wanted to come here without their permission.

Spinning in a few circles, Danika settled down in the wildflowers as I prepared the ritual.

Memories of my failed meditation taunted me, but I shoved them away. As always, my mind was my own worst enemy. The nightmare of the devouring flames had haunted me for years. I couldn't let it defeat me now.

Lighting a bundle of sage, I moved around the clearing to cleanse it. Inhaling its woody and herbal aroma, I allowed it to clear my mind and calm my nerves.

At least I wasn't doing this alone. Without Danika, I'd never have discovered any of this.

Me with a familiar. I smiled at the thought. I doubted any of the witches back home would believe it.

"Do cobalt vulpines bond with shifters?" I asked.

Witches prized familiars with an affinity for solar magic. But I'd never heard of a familiar with incompatible magic such as fire with water, or a witch with a lunar-aligned familiar.

Danika opened her eyes, peering up at me. *"Some bond to people with an affinity for lunar magic. We were crafted for the lunar witches, but without a bonded . . . we long to fulfill our purpose."*

Sorrow brimmed in Danika's mournful gaze.

A bone-deep ache squeezed in my chest, a void in my soul that longed to be filled. And then, in a blink, it was gone.

"I'm not judging you or your kin," I said, kneeling beside her and patting her head. "I'm just curious to know more about you."

"Oh." Her ears perked up. *"What would you like to know?"*

"You said you were created for the lunar witches," I prompted, pulling out my chalk to trace out the spell array.

"Mani, the son of Selene, brought us to life with a drop of his own blood. We were to watch over his children, protect and train them when their own kin rejected them. Many of our kind perished during the war when the lunar witches died. When Selene created her moon-blessed warriors, we aligned with them. Others sought out the shifter clans. Over time, we learned to bond with them, but it is still rare. Many of my kin fade without ever bonding."

The pain and longing that Danika and her kin must have endured for decades was unimaginable. No wonder she was so protective of me.

I paused, inspecting my array for any faults or errors. It was a five-foot star with a circle around it. At each of the points, I copied out the runes that would stabilize the magic and allow the moon's energies to flow into them.

"Do your kin live within the city?"

"No, I traveled here. Our seer had a vision that I would find my bonded within Arkirith."

"Do you miss them?" I asked, knowing she might sense the ache within my own chest. Leaving my family behind to start a life here had been harder than I'd imagined.

"Every day. But I do not regret it, and I'm confident you don't either."

"You can visit them whenever you like." I began drawing the phases of the moon, but sensed Danika's amusement like a tingling warmth in my chest. "I admit I don't know much about the whole familiar thing. At school, they were vague about how the bond works, but I don't want you to feel obligated to stay if you miss them."

"Thank you, Nyssa. Though they are too far away to reach through telepathy alone, I can visit sacred spaces to connect with them."

"Almost as convenient as a cell phone."

Danika chuckled.

Last, I placed my offerings within the quarter moon to match its current phase. Iron bark for strength, fresh twigs of willow for flexibility, moonstones for balance, and crystal quartz for clarity.

"Ready?" Danika asked.

The moon had risen above the treeline, and its light washed over the spell array.

I nodded. Gripping my conduit in one hand and a silver chain in the other, I stepped into the center circle.

Emptying my mind of all thoughts, I gathered my magic and, with a slow exhale, released it. My magic poured into the spell array and activated the runes one by one.

The fairy lights retreated as the array glowed. Danika was there with me, whispering words in my mind.

My eyes fluttered closed as I murmured the incantation in the old language.

The words fell from my lips; the chant vibrating through me until time no longer had any meaning. Heavy magic filled the air, calling on the power of the moon and harnessing its light.

Power rumbled deep within me—the wildness wanting release—but I focused on the spell, letting it anchor me.

Beneath the churning surface of my magic, I sensed something new. It thrummed with vitality that I could only sense now that I'd quieted the rest of my mind and magic.

I brushed against it, testing what lay at the core of my power.

It shifted at my touch, wrapping me in a welcoming embrace. It felt like peace. Fortitude and serenity.

A steady strength I'd never encountered before.

"Nyssa," Danika's voice swelled in my mind.

Her urgency made my concentration falter, but I held the spell before it could break. The foreign, yet familiar, power thrummed through my fingers.

"Release the spell."

Something was wrong. I gathered the magic, siphoning it off faster than I should. Distress thrummed through my connection to Danika.

More demonspawn?

Heat flared in my chest, and my balance wobbled. The flames scorched through my body. I ground my teeth as I gripped my magic to steady it.

"I'm here." A cool, steady presence wrapped around my chest as Danika's power merged with mine.

The magic stabilized enough that I discharged it as fast as I dared while the solar magic thrashed within me. Needles stabbed into the back of my eyes as the last of the spell dissipated, and I sucked in a gasping breath.

My head swam as I opened my eyes.

A faint silver aura lingered over my skin before it faded under the moonlight, but the array beneath me had scorched into the stone.

The surrounding flowers had blackened while others wilted in a wide circle around me.

Thankfully, Danika was unharmed.

"Goddess," I hissed.

I'd added extra stabilization runes and still almost lost it. But there were more pressing matters. I stood up, pins and needles flaring to life and the moon hung high above. Had I channeled for that long?

"What is it?"

"The fairies sent me a warning. Danger is coming."

Danika paced the edge of the circle, watching the perimeter. I grabbed my bag, leaving the rest of my offerings for the fairies as payment for the damage.

She took off faster than I could follow.

The forest was still.

Not even a whisper of wind rustled the leaves.

The fairy lights had disappeared, making the forest appear pitch-black.

Pulling out a glow vial, I gave it a shake until it emitted a soft green light and raced after Danika.

We crashed through the underbrush, and I hoped we didn't anger anyone along the way.

"Did they say what it was?" I puffed as I caught up to Danika.

"No, but I can sense the forest's distress."

Branches snatched at my clothes and hair, but I didn't slow. My lungs burned.

How big was this park? I pulled out my phone and called Rynac.

"Something's wrong," I blurted before he could say anything. "We don't know what, but the fairies warned us of danger."

"Where are you?" Rynac demanded.

"Heading toward the south corner," Danika said.

I repeated Danika's words because I would've said, "Surrounded by trees."

"I'm on my way. I'll check if any squads are nearby."

I tucked my phone away. The last thing I needed was to lose it in the middle of this park.

How many cookies would it cost me to get it back?

"Oh, no." Danika veered to the right, and I stumbled, trying to follow. My two legs were not as agile as hers.

"What?" I panted. But I couldn't keep up.

Danika disappeared, and I slowed down, trying to spot her.

Please don't let me get lost.

A bright light flew at me, and I jerked back.

Glitter dust splattered my face, and I wiped it away just in time to see a fairy fleeing deeper into the forest.

I ran in the direction they had come.

Bad idea, I know, but I hoped that was where Danika had gone.

I burst through the brush into a clearing and slid to a stop, fear slicing through me.

Demonspawn.

Chapter Nineteen

Fairies exploded into motion, some diving for the safety of the branches while others could only tremble where they hovered as the demonspawn lunged.

Its claws tore through the swarm of glowing silver, snapping at every streak of light.

If it caught even one, the rest wouldn't stand a chance.

A tiny scream cut through the air as the demonspawn batted at one. The fairy fell in a heap on the ground. The other silver fairies clustered around the injured one as if they could protect it.

Danika leaped, planting herself in front of the demonspawn, growling at the much larger beast.

"Get the fairy. The others won't leave it behind," Danika commanded, and then she launched herself at it.

I scrambled forward as she distracted the beast. My heart hammered in my chest as I ran closer to the demonspawn. Magic crackled around Danika, keeping it at bay. I scooped up the fairy with both hands and nestled it against me.

"Run!"

My head jerked up to find the demonspawn's undivided attention fixed on me.

Shit.

I spun on my heels and ran to the edge of the clearing. Which way should I go?

A guttural growl pierced the silence and sent a wave of dread through me.

The fairies swarmed around me.

For a moment, I feared they would attack, but they buzzed around like an angry swarm of bees.

A high-pitched yelp pierced the air. I stumbled as pain exploded across my right side.

My soul understood before my brain could catch up, and I whipped around.

My heart froze when I spotted her, unmoving a few feet from the demonspawn. The creature fixed its gaze on the fox, opening its massive mouth filled with jagged teeth as if to devour her whole.

"Danika!" I screamed, fear and desperation drowning out logic.

The demonspawn's head snapped to me.

"Come and get me, you ugly git!"

The beast surged toward me with breathtaking speed.

My senses caught up with reality, and I knew I couldn't outrun it. I fumbled with my bag, hunting for my vials as it gobbled up the distance.

My fingers wrapped around the large, bulky vial of sticky ooze, and I hurled it with everything I had.

Glass shattered as the vial smashed into the beast's head, ooze splattering over its face.

The demonspawn skidded as it snapped its jaw at the ooze, but that only coated more of its mouth until it couldn't open it anymore. It tore at its face, only for its claws to become stuck too.

A flash of red on its neck caught my attention as the beast flailed.

Wide-eyed, I could only watch in a mix of horror and disbelief, some faint part of my mind screaming I needed to run.

A dark shadow blotted out the moon. It hurtled toward me, moving too fast for me to escape, and I wrapped myself around the fairy.

Something sliced through the air, and I braced for the pain, but it never came.

A heavy thud hit the ground, then nothing.

The foul stench of rotting flesh hit me, and I gagged.

Why wasn't I dead yet?

"Are you hurt?" a voice asked.

I peered up to find a nephilim silhouetted against the moon.

It seemed to shine brighter behind him, like a lunar halo, but hid his features. He flared his massive wings, and the twin daggers he clutched dripped with dark liquid.

My eyes darted to the demonspawn lying in a heap by his feet, a black pool growing around it. Its eyes dull in the moonlight.

The creature's gaping jaw still coated in my ooze and filled with far too many teeth made to tear flesh from bone.

Another few seconds and . . .

The nephilim moved to kneel in front of me, blocking my view of the demonspawn with his wings.

The fairy.

I straightened, lowering my arms to reveal the fairy I cradled. The silver fairies descended, then lifted the injured one from my arms and disappeared deeper into the forest.

A few remained dancing just above our heads, their soft glow lighting the area. The last of my energy fled, and I sat down ungracefully.

"That was a handy trick with the vial. Again," he said.

I blinked.

The adrenaline faded, and my mind started working again.

Peering through the shadows, I wanted to groan as I recognized the angel-born from yesterday. Just my luck to run into him again.

Well, at least it wasn't the one who made me vomit.

"Ah, it seems you remember me then," Kaelan said, a hint of a smirk curving on his lips.

"Do people usually grimace when they recognize you?" I shot back. Much to my annoyance, he seemed to find that funny.

"They usually thank me for saving their life."

I narrowed my eyes. *Fat chance of that, bud.*

Kaelan pressed his lips together as if he were trying not to laugh. I guess Mr. Cool-calm-and-collected had a sense of humor. Joy.

He offered me a hand, which I ignored. I scanned the grass, but didn't see Danika anywhere.

My gaze fell on the demonspawn, and I remembered that flash of red.

"It had a rune on its neck," I said in a rush, moving closer to see if I could find it.

"What?"

"I saw it. When it charged me, its neck was glowing red like the rune on those thralls."

I crouched, not wanting to move too close in case it wasn't dead.

"There." I pointed. "It's black now, but it glowed red when it was alive."

Kaelan moved closer, reaching out.

"Don't touch it," I said, slapping his hand away. "Unless you want to be attached to a dead demonspawn for an hour."

The angel-born pulled out his phone and shone its light on the creature's neck. I squinted. Without the glow, it was hard to make out the shape of the rune. None of this made any sense.

"Why was this thing even here?" I asked. Was this the same one I'd encountered on my way to work? "I thought the UMC took care of them the other day. How many more are there?"

"That's why my unit is here with the UMC division. We're hunting them down, but it's best to use caution at night," he said.

Not very reassuring.

"This one was likely drawn to the lunar energies within these fairies. The one you saved was a moon fairy."

If it were because of lunar energies . . .

I swallowed hard and side-eyed the nephilim, not wanting to trust him, but he had saved my life.

"A client informed me that her shifter pack is being attacked," I admitted. "Some sounded like thralls, but if it's demonspawn too, no wonder they kept quiet. Could they be targeted as well?"

"It's highly likely." Kaelan rubbed a weary hand over his face. "Selene trapped the demons on the other side of the veil, and old grudges run deep. Demonspawn will always target those with lunar energy. But tonight, it's as if—"

"Nyssa?" Rynac's voice rang out.

I'd forgotten about him, and I didn't want him hurting himself again. I pushed to my feet, and the nephilim mimicked the movement.

"Am I allowed to leave?" I asked, glaring up at him.

The corner of his mouth quirked up.

Great, he thought my annoyance was funny.

"Of course. Try to stay out of trouble for one night."

Ass.

I jogged toward Rynac's voice, ready to go home and get away from anything likely to kill me.

Rynac swatted away a branch as he followed Danika toward me. I guess there were some benefits to being short.

"Are you okay?" I asked, kneeling down to check Danika for injuries. Her ears flattened when I pressed against her ribs—the same spot I'd felt her pain.

She rubbed her head against my hand. *I just need rest. Let's go home.*

"I was worried when she appeared alone," Rynac said, "but she led me here."

His gaze shifted past me.

"I'll explain at home," I said, turning him around.

I could feel the nephilim's gaze and didn't like it one bit. And if I didn't want them sniffing around, I needed to stay off their radar.

When we were far enough away, I gave Rynac the rundown. From the set of his jaw, I doubted he'd let me go anywhere alone ever again. But I didn't dare voice the real question I wanted to ask, not while he was around. It was chewing me up inside.

Only when I was back home did I confront Danika. "The nephilim said lunar energies attract demonspawn."

Danika opened her eyes and watched me from the nest she'd made of my blankets.

"Did it attack the fairies because of me? Was it my ritual that called to them?"

She was silent for a long time. *It is possible.*

I swore, dropping my face into my hands. This was all my fault. "I should drink that binding potion."

Nyssa, Danika scolded.

"What if the demonspawn are turning up because of me?"

Lunar magic created the veil between the realms. Just by using your magic, you cannot accidentally summon demonspawn. Only dark magic can do that, twisting the lunar energies with their runes.

"But what if I'm like a beacon calling to them? I'm putting my friends in danger."

"We'll work this out together," she said, but she didn't deny it. *"You're tired and have been under a lot of stress. Please, just rest."*

I sighed and dragged a hand through my hair, only to freeze when my fingers came away streaked with black demon blood.

Perfect.

At this rate, I needed a scalding shower and a year-long nap.

Just once, I'd like something in my life to go right before I ran out of shampoo.

Chapter Twenty

Perched on the edge of my bed, I clutched the binding potion so hard my fingers ached, weighing the choice I'd been running from. The one that plagued my every waking moment.

If I drank it, I might finally be safe.

If I didn't, those around me could be hurt.

That foolish hope that I could harness my magic had put people in danger. I'd come here to control the wild magic, but instead I'd awoken a new, far more dangerous power.

What would happen the next time I encountered demonspawn? Would I lose control and tear the veil again?

But if I drank the potion, what would it do to me? Would it inhibit my alchemy as well? And what about my connection to Danika?

As if hearing me think her name, the fox yawned, and I tucked the potion away. I didn't need to cause her any more stress right now.

Despite her claim to be uninjured, she'd been limping when we walked back from the park.

An hour later, Indra and Rynac came over claiming it was to eat lunch together, but I knew they wanted to check up on me. I pushed the food around my plate, my mind stewing over everything that was going wrong in my life.

"Nyssa." Rynac's voice cut through my thoughts.

I looked up to see them both watching me.

"You need to talk to us. Your thoughts are eating you up inside. We want to help you, but we can't do that if you don't talk to us."

A heavy sigh rushed out of me. "I don't know where to start."

"How about last night?" Indra said. "Tell us what happened. It might give us a clue to what's going on with the demonspawn. And it was a good thing Rynac called in the squads because we were fending off demonspawn all night."

"At the park?" My heart pounded in my chest as Indra nodded. "Was anyone injured?"

"A few," she said, not meeting my gaze. "Thankfully, the nephilim were there to support us."

With a shake of my head, I rose and headed for my room. I couldn't keep silent about this anymore.

They deserved the truth, and I couldn't keep calling them in to clean up my mess without being honest with them.

Danika watched me as I gathered up *The Lunar Codex* along with the binding and enhancement potions.

"You should join us," I said.

My voice sounded flat even to my own ears, but she followed without a word.

Their conversation died away as I placed the items on the table. I remained standing, still at war with myself.

They had offered me the benefit of the doubt and stood by me even after seeing the destruction my magic wrought. They deserved the truth. I rubbed a hand across my face, and my shoulders sagged.

"I guess I need to start from the beginning," I said.

Might as well get this over with.

"Witches manifest magic in their teens. It's a turbulent time for us as we struggle to learn how to control and contain our magic. I was no different, but over the months, it grew wilder and harder to control."

I swallowed hard against the lump in my throat. After all these years, I'd kept all this to myself, fearing it would be used against me.

"My parents searched for a way to fix my magic. Though we were able to suppress it, nothing we've tried over the years has been able to tame it. I learned not to use it unless I wanted disastrous results, and that I had to suppress it unless I wanted to be discovered."

A weighted silence pressed against me, and I shot a glance at Danika. My bonded sat patiently, watching me with an open and trusting gaze.

"In all magical races, anyone discovered with volatile magic has it stripped away. That's the fate that awaits me when I return home. My parents want me to give up my magic before it's taken from me. I've already had several encounters with Inquisitors—the witches who track down those with wild or corrupt magic."

"I can understand why you left," Rynac said. "If you give up your magic, you'll lose your alchemy too."

"It might not be much, but alchemy means a lot to me. I'd hoped to find answers outside the witch community, which is what brought me to Arkirith. I'd been researching a binding potion formula when I came across this book."

"What language is that?" Indra said, eyeing *The Lunar Codex.*

"I don't know, but I can read parts of it. At first, the only bit I could understand was a formula for a potion meant to cultivate my magic, which is this one here."

I tapped the potion.

"I drank it the night the thralls attacked us, hoping it would help. When I summoned that shield, I thought it had worked—until I lost control. But the magic I used for the shield wasn't the solar magic of witches, but lunar magic."

"As in shifter magic?" Rynac asked. "Is it possible to have two types of magic?"

"Not that I'm aware of," I said. "A child born from two different races is uncommon. And from what I recall, if the children do manifest, they take after one parent and only have access to a portion of their magical ability. That's how sirens and druids come about. Having both is unheard of, at least in the witch archives. Besides, both my parents are witches, so it wouldn't be possible to manifest lunar magic."

"And you're certain it's lunar magic?"

"That much we know. *The Lunar Codex* and cobalt vulpines only bond with individuals who have lunar energies."

"Bond?" Indra asked.

"When I woke up after the thrall attack, I could hear Danika telepathically. She's my familiar, but I could only hear her after I connected to my lunar powers."

"So what are you then?"

"Danika believes I carry the bloodline of the lunar witches," I admitted. "They were the children of a witch and Mani, one of Selene's descendants, but the Great War wiped out most of them. While Beylin believes I could be a moon-blessed. Have you heard of them?"

"Tales of the moon-blessed were popular when we were growing up," Rynac said. "Despite humans aversion to magic, they loved these stories of the heroes who protected our people."

"What's the other potion?" Indra asked. "It's unnerving just to look at."

"That's the binding potion. I crafted it the night after the thrall attack. I haven't tested it yet, but I'm confident that it will suppress my magic and keep it in check."

"How long does it last?"

"My guess is a day at most. I made a less potent version, hoping it would dampen the wild magic while still allowing me to cast low-level spells. It's not a long-term solution, but it's the best I've got."

"But your magic only acted up the first time, right?" Rynac said. "Why do you want to bind it?"

"It also flared one other time when I tried a lunar meditation. Then, last night I performed a ritual that was meant to help attune my energies, but I think it called out to those demonspawn."

"How would it do that? With all the magic users in the city, there would be more of a pattern if magic drew them in."

"The nephilim mentioned lunar energies attract them. Attacks have targeted my shifter client's pack recently. I fear that by channeling so much lunar energy, I became a beacon on a dark night."

Silence settled over us, each lost in our own thoughts.

"So where do we go from here?" Indra asked.

I shook my head. "I don't know. It hurts too much to hope that there might be an answer out there."

As much as I denied Danika's impossible claim that I was a lunar witch, a small part of me wanted to believe her.

"But if my magic never stabilizes, I'm going to lose it anyway. And if I'm the cause of the demonspawn presence, then I have to stop. What other option do I have?"

I plucked up the binding potion.

My magic shrank away as if it sensed the power within the magicked vial. My stomach hollowed out and my mouth went dry at the thought of drinking it. This had been my plan all along, but now that I was here, I hesitated.

"We need to take this one step at a time," Indra said as her warm, calloused hand wrapped around mine.

The softness in her expression and the way she had said "we" made my eyes prickle.

"Train and have patience," Rynac said. "Exhaust all other options before you take drastic measures. And we are here to help you."

"From personal experience, I understand how hard a new magic can be," Indra said. "Learning to control it is difficult, but suppressing it might only put off the inevitable. What if the binding potion makes it worse? Or, when it wears off, it's stronger and even harder to control?"

"I don't know. I just—" I rubbed my eyes, trying to hide my stupid tears. "For once, I just want something to work. I hate not knowing. I hate feeling scared. And most of all, I'm afraid I'll hurt someone."

Why couldn't I just be normal?

Warm arms wrapped around me, which only made the tears flow.

"I know how hard it is," Indra whispered, "for magic to tear through your life and turn everything upside down. We're here for you. You're not alone in this."

"You barely know me," I croaked.

Goddess, I'm a mess.

"Well, you're stuck with us now," Indra said with a wide grin.

"Thank you," I said. "I don't know how I would've managed all by myself."

Reaching out, I rubbed Danika's head. I'd been hard on her. All she wanted was to protect and help me.

"How has your magic been since the ritual?" Danika asked. *"You mentioned it had been acting up after the thrall attack."*

"I haven't noticed it," I said with a frown.

"Perhaps the ritual was effective then. And I believe Indra is correct. Suppressing your magic with the potion will only hinder your progress and make things worse."

"Fine."

I sighed, knowing they had won.

"She agrees with you about the binding potion," I explained to Indra. "But I will keep it on hand if it acts up. I've already had two encounters with the UMC. I don't need a third. And what about the demonspawn situation? I want to help, especially if I've made it worse."

"The potions you supply us with have already made an enormous difference," Rynac said.

"And I'll see if I can get any info from our captain," Indra said. "The UMC has been less than cooperative with the MEA, but after our help last night, maybe they'll change their tune."

"I guess I better get brewing then."

"Oh yeah, I want some of that sticky ooze you mentioned," Indra grinned. She turned to her brother. "I'm heading back to HQ. Are you coming for your checkup?"

"Will you be alright by yourself?" Rynac asked me.

"I've got Danika and plenty of training to do," I said, waving him off as I cleared the table.

I felt lighter, even though my situation hadn't changed. Was it getting all of that off my chest?

It'd been a long time since I'd opened up to anyone, voiced my own fears rather than just listening to everyone else's.

While I was still just as lost as ever, with this much support at my back, it didn't feel quite so terrifying.

That I could take it one step at a time.

I could only hope the path I chose wouldn't drag everyone down with me.

Chapter Twenty-One

The next morning I awoke with a pounding headache and sweat plastering my shirt to my back, as if I'd spent the night in a sauna. No fever. Just misery.

So I chugged a pain potion and dragged myself to work, fantasizing about calling in sick.

Too bad rent did not care how close I felt to death.

As I stumbled around the kitchen, I wished Thayna was back to help, but then felt guilty for such a selfish thought.

The ovens did nothing to aid my sour mood; their doors taking swipes at me when I didn't take the cookies out fast enough.

Six hours in, I wanted to die.

I went to cover the register for the afternoon rush, and the customer service smile I'd plastered on my face was faltering.

While most of the customers were pleasant—or at least tolerable—trying to be polite when a headache threatened to split my head in two was a challenge.

I placed the last two drink orders on the counter, shooting Voren a sympathetic smile. He sighed dramatically, then winked as he finished up the next order.

My feet added their complaint to my long list as I grabbed milk from the back to restock the bar.

A waft of cool air from the fridge felt like heaven against my skin.

"I don't know how you do it," I told Voren as I deposited the milk. "If I'd been on bar, I'd be a puddle on the ground."

"Just takes a lot of practice and good muscle memory," he said. "And I'm terrible with the till. How about your next shift we put you on the bar? A little trial by fire."

"That's a hard pass," I said, making a horrified face. My body already felt as if it were on fire.

"Maybe we can stop by *EtherFlow Lounge*. I'm sure the bartenders would be happy to give you some private lessons."

"What?" I choked.

Heat flushed my cheeks, and Voren chuckled.

"I'm never going drinking with you again."

"Stop trying to corrupt Nyssa," Zola chided.

"She doesn't mind," Voren said, winking at me.

I ducked down to hide my smile and pulled out the empty whipped cream canisters.

"Have you heard anything from Thayna?" I asked, hoping to steer the conversation away from me.

Pain flickered across Zola's face, and I regretted bringing it up. She shook her head, turning away to plate up a selection of pastries for the last customer.

Way to go, Nyssa.

I wished that there was something I could do for Zola and hoped Thayna would turn up soon.

The door jingled as new customers entered, and I groaned as I headed back to the register. Summoning my fake cheery expression, I glanced up and my mood darkened.

Nephilim.

The two who'd interrogated me. Kaelan might have aided me at the park, but he certainly hadn't earned any points.

Given their casual attire, they were likely off duty, and I resisted rolling my eyes.

Who did they think they were? And why did their V-neck t-shirts plunge so low? No one needed to see that much of their chest.

Their piercing gazes swept the area as if they expected danger.

A wave rippled over the cafe in their wake, their natural charm snagging the closest people's attention, before the patrons wrenched it back with annoyance.

One of their most annoying traits, that thankfully witches were immune to.

"Hello, what can I get for you today?" My voice exuded a false brightness while my eyes said, "Hurry up and go away."

Nathaniel's icy blue gaze sharpened as it landed on me.

"What are you doing here, witch?" He spat out the words as if they left a bitter taste on his tongue.

As charming as ever.

"I work here," I said dryly, resisting the urge to add, "Was that not obvious by the apron?"

Try not to antagonize the customers, Nyssa.

"We're searching for someone," Kaelan interjected.

He held out a photo of a smiling female with golden hair and light green eyes.

"Haven't seen her," I replied, annoyance building in my chest. "And this is a coffee shop, so why don't you try the enforcers? Or are you going to test me again, to see if I'm telling the truth?"

I was petty, but the angel-born had rubbed me the wrong way.

The muscle in Nathaniel's jaw twitched, but I met his fierce gaze head-on.

Kaelan cleared his throat. "She was investigating reports of . . . the creature in the park."

Demonspawn. I pushed my panic back down as I glanced to see if anyone else was listening. At least he had the decency not to say it out loud—the last thing we needed was people panicking.

"She hasn't reported in for over a week," he continued. "We tracked her magic, and the trail led us here."

I stepped to the pastry case, boxing up the last of the cookies before pushing them across the counter and holding out my hand toward the nephilim.

He eyed the box and then my hand.

"The seating area is for customers only," I said.

After a moment, he passed me his card, and I gave him my best customer service smile as I rang him up.

"Give me the photo, and I'll ask the other employees if they recognize her."

It would be better for me to ask, given their track record.

My shift was over in a few minutes, and I wanted the nephilim out of our hair.

Snagging the photo, I asked the staff on hand, then went to Beylin.

When I returned, the nephilim loomed by the bookcases; everyone gave them a wide berth.

"My boss recognized her," I said, offering the photo back to Kaelan. "Came in about two weeks ago, ordered a coffee to go, and left. Hasn't been in since."

"Thank you," Kaelan said, while Nathaniel shot daggers over my shoulder at where Zola and Voren waited for me.

Angel-born and demon-born had a long-held animosity, but this guy was acting as if Voren was a demonspawn in sheep's clothing.

Erebians and demonspawn might both have infernal energies, but it was like comparing humans to chimpanzees . . . if the latter were evil and hellbent on death and destruction.

"Do you have time for a few more questions about the other night?" Kaelan asked.

Ah, shit.

"I guess," I said, waving for my friends to head out without me.

Kaelan hissed something to Nathaniel, which he didn't take well. I glared at Nathaniel's back as he retreated outside.

Great, now he's going to scare customers away.

"I apologize for his behavior today and during our prior meeting," Kaelan said, sitting down at an empty table.

I didn't want to sit and chat, but my aching feet won out.

"He is concerned about our missing friend. Perhaps we can start over?" His eyes sparkled as he smiled, but his nephilim charm bounced off me.

I crossed my arms. Honeyed words and a sweet smile wouldn't get him anywhere with a witch.

"What are your questions?" I said, giving him a bland look.

"What were you doing at the fairy park that night I saved you?"

My eyes narrowed. "You didn't save me. I was dealing with it quite well on my own."

He arched an eyebrow, which made me scowl. A hint of a smile curved his lips. Did he enjoy riling me up?

"I thought you were another demonspawn. I was trying to protect the injured fairy. You should be thankful I didn't grab another vial of my ooze."

"That's true," he said, no longer bothering to hide his smile. "My team found out how effective it is."

Now it was my turn to try not to smile.

I hoped it was Nathaniel. He seemed like the type to ignore warnings. The least he deserved was to be stuck to a dead demonspawn after what he'd put me through.

"So why were you there?" he prompted.

"My business is my own, but the fairies granted me permission to enter."

He couldn't just butter me up to get his answers. I flashed him an oh-so-innocent smile.

"It wasn't anything illegal if that was your concern."

"Do you recognize this person?" he asked, pulling up an image on his phone.

My smile fell. "That's Ruby. Did something happen to her?"

My heart raced. Why else would a nephilim have her photo?

"Her pack reported her missing this morning. How do you know her?"

My fingers trembled as I stared down at Ruby's smiling face. "She's a client. I brew potions for her pack, and she picks them up."

"When was the last time you saw her?"

"Two days ago. She came in here that morning to pick up an order of potions."

"Did she seem worried or concerned to you?"

I furrowed my brow, trying to recall everything from that day. "Her pack is the one being harassed and attacked by thralls. I've been brewing them healing potions. We don't usually chat, but that day she brought her sister, so they stayed here for a bit."

"And you haven't been in contact with her since?"

"No. Although, I was expecting a text with her next order."

"Do you have any proof of the contract between you?"

"Yeah, everything goes through the Alchemy Guild," I said, my thoughts churning.

She had shown no indication that she was leaving or that something personal was wrong. But then again, I was just their alchemist.

I gnawed on my lip. "Is her sister missing too?"

"No, she's with her pack."

I shook my head. "Then something must have happened to her. She told me they'd lost their mother recently, and Ruby was doing her best to care for her sister. She'd never abandon her."

It was apparent from how she doted on Jade. And what about our contracts? It was my only one.

Guilt shot through me at that thought. A shifter was missing; that was far more important than earning an income.

"We are doing our best to investigate. There have been several unusual reports of people going missing."

I'd have to talk to Indra or Rynac and ask them if they knew about the missing people.

Could I do anything to help? I doubted it, but I could brew some potions that might assist the enforcers.

"I'll ask around," Danika said, as if she could read my thoughts.

She was always close by, with one ear listening out for me. I didn't know if it was the bond between us or the recent attacks, but neither of us dared to get too far apart.

"Was there anything else?" I asked.

"Not today," Kaelan said, sliding a card across the table. "This is my number if you think of anything else. But otherwise, I know where to find you."

I nodded and pushed to my feet, barely catching a word he said. My body went through the motions that led me out the door toward home . . . but the nagging weight in my gut wouldn't let go.

There was more to this.

I could feel it in my bones.

Chapter Twenty-Two

Steam curled against my face as I wiped sweat from my brow and eased back from the cauldron. The brew had to simmer for a few more minutes before I added the next ingredient.

Danika took her usual spot beside me, tail flicking in quiet warning.

If this went sideways, we both knew it would not be subtle.

Over the last few nights, I'd crafted a range of brews that I thought might be beneficial.

I'd told Indra and Rynac about my latest encounter with the nephilim and that Ruby was missing.

They promised to look into it and also confirmed that there had been an increase in missing persons reports.

Guilt gnawed at me. The nephilim's suspicions made me fear Ruby was missing because of me, though I didn't know how.

Pouring myself into my alchemy was the only way to occupy my thoughts. With utmost care, I tipped the bowl of magnesium strips into the cauldron.

The magical flames below might not burn me, but they would still react to the magnesium if I were clumsy.

A classmate had almost blinded half the class when he flicked a strip into his burner just because the teacher cautioned us not to. People like that were the reason for warning labels.

The brew gurgled as I stirred, and the liquid morphed into a rich yellow, indicating it was almost ready.

The awaiting vials were half the size of my thumb, and I only used them for high-potency potions.

I kept my hands steady as I began the arduous process of portioning the liquid out.

A drop of liquid missed the vial, and I tried not to flinch as the liquid collided with the table and flared.

The protective runes on my witch's hat activated, shielding my eyes from the bright light.

I blinked away white afterimages.

As I said, protective *and* stylish. And now I knew the brew worked.

I couldn't help but grin as I looked over my growing supply of offensive potions.

At least one thing was going right. I'd studied the codex on my lunch break, and it had offered a few new additions.

One improved night vision, another would reveal traces of magic, and the last harnessed the moonlight into a liquid that could be used to empower other brews.

Though for the latter, I needed a full moon to craft it.

Unlike the phases of the moon, my magic didn't ebb and flow, though tonight I fought for control as I brewed my next concoction.

The overwhelming sense that time was against me weighed heavy on my shoulders.

With one final push of magic into my second brew, I sensed the moment the liquid shifted from individual ingredients into one co-hesive potion. The last bubble popped with extra vigor, and I flinched as my witch's hat deflected the rogue liquid.

My shoulders slumped as a weary sigh escaped my lips.

I knew I was pushing myself, but my attempts to summon the astral shield had all failed. I'd gotten a few flickers before I lost control, which added to my headache.

I scrubbed a hand across my face and set to portioning the brew.

The MEA captain had offered me a temporary contract to brew offensive potions, thanks to the siblings.

The enforcers had been working double shifts with the growing demonspawn threat and needed any edge they could get.

While my potions were non-lethal, they could make a real difference out on the streets.

My phone rang, cutting through the silence of the evening.

Then my heart stuttered in my chest when Rynac's name popped onto my screen.

"What's wrong?"

"Hello to you too," Rynac said, sounding far too sarcastic and calm.

But why else would he call me?

"No, I'm not dying, if that's what you were wondering," he said in a flat voice, and then I heard a bark of laughter that could only be Indra.

"Is this a coded message? Are you not able to talk freely?" I jested.

"I'm fine," he snapped. "Do you think I'm that lacking as an enforcer?"

"Why else would you call me in the middle of the night?"

"You owe me a drink," Indra's voice echoed in the background.

Rynac sighed, and I imagined him rolling his eyes at his sister. "Do you want to come for ice cream?"

"It's midnight and you're getting ice cream?"

"Are you telling me you don't want some?"

"Of course I do, but I thought you were working?" I said. "And what about the demonspawn?"

"We're on a break and a block away. We'll meet at your place. You'll be safe with us," Rynac said with a confidence I wished I felt. "Unless you're too busy."

"Come on, Nyssa," Indra called out.

I let out a long sigh, despite the faint smile that curled on my lips. "You're exasperating."

It pleased me far too much that they had thought of me and that they wanted to spend time together. Sure, I'd saved Rynac's life, but this was different.

"Well?" he prodded, and I could hear the smile in his words.

I rubbed my gritty eyes.

Over the last week, I had been pushing myself hard, and it wasn't like brewing was going to get any easier tonight. I deserved this outing, deserved a treat.

And—if I was being honest—I wanted to hang out with my friends.

I shot a questioning look at Danika.

"I'll watch over the apartment. They'll keep you safe," she said before settling her head back down.

I was pretty sure she just didn't want to interrupt her nap.

"Yes, I'm coming to get ice cream. Who do you think I am?" I grumbled and rushed to pack up my supplies.

Chocolate hazelnut, mint chocolate-chip, and coconut ripple.

I was in ice cream heaven.

Who knew Arkirith had late-night ice cream shops? Now I knew where to go when I had cravings, which might not be a good thing. This cone was delectable, but it wasn't in my budget.

A sigh escaped me.

When I got my business off the ground, I would buy one of these every day.

A snicker pulled my attention back to reality. Rynac watched me with an amused expression as Indra tried to hide her laughter.

"You'd think she'd never had ice cream before," Indra said, shaking her head at me. "How can you eat that much?"

"It's a talent," I said with a grin. I likely had ice cream covered lips, but I didn't care.

We strolled along Rundle Street, where strings of little gold lights crisscrossed above the red brick road. The street was pedestrian-only and a hub for people day and night.

After all, Arkirith had a large nocturnal population.

Restaurants with every type of cuisine dotted the street, their tantalizing scents enticing hungry patrons. A few shops tempted me, from a quaint bookshop to a chocolatier with a window display of handmade truffles.

There was even a soap maker with hanging bundles of dried herbs and flowers that called to me on a deeper level.

"This is why I need locals to show me around," I murmured, watching as a chef made fresh pasta, mixing eggs into the flour by hand. "How have I never found this street before?"

"Would you say you owed us a favor?" Indra asked, a sly expression on her face as she nudged Rynac, who shrugged as if to say sorry.

I narrowed my gaze. "What kind of favor?"

"Answer a few questions for us?" There was a sparkle in her eye, but I didn't sense anything but curiosity.

"What do you want to know?"

The siblings shared a look I could only describe as gleeful.

"How does witch magic work?" they blurted out together.

Childlike excitement lit their faces. You would've thought they were twins.

I laughed, mostly out of relief. Here I had been bracing for a barrage of questions about my childhood or embarrassing moments, but no, they wanted to learn about magic.

"I know you told us a bit, but I'd love to know more," Indra said.

"Magic is different for each person," I started. "We have to test and train to gain an affinity and discover which branches of magic mesh with our powers. We start by learning runes or trigger words for spells, and most of us use a conduit to help direct our magic."

I pulled out mine and offered it to Indra.

While most witches would hesitate to part with their conduit, I had no apprehension. Plus, the wonder on her face was worth it.

"Those who have a stronger connection to a spell can learn to cast it without the trigger word or rune. Then there's ritual magic, which requires a spell array. Any magic that's channeled or needs to be sustained for a long time uses an array, like I use in my alchemy. Am I boring you yet?"

"It's fascinating," Indra said with a wistful smile. "The amount of magic right at your fingertips."

"Well, not mine."

"Excuse me? Who can brew potions and bake magic cookies? Who saved this walking meat shield from dying twice?" She bumped into my shoulder, and I fought the smile forming on my lips.

"I guess."

It was hard not to feel inadequate when surrounded by talented witches. But here my magic made a difference, even when I was just making potions or delicious baked goods.

And I *had* saved Rynac's life.

"I can't summon badass swords, like you."

"True," she said, "but swords can't solve every problem."

"Neither can magic."

That was a hard lesson I'd learned long ago. Growing up around witches, I believed magic was the answer to everything and had longed for the day mine would arrive.

Disappointment and heartbreak were all that followed.

On the bad days, I wondered if it would've been better to never have manifested than to have only a quarter of the magic other witches had.

Sensing all that power within my veins but knowing I could never wield it—that it didn't work right—had been torture.

It had taken me many years to accept it, and I tried not to think about it. The deep ache that I was defective was always there. I'd just learned to ignore it.

"Have you had any updates about Ruby or her pack?" I asked.

"We have a team working with the shifters," Rynac said, but his expression was grim. "It appears the packs around the city have been having issues for some time but didn't alert us, believing it was merely a dispute over territory. There's been a spate of attacks and kidnappings, but the last few rattled them when demonspawn turned up."

"When I talked to Ruby," I said. "It sounded like those attacking her pack were thralls too."

"I mentioned that to the team," Indra said. "We'll find her."

"I just feel so useless. I wish there were more I could do to help."

"This is our job," Rynac said. "And your potions do help."

As we continued to stroll down the street, Rynac attempted to lighten my mood, and I tried to enjoy my evening. Worrying would get me nowhere.

Chocolate ice cream dripped down my hand. I made a strangled noise as I attempted to lick it before it escaped. It would be a crime to waste any of this delicious treat.

"Someone needs to create a spell to keep ice cream from melting, otherwise what's the point of magic at all?" I grumbled.

Indra's phone dinged. Her amused expression dissolved as she read the message.

"Is something wrong?" I asked.

The siblings shared a glance before steering us down one of the side alleys.

Rynac took the lead, while Indra furiously typed on her phone before scanning the streets in the direction we'd come.

I opened my mouth to ask if someone was following us, but snapped it shut, fearing I might be correct.

Weaving through the back alleys, I could still hear the faint rumble of activity from Rundle Street, along with the occasional thrum of an engine. But the route we took was void of anything living.

Icy fingers crept down my spine as if I could sense eyes watching us, but I shook it off. My mind was playing off my fears.

With a nod, Indra veered left and disappeared from sight.

I'd lost all sense of direction as we twisted and turned. How did the enforcers not get lost?

We paused just before the alley intersected a larger street. Rynac peered around the corner, and my heart beat a little faster. Maybe something was following us.

My ice cream turned sour in my stomach, and for the first time in my whole life, I regretted finishing my dessert.

Without a word, Rynac waved me closer and took my hand.

"Ready?" he whispered.

I managed a small nod, though it was a lie. How could I be ready when I had no clue what I was about to face?

He squeezed my hand, then pulled me beside him. At a brisk pace, we walked across the street and into the adjoining alley.

I blinked. That was it?

We stopped just within the shadows of the alley.

Rynac pressed his back against the brick wall and peered down the street. I mimicked his position, craning my head to see what he was looking for.

A shadow shifted a few buildings down. If I hadn't been watching so close, I would have missed it.

My breath caught as the shadow appeared to move to our side of the street, then I lost sight of it.

What in all the hells was that?

Rynac stiffened beside me. At least I knew I wasn't losing my mind.

He seized my arm and hustled us down the alley. My eyes darted up at him. His brows were drawn low, and his jaw clenched as he scanned the area ahead.

When we slowed, he tugged me into an alcove. A hand lingered on the gun at his waist, which I hadn't noticed. Rynac's narrow gaze surveyed the area. And he didn't even have the decency to appear winded, unlike me.

"Your apartment building is just up ahead," he said in a low voice. "We need to get you back inside."

"What's going on?" Did he think that after our race home, I didn't deserve to know what was happening?

"It appears work followed us during our break." His lips twisted into a grimace. "It's not safe."

Rynac guided me forward, keeping to the shadows until we reached the back entrance to my building. I wanted to ask more questions, but he hurried me along.

I swiped my fob to unlock the door and stepped inside. Before I could turn to ask another question, Rynac darted back into the shadows.

Ensuring the door locked behind me, I trudged up the stairwell, my brain trying to sort out what the hell had happened. Was it demon-spawn, and he didn't want to scare me?

After my last display of magic, I didn't blame him. Even I was afraid of my power.

My phone rang as I unlocked my front door. I pulled it out but almost dropped it as I read the name of the caller.

Ruby.

Chapter Twenty-Three

"Hello?" I clutched the phone tighter.

"Nyssa," a voice whispered, too quiet to distinguish if it was Ruby. "Help me."

"Who is this?" I asked, straining to hear the voice over the sound of my pounding heart.

"It's Ruby. Please."

Why would Ruby call me instead of her pack?

What could I ask that only she would know?

"What did I give Jade the last time we met?"

"A salted caramel brownie."

It had to be her. "Where are you?"

"Lynock Sports Field," she whispered, desperation lacing her words. "Please hurry."

"Are there other people there? Are you hurt?"

I sped into my room, opening the drawer filled with potions. The streets might not be safe, but I wouldn't go unprepared.

"Ruby? I'll bring help."

Rynac and Indra had raced off, but I'd call the MEA for backup. I couldn't go alone.

The line crackled.

"If you notify the enforcers," a hard voice said, "I'll kill her."

The call ended.

I could only stare down at my phone.

What in all the hells was going on? Who would take Ruby, and why did they want me?

If they didn't want the enforcers involved, what other choice did I have? This was Ruby's life; I had to do something.

Stuffing my bag with as many potions as possible, I raced to the rooftop.

"Danika?" I called out, hoping my fox was close by and not dealing with demonspawn.

"What's wrong?"

I explained the call and about Ruby.

"I'll come with you."

"Where are you?" I asked. I didn't see any movement on the surrounding roofs.

"Out on the street," she said. *"I can hear you through our connection. You must be growing stronger. Try thinking something to me."*

Can you hear me? I said in my mind, feeling foolish.

"Better to feel foolish than to look weird talking aloud to yourself," she snickered.

Great, she can hear my thoughts. That would have been nice to know earlier. But I'd take sharing my embarrassing thoughts if it meant I could communicate with Danika at a distance.

Hesitating at the door to my room, I backpedaled to my drawers. I needed to be ready for anything, but worry knotted my stomach.

Swearing, I snatched up both the empowerment and binding potions. While I hoped I didn't need either of them, I wanted to be prepared.

Tucking them into the special pockets in my bag, I rushed out. I took the steps two at a time and found Danika waiting outside my building.

"Ready?" she asked.

"Nope. Let's go."

We sprinted through the streets as if demonspawn nipped at our heels.

Sweet baby vulpines, I hated running. Why did I have to sweat so much? I'd need to start packing a spare top.

My legs protested each stride as we ran toward the sports field. My lungs burned. At this rate, I'd be useless once we got to Ruby.

It was also my fault since I took the longer route to avoid crossing the Torrens River. I'd pushed myself faster to make up for it, but if I'd been forced to cross . . . well let's just say I'd probably still be there.

Stupid river.

As we approached, Danika took the lead, her nose and senses honed for detecting demonspawn. Yet she didn't find any. That should've been a good thing. It wasn't like Arkirith was crawling with the beasts, but it only added to the unease clinging to me like my sweaty top.

The sports field joined to the back of a high school. The weak light of the lampposts didn't pierce the darkness that had settled over the area.

"There are dark energies here," Danika said, her ears flicking back and forth. *"I'll scout the area and stay out of sight. Whoever kidnapped Ruby wants something from you. Best they don't know about our connection."*

I nodded, but the thought of confronting the kidnapper alone was terrifying. We hadn't seen anyone in this area and even now, I couldn't hear anything over my own breathing.

Did the dark energies Danika sensed keep people away? This sensation made me want to run in the opposite direction. But it was more than that.

As I strained to make out any noise, I found the complete lack of sound unsettling. No night birds or insects. Even the breeze had died down as if it was afraid to break the silence.

Why were sports fields so creepy at night?

The heavy air pressed in around me as I walked closer. The dim glow of the moon offered the only illumination, casting elongated shadows across the empty bleachers, as if the whole stadium was full of spectral spectators.

Downing my night vision potion in one gulp, I tucked the vial away. Tonight, I would be prepared for whatever was thrown at me.

I hopped the fence, and the compact dirt muffled my steps. A cloud passed in front of the moon, and for a moment, it plunged me into near darkness.

My throat constricted as I paused, scanning the area, fearing something was about to jump out at me.

I willed the clouds to part as I sensed eyes watching me. My gaze drifted up to the sky and the wispy gray clouds that shielded the moon.

Another breath and they shifted enough to allow me to see where I was going.

Something drew me closer to the looming stand that shielded the area below from the moonlight. I wanted to call out, but at the same time I feared my voice would break.

Some brave rescuer I was.

The world around me lightened as my potion kicked in—black turned to gray, and the shadows lessened.

The vice grip around my chest eased a fraction.

No demonspawn or thralls lurked there, waiting to ambush me.

But the potion couldn't pierce the darkness before me, and as I moved closer, I sensed the magic—a veil of night that wouldn't lift.

This silence was killing me.

"Well, here I am," I said, throwing my hands wide with far more bravado than I felt.

"Hello, little witch." A figure slipped out of the darkness.

"Carmen?" I squinted.

Even with the shadows coiling around her, I recognized her features. But it was her crimson eyes that pinned me in place.

"It was so terrible that demonspawn ambushed your altered friends," she said, a smile curving her lips. "How lucky they were that their witch came to the rescue. Such a shame if it were to happen again, but would you be able to save them this time?"

"You did that?" My eyebrows drew together. "Why?"

Dread coiled in my stomach. Had she lured them away tonight, too?

Carmen shrugged. "It appeared you needed a bit more of a nudge."

"A nudge to do what?"

"To set yourself free. How did it feel to harness that power deep within you? To wield the magic you long for?"

I bit my cheek to keep the words inside, but Carmen smiled as if reading my thoughts.

"Amazing? Exhilarating? Did you enjoy the rush of power after being weak for so long?"

"How do you know all this?"

"You've been suppressing a part of yourself, Nyssa. You've been doing it all your life. I know you long to be whole, to wield power like your family. Now it's just within your grasp. What's there to be afraid of? Isn't this the power you've always wanted?"

My mind raced. How did she know that? I'd never met her before I moved here, yet she knew such details about me.

"Do you want to be chained for the rest of your life?" she asked. "Living up to other people's standards of who you should be? Are you really going to bind your magic just so you can live the way your witches deem acceptable?"

"I don't want to give up my alchemy, just the wild magic. It can only destroy."

"Wild magic? That's what you think this is?" Carmen's harsh laughter grated on me. "Is that what the foolish witch council claimed? Narrow-minded as always."

"What do you know about witches?" I snapped back.

"Plenty," she said, her smile showing far too many teeth.

Her red eyes gleamed back at me as if waiting for me to put the pieces together.

If she consorted with demonspawn, she had to be a warlock. No one besides high-level demons from Terrarum or those bound to them could command their minions.

"What is it then?" I asked, despite myself.

My need for answers outweighed my caution.

Was it possible she understood me better than my family?

Carmen grinned like a predator about to devour its prey. "Your magic wars with itself. Solar magic, like its Goddess, wants to dominate and refuses to let anything outshine it."

I hated that her words rang true, but I had seen that throughout my life. Just as the sun dominated the sky, never giving others a chance. Only when it retreated could the stars and moon shine.

Could that be the answer to why my magic failed? The solar magic fought back whenever I tried to use my lunar magic?

"Accept who you are, Nyssa. Don't let them suppress you any longer."

I hesitated. "Why are you doing this?"

"Because you are the key."

Carmen's eyes bore into mine, leaving me paralyzed, unable to look away.

"I've seen those in power crush the rest of us beneath their feet, taking our magic away because they fear us—fear what we represent. I want you to understand there is another option. All I'm offering you are the words I needed to hear to break free."

"I'm not like you."

Carmen leaned closer, her voice soft yet intense. "Are you sure?"

"If it means harming innocent people, I refuse the power."

Carmen's smile was chilling. "Perhaps you just need the right incentive."

Chapter Twenty-Four

Carmen thrust out her hand and the air snapped, the power rolling off her making the hairs on my arms rise.

That was when I saw the crumpled figure at her feet.

Ruby.

She cried out, wisps of light flickering from her body and condensed into a ball in Carmen's palm.

"What are you doing to her?" I yelled, starting forward, but Carmen just smiled.

Ruby writhed as Carmen dragged more from her body.

"Stop! Stop hurting her. What do you want me to do?"

The moment the words left my lips, Carmen's head tilted toward me, Ruby stilled, her chest heaving for breath.

"There's a potion in your bag," Carmen said.

Her lips curved up in a satisfied smile.

The orb of white light bobbed in her upraised palm, casting a glow over her face, but it did nothing to brighten the darkness in her gaze.

"I have many potions," I said, my mind screaming.

I was in over my head. Was this all for my potions? How much damage could they inflict in the wrong hands? And I'd brought them right to her.

Shit. Shit. Shit!

So much for being prepared.

My heart bounced against my ribs, urging me to run, but I would not leave Ruby. It was my fault she'd been kidnapped.

"You know the one," Carmen replied, her voice a satisfied purr. "All you needed was a nudge. You overheard a single conversation about the Master's Only section at the Guild, and off you went. The codex was the first test. It's been waiting centuries for a worthy lunar magic user. The second was when you successfully brewed the *magiam augere* potion."

"How do you know all this?"

"We have eyes and ears everywhere, little Nyssa."

We?

Who was she working with? No, that didn't matter right now. The question was, would I trade the potion for Ruby's life?

"What will you do with it?"

"I want *you* to drink it."

"What?" Why would she want me to become more powerful?

"My master is growing impatient. We have so much planned for you."

What in the realms did that mean?

But if I drank it, would I be strong enough to fight her? "And then you'll let Ruby go?"

"Yes," she said, drawing out the word until it sounded like a hiss.

"Ask her to give her word that she won't harm Ruby again," Danika's voice whispered in my mind, and I almost jumped. I'd forgotten I wasn't alone.

Will that work on her?

"It should."

That wasn't reassuring, but it was better than nothing. To give your word meant swearing on your magic and honor. But a person who kidnaps and wields infernal magic couldn't be trusted from the start.

"Do I have your word?" I called out. "That you will release her and never harm her again?"

Carmen's grin widened into something frightening. "You have my word, witch."

I pulled my bag off my shoulder and knelt on the ground to rummage through it. Vials clinked as I rifled through them—I needed a better way to organize these.

I slipped a flash potion and a stinging nettle brew into my pocket before pulling the empowerment potion out. I'd almost grabbed the binding potion too, but feared Carmen might sense it.

"Drink it," Carmen said, taking a step closer as excitement glimmered in her eyes.

Danika? I thought as I lifted the potion.

"I'm with you. Trust your instincts. Don't fight your magic, and it shouldn't lash out. I'll help to stabilize you as best I can."

Easier said than done. I pulled out the cork, settling my nerves as I brought the potion to my lips.

A part of me wanted this—to step forward and embrace this magic—another part warned me of the consequences, the harm I could cause, and asked why Carmen and her master desired this.

"Bottoms up," I whispered and downed the vial.

Unlike before, when fear and panic had consumed me, I sensed the surge of magic. The liquid fizzed and bubbled in my mouth.

Magic zipped across my tongue, sweet and soothing like the nectar of the gods.

Sparks of magic buzzed through me, and I gasped as if taking my first full breath. I blinked wide-eyed. The shadows brightened as if a full moon were shining down, washing the area with its warm glow.

I wanted to explore this feeling more, to call to my magic, but Ruby was still in danger, and I wasn't safe either.

My gaze snapped back to Carmen. As I opened my mouth to tell her to keep her word, she waved a hand.

Growls and chittering filled the air. The shadows elongated as spindly limbs emerged as though crawling from the darkness itself.

The burning stench of sulfur hit me, and I gagged as my eyes watered.

Danika! I screamed in my mind as the horde of demonspawn crept closer.

I spun in a circle, but it was too late. They were all around me. Carmen had set a trap, and I'd walked right into it.

Dark, scaly skin glistened in the moonlight. All different shapes and sizes. Black horns adorned their heads. Grotesque faces twisted into snarls.

Jaws opened to reveal needle-sharp teeth perfect for shredding flesh.

I froze, paralyzed by fear, and they could smell it. A smaller one lunged, its deadly claws swiping toward me, and I stumbled backward.

Think.

What options did I have? I couldn't take on this many.

"Accept what you are, Nyssa," Carmen called. "Or you won't walk out of here alive."

What I am?

A failing witch who can't summon magic to save her life.

The demonspawn swiped again, and I darted to the side. It was toying with me.

All the others stopped as if content to watch this game.

Wait, was Carmen controlling them?

The demonspawn snapped at my legs but wasn't close enough to do any damage.

Yep, definitely toying with me. Could I survive until help arrived?

"What are you?" Carmen's sing-song voice called out as if I should know the answer.

"I'm an alchemist," I hissed.

Shoving a hand into my pocket, I pulled out the vials. This would either work or really piss it off.

I weighed the potions in my hand. Backpedaling, I watched the demonspawn stalking me and waited for the perfect moment.

It growled, opening its mouth to snap at me, and I hurled the potion right into its maw. It snapped its jaw shut.

Glass shattered, releasing my stinging nettle brew. The demonspawn howled, shaking its head.

Before the others reacted, I hurled my flash potion at the closest demonspawn who blocked my escape, and shielded my eyes.

Blinding light exploded and ear-splitting screams rent the air, but I ran, slapping my hands over my ears to block it out.

Daggers stabbed into my brain at the unworldly screeches.

I blinked away the afterimages and crashed into the line of demonspawn before they recovered.

Carmen hadn't moved, but a wide grin spread over her face.

"You'll have to do better than that," she said.

Dark energies crackled in her hand, and I skidded to a stop.

Even from a distance, my skin crawled, my powers recoiling at Carmen's twisted magic. Her other hand was still aloft, holding the glowing white light she had pulled from Ruby as if giving me a choice.

Which magic did I want to face?

I snatched up another potion and prepared to throw it, but Carmen was faster. A bolt of dark magic sizzled through the air and slammed into my arm.

Like acidic lightning, her magic coated my skin. My muscles spasmed, and I dropped the potion, a strangled cry caught in my throat.

"Use your real magic, Nyssa," Carmen scolded as if I were a naughty child.

The pain disappeared, but my fingers still twitched.

Clenching my jaw, I straightened. I risked a glance behind me.

Ice coated my veins as I took in the wall of demonspawn.

"Use your magic if you want to live," Carmen snapped, launching another attack.

I clawed for my power, feeling it swirl uselessly in my chest.

It wasn't enough. I threw my arms up as the spell slammed into me.

The impact ripped me off my feet, sizzling fire straight through my bones.

If I'd had any air left, I would've screamed.

I'm going to die.

The thought shrieked through my head.

Danika! I reached for her with everything I had, but my mind was silent.

No one was coming.

CHAPTER TWENTY-FIVE

"You gave your word," I said, gasping for breath, hoping to buy myself a few moments to recover. "You said you would release Ruby without harming her. But you're putting her in harm's way right now."

"Very well," Carmen said.

A thrall emerged from the shadows and picked Ruby up, carrying her to the far side of the field.

It was better than nothing, and at least now I didn't have to worry about harming Ruby with my magic.

"Will you play now?" she asked, tilting her head as if this were some child's game.

What do I have to lose?

I shifted into a balanced fighting stance, and Carmen's eyes filled with delight.

She hurled another bolt of dark energy, and I scrambled for my magic, but it slipped through my fingers.

I jerked out of the way, but was too slow. Pain erupted in my leg like a million needles poking into my skin, but I stayed upright.

The next spell was already heading for my chest.

I shoved my magic with everything I had, and the astral shield rippled to life in front of me.

Dark magic flickered across its surface as Carmen's spell collided with it.

Over and over, she hammered my shield.

I locked my knees, refusing to show weakness—not with a horde of demonspawn surrounding me.

Their lust for my lunar energies pressed in around me. Saliva dripped from their awaiting maws, serpentine tongues flicking out as if they could taste the sweetness of my magic in the air.

"More!" Carmen demanded.

Sweat dripped down my back. My arms shook as my shield flickered with each crack of her magic. I pushed harder, casting everything I had. But it wasn't enough.

I always failed.

Fire raced through my veins, and I didn't have the strength to contain it. A moment later, flames surged into my shield, shattering the iridescent wall into a thousand pieces.

Wild magic skittered through the air, and the backlash sent white-hot knives of pain slicing into my brain.

My knees slammed to the ground, and I swayed as the last of my strength drained from me.

"Not strong enough," Carmen snarled as she stalked closer.

I could only stare up at her, waiting for the final blow.

"You are still too weak. Too attached to the image of what a witch should be. You let fear control you. And you fail, like all the other lunar witches before you. Pathetic."

Carmen turned her back and walked away, but I knew this wasn't over.

I pushed to my feet, bracing for the next attack, waiting for her demonspawn to tear me to shreds.

She paused, the orb of Ruby's energy bobbing in her hand.

"I'll just have to make use of what I have."

Spinning on her heels, Carmen hurled the ball of light at me. It raced forward, and before I could even lift my arms, it slammed into my chest.

The force knocked the breath from me, and I reeled as white sparks exploded into the air. Power seeped into my chest, crackling through my body, and then ignited.

A scream tore from me as I crashed to the ground, ice plunging through my veins before a wave of fire pulsed after it.

I writhed, trying to tear this power from my body before it consumed me, but all I could do was brace myself for the next wave of agony.

A familiar voice echoed in my mind. I wanted to latch onto it, but words no longer held any meaning.

"Stop fighting." The voice wormed its way into my head.

Fire surrounded me, licking my body, hungering to consume me.

"Surrender to it."

No!

I wanted to scream, but another cry of pain ripped from my throat.

Whatever magic she had torn from Ruby, I wouldn't submit to it.

A wildfire burned through me, too fast to control.

I had to contain it, to snuff it out, before it destabilized my energies.

My nails clawed the hard ground, gouging into the dirt. I wanted to tear this magic out with my own hands.

My back arched.

Lightning sizzled through me—too much power brimming within my body. I couldn't contain it.

The ground shook. Someone cried out. Iron coated my tongue.

No matter what I tried, the magic refused to be contained.

Too volatile to release, or I'd risk shredding the veil, but if I held on, then I'd be the one shredded to pieces.

"Summon the image of the moon." Danika's words crashed into my mind.

I clung to them as my magic tried to drown me.

"Find its soft and steady glow within your chest. Find that slice of tranquility, present and indomitable."

I dove below the turbulent liquid fire that raged and consumed, deeper until my lungs burned. My arms shook as I tried to hold on.

"Help is coming."

It would burn me alive, but still I plunged deeper.

And then I broke through.

Silence surrounded me. Power brushed against my awareness and wrapped me in a comforting embrace.

Strong but subtle.

There was harmony here, one that called to a deeper part of me. But then cracks started to appear, the fire flooded in, and I lost control.

Warmth pressed against my side, grounding me. I stabilized my power, but I was barely hanging on.

At any moment, I would fall into the maelstrom that raged around me. Like being caught in a rapid, I clung to the warm presence as if it were the only thing keeping me afloat.

A heavy pressure settled on my chest. A moment of reprieve—like a dark cloud blocking out the scorching sun.

The tempest of fire slowed, weakening its hold on me. I gripped the silver light within, letting it wrap around me.

I gasped as my eyes flew open and I crashed back into my body. Shadows swam around me.

"Release it," a deep voice snarled.

I loosened my grip, letting my magic slip through my fingers.

The ground vibrated beneath me, but the magic subsided until it was nothing but a faint throb in my chest.

My imagination was playing tricks on me; I almost swore a silvery glow rippled over my skin before it faded to nothing.

The male sighed as he rubbed his neck. "It's kind of hard to fight when you do that."

"When I what—" Fire flared in my chest.

Fighting to find that calm, I wrestled with my magic as pain scorched through me.

My vision wavered. Of course, it couldn't be that easy.

"My bag," I hissed.

I had to stay awake to stop this, to avoid harming anyone.

Danika whimpered at my side as I fought to roll onto my elbows. She was siphoning off my magic, but her small body could only handle so much.

"What do you need?" he said between clenched teeth, one hand pressed against his neck.

My brain finally coughed up his name. Kaelan. Nephilim.

I'd deal with that later.

Retrieving the binding potion from its hidden pocket, I hesitated.

"I'm sorry," I whispered.

Pulling out the cork with my teeth, I hoped—prayed—this wouldn't hurt Danika.

The potion was thick on my tongue. I gagged, the harsh acidic taste coating my mouth like bile. It crept through my insides, smothering the magic, as if someone had doused me with a vial of ooze.

A groan escaped my lips, and my body shuddered as if darkness had wrapped around me and squeezed all the life out of my body.

Danika yelped. I was *hurting* her.

With the last dregs of my energy, I dragged myself away, hoping that breaking physical contact would release her.

My head throbbed. Distant snarls echoed all around. Demonspawn. I gasped for air. Strong hands held me in place, and I squeezed my eyes shut against the nausea.

"What was that?" Kaelan demanded.

I waved the question away. My head spun, and it took all my restraint not to vomit.

"Ruby?" I croaked.

"Nathaniel has her. Astrid went after the warlock."

Warlock.

A wave of excruciating pain crashed into me, leaving no room for rational thought. I tried to sit up, but hissed as the world around me whirled.

"We need to get you out of here," Kaelan said. "The demonspawn are fleeing, but the UMC unit will arrive soon."

I didn't fight as he scooped me up like I didn't weigh a thing, though I groaned as he ran.

Each jolting stride sent a wave of daggers stabbing into my head, and it was all I could do to remain conscious.

Chapter Twenty-Six

The world tilted as Kaelan lowered me down. A weak yellow light flickered over tiled flooring, changing stalls and cubbies.

A locker room.

Cold gnawed at my skin, wrong and lodged deep in my chest. My limbs felt heavy and oversized, but I forced them to move.

Because Ruby lay on the ground with the other nephilim . . . and she wasn't moving.

"Ruby?"

My legs wobbled as I slumped down next to her. She lay still and silent, no sign of injury, but her skin was far too pale, almost matching her dull and matted silver hair.

My hand trembled as I reached out. Her skin felt clammy, and beneath my fingertips, a weak pulse fluttered.

"She's stable, but will require a healer," Nathaniel snapped.

I winced, but couldn't blame him. I had caused all this.

With a gentle touch, I brushed the hair off Ruby's face and cradled her hand in mine. Deep shadows lay under her closed eyes, her face gaunt, as if she hadn't eaten in weeks.

I ran through all the potions I had on me, but without any idea of what Carmen had done, I couldn't help. At least she didn't appear to be in pain.

My mind jumped to Danika, and I panicked for a moment before I spotted her curled up in the farthest corner from me.

I'd be lying if I said that didn't hurt, but I feared the binding potion had harmed her just as much as it had me.

"Sit down before you fall down," Nathaniel said, but he wasn't talking to me.

Kaelan leaned against the wall, and by the looks of it, that was the only reason he was still upright.

Mud and black demon blood splattered both nephilim, who wore dark clothing tonight, the kind I'd expect motorcycle riders to wear.

Kaelan's jacket was in tatters, and he clutched at his side.

Nathaniel pushed to his feet. "I'll deal with the others. Just try not to die."

"I wouldn't give you the satisfaction," Kaelan shot back, but Nathaniel ignored him as he left.

A wave of agonizing pain rolled through me, hammering the back of my head, and I groaned, fingers digging into my temples.

"Are you injured?" Kaelan asked, but then he coughed, the sound rattling in his chest.

My healer alarm went off right as he slid down the wall. Shoving my pain away, I scrambled over to him.

Under the weak light, I hadn't realized how injured he was.

That wasn't mud, but a dull gold liquid—angel blood.

"What happened to you?"

I inspected the wound on his side. Whatever had hit him appeared to have dissolved the thick fabric; an inky blackness covered his skin and hid most of the damage.

For a terrifying moment, I feared my magic had caused it.

Reading my expression, Kaelan explained, "The warlock caught me with a spell when I was distracted."

I reached out on instinct. The darkness shifted and writhed, but Kaelan caught my hand.

"The magic is still active. It might harm you."

"Does it hurt?" It looked terribly painful, and I winced, knowing I was the reason for his distraction.

"I've been through worse." He smirked, but the strain around his eyes belied the truth.

And there was the arrogant nephilim.

"You are not to blame for this." His voice softened, as if he could read the thoughts hidden behind my eyes. "I'm sorry we didn't arrive before the warlock hurt you."

Carmen might have warned me against alerting the enforcers, but she never mentioned the nephilim. I doubted she'd even considered a witch might ask them for help.

And before today, I wouldn't have expected it either.

As we'd ran toward the sports field, I'd called Kaelan to tell him about Ruby. I wasn't foolish enough to think I could handle the situation alone.

Although I probably should've waited for them to arrive before rushing in.

"Where are you bleeding?" I asked, needing to do something rather than just sit there under his intense gaze.

Had they figured out what I was? Did they realize my unstable magic was causing all of this?

"I'll be fine," he said, trying to pull away but let out a hiss.

With a huff, I grabbed my bag and tipped out my stockpile of potions and supplies. I ran my fingers over the vials, searching for the right one, and I froze.

I couldn't sense the magic within them. A wave of dizziness crashed over me as the air turned thin.

Kaelan reached out to steady me. "What's wrong?"

"My potion was far more effective than I realized."

Brewed under a quarter moon, I hadn't expected the binding potion to cut off my entire connection to magic. I'd hoped it would be weaker, that I could guide it to only suppress that wild part of my magic. I'd been wrong.

My last chance at locking away the unstable magic failed.

What was the point of suppressing my power if it took my alchemy away too? I'd expected side effects, hoped I could work out the kinks over time, but it seemed to be all or nothing.

Could I learn to control my unstable magic?

Carmen believed I could, but then again, she was a warlock. She'd harmed Ruby and hit me with a painful spell that had caused my magic to flare.

"This should be a healing potion," I said, grabbing the vial with a red shimmer. "Or is it this one? Why did I pack these in the same type of vial?"

"Why didn't you label them?" Kaelan said.

I scrunched up my nose at the nephilim and his common sense. "I don't need to. Usually, I can identify my potions by touch. But I drank a potion that suppresses my magic to stop whatever Carmen hit me with."

"Carmen? You know the warlock?"

"I've met her a few times. She was a customer at Divine. I also encountered her as I walked to work one morning. I had run into a demonspawn, and Danika scared it off. Carmen appeared right after. It was odd."

"Who's Danika?"

"My fox," I said, nodding to the sleeping vulpine. Was she even mine anymore with our connection broken?

His gaze narrowed on the fox. "She's your familiar?"

Instead of answering, I uncorked the first vial and took a sip, focusing on the magical sensation running through me.

Despite my suppressed magic, I could feel the effects of the potion on me.

"This is for healing," I said, offering it to him. "And this one will help with pain."

Kaelan held them as if he didn't know what was going on.

"You drink them," I said, mimicking the action. "It will speed up your recovery."

He eyed them with suspicion. "Are you sure?"

I frowned. Was he doubting my brews? "Yes, though they won't be as powerful, it's better than nothing. Witch brews are compatible with all magicals, though they might give you a bit of a hangover tomorrow. So drink up. Unless you enjoy being injured."

What was his deal? Rynac had snatched them up, and he didn't even know how they would affect him.

"Where are you bleeding?" I asked again, opening my emergency first-aid kit.

He didn't appear to have suffered a severe injury other than the magical hit, for which he'd need an actual healer. But bleeding I could manage, and as I'd caused his wounds, patching them up was the least I could do as an apology.

Kaelan eyed me for a moment longer before downing both potions. I recorked the empty vials and tucked them away for later. My supplies didn't grow on trees . . . well, I guess cork does.

Whatever.

The nephilim offered me a curious glance before he pulled back the high collar of the jacket. Shimmering golden blood dripped from his neck.

Shit.

It couldn't have been a deep wound, or he'd be dead.

I shifted closer. His jugular pulsed with each thump of his heart, causing more blood to trickle down his neck. I ripped open a gauze pad and wiped it away, but I couldn't see an open wound, only a tattoo.

"What caused that?" I asked.

I pressed a fresh gauze pad against it, hoping to stem the flow, while rifling through my kit for a bandage.

I didn't sense any of Carmen's dark magic, yet it continued to bleed.

"It's a tattoo," he said.

I resisted rolling my eyes. Did he really think I'd never seen one before?

"Does your tattoo regularly bleed? That doesn't seem practical." I shot him a flat look, but he'd turned his head away.

It was only then that I realized how close I was. I guess nephilim detested witches as much as we despised them. *Rude.* I'd only been attempting to help.

I ripped the bandage open with one hand, but when I pulled back the gauze, my eyes snagged on the design—an intricate, detailed image of a full moon surrounding a crescent moon.

Whirls surrounded the design, forming runes I'd never seen before. Latent magic coursed through the marking.

I was so enraptured by it I didn't notice the wound had begun to bleed again until a drop of gold collided with my fingertip.

Images flashed through my mind, too fast to make sense of them. A dark forest. The exterior of Divine. A horde of demonspawn. The cityscape from above.

My mind reeled until one clear image appeared. I stared down from a high rooftop at the scene below. The full moon shone down on ten figures, most demonspawn, but my gut recognized that was me down there, facing off against Carmen.

"Is something wrong?" Kaelan's voice snapped me back to reality.

My head throbbed as I tried to get my bearings.

What in the realms had that been? A hallucination? A vision?

Damned angel blood. I gathered myself, realizing I'd been staring at his neck like a vampire.

"The bleeding has slowed," I said, hoping I sounded professional.

I affixed the bandage to his neck, doing my best not to touch his skin or any more blood.

A shudder crawled over me like nails scraping across a chalkboard. I shot to my feet, heart pounding.

I recognized that sensation. My necklace heated as it deflected an attempt to locate me through my magic. Fear empowered me, screaming at me to flee. I searched the room, finding only one way out.

"What is it?" Kaelan said.

The door burst open, and I jumped, my hand wrapping around my conduit.

On instinct, I reached for my magic, but doubled over at the gaping hole within my chest where it should've been.

A figure snapped the door closed, lifting her hands when she noticed my conduit. She wore the same black leather outfit as the others, midnight blue hair braided down her back, with striking features and a pair of wings that marked her as another nephilim.

"I'm with him," she said, nodding at Kaelan. "Inquisitors are coming this way."

Paralyzed with fear, I couldn't move. Couldn't think.

They were coming for me.

Chapter Twenty-Seven

"I'll hide you," the nephilim said. "The Inquisitors sensed the warlock's magic and whatever she did to you. These are people who 'deal' with a perceived threat and ask questions later."

"I know," I whispered.

Both times I'd encountered them, my parents or Tobin had protected me.

The Inquisitors would strip me of my magic without hesitation. But how could I endure living without magic for the rest of my life? I didn't think I was strong enough to survive that.

"I can help, Astrid," Kaelan said, grimacing as he tried to stand.

"No, you need to sit still and be injured," she snapped, then her gaze turned to me. "You'll have to trust me."

"Okay," I managed, my voice nothing more than a whisper.

What choice did I have?

Danika's whimper squeezed at my heart. Hadn't I hurt her enough tonight?

Astrid guided me back, wedging me behind a row of lockers. "They won't notice you, but don't move or make a sound. Okay?"

I nodded. Why was she helping me?

Darkness whispered across my skin, curling higher until it covered my body and the surrounding area. It was as if a shadow had swallowed me whole.

I was so amazed by the spell I forgot to be terrified.

Then the door creaked open, and I pressed my back harder against the icy wall, not wanting to glimpse the faces of the Inquisitors.

I hugged myself, locking my knees before they could give out.

From here, I could only see Ruby and Kaelan. But if the witches stepped any farther into the room, they'd spot me . . . or at least, the shadows surrounding me.

"As I already said,"—Nathaniel's hard voice echoed into the room—"both the shifter and one of my squad members suffered injuries. They'll be relocated once backup arrives."

"You observed no one else?" A harsh feminine voice split the air, not even trying to hide her disdain.

"Only the warlock, with the demonspawn she summoned."

"We sensed the unstable magic. How do you explain that, nephilim?"

"As *I* have said before," Nathaniel drawled. "We are under orders as part of the UMC special division. We do not answer to you. Take any issues or complaints to the council."

If I hadn't been so utterly terrified, I might have enjoyed Nathaniel's barb. Though witches sat on the United Magical Council, many—particularly the whole Inquisitor faction—despised the council for its interference in the witch community.

Footsteps echoed through the room, and I held my breath as they moved closer.

A witch in Inquisitor robes appeared, kneeling beside Ruby.

Kaelan shifted, and the blood drained from my face as I realized he was trying to hide my bag. Would the witches recognize a witch-brewed potion by sight?

My heart pounded so loud I feared they would hear it.

The Inquisitor waved a hand over Ruby, then stood. His eyes swept right over me as he stepped away.

I waited, expecting him to call out my presence at any moment. The door clicked shut. I remained motionless, not daring to even breathe.

"They're gone," Astrid said as she appeared in front of me.

The surrounding shadows dissolved, and I slid down the wall.

Curling up, I wrapped my arms over my head and took a shuddering breath.

That was way too close. Inquisitors were relentless. If they sensed wild magic, they wouldn't stop until they found the source.

How long would I be able to hide from them?

"Are you hurt?" she asked.

"You understand what they are, don't you?" I said, my voice muffled. I feared I'd fall apart if I let go.

"We do." The gentleness in her voice made my eyes sting.

I hated looking so weak, especially in front of the nephilim.

"Why did you hide me?" My voice sounded so small, but I forced my chin up to search her face for the truth.

She crouched before me, sorrow shining in her gaze. "Because we know what they do to witches. Whatever the warlock hit you with caused that surge of magic. You don't deserve to be punished for that. But I'm confident that *they* would punish you anyway. As long as you don't pose a threat, we won't expose you."

"Can I go home now?"

I didn't want to think anymore. About my magic. The warlock.

All this mess I'd gotten caught up in.

"Of course. We'll want to ask you a few more questions tomorrow after you rest. But clean up first."

Astrid nodded toward a sink in the corner.

She helped me stand before heading over to Kaelan. I struggled to walk. Why did I feel so weak without my magic?

I blinked at my reflection. I was a mess. Blood dripped from my nose. A mix of dirt and more blood caked my skin. I scrubbed my face with the cold water, wishing I had soap.

As the grime washed away, my reflection gave me pause.

Despite the fear and terror of tonight, an unusual brightness filled my eyes, as if a light glowed behind them.

I squeezed my eyes shut, not trusting my brain after all the trauma. Pain and fear did strange things to one's mind.

"What about Ruby?" I asked, drying my face with the cleanest part of my top.

The intense gazes of both nephilim bore into me. What had they been whispering about?

"We will take her to her pack," Astrid said as she handed me my bag. "Their healers will tend to her."

I scanned the room. "Where's Danika?"

She'd fallen asleep in the corner, but now she was nowhere to be seen. Had she left? Did she no longer want anything to do with me?

Blue flickered, and her form appeared right where I'd left her.

"Hiding from the witches, huh?" Astrid chuckled beside me.

Had she turned herself invisible? She'd never told me about that.

Then again, I'd never asked her anything about her magic. I'd discovered my familiar and hadn't even taken the proper time to get to know her.

Danika's eyes lifted to me expectantly.

"I'm going home," I told her, too scared to ask if she wanted to come with me.

If she rejected me . . .

The fox struggled to her feet and moved to my side. She wasn't close enough to touch, but a ghost of a smile curved my lips, knowing she hadn't abandoned me.

Yet.

I didn't say a word as I followed Astrid.

We stepped out into the night, the stadium behind us, and the path ahead empty.

What would I see this time if I returned to the spot where I'd lost control?

A shiver ran down my spine. Could the witches trace that magic to me, even if it wasn't all my own?

My skin crawled at the memory of the Inquisitor's spells, but the ripples I'd sensed earlier paled when compared to the full force of their powers.

The memory surfaced of Thaddeus Flamebury looming in the doorway, his severe features and lethal gaze freezing me in place.

The pure, unadulterated hatred radiating from him, and the sensation of his magic was forever seared into my brain. It'd felt like bugs were burrowing under my skin, while talons scraped at my mind.

My stomach soured, and I shoved the sensation away before I gagged. I'd only survived that encounter with the Inquisitor because Tobin had subtly cast his magic to shield the power within me.

If any Inquisitors found me in Arkirith, I'd be arrested on sight. I only hoped the enchantment on my necklace would hold against their tracing rituals.

Arms crossed, Nathaniel leaned against a car, his hard gaze tracking my approach.

"They'll drive you home," was all he said as he opened the door.

I peered inside, but a tinted divider separated the driver from the passengers.

I blinked. Where was the interrogation? The accusations?

Wait.

My gaze narrowed in on the angel-born. "How do you know where I live?"

"We'll see you tomorrow to discuss tonight's events."

"Well, that's not creepy at all," I muttered, sliding into the car.

Astrid snorted as Nathaniel shut the door. Danika curled up on the seat beside me as the driver took off.

When we were several blocks away, my shoulders sagged as exhaustion set in.

Too many thoughts whirled through my head, but I didn't have the energy to hold on to a single one.

I needed to keep it together, to wait until I was safe inside my apartment before I broke down, but my mind refused to comply. The relentless whispers grew louder with each passing minute.

This is all your fault. Innocent people are suffering because of you. One by one, you will harm everyone you care for and drive them away.

You deserve this. You're not worthy of your magic.

After what happened tonight, I knew they were right. I was just too stubborn to see it.

CHAPTER TWENTY-EIGHT

Danika wound around my ankles while I fumbled with the lock. The first light of dawn spilled over the horizon as we stepped into the apartment.

I attempted to suck in a deep breath, but the vice around my ribs squeezed tighter, and I rubbed at the ache there.

Since when did breathing feel like a losing battle?

A steady throb built in my head until I took another painkiller.

Last time, I'd crashed pretty hard after using the empowerment potion, but adding the binding potion to the mix?

I was in for a rough ride.

Fatigue gnawed at me. Sleep would help, but Danika yipped before I made it to my bed.

"I just want to sleep," I said.

She stared at me, and I knew she was saying something that I couldn't hear. Why did the silence between us hurt so much?

Danika poked my phone with her nose.

"You want me to call someone?"

I guess I should message Rynac and Indra.

They'd be angry I'd gone out after their warning, but I needed to tell them about Ruby and let them know there was a warlock in town. Not the easiest thing to send in a text, so I asked them to stop by.

Plus, with my connection to Danika disrupted, I didn't have any-one else to talk to about my magic.

My arms shook with exertion as I pulled my shoes off.

What was going on?

My fingers trembled, and my nerves felt like they were burning, as if a fire simmered just beneath the surface. And yet, I couldn't stop shivering as goosebumps prickled over my skin. So strange—shivering while burning up.

The gentlest touch was as if sandpaper were being dragged across my raw flesh.

My body was at war with itself.

Each breath labored as if a weight had settled on my chest.

The intense pain shoved all fear from my mind. Danika whined, jumping onto the couch beside me and pawing at my arm. I hissed. Even that light touch hurt.

My bones ached. Every joint in my body refused to move. And the pounding in my head throbbed with my rapid heartbeat.

I stumbled into the kitchen and put the kettle on to brew myself a healing tea.

My hands wrapped around the hot mug, and I sipped the scalding liquid. It soothed my chills for a moment, but then the fire inside me burned hotter.

Wrapped in my blanket, I huddled on the couch. I don't know how long I sat there before someone knocked at the door. It took the last of my energy to open it. I was so relieved to see Rynac that my knees gave out.

On second thought, the collapse was probably due to whatever was wrong with me.

Rynac caught me before I hit the ground, calling to his sister.

I flinched at the noise and his touch. Everything was too much.

"Nyssa," Indra hissed. "What happened? Do you need a healer?"

"Took another empowerment potion." I labored to force the words out. Each one demanded more effort than the last. "Drank the binding potion to suppress my magic. Warlock hit me with something."

I rubbed my chest as if that would ease the pain.

Indra pulled my shirt down, and Rynac swore. Thin white lines streaked across my skin, pulsing with each beat of my heart.

"That's beyond our healers," Rynac muttered.

"Nyssa, didn't your boss used to be a battle-cleric?" she asked.

"Beylin's a what?"

"Where's your phone?"

We arrived at Divine, entering through the back door, which saved me from the embarrassment of people witnessing Rynac carrying me.

"This way," Beylin called as he led us upstairs.

An examination table dominated the space, with an adjacent sink and bench. Shelves, filled with all kinds of medical equipment and supplies, lined the far wall. Why did the boss of a magical coffee shop have a fully kitted-out medical suite?

"What happened this time?" Beylin asked, as if this happened daily.

He motioned for Rynac to set me on the table, dimming the lights after I winced from their brightness. Then he pushed a steaming cup into my shaking hands, and I groaned, knowing what was to come.

I downed the dirt-flavored tea. Anything was preferable to the dizzying hot and cold flashes.

After a few minutes, the pain dulled, allowing me to recount the night as well as I could remember.

"First the enforcers, and now, you've gotten yourself involved with nephilim," Beylin grumbled under his breath. "And the warlock wanted you to drink the empowerment potion?"

He frowned, concern etching deep lines into his face. "Can I see where her spell hit?"

I unbuttoned my shirt, revealing the top part of my chest where the glowing lines pulsed.

Even without looking, I sensed the magic as it pulsed against my skin. The binding potion had to be weakening. But what would happen when its effects subsided?

"I don't know what the warlock did," I said, unable to speak her name. "But she drained Ruby and then hit me with the power she stole. My magic surged. I was unable to contain it and it hurt like hell. One of the nephilim suppressed it enough that I could drink a binding potion. But I was about to lose control."

"I know what type of magic this is," Beylin said.

His eyes met mine before he gave a subtle nod toward the others.

I sighed, knowing he was about to confirm my fears. "I've told them about my unstable magic and that I might have lunar abilities."

"Warlocks have the ability to drain energies from others, both magical and life energy. Given that it was a shifter and seeing how it affected you, I believe the warlock drained the shifter's lunar magic and tried to infuse you with it."

"But why would they do that?" Rynac asked. "What do they intend to do with it?"

"You know something else?" I asked.

Neither of them would meet my gaze.

"Last night, people reported demonspawn sightings all over the city," Rynac said. "We joined another team chasing them down, and they led us to a building. Inside, we discovered a handful of people who've been missing. Only a few were conscious. They couldn't remember much except to tell us that thralls and demonspawn had guarded them, but the initial report from our healers indicated that someone had drained them of their magical energies."

"You think it was the warlock?" I asked.

"Who else works with demonspawn?" Indra said with a scowl.

"While we couldn't identify them all," Rynac continued, his gaze shifting to Beylin, "most of them are shifters, but one matched the description of Quinn, and another of Thayna."

The floors shuddered beneath me and the shelves shook violently, yet nothing toppled from them to the ground. It took me a moment to realize Divine was in distress at the news.

"Thayna had been traveling home. How did she get caught up in this?" I asked, not expecting an answer. "And who is Quinn?"

I gazed between them, knowing I was missing something.

The dwarf rubbed his face. "Quinn is an employee. She's been absent for over a month, but that's nothing new for her. When we couldn't get a hold of Dira, her partner, I reported her missing. Thayna, Quinn, and Dira all have latent lunar magic."

The breath rushed out of me as my chest throbbed harder. "Why does the warlock want lunar power?"

"Selene's moon-blessed were the only reason humans, nephilim, and erebians escaped from Terrarum. They guard the divide between realms and are the only force able to keep the demon lords from invading. But any blessed with lunar abilities are enemies of the demons."

"But then why did they want to increase my power?"

"I can answer that," a feminine voice answered from the shadows.

Chapter Twenty-Nine

The enforcers drew their weapons, but Beylin waved them off. I could only blink as the nephilim appeared.

"Ever heard of knocking, Astrid?" Beylin scolded.

"You know her?" I asked.

"Old friend," he grumbled, which made her smile. "But she has more knowledge of lunar abilities than I do."

Beylin eyed our uninvited guest.

"How long have you been eavesdropping?"

She shrugged. "Not long."

Beylin scowled.

"I wanted to assess the situation, but that magical wound is concerning. May I?" she asked me.

"Why should I trust you?"

She might have shielded me earlier, but that could've been for her own reasons.

Sneaking into a building and eavesdropping wasn't very reassuring.

"I stopped by your apartment to check up on you. When I realized no one was home, I came here. I do apologize for sneaking in, but I am glad I did. I could sense the unstable energy from downstairs."

"What do you know about lunar abilities? I thought nephilim power came from their angel blood."

"It does, but I think you might also recognize this." Astrid exposed the inside of her wrist.

A moment later, a mark appeared.

A tattoo of a full moon with a crescent moon on either side. Just like the illustration in Beylin's book.

Wait. Kaelan's tattoo was a moon design, too.

"A moon-blessed marking?" I looked at Beylin, my eyes narrowing. "I thought you didn't know much about the moon-blessed."

"I know a few moon-blessed," Beylin said. "But their secret is not mine to reveal. I contacted Astrid for information, but didn't invite her here."

"I am part of the Lunar Order, a covert group of Selene's moon-blessed," Astrid said. "Knowledge of which is need-to-know. And I trust I have all of your words to keep it that way, along with everything else we discuss today?"

The enforcers nodded, taking this far better than me. I doubted my world would ever return to normal after weeks of feeling upside down.

"May I look at the injury?" Astrid asked.

The last thing I needed was to become further in debt to the nephilim.

I hissed as I pulled my shirt down.

"You said you knew why the warlock targeted me," I said through gritted teeth.

Astrid pursed her lips as she studied my wound. "Lunar witches can manipulate the veil between realms."

"I can what?" I blurted out.

Manipulate, not just tear. The UMC kept the information about those who could repair it a closely guarded secret due to its rarity.

"And why do you think I'm a lunar witch?"

I couldn't bring myself to deny it outright, even though it was still hard to believe. I guess Danika was more convincing than I realized.

The hole in my chest throbbed at the thought of my familiar. I didn't realize how accustomed I had become to her presence until the potion stripped it away.

"You're not?" She frowned. "Your magic saturated the area, and there was no denying it was lunar energy. I've never heard of a child of the sun with lunar abilities outside of the lunar witches."

"How do you even know about them?"

My gaze narrowed in on the nephilim. I'd lived my whole life never hearing a whisper about lunar witches, now everyone but me knew about them?

Danika, the warlock, and now a nephilim.

"Only two lunar witches survived the war, which wasn't enough to protect this realm. They created the Lunar Order to defend our home and maintain the veil. Those who join the Order learn our history, but most history books forget the sacrifice of the lunar witches."

Astrid frowned as a whisper of her magic curl around me.

"This injury is concerning. What was the warlock doing? Trying to create a lunar witch?"

"Do you know what's happening?" I asked.

"I believe your body is trying to protect itself from the magic that struck you. These white lines are lunar energies seeping into your body, but your binding potion is slowing the process." She shook her head. "If I'd known you had an injury, I wouldn't have sent you off so quickly, but I thought you'd be safer away from there."

"And when the potion wears off, will we have a repeat of earlier?"

I could feel its effects diminishing as a tingling sensation grew, vibrated from my chest down my arms and into my hands.

Astrid's face darkened. That was all the answer I needed.

"What can I do to stop that?"

"We could continue to suppress the magic, and I can attempt to siphon it off."

"Except that's what I've been doing my whole life," I snapped, unable to hold back the frustration. "Trying to manage my magic, looking for a way to fix it, but never facing the real problem. And look at where that got me. My magic grows more unstable, and now the Inquisitors are sniffing around again."

"Inquisitors," Beylin spat.

I guess no one liked them, but that didn't come as any surprise.

"Or," she continued, "you'll need to learn to control it while draining the excess magic from your body, which is something I can help you with."

I let out a humorless laugh. Learn control or suppress my magic. My options hadn't changed; my actions had just made things worse.

Magic was a part of me, one I didn't want to lose, but if I only hurt people with it, I'd have to give it up.

"The warlock wants my magic," I said. "She said she wants my powers to awaken. I have no interest in her plans, but I might need to learn about this magic. If I don't, she'll hurt more people I care about. If I surrender to the witches and let them strip away my magic, she'll only target someone else. This way, we can prepare for what's coming. And it might be the only way to stop whatever she plans."

Astrid offered me a faint smile. "I would agree, but only you can make this choice."

I glanced at Rynac and Indra.

"We will support you, no matter what you choose," Rynac said.

Indra flashed me a smile. "I think learning how to use your magic is exactly what you need. Plus, I don't want to lose my alchemist and all her fun potions."

"I guess it's settled then," I said, somehow both terrified and excited. "Does my mark mean I have to join this Lunar Order too?"

Selene might've marked me, but running around hunting demonspawn wasn't the life I'd envisioned for myself.

"You have a mark?" she asked, and I nodded. "Not everyone with lunar abilities bears Selene's mark, and even if you do, it's not mandatory to join the Order, but may I have a look?"

Lifting my hair, I twisted my neck to show her. Rynac and Indra shifted closer—I had never felt more self-conscious.

As Astrid ran her fingers across the nape of my neck, a shiver of magic skittered over my skin.

"It's more defined than before," Beylin said.

"I think it looks badass," Indra added.

"Good," I chuckled. "Because I can't see it."

"Interesting," Astrid muttered. "A waxing crescent moon. Our markings have significance, though it can take time for us to understand them. This is the mark of our Goddess. A witch with a lunar blessing. How unusual."

"My familiar believes I'm from a lunar witch bloodline."

"But you don't?"

I hesitated. "I didn't at first. How could I be something I'd never heard of? But after last night, it's hard to ignore all the evidence showing I have lunar and solar magic."

"A mixed bloodline makes more sense," Astrid said. "That you already carried latent lunar powers could be why the warlock is targeting you. Forcing lunar energies into a regular witch would likely kill them, just as when demons tried to obtain holy energies. The two powers conflict. Is that why your magic is unstable?"

"The warlock alluded to that last night. It could be the reason."

It made logical sense. Of course, I also had a fear of being burned alive. And of deep water. I was a walking oxymoron.

"I don't like how much she seems to know about you," Rynac muttered.

I had to agree; it was unsettling.

"We should start training right away," Astrid said. "If you'll allow me to train you."

I nodded. I trusted Astrid, even though I'd only just met her. Maybe it was my magic recognizing hers, or how she had protected me from the Inquisitors without hesitation.

"What about the other two?" I asked.

"They don't need to know unless you want them to."

"Okay," I sighed. "What now?"

"First, you need rest. I can keep the magic under control. Beylin—"

"Yes, I'll watch over her," he grumbled. "Come, I'll set you up in the guest room."

Indra wrapped me in a hug the moment I stood up, and Rynac joined in a second later.

"What's this for?" I asked, my voice muffled.

"To remind you that we're here for you," he said.

"We need to rest too," Indra said. "We'll be patrolling tonight, but contact us if you need anything. I anticipate things are about to kick up a notch."

"Please stay safe," I murmured, holding them both a heartbeat longer before trailing Beylin to the guest room. My mind wouldn't stop spinning; sleep felt impossible.

Then Astrid's spell slid over my skin, and Beylin sealed the ward around me.

The world blinked out as soon as my head touched the pillow, just like someone had flipped a switch.

Chapter Thirty

Astrid sat opposite me on the rooftop, legs crossed as a cool breeze whispered over us. I kept my eyes shut, yet I could still sense her, a steady pulse of calm strength.

Danika nestled in my lap, her warmth the only thing that felt easy.

Everything else was swallowed by a deafening silence so loud it made my chest ache.

I wanted to open my magic to Astrid again, to feel that familiar thread between us.

But if it was gone or if I'd damaged it . . .

I wasn't sure I'd survive the answer.

"Deep breath in," she said.

Inhaling through my nose, I focused on the air as it filled my lungs and pushed away the nagging thoughts.

"Breathe out."

The afternoon sun warmed my skin. Magic stirred in my chest, but I soothed it, letting it settle back into slumber.

Since returning home, I'd sensed it beginning to reawaken. Both potions were out of my system, but Carmen's spell felt like a ticking time bomb.

Why had I agreed to this? Oh right, the fate of countless lives depended on my ability to master my magic.

"Quiet your mind."

I didn't know how she sensed that, but I cast away the thoughts.

We'd only done regular meditation, but she thought I was ready to tap into my magic.

Astrid hoped attempting it during the sunlight hours would weaken the foreign lunar magic's attempt to rush into my system.

"By the gentle glow of Selene's light," Astrid chanted, and I repeated the words, feeling silly.

She assured me I didn't need the actual moon to connect to the magic within.

"I seek the magic of the tranquil night. In the moon's embrace, I shall find the power within my soul aligned. With each breath, I draw her near, lunar magic, calm and clear."

Power stirred in my chest, as if my words had called it out—subdued, but awake. I gathered it, guiding it into my hands, and sensed the magic pooling within my upraised palms.

Fire sparked within my heart like a dragon waking from a deep slumber. I pushed it away, focusing on my lunar magic.

"Steady, hold on to it," Astrid said.

My breathing was slow and light as I maintained the magic I had gathered.

Gentle, balanced, and calming. Magic that called to a deeper part of my soul.

Fire flickered, whispering that this power was weak. Nothing compared to the power my family commanded.

But I wasn't strong enough to wield the magic they summoned.

Heat raced across my skin. Images lurked in the depths of my mind, but I shoved them away.

Latching onto Danika's presence, I settled my mind, imagining the moon's soft glow.

Flames ignited in my chest, and I gasped as heat scorched through me.

The images flashed before my eyes. Fire surrounding me.

I choked, my eyes flying open as the air vanished from my lungs.

Astrid held out a hand toward me, then squeezed it into a fist. My magic sizzled and then snuffed out. Only when Astrid opened her hand could I breathe again.

"Sorry," she said. "Your magic flared. What happened?"

"I don't know. This happened when I tried meditating with Danika."

I raked a hand through my hair. I guess nothing had changed.

"Everything was fine. It was easy to summon the magic, but then my solar magic flared, and I couldn't control it."

Astrid frowned. "We'll keep trying. I know it's frustrating. Finding balance is difficult with opposing magics."

"Why do you fear fire?" Danika asked.

My heart skipped a beat at the sound of her soft voice in my mind. The connection was there. I hadn't destroyed it with the binding potion.

"What do you mean?" I said when my brain caught up.

"I could sense your emotions. That fear saturated everything."

At Astrid's curious look, I explained what Danika said.

"Why wouldn't I fear fire? It's wild and erratic. Once it gets out of control, it's near impossible to contain."

Only witches with a mastery of solar magic could pass through fire unharmed. But while they could summon fire, they still respected the magic, knowing that fire could easily escape their control and cause significant damage.

"There's more," Danika pressed.

I opened my mouth to refute it, but what if this was the reason I was having problems?

"I had a vision once," I said, licking my lips. "When I was thirteen, my friends and I sneaked out to the sacred lake for some fun. We'd heard a rumor that it would reveal your soulmate if you looked into its water under a full moon."

Despite the years, I'd never shared this with anyone after my parents dismissed it.

"But I caught a glimpse of my future. A wall of magical fire trapped me. My powers were the only thing holding it back, but they weren't enough. It was so hot I thought my skin was going to melt. When the vision ended, I was ten feet below the water's surface. It was a miracle I didn't drown."

I banished the painful memory from my mind.

"No one believed me when I told them, but I know what I saw."

"Do you think the fire was your own magic?" Astrid asked.

"Yes. It turned against me." More than that, it *wanted* to devour me. Hatred fueled that fire.

"*I believe you,*" Danika said.

"Have you had any other visions?"

"No, I avoid large bodies of water at night," I said.

Astrid snorted. "I don't blame you. But Selene is renowned for granting visions through divination. I was curious if she had granted you any others."

"I never asked." At Astrid's curious look, I explained, "I thought I heard a voice that night. It whispered, 'Ask, and it will be revealed.' But I thought my mind was playing tricks on me."

Why would I want to look again? I'd seen something else through those flames.

A brief glimpse of my soulmate, only to find their eyes burning with a deep-seated hatred. I never wanted to see my future again.

"I wonder if that's when Selene first marked you," Astrid said.

Shrugging, I rubbed the back of my neck. I remembered a phantom touch, as if someone had pulled me up to the surface.

"But if I already possess her powers, why would she mark me?"

"There's more to the mark than just Selene's blessing," Astrid said, her eyes distant as her fingers absently trailed over her own mark. "What did your friends say happened?"

"They said one moment I was there, the next I was gone. They rushed to get our parents, and when they returned, I surfaced in the middle of the lake."

"That's a long time to be underwater. Was there anything else?"

"No. When I pressed them for more later, they didn't recall the night at all."

"There's more to that night than you remember," she said. "Our marks represent an agreement with the Goddess. She offers us a second chance at life and grants us access to her magic. For some of us, that means serving as her warriors to protect the realm. For others, it means offering support and guidance. We all have roles to fulfill, even if it's unclear how we'll serve."

"What do you mean by a second chance?"

I'd been thirteen. My life hadn't even begun.

"Selene saves us from death," Astrid said. "The spot where she touched us bears her mark. She grabbed my wrist and saved my life. And she guided you to the water's surface."

"But I almost died because of her vision. And I don't remember agreeing to anything."

"I can't say for sure, but you carry the magic of her bloodline. Perhaps she simply wished to protect the last of the lunar witches."

Did something else happen that night? Something that I couldn't remember? I shook my head.

None of this was helping. I needed to get a handle on this magic.

My phone rang, saving me from a reply. I was almost relieved until I saw the name.

Dad.

CHAPTER THIRTY-ONE

"What's wrong?" I answered, pulse already spiking with unneeded anxiety.

Dad didn't call for chats.

He only called for emergencies or birthdays. And it wasn't my birthday.

He chuckled. "Can't a dad just call his favorite daughter?"

"I'm your only daughter," I grumbled. "I thought you were away for work?"

"Yes, but there's been some activity in Arkirith."

That was code for protection forces deployed, bad things are happening, but I can't say anything specific—the joys of my dad working with military intelligence.

The sensitivity of his job prevented him from calling often, even when he was away for months.

"I'm aware." I bit my lip.

How much should I tell him? He'd know more than me, anyway.

"They've warned everyone to stay off the streets at night, and the local enforcers have increased patrols. With a UMC unit here, I know they'll resolve the issue with haste."

Well, the last part was a lie, but it'd put him at ease.

"How do you know so much?" he said with thinly veiled suspicion.

"I am *your* child," I shot back. "And I'm friends with a few enforcers and have an alchemy contract with their division."

"That's wonderful, darling. Congratulations," he said. "But are you sure you want to stay there?"

"I like it here, Dad. I mean, it has its ups and downs," I said, rubbing at the throb in my chest, "but my friends will keep me safe."

"You can always come home, no matter what."

I hesitated. "Dad?"

As much as I longed to share everything and to ask him what he knew about the lunar witches, but right now, it wouldn't do any good. They timed and monitored all calls, and I didn't want to make him worry about me.

"I'll be careful. Maybe you can come visit when you're back?"

"I'd like that, sweetheart. I'll be home before the summer solstice."

Voices echoed on the other end of the line and I knew our time was almost up.

My eyes prickled.

Just hearing his voice reminded me how much I missed him. But deep in my gut, I knew leaving home was the right choice, despite everything else going on.

"I love you, Dad."

"I love you too, Nyssa." His voice so soft that my eyes stung more.

Tucking my phone away, I grabbed my water and took a long drink, keeping my back to the others.

Why was I being so emotional today?

"Do you need more rest?" Astrid asked.

Danika rubbed her head against my leg, and I scratched behind her ears.

"No, I want to keep going." The fever persisted, and my head throbbed, but there wasn't time to recover.

"Let's try something different," Astrid said, not commenting on the phone call. "You said you've struggled with solar spells."

"I don't have an issue channeling into an array, but any spell that I must shape myself either fails or is faulty. I can only summon a weak, short-lasting orb of light."

"Have you ever cast one with your lunar magic?"

"No, I haven't thought to try."

"From what I can sense in you, your lunar magic is far stronger. If you try to pull more solar energy than you have, you might tap into your lunar magic automatically. That might be the reason the spells are unstable. Want to give it a go?"

Her logic made sense. At school, we learned how to assess the magic within us, calculate how much power we had, and test our reserves. I knew my potential reserves matched my parents', but it always emerged volatile.

Could I be unconsciously channeling both energies into a spell and causing them to unbalance each other?

I nodded and cupped my hands before me. I reached out to my power, but this time focused on the cool, steady glow within me.

Closing my eyes, I summoned the image of the moon, allowing a trickle of magic to flow into my hands.

Power thrummed against my palms as the magic coalesced.

"Open your eyes," Astrid said.

My hands held a fully formed orb of light. The soft glow competed against the sun in the sky, but it was there. Whole.

Flames flickered over my hands.

No. I quashed the magic. The flames subsided for a moment, then resurged. Fire spread across my orb as if it could devour the magic within.

My magic shifted; chunks of the orb melted and dripped onto my skin.

Astrid's hands shot out as her magic surrounded my orb.

The flames died as if all the oxygen had disappeared, and my orb withered and faded into nothing.

As my magic winked out, I slumped forward.

"Thank you," I said between breaths.

Silence lingered as I braced myself, anticipating her realization that I was useless. That my magic was incompatible with spells. That I might have lunar magic, but would never wield it.

"What does it feel like?" Astrid asked. At my confused look, she rephrased her question. "What do your two types of magic feel like, and when they combine, does it feel different?"

"On its own, solar magic is hot and powerful, while lunar is steady and subtle. Together?"

I gnawed on my lip. What did it feel like? My panicked mind always had other, more pressing matters than the sensation. Carmen's words from the other night rang through my head.

"When I summon lunar magic, it's like the solar energies want to dominate it, like the sun's brilliance overshadowing the pale moon." I cringed. That must have sounded so stupid.

"I have an idea," she said, her face bright. "Do you know the runed band spell?"

"I'm familiar with it."

Not that I had ever cast it more than once. After inking a rune on their hand, the witch channeled their magic into it. It acted like temporary storage, so the magic was easily accessible when the witch was ready to command it.

"What if we give your solar magic something to do so that you can cast your lunar spells?"

"That . . . makes sense."

I scrunched up my face, trying to poke holes in her logic, but I couldn't find any. Racing back down to my room, I grabbed my grimoire and a vial of ink to draw the rune. I hesitated for a moment, then I picked up *The Lunar Codex*.

Before Beylin sent me home, he'd helped me plan out a spell array to hide its aura.

Once again, I realized how little I knew about my boss. He was far more than just the owner of Divine Coffee.

"This belongs to you," Beylin had said. "It is your greatest resource, and it would be foolish not to see what other guidance it offers."

As I sat down again, Astrid laughed, tapping the codex. "You can read this and still doubted you were a lunar witch?"

Danika shot me a knowing look as if to say, "I told you so."

"After spending my whole life searching for an answer to why my magic was unstable," I said with a wry smile, "accepting something so far-fetched is difficult, especially after so many failures."

"That's fair. If I hadn't witnessed your magic for myself, I wouldn't have believed it either."

Flipping open my grimoire, I found the rune I needed.

With careful brush strokes, I inked it onto the back of my left hand.

Even without summoning it, my magic stirred when I completed the rune.

I couldn't tamp down my excitement that this plan might work.

"Whenever you're ready," Astrid said. "I'll be here to contain your magic if you need me."

I dipped my head. Knowing I had someone I could trust and who could stop me before I lost control was an immense weight off my shoulders. Now I only had to contend with my fear of failing.

Even with my eyes closed, the latent magic in the rune called to my solar energy.

It thrummed, longing to be summoned.

I gathered the magic; it rippled like fire dancing across the surface of the sun.

As I focused, it became easier to separate the magic.

I channeled the solar magic down my arm and into the rune. Heat washed across my skin as the eager energies surged into it.

Warmth spread across my hand, but never grew so hot that I feared it would hurt me. I fed more of my magic into the rune, and my powers obeyed my command without resistance.

"Look," Astrid said, a smile in her voice.

I swallowed before I complied. My heart skipped a beat. There, wrapping around my wrist, was a ring of fire.

Pure solar magic.

A complete spell.

The breath rushed out of me.

I lifted my hand, wiggling my fingers; the magic responded, twirling through them. I couldn't help but grin.

"Well done," Astrid said. "Ready for the next test?"

I nodded, and she took my other hand, tracing out a rune I was unfamiliar with. But the moment she completed it, my lunar magic awoke. I tensed, but the solar magic was far too content circling around its own rune.

This time, I reached for my lunar magic.

Cool power flowed through my veins, a reassuring pulse that filled my arm with strength as if the magic empowered my body. It whispered over my skin like a cool evening breeze.

Only when Astrid made a noise did I realize the rune was at full power.

Shimmering moonlight curled around my wrist, and even in the light of day, it gleamed.

A weight pressed against my chest that had nothing to do with expending too much magic.

Danika peered up at me. Her nose twitched, then she rested her head on my leg, happy to watch my magic.

"I'd say that's a big success," Astrid said, her wide smile matching my own.

"What's next?" I asked, eager to keep going, to learn more. For so long, I'd missed out on this.

"Let's try the orb of light again."

A mere thought was all it took to summon the lunar orb as magic thrummed at my fingertips.

The solar flames flickered in response but continued to circle around my wrist, waiting for me to give them a purpose.

Following Astrid's instructions, I poured more power into the lunar orb until it glowed so bright I couldn't look at it.

I sealed off the spell and tossed it into the air. The orb bobbed, floating just above my head, casting its light over us.

"Now recall it and absorb the remaining power."

Without hesitation, the orb returned to my outstretched hand.

My eyebrows drew together, and I tugged, trying to call my magic back. It resisted, but then reluctantly dripped back into me.

My flames flickered, surging as the lunar magic filled me. I stilled both energies, took a steadying breath, and waited.

The lunar energies obeyed my will, but the fire simmered for a moment before relenting.

I sagged as the last trickle of magic drained away, sweat prickling over my skin as if I'd just sprinted around the block.

"That was perfect," Astrid beamed. "You wobbled but recovered right away."

"What's next?" I asked, excitement outweighing my fatigue.

"More practice, but tomorrow night we can try to tap into that excess lunar magic. It's stable enough to hold until then."

I stifled my disappointment. She was right, and I knew it.

Even bone-deep tired, energy crackled through me—excitement and something deeper, like the click of a lock turning.

All my life, I'd felt like I was pretending to be someone bigger, stronger, more magical.

Now, for the first time, I didn't feel like an imposter.

I felt complete.

And that changed everything.

Chapter Thirty-Two

An all-consuming fire blazed around me, so hot I thought my skin was about to blister and melt. But I had to hold on.

My arms shook as I channeled more magic. I couldn't stop, or the fire would reach me.

The flames flickered, a dance of green and gold.

They would have been beautiful if they weren't trying to destroy me.

I braced myself, knowing what was to come. Phantom claws dug into my heart, each slice sending a new wave of agony through me. I gnashed my teeth, refusing to let my body falter.

Sweat cascaded down my face, but I blinked it out of my eyes, knowing what I would see and fearing it all the same.

The flames parted as he shifted, but all I could see were his eyes.

Golden eyes, burning like the flames that surrounded me, and filled with pure hatred.

My magic faltered, and the fire rushed in.

I tried to scream, but liquid rushed into my mouth—water was everywhere, and I flailed.

Which way was up? My lungs burned.

Water filled my nose.

A force shoved into my back and propelled me. Then a hand cupped my neck, pulling me toward the surface. The full moon swayed above the rippling water, calling to me.

I broke through the surface.

Jolting upright, I gasped for breath.

The blanket tangled around my legs.

My heart hammered in my chest as I blinked and recognized my room. I swiped a hand across my sweaty face.

"Yeah, thanks," I hissed, glaring at the ceiling. "I don't need to be reminded."

Was that Selene's idea of a joke?

It had taken me years to stop having that nightmare. I should've known better than to dredge up the past.

My fever had yet to pass.

The relentless heat made me feel like I was being roasted alive.

Outside my window, the waxing gibbous moon had risen above the horizon. I'd slept later than normal.

Another reason I hated sleeping at night—my dreams were always far more vivid.

The last dregs of my nightmare evaporated when I remembered Astrid was coming again tonight. We would attempt to siphon off the lunar energy.

I stumbled into the bathroom. My hair looked like a literal coral reef, but I didn't care. I needed to see the glow on my chest.

Whatever Beylin and Astrid had done had slowed Carmen's spell. Fine white lines, which looked a little like veins, spread from the impact point across my chest.

The spell had left a mark as large as my fist, which glowed and pulsed in time with my heart.

I didn't sense any malevolence in the cluster of power, but it creeped me out. The sooner I got rid of it, the better. I wasn't a fan of having a ticking time bomb attached to me.

When I reached the rooftop, Astrid had already arrived, and Danika was lapping up her attention.

"Any updates?" I asked as I cleared a space for us to work.

Despite her smile, a sense of weariness rested on Astrid.

I felt a tad guilty at demanding more of her time when she was already stretched so thin, but the dire need to fix my problem outweighed my guilt.

If I lost control, I could do so much damage.

"No leads on the warlock," Astrid said, her frown deepening. "After the display at Lynock, we believe she's lying low or waiting for her spell to take effect. We've also seen nothing of the Inquisitors, but they tend to do their own thing. The UMC and MEA squads are doing their best to combat the demonspawn and thralls, but their attacks have turned random. They seem purposeless and possibly beyond the warlock's control."

"I hate being one step behind," I grumbled. "We're just sitting and waiting for her to attack again. I want to strike a blow back."

"It might not feel like it, but we are hitting back."

Astrid took up position opposite me, and Danika settled at my side.

"The spell she hit you with was deliberate. By managing that energy, we will hinder her plans. Strengthening your magic and learning control will aid us later. She wants you weak and unstable, so it will be easier to use you."

"Any ideas on what she plans?"

"Only a theory," Astrid said, her words cautious.

Whatever it was, I wasn't going to like it.

"Selene crafted the veil that traps the demons within their own realm; warlocks can create a small tear which allows low-level demonspawn to pass through. As the warlock is gathering lunar energies, we believe she is attempting to create a portal capable of allowing more powerful demons to enter our realm."

"Well, that sounds like a riot."

The MEA was already struggling against the demonspawn. How could they fight more powerful demons?

"Where do I come in?"

Astrid gnawed on her lip as though debating how much to tell me. "It wasn't the battle that wiped the lunar witches out. They sacrificed themselves to create the veil."

My mouth opened, but I snapped it shut.

All of those lives lost to protect us from the demons. The lunar witches made the ultimate sacrifice for us, and we didn't even remember them?

My mind came to a shuddering halt.

"If lunar witches created it . . ." The words stuck on my tongue.

Astrid nodded, pain rippling across her face. "Then they can tear it down. Not just tear holes but destroy the only thing protecting us. It's already weakened, allowing demonspawn to slip into this realm, but if the entire spell shatters, we'll be overrun. Nothing will hold the demons back from ravaging this realm like they did ours."

Goddess.

The world around me stilled.

My mind struggled to process her words as I stared sightlessly. I was a danger to everyone and everything in this realm.

I might've longed for powerful magic, but not this.

As much as I wanted to deny it, I couldn't. Why else would Carmen keep me alive?

She could have killed me several times, but she wanted me to grow stronger and gain control. Just so I could tear down the veil?

"Danika?" I looked down at my fox. She'd remained silent. "Did you know about this? Is it true?"

She peered up at me, sorrow filling her gaze. *"Yes. The lunar witches created the veil. I don't believe a lone witch could destroy it, but they could likely create a permanent tear."*

"Which, I'm guessing, would kill me?" I asked, already knowing the answer.

"Yes."

"Fucking hell," I hissed. "Literally."

I rubbed a hand over my face and relayed the information to Astrid.

"We will not let that happen," she said.

She spoke with such conviction, but did I have a choice? I shook my head. No, there was always a choice.

My mother's words echoed through my head. I couldn't control the actions of others, only how I reacted to them.

"No. I won't."

Now that I understood what was coming, I would be prepared. I would do everything in my power to thwart her.

"I could turn myself in to the Inquisitors and have them strip my magic away."

"What?" Danika hissed, surging to her feet.

My stomach soured at the idea, but if our realm's protection was at stake . . . I'd been fighting so hard to fix this magic, to learn how to control it, but maybe I was fated to be magicless.

"The damage this magic can do," I said, staring at my hands. "The last lunar witches sacrificed their lives to protect the realms. I can't undo that."

"You're also the only one who can strengthen it. That's the magic of your ancestors, and the same energies are within you. If anyone can empower the veil, it would be you."

"I can?" I asked Astrid, explaining what Danika had said.

This was so much bigger than me. I was just one witch.

"I don't know. Knowledge about the lunar witches has been guarded to prevent it from falling into the wrong hands. But it makes sense. Many within the Order can repair smaller tears, but those areas remain weakened, and we monitor them for activity. Someone who could fully restore the tears would be invaluable."

She was silent for a long moment; her gaze distant.

"While I understand your selfless motive for forfeiting your magic, I think it would do more harm than good. You bear Selene's mark. She doesn't bestow her blessing for no reason. If she wanted you to live—to harness her magic—then we have to trust in her."

"That's a relief, but also terrifying."

These powers were a double-edged sword. As long as I had them, Carmen would try to use them to weaken the veil, but if I gave them up I might be sacrificing the only magic that could heal it.

There was no simple way out of this, and I'd never been one to pick the easy route.

Astrid and Danika believed in me. Selene believed in me. I would find a way.

We would find a way.

"Okay," I said, letting out a heavy breath. "Putting aside the potential apocalypse. Shall we get to work?"

We began with breathing exercises because—for some reason—I was stressed.

I traced the rune on my hand again, summoning my solar energies, which were eager to comply.

Tonight, the lunar magic flowed through me like a soft summer breeze, responding to my touch with no resistance.

Erring on the side of caution, Astrid inked the lunar rune to aid in controlling the power.

"Close your eyes and gather your energies in your hands, just like in the meditation."

I tapped into my solar magic first, imagining the sun in my grip. It crackled across my skin, then heat washed over my palm.

I fed a trickle of my magic into my left palm to create an orb. I poured every drop of solar energy into the rune until none remained to unbalance me. Then I moved to the lunar energies.

The cool caress washed through me and pooled in my fingertips.

"Good," Astrid said. "Now focus on the energies. Sense the difference between them: the heat and warmth of the solar power, the pulsing ebb of the lunar power. Follow the flow of lunar power back to the core."

The lunar energy flowed through my body like a river after the winter melt. It weaved through my veins like it was my lifeblood until I found the source. It was like a wellspring bubbling up from my chest.

I nodded to Astrid, keeping my eyes closed.

"Reach out with your awareness. Let your mind flow with your magic. Seek more of that power, one that doesn't resonate with yours. That should be the foreign energies."

It was easy to find now that I understood my own magic. It thrummed not quite in time with my body.

The power resonated—reaching for me—but my lunar magic resisted.

It was like a phantom heart within my chest, but out of sync with my energy.

"Try to direct that magic, push it toward your hand."

I nudged at the power with my mind, encouraging it into my palm.

A small trickle detached.

When it touched the lunar magic pooled within my hand, the two melded together like a drop of coloring in a cup of water.

"Good, now siphon off the magic you hold. Let it slip through your fingers and return to the world."

I eased my grip on the power, letting it flow from my control.

All witches learned this technique of safely dispelling gathered magic when they couldn't reabsorb it.

The magic trickled through my fingers, slow enough not to cause discharge, but power clung to my skin like tar.

I poked at it, encouraging it to follow; it resisted. I shook my hand, attempting to physically fling it off.

Frustrated, I released my hold on the power and sagged, staring down as if I could see the stolen power clinging to me.

"Rest for a moment, then we can try again," Astrid said.

Over and again I tried, but the foreign energies refused to leave me. My own reserves drained with each attempt.

"If we can't siphon it off, perhaps we can harness it and burn it up in a spell," Astrid said. "Do you remember the moonbeam spell?"

I'd stumbled upon the spell in *The Lunar Codex* yesterday and asked her about it. It condensed lunar energies into a beam of moonlight, which had multiple effects.

At lower levels, it offered illumination and a calming aura, while more powerful spells fortified, healed, and even became a weapon that could be used against demons.

"Gather and mix the lunar energies again. Then I want you to summon a moonbeam of light."

I slowed my breathing, calming my mind until it flowed in time with my magical energies.

Opening myself to the surrounding moonlight, I focused on the soothing sensation, willed it to gather, to mix with my magic and form a beam in front of me.

I infused my magic with the singular purpose of illuminating the darkness, bringing light and casting off shadows.

Power flowed from my chest, coursing through my veins and pouring out of my hands.

Even with my eyes closed, I could sense the light growing brighter.

I strengthened it, adding more of my magic.

The stolen energies gathered in my hands but refused to move any farther, resisting my command.

I opened my eyes, mesmerized by the shimmering silver light that glowed, and then I released it.

"That was an impressive first try," Astrid said with a smile.

"But the other power wouldn't leave me." I wanted to enjoy her praise, but the failure tainted my triumph.

"I fear the warlock put precautions in place, wanting to ensure you absorbed the energies."

"What would happen if I did?"

"Hard to say if it's harmless, as the warlock's true intentions remain unknown. There are safe ways of sharing magic between people, but she tore them from Ruby."

Anger clawed at my chest. Another innocent caught up in Carmen's actions, her stolen magic trapped within me.

"We'll leave it here for tonight," Astrid said, reading the guilt on my face. "Get some rest, and we can resume tomorrow."

The nephilim vanished into the dark and I exhaled.

The moon hung overhead, bright and distant as I glared up at it.

"Just once," I muttered under my breath. "Could something in my life go right?"

Chapter Thirty-Three

Beylin grumbled the second I walked into Divine and refused to allow me to work more than a half shift, which, naturally, I complained about on principle.

"I need the distraction," I said, absently rubbing the ache in my chest that refused to subside.

Ruby's pack was silent, and I didn't expect that to change. At least I'd scraped together enough for rent.

Everything else I'd deal with when it came crashing down

"Fine," Beylin sighed. "We could use the coverage. Thayna regained consciousness, though we're still uncertain what happened to her. I know Zola is desperate to visit her. If you think you're up for it, I'll give Zola the time off."

"I am." And even if I wasn't, I'd remain silent.

Guilt gnawed at me like a hungry beast. I blamed myself for the disappearance and attacks, despite what others said.

I was at least partly responsible for it, and I needed to do whatever I could to help.

If Carmen wanted something from me, could I keep her attention fixed on me so that she would leave the others alone?

Were the demonspawn attacks and Carmen's plan for me even related?

The number of demonspawn a warlock could control remained a mystery. But what if their goal was chaos, not control?

To release demonspawn into the city to keep the MEA and UMC busy, to distract them from the warlock's true purpose.

I threw myself into my work, needing to burn off energy and occupy my thoughts.

Astrid had given my magic its first real workout.

And though I felt like a limp noodle, I craved it again, to tap into my real power once again.

After a few hours, my body turned sluggish.

Perhaps Beylin was right.

Carrying my next batch of cookies to the display, I frowned at the café. It appeared more subdued than normal. Mornings were always a hive of activity.

"It's been like this for the last few days," Voren said, leaning on the counter. Even the playful glint in his eyes had diminished. "Word spread quickly about the threat lurking on our streets."

It was good that people were being cautious, but Divine appeared dimmer without them. I missed the hum of conversation, the warm atmosphere that permeated the shop.

"How are you holding up?" Voren asked.

I hadn't mentioned my latest adventure or my latest failure. Would my friends at Divine avoid me if they knew there was a warlock targeting me?

Bringing up the nephilim would only darken Voren's mood, yet I didn't want to lie. He'd asked out of genuine concern.

How could I explain how turbulent my life was right now?

"Rough," I said with a dry laugh. "That's about the best way to sum it up."

"I bet. I'm glad you're helping the MEA with your potions. They're the only ones trying to keep us safe."

Voren raked a hand through his hair and let out a heavy breath.

"In times like these, we have to look out for each other. But sometimes I feel so useless not being able to offer any aid."

I bumped my shoulder against his, a sad smile twisting my lips.

That was a feeling I knew all too well.

"Maybe you just need a distraction. This Voren is kind of depressing."

He huffed. "Zola's stressed, especially after we heard about Quinn and Dira. I've been staying at home just to put her mind at ease. But I'm not a homebody. I miss the nightlife. Still, I guess staying safe is more important."

Voren sighed dramatically, and it was hard not to laugh.

The door jingled open, and Rynac stepped into Divine.

"I'll be right back," I called out to Rynac before muttering to Voren, "Try to be nice this time."

He flashed a smile that showed off his incisors.

I needed to hurry.

Rushing to clean up the kitchen, I packed all my supplies away and wiped down the counters.

The MEA captain had requested a meeting with me, and even though there was still daylight outside, Rynac wanted to escort me. I didn't complain.

Danika had become my guardian of late. With the spell array around the codex, she followed me to and from work.

After the other night, I couldn't blame her.

No matter how I tried to hide it, I was on edge, jumping at shadows.

Finally done, I rushed to clock out, not wanting to keep Rynac or his captain waiting.

The enforcer leaned against the bar, sipping his drink and chatting with Voren, much to my surprise.

Then again, no one resisted Voren's charms for long. And after his last encounter with Rynac, it was a positive change.

Slipping out from behind the bar, a grin spread across my face.

"Stop flirting with my escort, Voren," I chided.

They both froze, and I did a double take. Was that pink coloring Voren's dark skin?

"Or not. Um, don't mind me."

Abort. I stepped back, but it was a bit late for that.

Rynac cleared his throat, looking anywhere but at either of us. "We should be off."

He guided me toward the door and I side-eyed him. His gaze met mine, then darted away.

Shooting a look over my shoulder, I found Voren diligently cleaning the already spotless bar. He flashed me an innocent smile.

"Do you want his number?" I asked Rynac, trying to suppress my grin.

One distraction coming right up.

"Nyssa," Matti called out, waving for me to follow as we entered the MEA headquarters.

He appeared far more haggard than the last time we'd met, as if the weight of the world pressed down on his shoulders.

I hadn't considered how the enforcers were faring with the demonspawn and thrall activity.

Leaving Rynac behind, Matti led me down the hall and past the infirmary.

My eyes strayed through its doors.

Last time, the ward had been empty, but now it was at capacity. A band wrapped around my chest and squeezed.

The enforcers put their lives on the line every night, risking themselves to protect us.

Matti ushered me into a side room off the medical ward.

The sharp scent of antiseptic stung my nose the moment I stepped inside. Stainless steel benches lined the walls, loaded with medical supplies ranging from the mundane to the magical.

My magic stirred, responding to the power in the vials that were lined up on the bench. These were my healing potions.

Had the testing concluded?

I whirled on Matti, but he remained silent, his lips pressed together as if that was the only way to keep the words inside.

The captain strode in with a stern look, but there was a slight spark in his eyes.

"I believe congratulations are in order," the captain said by way of greeting.

Was that the hint of a smile curving his lips?

"Our trials have concluded, and we have deemed your brews safe."

Fizzy energy zipped through my veins, my breath coming too fast as I stared at the captain.

A wide grin split Matti's face as he nodded, convincing me this was real.

"The potion had no adverse effects, and most patients experienced milder-than-usual side effects. We've added them into circulation. As you may have noticed, they're in high demand."

His smile faded before he ran a tired hand over his face.

"I have a full contract for you, if you're still interested," the captain said. "Which includes your offensive potions. Our squads are being pushed hard of late. We need every edge we can get. All your brews have been invaluable for protecting the lives of my enforcers."

I flashed the captain my brightest smile. "I happily accept."

"Good," he said, shaking my hand. "Come to my office when you're done here to finalize the contract. And I have another matter to discuss with you."

Well, that's foreboding.

Matti reviewed the test results with me. All my potions had passed with flying colors.

"We've been rationing the few potions left for the most critical patients," Matti said.

I scanned the long list of potions he had compiled. "Then I'll start brewing tonight."

"Thank you."

At least I made a difference here, but it still didn't solve the greater issue. I'd gained a major contract, the first step toward establishing my business.

Amidst the chaos, I had limited time to review my alchemy business plan.

Now I just needed to find time to brew between training my magic, working at Divine, and figuring out Carmen's schemes.

There was no doubt in my mind she'd strike again.

If she'd orchestrated the attack on Rynac and kidnapped Ruby, it was only a matter of time before she found another way to twist my arm.

After knocking, I entered the captain's office and took the seat he offered. My hands trembling as I accepted the paperwork.

It was hard to contain my excitement while looking over the offered contract.

What more could I ask for?

With this kind of income, I wouldn't have to worry about missing my rent payment again. And if I conserved my money, I could afford the first payment on the shop I wanted to lease.

"No floral crown today?" the captain asked as I signed the contract.

My cheeks burned, and I wanted to sink through the floor.

Despite the glint in his eye, I was pretty sure it was a joke, but all I managed was a small shake of my head.

"There is one other matter I wished to discuss," the captain said, as he accepted the contract back.

I braced myself for the reprimand. Did this concern the night Rynac and I were attacked, or the UMC investigation?

"A wolf shifter pack has requested to meet with you."

Oh, shit. Had he learned about my involvement at Lynock sports field? But he'd already offered me the alchemy contract.

"I believe you have a brewing contract with them," he continued. "They also wanted to meet with me, formally requesting protection. Do you know anything about this?"

"They did?"

Had the elders listened to Ruby or had the attack convinced them?

"I chatted with Ruby, one of their pack couriers who transported my potions. She mentioned strange attacks on her pack that sounded similar to the thralls I encountered, so I encouraged her to contact the MEA for help."

"I appreciate your concern and that you directed them toward us, rather than trying to solve the problem yourself."

I kept my mouth shut. Guess he didn't know about my run-in with the warlock.

"An alliance with a shifter pack will be beneficial for all of us and aid in building stronger connections within the community."

"I'm happy they reached out. I understand you're already stretched thin."

"That we are," he said, his gaze turning distant. "If you don't have any prior engagements, we can head to the pack's den now."

Now? Me going alone with the enforcer captain into a literal wolf's den?

"Okay."

What choice did I have?

Chapter Thirty-Four

The building that loomed in front of me was huge, the kind of place that should've housed tourists and conference rooms, not a pack of shifters.

Its peculiar architecture jutted and curved in ways the neighboring skyscrapers didn't dare imitate. In the center of the city, it looked less like an apartment complex and more like a fortress.

I didn't know what to expect from a shifter den, but it hadn't been this. Ornate columns and wrought-iron balconies coexisted harmoniously with sleek, modernist glass walls that shimmered in the sunlight.

The weight of unseen eyes bore down on us, but I couldn't spot where they hid.

A handful of individuals stood in the manicured outdoor courtyard, ready to receive us.

The eldest of the shifters stepped forward to greet the captain. A mane of silver hair cascaded down his back.

Unlike Ruby, age had whitened his hair, a stark contrast to his dark, weathered skin that spoke of countless seasons under the open sky.

Deep lines were etched in his face, each wrinkle telling a story of a life well-lived. While his eyes, the color of the stormy sea, seemed to hold a world of knowledge within their gaze.

"Welcome to our home." He greeted us with a raspy voice. "I'm Elder Talaar. Thank you for meeting with us."

The elder exuded vitality and strength, despite his advanced age. His posture was regal; each movement deliberate and graceful as he waved for us to follow.

As he led the way, two other shifters fell in step behind us.

Despite the building's weathered appearance, the grand entrance remained imposing. Intricate carvings hinted at mysteries within and conjured memories of my home.

Witches favored older architecture, building on grand scales to invoke beauty rather than adapt to the modern era.

A shudder of magic crawled over my skin—unnerving, but not hostile—as we crossed the threshold and spilled into the atrium.

Tables and couches adorned the spacious area, a massive handwoven rug covering the stone floor and a rich variety of artwork gracing the walls.

"Idris." Elder Talaar waved to the shifter beside him. "Please escort Captain Everson to my office. I'll be along shortly."

With a short bow, Idris motioned for the captain to follow, leaving me alone with the two shifters.

"So you're our alchemist," the elder said, looking me over. "Quite young, too. I wanted to extend my personal gratitude not only for your expertise but for aiding our pack in our time of need."

"I'm happy that I could help," I replied. "That's why I am an alchemist. Making a difference in people's lives is all the thanks I need."

The elder smiled before taking my hand. "And I want to thank you for helping to return Ruby to us. The nephilim mentioned you were the one who alerted them to her location. I'm thankful Ruby has a friend like you looking out for her. Her little sister can't seem to stop talking about you either."

My smile felt weak. Some friend I was. I was the reason they had taken her. "The nephilim did all the hard work."

"Nonsense," he said, waving off my words as if I were being modest. "Lainie here will take you to visit Ruby. She hasn't awoken, but I'm sure your presence will comfort her. And Jade would be grateful too."

I could only nod as the elder departed. It wasn't as if I could decline.

Lainie, the dark-skinned shifter, regarded me with unflinching quicksilver eyes.

Her short-cropped white hair was almost as severe as her expression. Twin daggers hung at her waist, and the hilt of a sword peeked over her shoulder.

That wasn't intimidating at all.

Pivoting on her heels, Lainie strode off without waiting to see if I followed.

I hurried along, following her up two flights of stairs and down a long corridor. I struggled to match the shifter's strides and was puffing by the time we paused.

Lainie gave me one sharp look before pushing through the door. What was that about?

A thick, rusty-red carpet muffled our steps as we walked down the hallway. A heavy silence hung over the area, as if even the walls held their breath.

The shifter paused to knock on one of the many doors before opening it.

A single, muted lamp cast its soft glow over the room. A few serene landscape paintings adorned the pale blue walls, giving a touch of serenity to the somber atmosphere that weighed down the room.

The single bed caught my attention, with Ruby tucked under its crisp white sheets.

A quilted blanket covered her body, which seemed so much smaller than before.

The shimmer of her hair had dulled, and her skin was too pale. My chest throbbed as if her stolen magic longed to return.

This was all my fault.

I stepped closer, picking up Ruby's hand to squeeze it.

My fingertips tingled with magic, and I willed it to return to her, but it didn't respond.

On a nightstand beside the bed stood a vase of fresh flowers, but even their vibrant colors appeared muted.

Why hadn't I thought of bringing flowers? Something to say that I was sorry. That I hoped she could one day forgive me.

"Nyssa?" Jade said as she hurried through the door.

I managed a smile as the little shifter rushed over.

"Did you come to visit Ruby?"

"And you," I said, crouching down to her height. "Though I'm sorry, I didn't bring any treats today."

Lainie nodded before stepping outside, but I sensed her lurking nearby. I wasn't a fan of having the armed escort loom over me.

"How are you doing? I know this must be so hard for you."

Jade nodded. "She'll wake up soon. She promised to take me back to the coffee shop, and she never breaks her promises."

"Maybe I can have some treats delivered, then you can enjoy them with Ruby."

"I still want to visit. Do you think that barista with the beard would make me another special drink?"

"I'm sure he'd love to," I said with a smile.

Kain had found himself an admirer.

"Oh, I drew you a picture. I'll go get it!" Jade raced away, and the weighted silence returned.

The shifters would do everything in their power to heal Ruby, but with all the other attacks, they had their plates full. And Jade deserved her sister back.

Pushing myself upright, I pressed Ruby's hand against my chest, where her magic pulsed.

I let my eyes fall closed and sought the balance within me and stilled my mind.

Gathering up the lunar energies—both mine and Ruby's—I pushed them into the surrounding air, willing them back to her body where they belonged.

They swirled around me like a light breeze, but the stolen lunar energies refused to return to their owner. They clung to me like my vial of ooze and refused to detach.

Pain built in my skull, daggers pricking the back of my eyes as I pressed harder.

Hissing out a breath, I released the magic. The soft silver aura in the air faded and receded back into my skin.

My shoulders slumped.

I knew it had been a long shot, but I needed to try. I never wanted to steal her magic, but Carmen had cursed me into accepting it.

Would Ruby be able to wake up without her magic?

Placing her hand back down, I stepped away.

As much as I longed to fix my magic, it was never at the cost of someone else's.

"I'll find a way to heal you, Ruby. No matter what it takes. I'll undo what they took from you."

"I've got it!" Jade called out as she burst back into the room.

"Child," Lainie scolded. "What have I said about being loud?"

"I've got the drawing," Jade said in a quiet voice.

"Oh, this is lovely," I said, smiling down at the paper.

"This is me and Ruby. That's you," she said.

My drawing happened to have crazy pink hair. Close enough.

"And is this Kain?" I asked, pointing to a stick figure with a beard. Jade ducked her head.

"It's for you," Jade said. "Ruby said it would be a nice way to say thank you. I was going to bring it next time."

"I love it, thank you."

"Time to go," Lainie announced. "Your captain is waiting."

I nodded, not bothering to correct her. "I'll see you soon, Jade. Take care of your sister, okay?"

Jade nodded, waving goodbye as I followed Lainie out.

My heart broke a little more with every step, my control fraying at the edges.

I'd tried to give Ruby's magic back. I'd tried to drain it away. Both times, I'd failed.

There was only one thing left.

Do what Carmen had planned all along—absorb the magic.

If that was the only way to end this and stop her, then fine.

Ruby's sacrifice would not be for nothing.

Even if it meant I was the next one Carmen attacked.

CHAPTER THIRTY-FIVE

Long before the sun dipped below the horizon, I was already preparing ingredients for tonight's alchemy brews.

Danika watched me from her nest beneath my table as I rushed around, not willing to waste a minute of moonlight.

The MEA's extensive list was my top priority, along with more batches of potions I could keep on hand.

I couldn't work fast enough, as if I sensed a change in the atmosphere, the weight in the air that signaled a storm brewing.

Unable to prevent it, I would be prepared when it struck.

No "if" remained in my mind.

She would strike.

Carmen was driven by a strong conviction. She believed in what she was doing and in her own cause. I had to keep Carmen's attention fixed on me to avoid anyone else becoming entangled.

No more collateral damage for just being associated with me.

I debated all afternoon, but I couldn't settle for half measures.

Once the moon reached its zenith, I brewed another empowerment potion, splitting it in two again.

Carmen had used my last one against me; this time I would use them against her.

Astrid arrived deep in the twilight hours.

Her dark wings blended into the sky like a shadow against the stars, then drooped before she tucked them away. Her smile was strained as she settled into her usual spot.

Danika padded over to greet her and to get a head rub.

Sending another trickle of magic into the spell arrays, I stepped away from my two cauldrons.

With the full moon several days away, I pushed myself harder.

I didn't find it taxing to maintain both; it was as if I was barely skimming the surface of my power. It helped that I no longer had to monitor my magic for flares. Both solar and lunar magic seemed content when it came to brewing.

"I want to absorb the magic," I said, joining the others in our circle of cushions. "This afternoon I visited Ruby."

A heavy sigh escaped me. Her pale face still haunted me.

"I tried to return her magic, hoping she'd awaken, but it was like last night. Maybe there's another way, but I fear time is running out."

"I suspect you're right," Astrid said.

The last few nights had taken a toll on her, and I worried she wasn't sleeping enough. Her movements had slowed, as if burdened by the weight of the world.

"There's an unsettling quiet on the streets. The demonspawn and thrall sightings have reduced, but they're spread across the entire city. It's been impossible to keep up, even with wings."

"Can I help in any way?"

"I'd say you're already doing your part."

Astrid nodded at the cauldrons.

"Keeping the enforcers well stocked is more valuable than you realize. Their knowledge of the city and their squads has been invaluable. They're an asset to Arkirith. Without them, I doubt we would've kept the casualties to a minimum."

"Casualties?" People had been killed?

I should've known. I'd seen the enemy's destructive force and the deaths of those who'd been transformed into thralls.

"We do our best, but it's impossible to protect everyone from harm," Astrid said.

She clearly hated that reality as much as I did.

"Training your magic is a vital part of all of this. You must be prepared. We both know the warlock will come after you again."

I nodded. Her words reinforced my own thoughts.

"How has your training been going?" Astrid asked.

"My moonbeam is getting stronger, though I don't think it can do much besides offering light."

Every chance I had, I'd been practicing my spells with Danika monitoring my magic, and so far, I hadn't slipped up.

Nothing like in the alley or at the sports field.

"It takes time and the right mental force behind it. And the light still act as a deterrent to demonspawn, even if it doesn't harm them."

"I've had little luck apart from the astral shield."

As Astrid had suggested, I'd practiced during the daylight, like resistance training for lunar energies.

To challenge myself, I'd summoned shields of different sizes and moved around while actively casting.

"Better to master a single spell first, then learn new ones," Astrid said. "I can test your spells afterwards if you would like. But we should prioritize absorbing the magic first."

I nodded, excitement and trepidation twisting in my stomach as I focused on finishing my potions. I didn't want to split my concentration, especially if Carmen had left any traps or triggers hidden within her spell.

Wiping my forehead, I sat back down as my heart raced.

"Do you still have a fever?" Astrid asked.

"It never subsided."

To other races that'd be worrisome, but to a witch they were merely annoyances, similar to headaches.

"Fevers are common with witches. It means there's an imbalance in our magic."

"Hmm," was all Astrid said.

It was easy to fall into a state of meditation, quieting my mind and focusing on my body in the present moment.

Astrid placed her hands on mine. Her touch provided a comforting warmth.

A tingle brushed over our joined hands as a vibration shivered through my arms and filled my body.

I followed the tingle as it moved; my magic swirled around it, and it responded in kind. Astrid's magic.

My own powers recognized it before I did, like calling to like.

I wasn't alone anymore.

Singled out for having wild magic, it had been lonely growing up. It was isolating, knowing every witch around me couldn't understand what I was going through.

But now, I knew the truth in my blood.

I might be the only lunar witch left, but all moon-blessed were my kin in magic. They would guide me forward.

Astrid's magic fluttered against the stolen energies.

Heat flared in my chest like a barrier protecting me from harm.

My temples throbbed as I tried to stabilize my mind, but flames licked over my skin and sweat prickled on my forehead.

"It's the solar magic again, isn't it?" I said, when Astrid broke the connection.

Who knew such a small amount of magic would cause me so many issues?

"Yes, but it's trying to protect you," Astrid said with a crooked smile. "I believe it's also causing the fever. Your solar magic is acting like a defense system to protect you from the foreign magic, which isn't a bad thing. However, I agree that the only solution is to absorb the magic."

"How do we get past it, then? It clearly doesn't want to listen to me."

"Let's test the runed band and see if it suffices. But even then, it will probably fight you once you start to absorb it."

"I might need this as a tattoo," I said, gathering the supplies.

Astrid chuckled. "I'm hoping with more training you'll gain control over both, but we'll keep it as a backup plan."

We settled into the next meditation ritual, Astrid guiding me. Her soothing voice led me through the steps, offering me strength and putting me at ease.

This time, all it took was a simple thought, and my solar magic raced to fill my rune with its power.

"Just as with your alchemy," Astrid said, "keep feeding that magic into the rune. Don't give it a chance to escape."

I nodded, twisting and weaving my solar magic into an endless loop.

"Focus on the ebb and flow of both the lunar energies. See if you can align them and draw in the magic."

I lost track of time as I turned all my focus inward, sensing every detail in the sway and movement of my power.

The magic fire was warm and comforting, at least when it didn't want to consume me. It danced through my runed band, its movements mesmerizing.

But the lunar energies were at my core, what resonated so deeply with my soul.

They'd always been there, under the surface, waiting to be awoken.

But now, as I flowed with their soft rhythm, I sensed the power everywhere.

Rippling like a slow tide through my body, it was only when I dimmed the bright solar energies that I sensed their power and beauty. Like turning off a bright light and watching the stars spring to life in the velvet sky above.

My awareness brushed against the foreign lunar magic, listening to its thrum until my own energies pulsed in time with it.

I pressed again, and this time, the barrier that separated the lunar energies parted, allowing me access.

My solar magic stirred, flaring brighter in my hand, but I clamped down on it. Still, it tried to fight back.

When I released the lunar magic, the flames settled. I'd been doing this all wrong. I was trying to control the fire, to suppress it, but that only made it aggressive.

This drop of solar magic was part of me. I couldn't hide it away.

No, I needed to give it a purpose.

I needed to demonstrate that it also had a place in me.

Heat pooled in my hand as I summoned a flame.

In my mind's eye, I watched it flicker and dance.

Heat, light, warmth. Purpose.

Then I returned my focus to the lunar power.

Opening myself, I welcomed the foreign lunar energies.

My magic shivered over the surface. Then I allowed the foreign magic to join with it, to enter my heart and become united with us.

This new ethereal power flowed like a soothing river that burbled through me.

Unlike my wild flames, this magic was a subtle, constant presence that seeped into my soul. Whispering like an evening breeze, it pulsed with the flow of the tides.

Deeper, I sensed the quiet yearning of the stars themselves.

My breath caught, and for a moment I teetered, filled to the brim with the divine magic of Selene.

It was as if the universe whispered its secrets to my soul, as if I hung between the stars as the celestial bodies danced through the heavens.

Air rushed out as the universe slipped from my grasp, and I became myself once more.

Just Nyssa.

"How do you feel?" Astrid asked when I opened my eyes. A look of wonder shone in her gaze.

"I don't know."

Dizzy but energized. Wonky yet centered.

None of that made sense.

I tugged my shirt collar down; the white lines had vanished, leaving no trace of the mark.

"Good, I think."

Astrid flashed me a bright smile. "The energies feel steady to me. I think you should eat and get some rest. I'll stay for a bit to ensure there are no side effects or other surprises."

"Thank you for everything." I wrapped my arms around the nephilim and squeezed. "This wouldn't have been possible without your help. Or you, Danika."

My familiar butted her head against me, and I chuckled.

My life had changed so much since I arrived in Arkirith, and in ways I never would have imagined. And I couldn't imagine it any differently.

Now, I had a warlock to stop.

Chapter Thirty-Six

The air vibrated with familiar magic as jars and spices levitated from shelves before portioning themselves into the awaiting bowls. I grinned as I fastened my apron.

"You're eager today," I said to Divine.

Over the few weeks I'd been here, Divine had begun using more magic in my presence, which I hoped meant they were comfortable around me.

"I need all the help you can give me. I've been training with my magic all night, and I'm exhausted."

After absorbing the stolen lunar energies, I'd trained hard with Astrid. My solar magic hadn't flared up since I'd used the runed band, though it still grumbled when I summoned my lunar magic.

Though my success felt hollow because we hadn't found any leads on Carmen or the demonspawn.

My third batch of cookies was baking in the oven when the front door chimed, signaling the arrival of the first shift.

"Morning, Zola," I said, but my smile faded as I took in the dryad.

Her usual bright green hair was dull and motionless, and dark smudges shadowed her eyes.

"What's wrong?" I rushed over. I'd never seen her looking anything less than vibrant.

She shook her head, tears glistening in her eyes.

"Sorry," she mumbled, swiping at the unshed tears. "I went to visit Thayna yesterday."

"How is she recovering?"

"Slow. It was hard to see her like that," Zola sighed. "I don't know what they did to her, but she's only a shadow of her former self. And Quinn is still unconscious. But worse is that her partner, Dira, is still missing. No one knows where she is."

"Is Dira a druid too?" I asked.

"No, she's an oracle. Well, former oracle. Leaving her life as a priestess of Selene, she came to live with Quinn."

A heavy stone dropped in my stomach.

There could be no doubt about who had taken Dira.

No one with lunar magic was safe in Arkirith, not while Carmen and her demonspawn stalked the streets.

"I need to get started on opening," Zola said.

I wrapped her in a hug.

Had the warlock been hunting for my magic and settled for the others because I couldn't access it yet?

"I'm sorry," I whispered before releasing her.

Zola offered me a small smile of thanks. "Is Voren here yet?"

"No. He didn't come with you?" They worked the same morning shift and typically walked together.

Zola shook her head. "He had a date and left before I returned from visiting Thayna. He wasn't in his room when I woke up. I assumed he stayed elsewhere."

My insides turned to lead.

Date.

I fumbled for my phone. Voren was only a couple minutes late, but it was unlike him. I bit down on my lip as worry wormed its way through me, then I hit dial and put it on speaker.

"Nyssa?" a groggy Rynac answered.

"Is Voren with you?" I blurted with little tact.

"No, why?"

"When did you last see him?"

"Around eleven. I walked him back to his place and headed out on patrol. What happened?"

My gaze lifted to Zola.

"I was asleep by then," she said.

"Could he have headed back out after?" I asked.

"I don't know," Zola whispered, her hands clasped against her chest.

"Get Beylin," I said to Zola.

I didn't care if I was overreacting. Something in my gut told me to fear the worst.

"Heading to their apartment right now," Rynac said.

His voice sounded muffled, and I guessed he was throwing clothes on. I tucked my phone away and paced to the front door, scanning the street for Voren.

Restless energy surged through me. I needed to move, to act, to do something, anything but wait. The chairs and tables rattled, and I realized Divine was as worried as me.

"Don't worry, I'll find him no matter what."

Beylin, Zola, and I rushed up the stairs of the apartment building ten minutes later. Kain remained to watch over Divine in case Voren appeared.

Rynac paced the narrow corridor, his hands clenched into fists at his side. He offered a tight nod of greeting to the others, but I gripped his hands until he relaxed them.

"Is this because of me?" he asked in a low voice.

"No," I said. "I think it's because of me."

Rynac hissed out a breath and wrapped me in a fierce hug. "We will fix this."

I clung to Rynac and his determination, wishing it would be true.

"Don't touch anything," Beylin warned as we stepped into the apartment.

He waved a small device through the air as the rest of us gathered behind him. But my attention was on how beautiful their home was.

It was an extraordinary fusion of natural beauty and otherworldly aesthetics.

The morning sun filtered through the gossamer curtains, bathing the plethora of plants in warmth.

Vines twisted up the walls as if the apartment were alive. The furniture blended natural wood with plush, dark velvet upholstery.

A gorgeous hardwood dining table dominated one side of the room. A dryad's ownership of such things may have seemed odd, but their understanding of the cycle of life surpassed all other races.

We all served our purpose.

When our bodies died, we returned to the soil, providing for the next generation.

It made sense, but seemed morbid if I dwelled on it for too long.

"Not picking up anything here," Beylin said. "Be vigilant for anything unusual. Which bedroom is his?"

Zola pointed to the far end of the hall. I tapped into my magic, letting its calming pulse settle my nerves.

Beylin opened the door, and a faint hint of magic tickled my awareness. If I hadn't been searching for it, I would've missed it.

"I sense something," I whispered, my eyes roaming over Voren's bedroom.

The room was a captivating embodiment of darkness and intrigue, a stark contrast to the rest of the apartment's natural charm.

"It's weak, but this magic isn't Voren's," Beylin replied. "Tread carefully."

Entering his room felt like stepping into a realm where shadows held dominion.

The air carried a subtle, smoky scent, and a massive four-poster bed dominated the space, looming like an obsidian throne.

Covered in rich shades of crimson and onyx, it felt as if I were intruding on a personal sanctuary. This was Voren's private space, and here I was poking around.

Weak magic prickled over my skin, but I couldn't pinpoint its location.

"Here," Zola said, pointing to something on Voren's bed.

Nestled on a pillow was Voren's earring.

The silver hook glistened in the sunlight while the delicate black raven feather devoured the light.

"Why would it be here?"

"It was deliberate," Rynac said, the muscle in his jaw ticking. "I'm sure they left it for us to find."

"There's magic on it," Beylin said, moving his device closer. "It could be a trap."

I rifled through my bag, vials and jars clinking together.

"I have a brew that can help me detect traces of magic," I said. "Unless anyone has a better idea."

The others remained silent, so I downed the potion.

It fizzled over my tongue like the faint memory of soda.

Magic surged within me, and I wobbled on my feet.

Faint shimmering lines crisscrossed the room, revealing traces of magic, but I couldn't figure out what they meant.

I tilted my head, and the room swam, but nothing changed.

My gaze snagged on the earring, power glowing within it. I reached for it; deep in my bones, I knew it was the missing piece that would bring everything together.

"Nyssa," Beylin warned.

"I know. Terrible idea." My head was spinning from this magic, but I had to try. "Get everyone out of the room. I know this will trigger something."

Beylin swore, but he ushered Rynac and Zola into the hall.

I reached for the earring, my fingers trembling even before they brushed against the metal.

Dark magic jolted through my arm, conjuring phantom pains from Carmen's last assault.

The room shifted, coated in a ghostly silver light.

My head snapped up at the sound of the door.

The others were barely visible as the silver ghost door opened and Voren's wispy shadow appeared.

My breath rushed out.

"What do you see?" Rynac asked.

"A memory, I think," I said, padding over to the glowing form of Voren. No, that wasn't right. "It's an echo of the magic here."

Echo-Voren closed the door, slumping against it with a smile. His fingers traced over his lips, his grin growing larger.

With a shake of his head, he pushed himself away from the door and unbuttoned his shirt, then stopped dead.

His gaze locked onto something across the room. I moved behind him, but he appeared to be staring out the window.

Voren whirled around, his eyes wide as if he could see me.

A silver claw shot through my body, and I jerked back as it gripped his throat.

"What is it?" Rynac demanded, but my lips refused to form words.

A massive demonspawn lifted Voren off his feet.

Its growl reverberated in my chest.

Voren gripped the claw as if he could pry it off.

His panic pulsed in my chest as if I were the one dangling mid-air.

"Now, now. I do want him whole," Carmen's voice echoed through the air, sending a shudder down my spine.

Her silver form stepped forward as she eyed Voren as if he were a delectable treat to be gobbled up.

The demonspawn lowered him to the ground, and Voren struggled to free himself.

"What do you want?" Voren hissed.

Carmen prowled closer, lifting her hand toward him, but he recoiled.

"If you comply, this will hurt far less," she said.

Her grin widened, delight sparkling in her dark gaze.

"But I do enjoy it when they scream." She ran her nail down Voren's face. *"Which shall it be?"*

He remained silent, his lip curling into a snarl.

She shrugged, and the demonspawn slammed Voren into the ground as if he weighed nothing.

One claw still wrapped around his throat, the other pinning his body down.

Carmen reached for the earring, her fingers wrapping around it while her other hand covered his mouth.

Dark magic rippled from her, pouring into Voren. Her hand muf-fled his scream as he thrashed. But he had nowhere to go.

The magic ebbed and Voren went slack.

She pulled out the earring, setting it on the pillow like a trophy.

The demonspawn lifted Voren and disappeared.

"If you care about him," Carmen said. *"You'd better track him down."*

I shuddered, knowing she was talking to me. She had planned all of this.

"That is, if you wish to see him in one piece. Take too long, and I'll feed him to my pets. See you soon."

The echo of Carmen faded. I squeezed my eyes closed, willing the rest of the ghostly scene to disappear.

My chest throbbed; my breath coming too fast.

"Easy," Beylin said in a soothing voice as he rushed over.

He gripped my arms to keep me steady, then guided me out of Voren's bedroom. I slumped onto the couch, trying to gather my scattered thoughts.

Rynac brought over a steaming mug of tea while Beylin talked to Zola.

"He wants her to stay with friends until we can sort this out," Rynac explained. "The warlock took him, didn't she?"

I nodded.

"Figured as much." Rynac wrapped an arm around me, and I leaned into the embrace.

Beylin joined us as Zola disappeared into her room to pack. It was better that she didn't hear what I saw, especially since it happened while she was asleep in the next room.

I recounted what the spell had shown me, down to the smallest detail.

We fell into a silence, my thumb rubbing over the earring.

"We'll get him back," Rynac said, squeezing my hand.

"I don't know how. How am I supposed to track him?"

"There are numerous tracking spells," Beylin said. "We possess an item linked to our target. We just need the right spell. May I?"

He extended his hand, and I placed the earring in it.

Laying it on the table, Beylin muttered something, his hands weaving magic over it. He shook his head, then tried again.

The dwarf attempted several tracking spells, but there was no response.

"If he's being kept at a warded location, it'd block these spells," Beylin said as he glared down at the earring.

"What else did the warlock say? Maybe there's a clue we missed," Rynac asked.

"She's after me. It has to be a spell I can cast," I said, chewing on my lip. "Oh."

Dread sank like a heavy stone in my stomach.

"What is it?"

I shook my head.

Carmen knew who I was and appeared to know my history. She knew about the incident at the sacred lake.

"Divination. Powerful enough, it might bypass the wards."

"Can you cast that?" Beylin asked, and I nodded weakly.

Did I want to? Hell no. Would I if it meant saving Voren's life? What other choice did I have?

Carmen's trap tightened around me. I'd face all the demons of my past if it kept my friends safe.

"We are going to need Zola's help."

CHAPTER THIRTY-SEVEN

Sunset burned along the horizon as I stood on Divine's rooftop, the city below twinkling to life. Yet I felt untethered, like one wrong breath would send me drifting off the edge.

Leaves rustled in the rooftop garden, a tranquil sound that didn't match the storm tightening in my chest.

Ivy climbed up trellises that arched overhead, casting intricate shadows on the ground.

I paced along a winding path, the soft crunch of gravel underfoot. Potted roses, their petals a deep crimson, spilled over the edges of decorative urns.

But nothing could soothe the fear churning in my gut.

My worry about Voren and fear of divination clung to me like bloodsucking leeches.

I'd messaged Astrid earlier but hadn't heard anything from the nephilim.

Rynac and Beylin emerged from the side door, followed by Zola, who carried a carved ceramic pot.

When I asked her for sacred water, she was happy to assist.

The only blessed lakes I knew of were hours away. But nymphs resided near sacred water—not that they would ever explain why—and offered small amounts to outsiders, typically for healing.

Though I'd spent the rest of the day searching my grimoire and *The Lunar Codex* about everything related to divination, I was woefully unprepared.

To perform the ritual, I only needed moonlight and sacred water.

Though I collected a few extra reagents anyway, desperate for this to succeed.

Beylin motioned for us to follow, leading us out into an open area.

Stepping stones wove a path through the meticulously raked gravel.

The others were silent as I set to work, likely consumed by their own turbulent thoughts.

Everything was riding on this spell.

Danika brushed against my leg as if she sensed my fear. I rubbed her ear, thankful for her unshakable faith in me.

Selecting the largest rock, I poured out a circle of crushed moonstone for insight and stability.

At the center, I positioned a pewter bowl, swirling runes engraved on its rim to aid in gathering and containing magic.

Beside it, I placed an eagle feather for clear vision, and a vial of lunar dew for increased perception.

By the time I set it up, the moon had graced us with her presence.

Zola offered me the pot in her arms, which contained the last ingredient—sacred water.

The liquid glistened under the moonlight as it cascaded into the bowl.

Magic saturated the air.

The water's aura thrummed with vast potential.

My memory of the sacred lake was hazy, but the sheer power exuded by the water was undeniable.

Stepping into the circle, I sat before the bowl as fear clawed its way up my throat.

What would I see this time?

I silenced all my thoughts and fears. I'd face the fire again if it showed me where Voren was.

Last, I pulled out his earring and dropped it into the water.

Closing my eyes, I drew in a deep breath, pushing all thoughts from my mind and allowing the crisp air to wash everything away.

Just like when I meditated with Astrid, I found that calm deep within my chest. I brushed against my magic, allowing it to course through my veins until I was brimming with power.

With a gentle nudge, the magic flowed through my hands and into the bowl.

Keeping my eyes shut, I summoned the echoes I'd seen in Voren's room and held an image of his face clear in my mind.

Letting a wisp of magic coat my tongue, I recited a chant.

"Under your moonlight, I ask for a blessing. By your divine grace, we bask in your glory. In these sacred waters, reveal to us that which we seek. Show us that which was stolen. Guide us to recover, our treasured friend."

Magic hummed, brushing against my skin as if it danced through the air.

I repeated the chant, opening my eyes for the first time.

My voice wavered, struck by my surroundings, and the magic wobbled. I pressed on, trying to regain my flow.

The magic balanced out, but it was nearly impossible to drag my eyes from the rippling colors.

Shimmering hues of green, pink, and purple swirled and twisted in a dome above me. Like ribbons of celestial light that shivered under the moonlight, the colors shifted and merged in a mesmerizing display.

The magical light called to me, awakening a deep ache in my chest, as if a part of me was missing and it was the last piece.

An opalescent glow coated my skin.

Tiny flares curled up as if longing to join the magic above.

I tore my gaze away and fixed it on the sacred water.

The last words of my chant spilled from my lips and buzzed through the air.

Magic prickled the nape of my neck. A weight settled on it as if a hand rested there.

Power blazed into my eyes, and I blinked as my vision swam.

The weight on my neck increased as if a hand guided me closer to the sacred water.

I resisted for a moment, memories of drowning flooding my thoughts, but I shoved them aside and leaned over the bowl.

Although there was no breeze, the water rippled, distorting my reflection.

The moon shone into the water; the distortion causing my own eyes to blaze with its silver light.

The water settled, and I strained to glimpse the image it now reflected.

A dark room. Underground. Thick concrete.

I didn't understand how I knew these things, but I opened myself to anything the water offered.

Lights flickered on. Voren's body lay on plain concrete, other people surrounding him.

All were unconscious. Shifters. Oracle. Moon-touched.

The information filled my thoughts as if the Goddess herself whispered in my ear.

Golden runes flickered on the walls, shielding them from tracking magic. But my divination slipped through. Or had Carmen left that loophole on purpose?

Darkness crept in.

The image began to fade.

But I needed more information to locate them.

I pressed myself harder, channeling more magic into the bowl.

Show me more.

The image disappeared, leaving only clear water.

No.

I thrust my magic into the water; twin daggers jabbed into the back of my eyes, but I didn't stop.

Heat scorched the nape of my neck, as if a red-hot iron brand pressed against my skin.

I needed more.

Where are they?

I had to find them.

An unsettling sensation crept over me, as if incorporeal hands were inside my chest, weaving magic through me.

The air rushed out of my lungs; something squeezed me tight before it released.

My magic faltered, and the spell slipped from my grasp.

I shuddered. Taking a deep breath, I blinked at my surroundings.

Color vanished with the magic, leaving only the blacks and grays of the world.

My heart ached for the vibrant dance of colors. The world appeared dimmer without them.

"Nyssa?" Rynac said, taking a tentative step toward me. "Did you find him? Did it work?"

Denial was on the tip of my tongue.

Then something shifted inside me.

A soft thrum pulsed in my chest, in time with each beat of my heart.

No, that wasn't right.

That wasn't my heartbeat.

Though my brain reeled at the loss of magic, I summoned the last of my focus and the dregs of my power.

There!

A silver thread shimmered in the air, starting in my chest and then leading away.

I lifted my hand, and my fingers passed through it, but when I touched it, I could feel that pulse—it called to me, tugging me.

A phantom heart beating in time with my own. I pressed a hand against that pulse.

Nyssa. A voice whispered in response.

Voren's voice.

Chapter Thirty-Eight

By the next morning, sweat was trickling down my spine, and it wasn't from the brutal sun overhead. I shut my eyes and chased the faint, incorporeal tug in my chest, willing it to pull harder.

An hour of aimless wandering later, it was still no more than a whisper.

"It's still pulling north," I grumbled.

"Then we keep going north," Rynac said.

But how much farther north could we go before we left the city?

I squashed the doubt that flickered in my chest, the fear that they were keeping the captives somewhere outside of Arkirith.

"Do you need a break?" Lainie asked as she materialized beside me.

After I'd relayed everything I'd seen, Beylin had forced me to rest while the others prepared.

Rynac contacted his captain, who was assembling a team for when we discovered the location.

But—unbeknownst to me—he'd also contacted the shifter pack. They'd agreed to offer support if it meant recovering their missing people and sent a group to help scout and offer protection.

And so here we were, the start of a bad joke: a witch and an enhanced, with shifter bodyguards searching for an erebian.

Lainie scanned our surroundings as if she expected danger around every corner.

While her sword and daggers were missing, I doubted she'd come unarmed.

What was more surprising was that she hadn't even complained about her assignment, and she'd almost been nice.

"No, I don't have time for a break," I grunted.

Rest was impossible, I was the sole person capable of locating Voren and the others. If I could even do that.

And where were the angel-born? The one time I wanted them around, but neither Beylin nor I could reach them.

Lainie's gaze swept over me, but she nodded.

Not for the first time, I wished for a stronger connection to guide us. But no, I only had these tiny tugs that demanded greater concentration with each passing minute.

I set off down the street before anyone noticed my flagging energy.

This area lay on the edge of the industrial district.

Investors had converted the ground floor of old warehouses into trendy restaurants with apartments on the second level.

It seemed at odds with the practical buildings a few blocks ahead. But the need for housing pushed developers to be creative.

I allowed myself only a few wistful glances through the large windows into the cool interior.

Exposed beams and hanging lights maintained the industrial feel, while the area below had been transformed into a chic, modern restaurant.

"Give me a minute," Lainie said, not waiting for my response before she stepped inside a juice bar.

Not that I'd argue with the shifter.

Rynac took up position beside me, his face composed, but tension rippled beneath the surface.

Leaning against the light pole, I reached out to that connection again, but it felt the same as before.

While we waited, I played find-the-shifter.

Since they'd joined us, I'd only caught fleeting glimpses of the six shifters that accompanied us.

Even though I knew what they looked like, I struggled to spot them. How did they blend in so well?

"Here," Lainie said, holding out two cups of an orange concoction.

"Thanks," I said.

Enjoying the tropical flavors, I paused to savor the drink before I re-centered my focus.

"It's delightful."

Lainie sipped her own white blend as we started off again, but didn't hide her smirk.

A twang vibrated in my chest, and I stumbled to a stop.

I rubbed a hand against it. Had that been real, or had I imagined it?

"Sense something?" Lainie said in a low voice, stepping closer as if she feared I might topple over.

"Yes."

My voice trailed off as a softer vibration resonated in my chest, the tug more demanding. It felt like the connection had been asleep and had now awoken.

"It's stronger. I don't know how long this will last."

We hurried along. I didn't have to focus as hard on the connection, almost like it wanted me to reach my target.

"Do you think they have some sort of shielding or suppression magic?" I asked, wincing when I gave myself a brain freeze.

It wouldn't look very professional to be holding juice while infiltrating a warlock's lair, and I wouldn't waste it.

"It's highly probable. All our attempts to locate our missing pack members came up with nothing."

We wove through the streets, Rynac alert, Lainie watchful, and me looking weird, turning my chest in every direction, like I was an antenna trying to get a signal.

The scent of oil and machinery permeated the air. Smokestacks and chimneys punctuated the skyline, releasing intermittent puffs of thick, dark smoke that painted the air with a subtle haze.

The acrid stench made me miss the fancy renovated area, but at least I didn't have a shifter's sense of smell.

The streets were wide and deserted, except for an occasional delivery truck or forklift trundling along. We stuck out like sore thumbs; the drivers gave us curious glances as they went by.

With each block we passed, the connection grew stronger until it buzzed in my chest.

The warehouses here appeared long abandoned, the few unbroken windows yellow with age and coated in grime.

This place was creepy even in daylight.

My steps slowed as we passed a set of arched warehouses. Their cold, metallic exteriors showed the wear and tear of time, adorned with streaks of rust and patches of peeling paint.

The tug shifted as we passed, but I didn't pause, fearing someone might be watching us.

When we were out of sight, I slipped down an access road.

"They're in the third warehouse back," I whispered.

"You're sure?" Lainie blinked at me. "I didn't sense anything."

"My connection shifted right as we walked by it," I said.

Lainie considered the surrounding buildings. "Let's loop around the other side to double-check."

My stomach knotted as we headed off, avoiding thoughts of what this meant.

It was impossible not to stare at the metal monstrosity, to search for some confirmation that I wasn't crazy.

"No windows, concrete foundation," I said under my breath.

Rynac gave a slight dip of his chin, but otherwise appeared calm and collected.

As we walked closer, I could sense the underlying tension rippling off him. I hoped I was right about this.

Electricity jolted through me.

My heart beat faster the closer we walked.

Please. Please be here.

The warehouse loomed over us, blocking out the sun, and a shiver ran down my spine.

A rusting chain-link fence enclosed the area, but the padlock on the gate looked new. That might not mean anything. The owner could have just replaced it.

Passing the midpoint, my stomach clenched, sweat prickling on my forehead as I concentrated on the pull.

There.

It shifted again, pulling down slightly toward the structure's center. With a subtle gesture, I tapped Lainie's hand to mark the location.

My heart thumped against my ribs.

He was here.

My skin crawled as if we were being watched.

I couldn't shake the sensation even as excitement bubbled up.

After we put three blocks between us and the warehouse, we stopped and Lainie signaled someone.

A shifter that had been trailing us appeared. I scratched the back of my neck as Lainie described the warehouse to them.

With a nod, they vanished the same way they had come.

"What now?" I asked.

"We stake out the area," Rynac said, and Lainie nodded.

I suppressed a smile at seeing firsthand the shifters and MEA working together.

"While I'd prefer daytime, when the demonspawn are weak," Lainie said, "night will allow us to get closer before alerting them to our presence."

"Until then," Rynac said and hailed a taxi for us. Lainie disappeared as I slid inside.

"Am I going to be able to persuade you to stay home tonight?" he asked, taking a seat beside me.

I shot him a hard look.

"Yeah, I didn't think so. But it was worth a try."

I huffed. "I thought I'd proved myself already."

"You have." He scrubbed a hand over his face. His shoulders sagged. "But I still want to keep you safe."

Taking his hand, I rested my head on his shoulder.

I didn't know if I deserved such friends, but I wouldn't have made it without their support.

I should've been terrified about tonight and exhausted after expending so much magic.

Yet I felt energized in other ways.

The thought of freeing captives and guarding the city took the edge off my worry.

My true magic was awake now, and I finally had a chance to use it for more than careful brews and healing tinctures.

For the first time, it felt like who I was and what I could do actually aligned . . . and made a difference.

Chapter Thirty-Nine

Each step up the MEA headquarters stairs thudded in time with my racing heart. I'd left Danika behind, and the absence of her warm weight at my side felt wrong.

I hated to leave her behind, but we both agreed it would be risky, unless I wanted to explain to everyone that she was my familiar.

With so many enforcers taking part in tonight's raid, she also wanted to be ready in case the warlock struck elsewhere. She was staying with Beylin at Divine, and I already missed her presence.

Lugging a bag crammed with as many potions as I could fit, I waved to the siblings. We headed into a private room to prepare.

Sharp tension filled the air as we moved through the building.

This was the largest assault the enforcers had ever undertaken.

"This question might surprise you," I said, once the door closed, "but how does one dress for a secret assault?"

Indra laughed. "Don't worry, I'm one step ahead of you. Keep the boots, but ditch the rest."

I'd picked a pair of durable jeans and a tee, attempting to be practical. She laid out black utility pants and MEA shirts of various sizes, along with a thick jacket. After I changed, she handed me a special-looking belt.

"What's this?" I asked.

"Something we commissioned for you," Indra said. "To say thank you. The enforcers have their own belts for weapons, but yours has smaller spaces—perfect for your potions—and even a spot for your conduit."

"You had this made for me?"

I don't know why, but my breath caught when I saw it. It was practical, thoughtful, and customized for me.

Why did it mean so much?

Dear Goddess, why are my eyes prickling?

"You need something better than that bag when we get into a fight," Indra said, either unaware or pretending not to notice my rollercoaster of emotions.

She guided me to a seat, then braided my hair while Rynac went over tonight's details.

My role, besides searching for magic, was to stay behind everyone else and not do anything dangerous. I could manage that.

The only reason the captain hadn't flat-out refused my involvement was that they needed people who were sensitive to magic.

The more people watching for magical traps, the safer tonight would go.

"Have you heard from the shifters?" I asked.

Going up against demonspawn, I wanted as much backup as possible. The angel-born had not contacted me either. I didn't know if I should be worried.

"They'll be meeting us there," Indra assured me.

I couldn't help looking myself over in the mirror one last time. Black clothes, hair tied back, and the array of potions tucked into my new belt. I looked ready to kick some butt.

Not that I could, but it was fun to pretend.

"Are you ready?" Rynac asked.

Ready to walk into a lair filled with demonspawn and feeling wholly unprepared?

Despite everything, I smiled.

"At least you haven't asked if I'm sure about this. Let's go."

I almost blended in with the enforcers surrounding me, our dark clothes helping us disappear into the shadows.

My fingers trailed over the potions on my new belt. I hoped I wouldn't need them, but having them nearby brought me a sense of comfort.

Waiting was the worst part.

Adrenaline and anxiety coursed through me with no outlet as we waited for the signal to breach the warehouse.

Minutes stretched into hours, and it seemed like half the night we stood there waiting.

I rolled my night vision enhancement potion between my fingers, ready to drink it at a moment's notice.

Maybe I shouldn't have insisted on coming along.

But as the first team approached the warehouse, all my senses sharpened.

Magic twisted in my chest, urging me forward.

Moving with the precision of a well-oiled machine, the first team breached the warehouse.

They poured inside as if they were connected, everyone in sync.

When the last one disappeared through the door, I held my breath.

Rynac had explained that they would sweep the ground level before signalling our group to move in as the second wave.

Only when the whole area was secured would the last team of healers enter.

Shifters monitored the area, positioned to alert us to any movement.

If demonspawn converged on us, we'd have a warning. But so far, there'd been no signs of activity.

Two more teams of shifters stood with the enforcers, ready to breach the building in the second wave. Like the enforcers, they carried weapons, and when I'd asked earlier, Lainie said that transforming required a large amount of magic.

Unless their animal form was needed, they would remain unchanged.

Indra gave me a nod. Our turn.

My group emerged from the shadows, slipping through the breached chain-link fence.

When we stepped inside the warehouse, only looming shadows greeted us. Even with enhanced night vision, I struggled to see much beyond the glow of our lights.

The first team held position ahead at a doorway that led below, weapons at the ready.

I swept the area with my awareness but didn't sense any foreign magic.

My group fell into a defensive formation and joined the first wave. There was nowhere to go but down.

The two enforcer teams communicated with each other with hand signals I didn't understand, but it was clear they were ready.

Weapons drawn, the first team opened the door, and the second descended.

A few seconds later, the rest of us followed.

Our footsteps echoed off the concrete; the corridor was almost twenty feet across, but even the faintest sound bounced off the empty walls.

My nerves prickled more than on the upper floor.

With military precision, the scouts checked each room.

My eyes remained fixed on the far end, where my magic was pulling me; but we had to sweep every room first.

The air was filled with a constant hum of power from the magic users around me, but beyond that, nothing stood out.

Empty rooms greeted us, containing only a few dilapidated machines and broken crates.

My stomach churned, twisting more with every vacant room. What if I were wrong and nobody was here?

Rynac, never more than half a step away, nodded for me to follow him toward the front.

Reaching out with my awareness, my hand hovered a breath from the door. But I sensed nothing beyond it but a void.

My heart faltered.

I couldn't pick up the thrum from my connection to Voren.

With a single nod to Rynac, I stepped to the side. I prayed there were no hidden magical traps.

Everyone shifted into position, and the seconds dragged on.

It was too quiet.

The slightest rustle of fabric, even the sound of my heartbeat, was deafening in my ears.

I held my breath as an enforcer swung the last door open.

We had found them.

The captives lay sprawled on the ground, motionless. Were they asleep? No, they were too still for sleep.

I squinted into the darkness, waiting for my eyes to adjust.

My heart lodged in my throat when my eyes found Voren's form.

Oh, Goddess.

All I wanted was to rush to him and ensure he was breathing, but I had to wait.

Why are they alone? Where are the guards? The thoughts rattled through my head.

My magic still couldn't sense the captives.

This was wrong. They were literally right there.

As I scanned the walls, a heavy weight pressed against my chest. A shimmer of gold caught my eye, a rune to ward against basic location spells.

But that was it.

Every one of my senses screamed that this was wrong.

I needed more light. The enforcers retreated to give me room as soon as they confirmed the area was clear of physical threats.

I grabbed my glow vial from my belt and shook it vigorously until it activated. The soft green glow grew brighter, and I shone it toward the captives while still not passing the threshold.

"It's clear," one of the magical enforcers called.

I shook my head.

"What is it?" Rynac whispered.

"I don't know." I frowned, my eyebrows furrowing as I squinted into the shadows.

Soft footfalls behind us signaled that the medical extraction team had arrived, and I shifted to allow them through.

The shadows flickered, and I saw it.

A rune scrawled in black. Hidden in the shadows.

"Wait!" I called, reaching for the first of the medical team.

But their foot had passed over the threshold, and magic snapped. Like a chain reaction, spells crackled to life, one surge after another.

Too fast to track, it rippled past us back the way we had come.

Growls echoed around us. The nearest door was ripped off its hinges, revealing demonspawn in one of the rooms we had just cleared.

Enforcers freed their weapons. Shifters transformed into wolves.

And I could only stare at the massive beasts, which were double the size of an actual wolf.

Their fur shimmered with drops of moonlight, mirroring the exact shade of their hair before the change.

"Get to the captives!" Indra barked.

The enforcers and shifters formed a shield around the medical team. Indra's voice snapped me out of it.

Duty called.

Leading the medical team, I rushed into the room, sweeping my magic to probe for any remaining traps.

"It's clear as far as I can tell," I called out, "but move with caution and watch for any runes."

They stepped inside as I rushed over to Voren and pressed a hand against his neck.

A flicker of magic still pulsed through his body, yet his skin and hair were dull. Was this a result of being held captive, or had they done something to him?

I shook his shoulders, then rubbed his sternum with my knuckles like the healers had shown me, but he didn't wake up.

Dried blood coated his ear where Carmen had yanked out his earring.

My blood boiled.

She had hurt Voren to get to me.

Shouts from the enforcers rang out, and my head snapped up.

The breath rushed out of me. Demonspawn flooded the area, attacking from all sides.

The enforcers fought back, firing their guns at the enemy, as shifters tore apart any that strayed too close.

They did their best to hold them back, but we were outnumbered.

"Something is keeping them under," Matti yelled over the fighting. "Move them closer to the walls so we can protect them."

Hooking my arms under Voren, I dragged him to the side. I just hoped we could protect them until the backup team arrived.

What was taking them so long?

Something scraped across my senses, sending a shudder down my spine.

Dark magic.

A bolt sizzled through the air, slamming into an enforcer. He screamed as green flames licked his body.

"Warlock!"

CHAPTER FORTY

I ce seized my lungs. Where was the warlock? I peered out the doorway, trying to make sense of the chaos of bodies.

The shifters and enforcers continued fighting, but they were losing ground, backing closer to the captives.

A demonspawn slipped through, but Rynac moved from his position guarding our door. He sliced through the creature with one powerful sweep of his sword.

If he used his gun, he'd risk injuring one of our people.

Swords and claws were far more effective at cutting down demonspawn, and I had neither.

A massive ball of green flames slammed into several fighters, engulfing them in infernal fire.

They'd all be slaughtered, and we would be next. Keeping low, I rushed to Rynac's side.

"How do you defeat a warlock?" I shouted over the fighting.

He shook his head, his eyes transfixed on the battle. "With an army of magic users."

"Can we alert the UMC?"

My gaze swept over the fighting, my focus narrowed on locating the warlock.

I needed to see her for myself.

"As soon as the demonspawn appeared, we sent a distress signal," Rynac said.

His white knuckles gripped the sword, as if it were the only thing keeping him from sprinting into the fight.

"But we won't last that long. Not against a warlock."

I had to do something. One warlock had already disrupted Rynac and Indra's lives, and now they had to confront another.

Before I could think, I raced forward.

My fingers skimmed across my potions, hunting for an idea. I wouldn't allow these enforcers and shifters to die right before my eyes.

Magic coursed through my veins. While I might not have learned full control, I had to try.

Solar magic pounded through me, longing to be used, but I channeled it into my runed band.

Surrounded by concrete, I longed for the light of the moon. I pictured its cool glow washing over me as it shone high in the inky black sky, like a beacon calling to the lost.

The magic in my chest swirled in response, then settled into my waiting hands.

Light pooled around me.

I tried to block out the snarls of the demonspawn; their gazes fixed on me the moment they sensed my magic.

I shoved my hands forward, willing a shield into existence.

Nothing happened. I pressed harder.

Magic crackled around my fingers as if it didn't understand my command.

"Come on," I hissed.

A headache built behind my eyes, a relentless pressure that only eased when I released my spell.

Why wasn't it working?

I would fail, everyone would die, and it would be my fault.

A heavy weight pressed against my skin, and I lifted my gaze to find the warlock watching me.

Carmen, swathed in a black cloak, kept her face hidden within the shadows of the hood, but I knew she was watching me.

My skin crawled under her gaze, and I sensed the grin on her face as my magic failed.

Green flames flickered in her hands.

For a moment, it illuminated her face before she tossed the spell, but my mind snagged.

That wasn't Carmen.

The warlock's eyes were a pitless black like the demonspawn, and their features were gaunt. But how were there two warlocks in Arkirith?

They lifted a gloved hand; magic sprang to life, a crackling ball of infernal fire.

It twirled at their slightest touch, as if it were a children's game.

They were taunting me, mocking my weakness.

Then they lifted their spell high, making sure I was watching, and then hurled it toward Indra as she battled demonspawn.

"Indra!" I screamed.

I threw my hands out in front of me again and channeled every ounce of my being into my magic.

Surrendering to my fear, I willed the lunar light to guide me.

Like a shimmering moonbeam, my shield sprang to life and formed a wall between our side and the enemy.

The warlock's spell slammed into my shield, showering flames over the demonspawn.

Enforcers and shifters retreated while the demonspawn prowled, seeking an opening.

The warlock summoned more balls of fire, but I was ready.

One by one, they collided with my shield, each one bouncing off and splashing the demonspawn—but the flames didn't harm them.

"Hold on, Nyssa," Indra said as she came up beside Rynac.

Black blood covered her, but determination shone in her eyes.

"Backup is coming, just hold on."

I nodded as a bead of sweat trickled down my face.

The runed band flared on my left hand, but it didn't inhibit the stream of lunar magic I funneled through it—a small relief.

My arms trembled with the sheer amount of magic I channeled, but I refused to falter, otherwise the warlock would annihilate us.

I had the sinking suspicion they were just toying with us.

That if they wanted to, they could've wiped us out already.

A larger fireball crashed into my shield. The impact hit me like a physical blow, pushing me back a step.

The flames licked at the iridescent magic until it dulled, but it didn't break.

Blood coated my tongue, but I gnashed my teeth.

Just a bit longer.

A new flame ignited in the warlock's grasp when they tilted their head as if listening.

I braced myself, ready for the impact. But the warlock snuffed out their spell.

The demonspawn snarled, launching themselves at my shield.

Claws and teeth raked across my magic, and I winced, trying to repair the weakening shield.

The flames on my left wrist crackled as I struggled for control, and I lost sight of the warlock.

Were they still there, waiting for me to weaken?

"Rynac." My voice cracked. "Get everyone back. If the spell shatters—"

I braced my shield, but I couldn't hold on any longer.

Rynac shouted out to our team, as Indra guided them back enough to protect them from the blowback.

"Let the spell go," he said. "I can't spot the warlock anymore, and you can't keep this up."

I gave a tight nod.

Nice and slow, just like an exhale.

Which wasn't the easiest thing to do when a horde of bloodthirsty demonspawn snarled, waiting to attack the moment I dropped my shield.

Taking a deep breath, I held it for a moment, then exhaled, letting my shield shrink in.

The enforcers clustered to the sides, still standing away from my shield, and raised their guns to fire on the exposed demonspawn.

The shield, now only twelve feet wide, funneled the demonspawn to the awaiting fighters. I could almost release it.

And then a force hit me, like white-hot talons raking across my chest. I gasped, struggling to maintain my spell.

"What is it?" Rynac yelled, but I could only shake my head.

The demonspawn shifted, revealing the warlock again. They raised a blade and slashed through the air, leaving a trail of liquid darkness.

The agonizing pain hit me again.

My vision swam, knees threatening to give out. If I took another blow like that, my spell would shatter.

The liquid darkness grew like fracture lines through the air.

Deep in my soul, I knew what this was.

The fabric of the veil was tearing.

The gap widened until I glimpsed the infernal hellscape and the awaiting demonspawn.

The moment it was large enough, the warlock dove through the tear in the veil as the enemy's reinforcements clawed to come through, making the hole wider.

Instinct compelled me forward.

My shield shoved the demonspawn back. I had to close it.

Each inch it grew, I felt as if my soul was being shredded.

But I needed to stitch it back together before the demonspawn overran us. My arms shook with the effort.

In theory, I knew what to do. Knew how to repair someone else's spell, though I doubted anyone had ever used it to repair the veil.

But I hesitated. Could I do this? Would they recognize my true nature if I revealed my magic to them?

I shook the doubt away. Saving lives and stopping the demonspawn, that was all that mattered.

Selene granted me these abilities for a reason.

This was my purpose.

I was a lunar witch. I knew it deep within my soul.

Selene's grace guided me.

Teasing out a thread of magic from my shield, I wrapped it around the edges of the tear, stopping it from growing.

Then I wove the magic in and out as if I were stitching a spell back together, not trying to mend the fabric of reality.

A menacing hiss erupted from the demonspawn as their claws grazed the stitch, and I prayed they wouldn't be able to break it.

Those already through surged forward as the fighters closed around me, but we were losing people too fast.

"It's working," Rynac whispered in disbelief.

I blinked sweat from my eyes.

My shield was now only a few feet wide. I didn't have enough lunar energy to fully repair it.

Would my stitches hold if I stopped casting?

The thundering thud of boots reverberated off the concrete.

"The UMC soldiers are here," Rynac shouted.

But relief eluded me as I focused on my spell, maintaining its continuity as I let the magic weave into the tear.

Soldiers flooded in behind the demonspawn who peeled away to attack the new threat.

An explosion boomed overhead.

Dust rained down around us as the ceiling fractured.

My magic wobbled, threatening to shatter.

Cracks spread across the concrete, and I feared we'd be crushed to death, but then the ceiling flew up and away.

What in the world?

Magic sizzled through the air, heading straight for us, but I couldn't do anything as it slammed into my right arm.

A band of power coiled around my wrist and squeezed until my power fizzled out. My magic wavered again, but this time, the enforcers and UMC soldiers were too close.

The backlash of my spell shattering would hit them if I didn't hold it together.

"Nyssa?" Rynac shouted, shifting into a defensive position.

But words were beyond me.

My right hand went numb as the black band gobbled up all the magic I poured into it.

While the left shook as I funneled all the magic through it and the power within the runed band surged.

I couldn't concentrate.

A whisper of my flames slipped free before I could contain them, mixing with the lunar energies.

No!

Urgency pulsed through me; I needed to work faster before the solar energies destabilized everything.

I braced myself as power rippled through the air, but it sliced through the demonspawn.

Of course, the UMC soldiers would have magic users with them.

The beasts faltered beneath the fresh assault.

Whatever spell hit me stung. But I didn't have time to see who cast it, needing to focus all my concentration on the lunar spell while holding the solar energies back.

I sensed more than saw the next spell hurtle toward me.

Indra moved and cut through the spell before it could reach me.

Sweat dripped down my back, plastering my shirt to my skin.

The sharp tang of iron coated my tongue as warmth dripped from my nose.

Just a little bit longer, I hissed to myself.

My magic crackled and hissed as I finished off the last stitch, praying it would hold, that the solar magic that slipped through wouldn't unravel what I'd done.

The yells of soldiers and the snarls of demonspawn swelled around me as I cut the thread of my magic.

My whole body shook as my knees threatened to give out.

Fire raged through me, demanding release, but I held my breath as the seconds trickled by.

My stitches held. It had worked.

Elation swelled in my chest as the soldiers cut down the last of the demonspawn.

We'd done it!

Heat surged through me like a tidal wave, snapping me back to reality.

I needed to get away from everyone so I could safely discharge the pent-up solar magic.

The ring of fire around my wrist crackled and flared, demanding release, when a force crashed into it.

A band of magic twirled around my wrist, and the flames guttered.

It snapped shut like a shackle; my magic guttered, trapped within. The breath whooshed out of me as if I'd been gut-punched.

I slumped to the floor as if my tethers to the world had been severed.

My mind and magic trapped, while my body refused to respond to my command.

Pain spiked through me as the solar magic tried to fight back, but I was unable to even cry out in agony.

Tears spilled from my eyes as hot pain sliced through my body as if I were the veil cracking open.

"What are you doing to her?" Rynac screamed as he knelt beside me. "Nyssa!"

I couldn't form words, couldn't even look at him.

A heavy silence pressed in around me, broken only by the groans of the injured and then the clipped steps of heavy boots coming closer.

"Nyssa Thornheart," a commanding voice said. "By the power of the witch council, you're under arrest for the use of unstable magic and disregard for life."

Inquisitors.

"What?" Indra shouted as the witches hauled me up.

Control of my body returned, but a deep weakness lingered. Either from expending too much power or from knowing what was to come.

"She did nothing but protect us. Why aren't you hunting down the warlock who attacked us?"

"Where are you taking her?" Rynac demanded.

The Inquisitors ignored them both.

I opened my mouth to tell them it was alright when the witch beside me flicked his finger and a black band of power wrapped around my throat, silencing me.

The witches dragged me forward, and I stumbled along with them.

I fixed my gaze on the ground, fearing what I'd see on the faces of those around me.

Volatile.

Dangerous.

Broken.

"Nyssa!" Rynac yelled as he raced after us.

I tried to turn, to shake my head, but the Inquisitors tightened their grip and dragged me away.

Don't fight for me. I willed them to hear the words. It would only make this harder.

The warlock had escaped. The demonspawn were dead. And the enforcers and shifters were tending to their injured and the captives.

No one dared question the powerful witches who dragged away one of their own.

Only Rynac and Indra stood watching.

Tears blurred my vision as I took one final, lingering look at my friends. There was no point pretending anymore.

I knew my fate.

The Inquisitors would haul me back to Myrite, dress it up as a trial, and call it justice when they convicted me.

After that, they'd sever my connection to magic and slice away the one part of me I had finally claimed as my own.

CHAPTER FORTY-ONE

An icy shudder tore down my spine, snapping every pain back into sharp focus. My shoulders pounded, trapped in a position I couldn't break, and I'd lost all feeling in my fingers long ago.

The Inquisitors had wrenched my arms behind me, bound them, and shoved me into a cramped room.

If this was only the beginning, I dreaded what came next.

Huddled in the dark, my mind replayed the night's events over and again. My fire seethed just beneath the surface, but their spell trapped it within my body.

The magic that silenced me had disappeared, but even though my throat rasped with each breath, I didn't call out or ask for water. The Inquisitors would offer me no sympathy.

Everything had been a blur after they hauled me away. They'd transported us into some building, then sealed me in this room. I knew I had to be within Arkirith. To travel farther would've required a spell array to summon a portal.

Not that it made it any better. I remembered Rynac and Indra's faces vividly; their sadness and confusion burned into my mind.

Would I ever see them again? I doubted it. After they stripped my magic, it was unlikely the council would allow me to leave. A witch with no magic was a stain upon their people. Allowing the world to know we existed would damage their reputation.

My future was sealed. But what of the others? Were the captives recovering? Had I hurt anyone when my spell shattered?

I wanted to apologize to Voren for getting him tangled up in this. To say my goodbyes to my friends before I left for good. I doubted I would be given such a luxury. In the eyes of the council, I was a rogue witch. I was already guilty. The trial would just be for show.

And Danika?

Did she know what happened to me? The binding potion had hurt her, but what would happen when I lost my magic?

The thought stole my breath. Would she even survive?

How had everything gone so wrong?

I'd only just unlocked the truth of my magic. Gaining control, recognizing the immense power I held to make a positive impact, and safeguarding countless lives. All to be ripped away.

Another cruel twist of fate.

The prospect of losing my magic before had scared me. The potential of losing my alchemy shattered my heart, and I had come to terms with that. But everything had changed since then.

My heart squeezed so hard it threatened to burst.

Hope had ignited in my chest over the past few weeks. The spark had taken hold and turned into a blazing fire.

After almost a decade, I'd finally glimpsed a future free from the fear of surrendering my magic. I'd found friends who cared for me, who accepted me for what I was.

For the first time in my life, I'd felt empowered, as if I had a true purpose.

Finding these missing people, protecting the enforcers, standing against those who threatened the lives of innocents.

That was where I belong.

Harnessing this power to shield and protect.

My alchemy had been the first step, giving me a taste of the positive impact I could have.

But embracing my lunar magic?

Everything about it felt right. As if all the pieces of my soul had aligned. As if the threads of destiny had guided me.

I understood why Rynac and Indra were enforcers. Why the nephilim risked their lives to protect this realm and its people.

This new life . . . it was the happiest I'd ever been.

It had bloomed before my eyes, unfolding into countless possibilities. Now, every single one of them crumbled.

Once again, waiting was the worst part. Wallowing in all my failures, remembering everything I was about to lose.

I had no idea how many hours passed, but it seemed like an eternity.

The door snapped open, and I flinched.

The Inquisitors hauled me upright, their grips tightening on my arms as if they feared I would try to run.

I winced against the light, stumbling to keep up.

They pulled me into a large room, the area cleared, leaving only the bare wooden floor where a spell array awaited. My gaze snagged on the rays of moonlight shining through the window, just beyond my reach.

I eyed the runes. The array extended almost twelve feet across, dominating the room.

Was this the portal home?

Despite the emptiness in my heart, part of me found solace in the knowledge that it would be over soon.

The Inquisitors placed me inside the array, and it snapped around me like a prison cell. I sank to the floor as its power whipped around me, dragging me down and holding me in place.

"We should strip her power now," one Inquisitor said. "It's far too dangerous to transport her back with that kind of magic."

Even though I'd anticipated it, hearing the words spoken aloud was a gut punch.

Their robes, long and dark, swirled as they moved to the far side of the room. I scanned their faces and swallowed hard as I recognized the leader. Thaddeus Flamebury.

Ruthless. Power hungry. I'd encountered him once, and his face haunted my dreams for months.

"She needs to stand trial before the council, Elara," the other Inquisitor said. "We will bind her magic until then."

"You think binding will do anything against dark magic, Cassius?" Thaddeus snapped. "She's a threat that needs to be removed."

"Dark magic?" Elara asked while Cassius frowned.

"You weren't there. I sensed it. She cast it." Thaddeus pointed an accusing finger at me.

"What?" I spat. "That wasn't me."

"You were the only one casting when we arrived. You tore the veil."

"That was the warlock," I shouted.

How in the world did they think that was me?

"Go ask anyone else who was there. I was trying to protect innocent people."

"What did the other witnesses say?" Elara asked the others.

"We don't need the statements from shifters or altered humans," Thaddeus hissed. "My word is enough."

I hated pleading, but my magic was on the line. "I was casting a shield, and trying to seal the tear the warlock opened. What kind of dark magic makes a shield like that? And why was it hurting the demonspawn? They are beings of dark magic."

"That is true," Cassius said. "She wasn't trying to hurt anyone. And her shield did harm the demonspawn."

"Don't let her magic-laced words twist your thoughts," Thaddeus said. "Whatever magic she was using, it wasn't our magic, was it?"

"The only other magic a witch can wield is dark magic," Elara said.

"No, I'm a lunar witch," I protested.

"A lunar witch," Thaddeus spat each word back at me as he stalked closer. "Those traitorous half-breeds? We would be doing our people a service by eradicating your tainted magic."

His hate-filled words snaked around me and squeezed until I couldn't breathe.

Half-breed?

Both my parents were witches. Everyone in the coven was. None of it made sense.

"She's a Thornheart," Cassius hissed, tugging him away from me. "If we act before a trial, Ambassador Thornheart will have our hides. Don't let your personal feelings cloud your view."

The Inquisitors retreated farther away, still arguing with each other. But whatever choice they made, it was out of my hands. Whether right now or after the trial, they would sever my connection to magic.

There was no way out.

"Now, this just won't do?" Carmen's voice purred a moment before she stepped into view.

All the warmth drained from my body.

Chapter Forty-Two

Carmen strolled toward me, lips curved in a smug, almost gleeful, smile. The pieces clicked together with a sickening lurch. Was this her doing?

Had she set the board, moved the pieces, and delivered me straight into the Inquisitors' hands?

My gaze darted back to the Inquisitors, but they continued arguing as if they hadn't even noticed the warlock.

Carmen crouched in front of me, and I tried to pull away, but the spell array held me in place.

"For all their claims to hunt dark witches, they're not very good at distinguishing the difference between magics."

Carmen shrugged.

"But I guess it worked in my favor today."

"You were a witch?"

"I still am," she snapped. "All of this is my magic. The demons only revealed the knowledge that has been hidden from us. The true power we can wield."

Dark witch or warlock, it was all the same.

They were bound to a demon lord, their magic corrupted.

"What do you want with me?"

I looked past Carmen to the Inquisitors. A choice between them or a dark witch wasn't a choice at all. More like picking my poison with extra steps.

"They won't be able to hear you," she said, grinning as if she wanted me to try to call out. "They might think they are high and mighty, but the Inquisitors are just as fallible as anyone else. Easy enough to influence, too—you just need the right pressure points."

"You didn't answer my question."

If she had that kind of power, how could we resist it?

I attempted to keep her talking, hoping her spell might weaken enough for the Inquisitors to break free, but that would still leave me right where I started.

"What do you want with me? You put me here after all."

"To open your eyes to the truth. The power waiting to be seized. I want you to take hold of the magic within you. Everything I told you before was true. And now you've seen it for yourself."

She flicked her hand at the bickering Inquisitors.

"This is what the witch council thinks of anyone who deviates, anyone who doesn't fit their mold."

I shook my head. Would I recognize her influence over me? I couldn't trust my mind, even if there was a grain of truth.

"So, what will you do to save yourself?" Carmen asked.

The Inquisitor's conversation had subsided, and they turned back toward me.

"Are you going to let them steal your magic? Strip away who you are? Or will you fight?"

Magic rippled through the air, prickling over my skin, as the Inquisitors drew upon their power.

My chest hollowed out, my body as paralyzed as my magic, unable to defend myself.

Power shuddered around me as the Inquisitors assumed their positions.

The bonds around my hand shifted and eased their hold. A whisper of magic curled through me, slipping past the suppression.

What could I do? Allow them to take my magic or fight back and be hunted?

I couldn't bring harm to these witches even as they attempted to strip away my magic.

Was that naïve? Foolish?

Most likely, but it was a line I refused to cross.

Kill them, Carmen's voice whispered in my mind. *Hurt them before they can hurt you. Fight. Fight for what you know in your heart.*

I shook away her voice. They believed I wielded dark magic and would strip my powers.

But in my heart? I knew the truth.

Despite their misguided belief, I wouldn't harm them. But that didn't mean I wouldn't defend myself.

I summoned the few drops of magic that had escaped and wove it into an astral shield.

It was too small to break their hold, but I wrapped it around my core—the source of my magic.

I closed my eyes, holding tight to the image of a shield, and prayed this would work.

The codex had mentioned how some magic users created an astral shield like a second skin. I didn't have enough power for that, but as long as they didn't reach my core, they couldn't sever my connection.

The spell array activated, stealing the breath from me.

Their magic sank into me like the claws of a demonspawn, ripping through my body and latching onto the power that flowed within.

The runes held me in place even as my body shook, pain raking through me.

"Hold on, Nyssa!" Danika shouted into my mind.

My focus slipped. Magic spilled through the hole in my shield.

White hot pain stabbed into my chest as part of my magic was sliced away and I scrambled to seal the break.

Hurry, I whispered. *I can't hold on much longer.*

The door behind the Inquisitors slammed open, the force knocking it off its hinges.

People flooded into the room. Faces I knew. Indra. Rynac. Lainie. Beylin. Enforcers. Shifters.

They'd come for me?

The witches' magic faded from the array, yet they maintained their hold on their power.

My body swayed, head spinning, the array's runes the only thing keeping me upright.

No, they couldn't . . . would they attack innocent people?

I wrestled with the magical bonds around my wrists and the spell that immobilized me. I had to stop them. The thought of anyone harming my friends ignited the fire within me to fight.

Shouts erupted as UMC soldiers poured into the room.

"Well, now it's a party," Carmen said, crouching next to me again.

Mischief twinkled in her eye as she grinned, excited for the fight to come. Her form faded. Was she just a figment of my imagination?

Everyone was yelling, and for a moment, the Inquisitors forgot about me. I had to get out of here.

I twisted my wrists, and though my bonds cut into my raw skin, they loosened until I could almost pull one hand free.

Something bumped into my knee, and I blinked down at a metal ball with dwarven runes engraved on the outside.

A thick substance covered it, and the dark liquid had spilled across the ground, distorting the spell array and weakening its hold on me.

"Open it," Danika whispered.

I couldn't sense where she was, but the tangle of fear and adrenaline pressed against our connection.

"I retrieved your potion."

I jerked my hand free of its bindings and tossed them away, then snatched up the ball and cracked it open.

It was just large enough to fit a single vial.

Still groggy, my power was slow to respond to my call, but the magic within the vial called to me. It was an empowerment potion. One made by my own hand.

Beylin nodded, encouraging me to drink it.

The shouting was growing louder; the Inquisitors clustered together, facing off against both groups.

Tension thickened in the air.

This hostility wasn't normal. Was Carmen still twisting them?

Regardless, I wouldn't let my friends come to harm because of me.

Downing the potion, I pushed myself up onto unsteady feet, hoping the boost would be enough. How was she influencing them? Could I interrupt her spell?

Magic fizzed through my veins, infusing strength into my body. Lightness bubbled up in my chest, and I rubbed a hand against it. I'd thought I would never feel the swell of my magic again.

Soldiers shouted, hands on their weapons.

Two of the Inquisitors took up defensive positions, but I watched Thaddeus, whose anger simmered just under the surface.

As I stepped out of the array, potent energy buzzed through me as I summoned my magic.

The fire responded in an instant, racing down my arm even in its diminished state.

The lunar energies throbbed with power, surging like an ever-rising tide.

Magic surged through my hands and I cast it out, my astral shield bursting to life between the Inquisitors, soldiers, and my friends.

"Stop!" I commanded.

Fire curled around my hand, quivering, longing for me to wield it. I poured more into the shield.

A silver glow coated my skin and grew brighter with each passing moment.

"What is the meaning of this?" Elara hissed.

"Only dark magic can break free from that spell and compel all these people," Thaddeus barked.

I stepped back toward the moonlight streaming through the window. Its silver glow offered me the power I needed to end this before the witches hurt anyone.

The Inquisitors' magic flared, wreathing around their hands as I took another step.

The air stilled, as if the world held its breath.

Lights flickered and went out.

Only the glow of our spells lit the room.

The blood drained from my face.

The Inquisitors' fire flared, illuminating the shimmer of gold that covered the ceiling in intricate runes.

"Don't—" I yelled, but Thaddeus had already conjured a ball of fire and stepped too close to a golden rune.

Like a hair trigger, magic cracked as the hidden spell array activated.

His magic fizzled as the array snatched the fireball like a hungry predator and devoured it all.

Unseen claws pierced into me, ensnaring my magic in an unyielding grip and rendering me powerless.

The insatiable runes gorged on my power as if it were lifeblood.

I crashed to my knees, fighting against the drain, but it was futile. Each drop of my magic increased its power, widening the array's perimeter.

The Inquisitors stumbled as it ensnared them.

The magic was too strong. None of us could escape.

Once an array was active, there were only two options; disrupting enough runes, which might cause a magical backlash, or letting it finish its purpose.

"What's happening? What can we do?" Indra shouted across the room.

I shook my head, all my concentration focused on slowing the magic being torn from my body. But it was too late.

The air crackled as more runes blazed to life, covering every surface.

One giant trap painted in angel blood.

CHAPTER FORTY-THREE

"Don't move," I yelled. Black and gold runes burst to life across every surface, causing my head to ache as I tried to decipher them. "You might trigger the runes."

Potent power thrummed through the air.

My frantic gaze darted between runes, hunting for a weakness. However, being trapped within a magical bomb made it hard to think, any movement might set it off.

"Stop whatever you're doing!" a UMC soldier barked.

"This isn't me," I yelled back.

Why did everyone always blame me? The soldier motioned to the two beside him, who stepped toward me.

"No—watch out!"

It was too late.

The moment their feet touched a rune, the air shifted.

Magic shattered, and the world tilted.

Power crackled as our stolen magic coalesced into an inky black pool. Like a deadly vortex, it swirled, devouring any magic or light that touched it.

"Portal!" someone shouted, and chaos erupted.

The UMC officer barked out orders, and his soldiers complied, setting off more runes.

Demonspawn poured from the portal, saturating the room with sulfur and brimstone.

Amidst the snarls of demonspawn and growls of shifters, screams of pain punctuated the air. Blinding flashes flared up as the enforcers fought to dispel the runes.

The Inquisitors snapped into action, and a dome sprang to life over the portal, trapping the newest demonspawn. But the spell wavered, their magical reserves sapped.

I pushed to my feet. My head was spinning, disoriented by the sudden loss of magic.

But what could I do? No magic. No potions.

Rynac and Indra rushed toward me. The runes ahead of them winked out as a shimmering blue magic cleared a path.

Soldiers pressed forward, either toward the portal or me.

"The ward is about to fail," I called out.

The Inquisitors struggled to maintain the dome as the mass of demonspawn caught within it clawed at their spell.

Rynac and Indra gripped my arms to steady me before turning to face the threat.

More demonspawn tumbled through. We had to close it.

Darkness spilled out of the portal, sending rippling shadows across the room.

Rynac stiffened, and my breath fled as I recognized it too.

Malevolent smoke rushed across the floor toward the soldiers and our allies.

The portal winked out, the power in the array spent.

"Get the dark witch!" Thaddeus bellowed at the UMC soldiers. "Before she can summon more portals."

"What?" I hissed.

After they all witnessed it, he was still going to blame me?

My rage and frustration caught in my throat as fear squeezed it.

Sinister magic twirled around everyone's feet, the trapped demon-spawn snarling as the others fought on.

Five soldiers broke away, their weapons raised. Pointing at me.

"We need to go," Rynac whispered to his sister, pressing me behind him as we moved closer to the wall.

"No," the word tumbled from my lips.

I raised a hand, but no magic responded to my call. I could only watch as dark magic speared the closest soldier.

His scream splintered the air, his skin blistered and cracked as the inky black tendrils twisted over him.

More cries of pain filled the air, as one after the other soldiers and enforcers transformed.

Their now blackened gaze hunting for a target and they turned on their own.

"Danika!" Indra yelled as she backpedaled, keeping herself between me and the soldiers with guns trained on us.

My nails dug into Rynac's arms, trying to hold myself back as thralls tore apart their former allies.

An explosion shook the ground.

Coughing on dust, I squinted through the haze and discovered a newly formed hole in the wall.

Rynac pulled me forward. We jumped through the gap, and the cool night air greeted us.

I stumbled out onto the rooftop, running after Indra as she led the way through the maze of metal air ducts.

The shouts of the soldiers and screams of the fallen chased after us.

"Oh Goddess," I swore as I launched myself over another duct. "We have to go back."

"The enforcers and shifters can hold their own," Rynac said, pressing me faster.

I could only hope he was right. There was little I could've done, but running away still felt wrong.

A blur of blue darted across the roof, and I stumbled as Danika zipped between my feet.

"You didn't think we would leave you to the Inquisitors, did you?" Danika said. *"We had many contingency plans, though the explosion was my favorite."*

Except now I'm running for my life, and they think I'm a dark witch, I thought back, having no breath to talk.

"Yes," she growled. *"The Inquisitors are quite stupid. But we will stand by you and sort this out together."*

"This way," Indra called, darting around a corner.

Skirting around the building's edge, it was impossible not to stare down at the two-story drop as we crept along the narrow ledge.

Rynac's presence at my back was the only thing that kept me moving. If I didn't hurry, he'd be the only obstacle blocking me from the soldiers' view. Would they shoot him just to stop me?

"Quick," Indra hissed.

My legs wobbled, but I pushed them to move faster. She grabbed my hand, helping me down, then pointed to the edge of the roof.

Under the glow of the moon, I made out the twisting vines. Only as thick as my thumb, they wove together, forming a ladder that led down to the ground level.

"Oh, I'm going to be sick," I muttered.

I guess I needed to add fear of heights to the list.

"Zola claimed they're strong enough to hold two of us," Indra said. "So hurry down."

Swallowing the lump in my throat, I sat on the edge and gripped the vines. They shifted under the weight of my foot but held firm.

I hate this! I chanted over and over in my head.

But it beat falling back into the Inquisitors' clutches. Or fighting thralls and demonspawn. My friends had come here risking their lives for me. I couldn't let them down.

The ladder swayed as Indra started her descent, and I jumped the last few feet.

The accessway was too narrow for my liking. If I reached out, I could touch both sides with my fingers.

Indra landed next to me a moment later, and Rynac was halfway down the ladder.

"What about Danika?" I asked.

My fox waited at the top, peering down as she watched Rynac.

"We know what we're doing," Indra said with a smirk.

She headed down the alley, never hesitating despite the lack of lighting.

A thud had me whirling around, but it was just Rynac landing.

He signaled to Danika. She bent her head toward the vines, and a moment later, they snapped and tumbled to the ground.

I shuddered at the sound. Danika disappeared from view, and I whipped back around as the yells of the soldiers grew louder.

My eyes glued to Indra's back, I pushed my legs faster through the twists and turns.

"Where are we?" I asked.

"The convention center along the Torrens," Rynac answered a few steps behind me.

This place was unfamiliar to me since it was across town from where I lived. The massive, multi-level building occupied a block and a half, and included a hotel which we might have just blown a hole in.

We emerged into a courtyard that ran alongside the building, manicured shrubs lining the path.

Indra dove into one and pulled out a bag.

"Put these on," she said, shoving a black hoodie into my arms along with my belt full of potions.

It was only when I pulled the hoodie on that I realized how cold I was. She slung another bag over my shoulder.

"More supplies and your codex."

"You came prepared." I had to smile.

They'd done all this for me. After the assault to free the captives, they must have scrambled to find me.

Dawn couldn't be too far off. The sun's rise would force the demonspawn into hiding.

We took off again, and I sprinted after Indra with everything I had.

We needed to get out of sight. And then—no, one problem at a time.

All that mattered was not being captured. I'd deal with the rest later.

"There's a courtyard just ahead," Indra said over her shoulder.

I whipped around the corner and slammed right into Indra's back.

Five demonspawn blocked our path; the two in the back near seven feet tall and both built like a house.

But it was the slight figure behind them that snagged my attention.

Carmen.

Chapter Forty-Four

"Do you see now?" Carmen called out. The snarls of her demonspawn sent a shudder down my spine. "Do you understand why I tried to warn you? They fear us. They refuse to learn or understand. Look at how they hunt you."

"Yeah, because you set me up," I yelled back.

"Was that before or after they planned to strip you of magic?"

"Before," I snapped. "Because now they want me dead."

"Come join me then," she beckoned, offering her hand to me.

"Be ready to run," Danika whispered.

I held Carmen's gaze, hoping she wouldn't sense Danika, even as the drum of the soldiers' feet grew closer.

My fingers trailed across my potion belt, searching for something that would help us.

A blur of cobalt launched itself through the air, magic crackling around her.

"Now."

I hurled the smoke-bomb vial at my feet, grabbing Indra's arm and dragging her to the side as the smoke curled around us.

Rynac was one step behind as I raced toward a doorway.

Indra grabbed the handle, rattling the door, then slammed it with her shoulder, but it wouldn't budge.

"Up!" she yelled, but the wall was ten feet high.

A snarl had me spinning around as a hulking demonspawn charged.

The smoke was already dissipating; soldiers and demonspawn locked in a bloody battle, but once again, Carmen was gone.

"Nyssa, go," Rynac snapped, lacing his fingers together to offer me a boost up.

"But—"

"But nothing! That warlock is here, and the Inquisitors will arrive soon. You have to run."

I swore. It didn't matter that he was right.

The thought of abandoning them twisted in my stomach, but they'd done this for me and I wouldn't waste their sacrifice.

Stopping Carmen was the most important thing, and I couldn't do that if they locked me up or I lost my magic.

Stepping into his offered hands, I gripped his shoulders for balance as he straightened up.

The wall rushed by, and I reached for the roof. With one last shove from below, I hauled myself the rest of the way up.

"Nyssa, watch out!"

Movement on the roof caught my attention.

I scrambled to my feet as Carmen walked toward me, a pair of imp-size demonspawn at her side.

I didn't hesitate. Spinning on my heels, I sprinted in the opposite direction, darting across the rooftop.

No time to think or plan. I had to escape.

The creatures shrieked, and my head whipped around to see them charging toward me.

Their wicked talons scraped the roof, their gaping jaws open wide as saliva dripped from between sharp teeth.

I ran with everything I had, which wasn't much right now.

The last forty-eight hours had been rough, fatigue weighing my limbs, my magical reserves utterly drained. Twice.

Vaulting over a railing, I stumbled as pain stabbed my side.

A chilling sensation washed over me, convincing me she truly had orchestrated everything. That every choice I made was the one she expected.

The first hints of dawn, a smudge of gray brightening the horizon, should've brought me hope. Yet, it would be too late to weaken the advancing demonspawn.

I hurled the one offensive potion I could find. A demonspawn yelped, but it didn't even slow them down.

Skidding to a halt as the building ended, I peered over the edge at the drop below.

Surviving the fall was possible, but not without broken bones.

I jerked back right as the first demonspawn reached me. It launched itself into the air, but I dropped into a crouch.

Pain sliced across my shoulder as the demon sailed over me and off the rooftop. I didn't wait for the second to catch up as I scrambled away, hunting for an escape route.

Carmen and her demon stalked behind me, knowing I was trapped.

My gaze fixed on the path ahead, over the bridge linking this building and the next one.

And below, the churning waters of the Torrens River.

My heart wanted to escape my chest as the racing water tried to hypnotize me.

I'd avoided the river like the plague and now it taunted me.

My shoulder ached, warmth trickling down my back, but I didn't have time for that. I downed a healing potion, hoping for the best.

"Come now, Nyssa," Carmen called.

I swung my legs over the railing, my knees weak as I pushed upright.

There were no guardrails up here, just six feet of curved roof and me: the idiot trying to cross it.

The metal roof was slick, and my shoes slid an inch to the side with each step.

Don't look down.

I threw my arms out for balance, keeping my eyes fixed on the building ahead.

The roar of the river grew louder, bouncing off the building walls.

Almost halfway across, I thought I was going to make it, but a dark form blocked the way forward.

I stumbled, nearly tumbling off the side. A massive demonspawn waited on the other side of the bridge.

A glance back revealed Carmen waiting for me, a faint smile as if she knew she had won. The sun was still too low to subdue the demonspawn. I doubted Carmen would have the patience to wait.

"You've nowhere to go, Nyssa," her voice called out over the river. "Come back to the safety of the roof. You know this is what you want."

"What I want?" I said, more to myself than her.

I wanted to avoid falling into a river. To not be hunted by a dark witch and demonspawn, Inquisitors and soldiers. To explore my magic without the looming threat of losing it hanging over me.

I'd lived half my life fearing discovery, desiring to blend in.

Now, I wanted to embrace my true self.

I was no fool. Whatever Carmen's true motives were, I wouldn't help her fulfill them.

"You want to be strong and powerful," Carmen called out. "To no longer fear your magic or yourself. You want to live a life where you are free to make your own choices. To help people, to protect them. I can help you do all of that. No one else can."

I shook my head, but I couldn't deny she spoke the truth.

"Then I guess we'll do this the hard way," Carmen said.

Metal screeched, and the roof shuddered as the hulking demon-spawn stepped forward. The structure protested every step it took.

"You refuse to see the truth right before you. After all I've done for you, helping you awaken your true power, I thought you would finally understand."

"Understand what?"

I backed up on instinct, but that way was toward Carmen.

Although her imp demonspawn was under control, its owner posed a greater threat.

"You're destined for greatness," she called out.

I skittered back a few steps, my feet slipping on the slick surface.

The water below churned and roared, hungry for its next meal.

Fear coiled around my chest until I gasped for air.

"The veil is weakening." Carmen's voice sounded almost pleading, but I shook my head to dispel her influence-laced words. "You've seen for yourself how easy it is to tear, for feral demonspawn to spill through. But what will happen when the stronger ones breach the veil? What happens when the entire veil crumbles and chaos ensues?"

She sounded far too excited about that prospect.

"And if I help you, how would it be any different?"

"The Great One's plan is already in motion," she said as if I hadn't spoken. "There is nothing we mere mortals can do but choose which side we will be on. Join me. Discover the truth. Taste the real power only the faithful can wield. The full moon approaches, and this is our chance to prove ourselves worthy."

My skin crawled. "Well, as delightful as that all sounds, I'll pass."

I eyed the turbulent waters below.

My knees locked, refusing to move.

Shouts and the hammering of boots filled the air.

I wobbled, trying to regain my balance as the Inquisitors, surrounded by a unit of soldiers, raced closer.

Their weapons raised as they looked between Carmen, me, and the demonspawn.

Hope swelled in my chest. How else could they interpret this situation other than me being the victim?

"Arrest them all!"

I should've known better.

The hulking demonspawn bound forward as Carmen's dark magic saturated the air.

No matter how I looked at it, the odds sucked.

"Fuck it." I jumped off the bridge.

CHAPTER FORTY-FIVE

The river swallowed me in one icy gulp, stealing the scream from my lips. Weight yanked me under—bag, clothes, everything—while the current spun me end over end.

I kicked and flailed, trying to guess which way was up.

Each movement sent a searing pain through my right shoulder, but if I stopped fighting, I'd never resurface.

I clawed at the water. My lungs burned, aching for air, while my mind froze in panic.

Gray light rippled above. I kicked with every bit of strength I had.

My head broke the surface, and I gasped for air, only to plunge underneath again. I fought back up, gulping in as much water as air.

My arm snagged, tangled in the roots of a tree.

I latched onto it, willing my numb fingers to hold on.

The base of an ancient willow tree held the rocky bank together, its roots like fingers reaching out to trail across the river.

My arms shook as I heaved my body out, struggling for breath as I coughed up the water.

Above me, stars winked out as dawn's first rays painted the sky.

Shivers wracked my body as I dragged myself out of the water.

I needed to get out of sight. No doubt they already hunted me.

But where would I go? Nowhere was safe, but I couldn't face Carmen alone.

I stumbled over the roots and collapsed onto the grass.

I'd never been so happy to be on solid ground before.

A shadow fell over me.

I jerked away from the looming figure.

"Shit," I hissed, scrambling to my feet before they could grab me.

How had they found me already?

I had no way of fighting; my magic was spent, fatigue weighed down my limbs, and my most effective potions were gone.

But I blinked as I took in Nathaniel, hands on his hips.

He worked for the UMC but he'd also helped me before. Which was it this time?

"Not the usual reaction ladies have when they see me," Nathaniel drawled.

He stepped forward, reaching for me, and I flinched.

"I'm here to help," he said with a frown, backing up a step with his hands raised.

"Sure you are," I snapped.

My teeth wouldn't stop chattering, and I'd lost feeling in my hands.

How in all the hells could I escape a nephilim?

He tilted his head as if I were a puzzle to be solved. "We've been looking for you since we got your message. But by the time we arrived, the Inquisitors had captured you."

I narrowed my gaze. Had the UMC sent them to hunt me down? "How did you find me?"

"Tracked your phone," he said, not noticing the horrified look on my face. "Which led us to the horde of demonspawn battling enforcers, shifters, and the Inquisitors. Beylin filled us in. From there, it was easy. Trouble seems to follow you. I just had to listen for the next fight. But then you jumped into the river. Pretty ballsy move."

"I'm not a fan of being a prisoner," I said dryly.

"Understandable. But we need to go before the UMC squads start swarming around."

"Why? You work for the UMC. Don't you want a reward for bringing me in?"

"I'm trying to keep you safe. We might work alongside the UMC, but our objectives are our own." When I didn't budge, he added, "You can trust me."

"Trust a nephilim?" I scoffed. "One who's generally been an asshole, and who made me vomit the first time we met?"

Yeah, I held a grudge.

"That is people's normal reaction when they first meet Nathaniel," Astrid said as she landed beside us.

"Fuck off," he shot back at her.

"I know you've been through a lot," she said to me. "But we are here to help. We understand the significance of your magic."

"And you're our best bet at finding the warlock," Nathaniel added.

"It's not just a warlock, but a dark witch, too," I said.

"What?" Astrid hissed.

"When the Inquisitors held me, Carmen came to taunt me. Or at least an image of her. She claims to be a witch, and I believe the Inquisitors have been hunting for her. Dark witches have magic prior to turning, unlike warlocks, which makes them far more dangerous. And these two are aligned."

"Dealing with both will be challenging. Will you help us?" Astrid asked, offering me a hand. "You can trust us. We'll keep you safe."

What choice did I have? I couldn't go home. I didn't want to risk endangering my friends by showing up at their doorstep.

And without Astrid's help, I never would've survived the infusion of lunar energies.

Now, more than ever, I needed powerful allies if I was going to rescue the captives and foil Carmen and the warlock's plans.

"Fine," I said.

Why were my legs so weak?

My fingers brushed over my aching shoulder. It didn't feel right.

When I pulled my hand away, blood coated it.

"Oh." And then my legs gave out.

Murmuring voices roused me, my mind and body too sluggish to respond, so I just lay there, hoping sleep would claim me again.

"She's been asleep for fourteen hours!" a deep voice said. "Don't you think we should check on her again?"

"Her magic was drained."

I recognized the second voice as Astrid.

"She's had rather an eventful few days. It doesn't surprise me."

"But the wound—" Kaelan protested.

"Was not deep and is already healing," Nathaniel butted in. "If there were a problem, zappy over there wouldn't be sleeping."

Right, the nephilim.

Reality crashed back down around me.

What in the hells had happened to my life?

Unsteady legs supported me as I pushed myself out of a bed in a foreign room.

I gathered the strength to stumble toward the door, driven by the need to uncover the truth. Were any of my friends injured? Was the UMC still after me?

Heat prickled across the nape of my neck, and all my aches and pains flared back to life.

My head felt stuffed with cotton wool and throbbed with each beat of my heart.

Gripping the door frame, I glared at the three nephilim. "You all talk loud enough to wake the dead."

As one, they turned to stare at me. My brain hurt too much to figure out their expressions.

"Come sit before you fall down," Astrid said. "Are you hungry?"

I nodded and took her offered arm. "But I also need answers."

"And some pants," Nathaniel added.

Frowning, I looked down to find I was only wearing an oversized t-shirt that reached my thighs. "Where are my clothes?"

"You were soaking wet," Astrid said, helping me onto the couch.

A pair of sapphire eyes blinked up at me from a pile of blankets.

"Danika." My breath fled as my bonded crawled into my lap.

I wrapped my arms around her, listening to the soothing beat of her heart. It weakened the grip I had on my emotions, and tears tumbled down my face.

All my thoughts jumbled together—fear she'd been hurt, relief she was safe, and an underlying sense of dread about the chaos that consumed my life.

"It will be all right*."* Her sweet voice soothed my soul. *"We are together. We will face this together."*

I took a shuddering breath, trying to compose myself.

The nephilim pretended they didn't just witness my breakdown.

Kaelan placed a glass of water and some pain pills on the coffee table, which I took without hesitation.

"What happened after the demonspawn attack?" I asked.

A heavy silence hung in the air, none of them wanting to answer.

I rubbed a weary hand across my face. "Spit it out. I need to know."

"The dark witch escaped, and the Inquisitors and UMC units are actively hunting you," Nathaniel said, ignoring the glares from the other two. "They claim you were the one to open the demonic portal and create the thralls. You've been charged with the use of dark magic."

I swallowed hard, conscious of the three angel-born who surrounded me.

Only, if they believed those claims, I wouldn't be sitting here.

"But you don't?"

"Even without seeing the spell array, we know it wasn't made by your hand," Nathaniel said. "I mean, how would you know where the Inquisitors would bring you and plant that array there?"

Guess that was an improvement over his initial hostility.

"Besides, only demons and angels know how to harness the magic within angel blood," Astrid added.

"What about those who battled the demonspawn and thralls? My friends?" I asked.

"We helped to dispatch the last of them when we arrived," Kaelan said. "Though your friends fought off the demonspawn, several of the UMC soldiers sustained injuries."

"The dark witch took captives, including your enforcer friends," Astrid said, gripping my hand. "Indra and Rynac were unconscious when they carried them into a portal as the demons retreated. By the time I landed, it was closed. The one remaining soldier said the dark witch wanted them alive."

Tears prickled my eyes. Carmen had taken my friends on purpose. I knew it in my heart.

She would keep them alive, at least for now. But that didn't mean she wouldn't hurt them to get me.

No matter what I did, I was trapped within her web.

My world had turned upside down, all my hard work ruined. The life I'd tried to build here was shattered beyond repair.

The Inquisitors would never stop hunting me, and the UMC appeared to align with them.

How quickly would word spread in the magical community? How would my family react?

Would I ever be able to clear my name?

Everyone feared dark magic. I doubted they would allow me to explain myself first.

They would take my magic without hesitation. The Inquisitors had already proven that.

I'd spend the rest of my life running, always looking over my shoulder. I shoved my spiraling thoughts away. They'd get me nowhere.

"I promise you we will find your friends," Kaelan said. "But you must stay here where it's safe. Once we capture the warlock and dark witch, we can clear your name with the Inquisitors and the UMC."

"No. I will not hide away," I hissed back, "or let fear dictate my life. For too many years, I've hidden myself. I'm done fearing my magic, fearing what I am. I will be true to my heart and not let my fears, or anyone else's, stand in my way."

"But—" Kaelan started.

Of course, he was the only one foolish enough to argue.

My eyes locked onto his, and I summoned all my resolve. "What matters right now is stopping Carmen and protecting this city from whatever she has planned. On the bridge, she mentioned something about the full moon. That it was a chance to prove ourselves. Taking my friends must be her insurance for my compliance."

Danika shifted to my side as I rose to my feet, my fists clenched. I met each one of their gazes.

"I will not sit idly by while she kills the people I care about," I said, biting out each word. "Even without me, she could inflict serious damage on the city. Either you are with me on this or I'm leaving now."

The gauntlet thrown, I braced for a challenge.

"I am always by your side," Danika proclaimed.

Astrid dipped her head, followed shortly by Nathaniel—which shocked us both.

My hard gaze swung to Kaelan as he moved, his eyes searching mine.

"Are you sure about this?" he asked, resting a hand on my uninjured shoulder. "This will be dangerous, and you're unprepared and injured. We understand if you decide to back out."

I narrowed my eyes. The faint hint of magic tingled in the air.

Was he trying to use his charm on me to convince me to back down?

I stepped closer, glaring up at him despite the six inches he had on me, and growled, "I am."

He hesitated for a moment before nodding and retreating a step.

I hissed out a shaking breath, the three nephilim were silent, clearly waiting for me to give them orders.

"We need every advantage if we want to defeat a dark witch, a warlock, and their horde," I said, desperately trying to come up with a plan. "We'll need to see what information the UMC has, what location spells they're using, and I'll need supplies from my apartment."

I refused to be sidelined. I wouldn't back down.

"Someone should contact Beylin and the enforcers to see what they know. Carmen will probably leave a message with them when she can't locate me. With time slipping away, we can use her desperation to our advantage. Set our own terms."

This time, I'd take the fight to Carmen.

Chapter Forty-Six

Hours later, I stood with a groan, trying to stretch away my aches, feeling like I'd gone toe-to-toe with a brick wall. The nephilim rotated between missions, never leaving me unguarded.

Midnight approached, but despite the need to rest, tomorrow night marked the full moon, and I was nowhere near prepared. I'd poured over my grimoire and had a few potential ideas, but nothing concrete.

And it was impossible to keep my mind from wandering to Indra and Rynac, fearing what was happening to them.

The glowing moon hung heavy in the inky black sky, her silvery light washing over the city. With each passing second, the tug in my chest grew stronger.

Before I realized it, my feet had carried me out onto the balcony, the cold metal railing cut into my stomach as I leaned closer.

My eyes fluttered closed as moonlight embraced me.

The sensation similar to what the sun had once evoked within me, when the first rays of dawn caressed my skin, wrapping me in a warm embrace and filling me with strength.

But Selene's touch differed from her sister's. It was like a cool breeze on a long summer day.

My skin tingled as if energy danced across it before it seeped into my bones, the moon's aura infusing me with renewed energy.

I could almost sense Selene's steady presence, as if she stood beside me, her hand on my shoulder, reassuring me we would face this together.

Time slipped away, and when I opened my eyes, the moon had begun her descent.

As a shadow beside me moved, I jerked back.

"We need to work on your situational awareness," Kaelan mused.

"How long have you been there?" My face heated as I willed my racing heart to calm, mortified that he'd been watching me while I remained oblivious.

"I was ensuring you didn't tumble over the railing. Witches aren't known for their ability to fly."

"Wha—" And then I looked down.

Only a thin metal railing stood between me and a ten-story plunge.

I squeezed my eyes shut.

My knuckles turned white as I clenched the rail harder.

"Of course, bloody nephilim would choose the highest floor."

Kaelan snorted, which he then tried to turn into a cough when I shot him a dirty look. "How is your shoulder doing?"

"Fine," I said through gritted teeth.

I wanted nothing more than to get inside, but with Kaelan watching—Goddess, that would be embarrassing.

Not that I hadn't already displayed all my best qualities for the nephilim. I just didn't want to add to the list.

"It takes time to recover. Don't push yourself too hard."

Was that kindness or a slight toward witches being fragile?

I side-eyed the nephilim.

"*You* seem perfectly fine, and you took a dark magic to the chest."

Kaelan unsuccessfully hid his amusement at my annoyance. "That was almost a week ago. A severe injury is nothing new. In my line of work, it's just another day."

He shrugged and I willed him to leave, but nephilim were never compliant when it concerned the needs of witches.

"I never said thank you for the potions and tending to my injury."

My gaze narrowed. "What do you want?"

"What?" Kaelan blinked down at me. I guess he was good at feigning innocence, too.

"You expect me to believe a nephilim would thank a witch with no ulterior motive?"

"I do, especially when said witch aided said nephilim without an ulterior motive. Unless you're hiding something."

"I'm an alchemist," I protested. "It's my job to aid people. I won't let anyone suffer when my potions can help."

"If you say so, little witch."

I opened my mouth, a retort on the tip of my tongue.

"You're trying to distract me," I blurted as the realization clicked.

Kaelan fought a smile as I glared at him. "It's working, isn't it? And it's quite entertaining to watch every emotion ripple across your face."

"Asshole," I said under my breath, even though I was a hundred percent sure he heard it. "Are you so bored that you decided to torment your prisoner?"

He bristled. "You're not a prisoner. We're protecting you."

I rolled my eyes.

He can give it, but he can't take it.

"But you don't deny tormenting me. A nephilim specialty?"

"Our divine duty."

I snorted. And then hated that he'd made me laugh, especially when he looked far too pleased with himself.

"If you must know, I was trying to be chivalrous by distracting you, as you clearly hate heights. Moonlight will speed up your recovery."

"But why would you want that? You don't want me going after my friends, and as your charm didn't work, I'm guessing you have another trick up your sleeve."

"I apologize for that."

"That you tried, or that it didn't work?" I shot back.

"Charm isn't something I use lightly. I only wanted to keep you out of harm's way, but it caused offense."

Apologies were not his forte. "So you'll not stop me or stand in my way when I go to help my friends tomorrow?"

"Turning yourself over to the dark witch is exactly what your friends were trying to prevent."

"That's why I must be ready. It's not just my friends, but all the captives they've taken. I can't continue with my usual life knowing that they're suffering, that I could help them, but didn't because I prioritized my safety instead."

I'd never been able to stand by and do nothing when I could help others.

"They risked everything to save me when the Inquisitors took me. And I'll do whatever it takes to free them, no matter the cost."

"But it's not only that," he snapped, though I couldn't tell if it was me or my words that pissed him off. "You can't risk yourself. You're too important."

My head jerked up, but Kaelan gave me a flat look.

"Did you think we wouldn't figure it out?"

"I . . ."

"I mean, it took us a bit," he conceded, talking more to himself than to me. "And I've never met a moon-blessed witch. Didn't even realize it was possible. But you could've told us. Was it because we are nephilim?"

"Well," I started, having zero idea where I was heading with the sentence, "you were interrogating me the first time we met."

Kaelan crossed his arms with an irritated grunt, staring out at the moon as if it held the answer.

It seemed that Astrid had been true to her word and hadn't mentioned her suspicion that I was a lunar witch.

Only a select few friends were aware, and I wanted to reveal the truth on my own accord.

The silence lingered.

I didn't know why, but I wanted to explain myself. "I wasn't aware I was moon-blessed then. Even now, it's kind of hard to believe."

"How long ago was your . . . marking?"

Thanks for not saying death.

Even that was near impossible for me to wrap my head around.

"I think it might've been when I was thirteen."

Kaelan stilled beside me. After a long moment, he said, "I'm sorry you experienced that at such a young age. It's hard to understand Selene's offer, though I'm surprised nobody explained it to you."

"I don't remember her offer at all."

He pursed his lips. "But you have a mark, right?"

"Yes," I said, self consciously rubbing the back of my neck.

I hadn't tried to look at it again. Would it appear any different? More like a crescent moon?

Astrid's mark had been so prominent—I froze, as another moon tattoo popped into my mind.

My gaze lifted to Kaelan's neck. It had to be his moon-blessed mark.

"Took you a while," he chuckled. "And to answer the question you're thinking, yes, that is mine."

"Will mine bleed?" I whispered in horror.

How in all the hells would I explain *that* to people?

"No, it's a very rare occurrence," he said.

I wanted to ask more, but he focused on the skyline again, and I took the hint.

"How do you know I'm moon-blessed?" I asked instead.

Despite everything, this seemed like a dream, as if reality could shatter and crash down around me.

"We can sense it through our marks, though in your case, it was only when you channeled lunar energies that the connection awoke."

"Connection?"

"The moon-blessed marks link us together. With time, the bond can grow stronger, but the link is always there. We can use it to locate each other, though warding can disrupt the tracking."

My mind snagged.

The moon-blessed marks linked me and the nephilim.

Could I use that connection to alert them to my location if Carmen took me?

"Kaelan, that's brilliant," I said, wide-eyed.

I needed to plan so that I could test it.

A laugh bubbled up. Simple and effective. Carmen would never expect it. I patted him on the arm before I raced back inside.

"The Inquisitors have trip-spell alarms all over your apartment and on the rooftop," Astrid said early the next morning, handing me a bag brimming with my supplies. "But I retrieved everything."

"Thank you."

I started marking the corks so I could identify them at a glance. I hadn't wanted the nephilim getting caught up in my mess with the Inquisitors, but rather than a threat, they viewed it as a challenge.

Unable to brew new potions, I still had plenty to work with, though only one empowerment potion remained.

I'd scoured *The Lunar Codex* and my grimoire, searching for any mention of strengthening connections, then I tested it with Danika.

If she'd been able to find me hidden beneath the nephilim wards, I hoped she could do the same when I surrendered to Carmen.

My head snapped up as something thudded on the balcony, but it was only Kaelan and Nathaniel.

But my excitement crumbled when neither met my gaze. I refocused on my potions, steeling myself for the next blow.

A heavy silence pressed down around me and I feared I'd suffocate, waiting for them to speak.

"How are they trying to track me?" I asked.

"The Inquisitors are working on a spell array," Nathaniel said, passing me a paper detailing the specific runes. "While the UMC casts spells nonstop, using every variation they have. They're desperate."

"Good."

I looked over the paper. I'd never seen such a combination, but they were the expert trackers.

"We can use that to our advantage."

"And we have a full team forming. They'll be here tomorrow," Astrid said.

"By then, it will be too late," I said. "What about the enforcers or Beylin?"

Kaelan handed me a slip of paper. "Found this at Divine Coffee. I've already checked it for tracking magic."

"It's blank," Nathaniel said as I hunted for any markings invisible to the eye. "How does that help us?"

I pointed to the bottom of the paper. "Because it's from a pad of paper supplied by the Nemea hotel where the Inquisitors held me."

I held it up to the light and squinted. She'd hidden the rune well.

The moment I pushed a drop of magic into it, and a dark script flowed across the page.

Your life for theirs. Find me when the full moon rises. Come alone.

I dropped the paper as flames devoured it.

"How dramatic," I muttered, rolling my eyes.

"What in the hells was that?" Nathaniel hissed. "A location spell?"

"No, didn't you ever pass secret notes in class?" I said.

Their expressions told me the answer was no.

"It was a basic spell to hide a message. Usually, you just make the words disappear, but I guess Carmen wanted a bit more flare."

"But where do we go?" Astrid asked. "She doesn't mean to meet at the convention center after yesterday, does she? It's still sealed off by the UMC."

"Yes, but they wouldn't expect us to return." I shrugged.

A memory flashed through my mind from when I'd touched Kaelan's blood. How I'd been standing on a rooftop facing off against demonspawn.

Despite the scant information, my heart was certain.

This was it.

"We don't have the numbers to take her by force," Astrid said.

"No, but we will."

"You're going to use yourself as bait," Kaelan said, his face unreadable as he surveyed me.

I grinned. "Exactly."

Chapter Forty-Seven

A blustery wind wrapped around me, and I pulled my borrowed jacket tighter, pretending its thin fabric could protect me from what waited ahead.

Clouds swallowed the setting summer sun, weighing down the sky as Kaelan and I waited on the rooftop near the convention center.

The nephilim was silent beside me, a strong and steady presence, while the other two kept a close watch on the area.

Only distance would delay their arrival if they needed to intervene. I refused to let them get closer, worried about Carmen or her demon-spawn sensing them.

But I wasn't here to pick a fight; I was here to surrender, to free my friends, and stop whatever Carmen was planning.

"They're here," Danika said.

I hissed a breath out between my teeth, pulled off the jacket, and handed it back to Kaelan.

We'd spent all day planning for every contingency, drilling them into my memory.

"Are you sure about this?" he said, as if we hadn't had the same argument ten times already. "You can still change your mind."

Do you see Indra and Rynac? I asked Danika.

"They're both here."

I squeezed my eyes shut, the vice around my chest easing a fraction.

"There's no choice to be made," I said. My life in exchange for my friends; it was a worthy trade even if my plan failed.

"I don't like this."

"You don't have to. Just make sure you find me before it's too late."

He raked a hand through his hair, his jaw clenching as if he wanted to say something else.

Deep in my heart, I knew the chances of the nephilim succeeding were slim. I couldn't rely on them to find me. I'd be on my own.

For the first time in fifteen years, I unclasped my necklace and handed it to Kaelan, surrendering the one protection I'd sworn to my parents that I'd never take off.

My fingers trailed over my bare neck, and I shuddered as I sensed the tracking magic press against my skin, even with the wards on this rooftop. I prayed this plan worked.

I swallowed hard as I tried to ignore feeling so exposed, so vulnerable. And yet, my magic stirred in my chest.

Not the volatile power that latched onto my unstable emotions, but something calm and steady. Almost as if it were unfurling, trickling through my body to reassure me it would be there when I needed it.

Vulnerable yet powerful. My soul laid bare for the world to see.

Kaelan took my hand, snapping me out of that odd sensation, and pulled out his dagger.

I met his gaze and nodded at the question in his eyes.

Faster than I could follow, his blade sliced across my forearm.

Glistening red beads of blood bloomed, and he touched the pendant of my necklace to it. Then his thumb dragged over the wound, followed by a tingling warmth, his magic knitting the skin back together.

"Thank you," I breathed, reluctant to pull my arm from his grip.

My blood and a sentimental item, a fallback to locate me if our moon-blessed connection failed.

"Can I offer you one last safeguard?" Kaelan asked, not meeting my gaze. "It's a powerful protection rune, one that I don't use lightly."

"Why are you bringing this up now? Are there consequences for using it?"

High-level runes could be dangerous. Many took something more from the caster than just their magic.

"It's an angelic rune and requires angel blood. The only consequences will fall on me, and I can handle them."

"Why are you offering me this?"

I didn't want to brush off anything that might offer me an edge, but angelic runes were a highly guarded secret.

To offer one to a witch? I'd expect hell to freeze over first.

"You're a moon-blessed," he said. "You are one of us. It's my duty to protect you."

Conviction shone in his gaze, powerful enough that I believed his words, that I would trust him with my life.

"I accept." The words tumbled out before my brain caught up.

Kaelan nodded, stepping closer.

"Here." He tapped just above my heart. "Where they won't see it."

I swallowed and pulled down the neck of my shirt to expose my skin. He didn't even flinch as his blade sliced his flesh, shimmering golden blood welling along the cut.

Dipping his finger into his blood, he met my gaze and waited.

If I admitted how terrified I was, the last of my resolve would crumble.

How could I refuse one last protection?

I nodded, uncertain what I was agreeing to. But that was a problem for future Nyssa—if I even survived the night.

My skin prickled, Kaelan's touch leaving a trail of heat in its wake.

He murmured as he traced out the rune. I couldn't understand his words, but they sent a shiver down my spine.

Power wrapped around me as Kaelan's musical voice filled the air.

The sound was mesmerizing. Then the realization hit me—*that* was the language of the angels.

The words faded, and I mourned their loss as if the world was duller without them.

But when Kaelan lifted his gaze, his green eyes glowed as if the light of the angels shone from within him.

Like an angelic beacon, it tugged at me.

Kaelan straightened and stepped back, shattering the spell. But the strength that surrounded me remained.

I was safe. Protected.

"Thank you," I said when I found my voice.

Without looking, I pulled my top back up to cover the rune.

I had to get moving, or I'd stay on this rooftop forever.

My friends needed me, and if Carmen didn't get whatever she was looking for from me, she would take it from them. I couldn't allow them to make that sacrifice for me.

Kaelan remained still and silent as I headed for the fire escape. I was almost relieved he didn't try to persuade me to stay again.

I climbed down the stairs and walked across the street toward the convention center.

We had planned this route, the angel-born drilling the twists and turns into my mind.

I didn't want to get lost on my way to turn myself in.

The weight of someone's stare bore into my back, but I resisted turning to discover who watched me.

Danika remained silent.

I wanted to reach out and say something to her. I knew this hurt her as much as me.

She'd just found me, and now I might be taken away. But I was grateful to have her beside me.

We would face this together.

A warmth pulsed in my chest, and I pressed my hand against it with a smile. She must have sensed my thoughts.

The full moon had risen high enough to light my path as I climbed up the ladder to reach the roof.

I wish I'd known about this last time. Might've saved me a dip in the river.

A shudder crawled over me as the acrid scent of sulfur enveloped me.

Did the nephilim ever get used to that stench? Did they ever face a horde of demonspawn and not feel terrified?

Six pairs of soulless black eyes fixed on me, tracking my every movement as I crossed the roof to where Carmen waited.

"I'm here," I called out. "Release them."

A wide smile graced her lips, setting my teeth on edge.

Rynac and Indra were on their knees in front of her, their wrists bound behind them and blindfolds covering their eyes. Dried blood caked their clothes.

I narrowed my gaze at Carmen. She had hurt them, and I would make her pay.

Tapping into my magic, I twined the solar and lunar energies around my wrists at a single thought, and their gold and silver glow washed over me.

"I said release them."

Carmen's laugh cut through the air, grating on my nerves. "You're not in any place to bargain. Do you think you're powerful enough to take out all of my demonspawn?"

No, I didn't, but I wasn't going to tell her that. And by channeling my powers, I hoped to be a beacon.

By now, the enforcers should have informed the UMC that they'd spotted me near the convention center.

I counted on the Inquisitors' moles to be quick.

If things went right, they'd start scrying for my magic, and hopefully, they'd arrive before I had to leave with Carmen.

"I'm here to make a deal. Release the enforcers, and I'll come with you quietly."

"What makes you think you have a choice? You came here aware of the inevitable outcome. At every crossroads along the way, you've done exactly what I wanted, thinking it was your own free will. Every little nudge, and every big one, too. They've all been me. You wouldn't have achieved any of this without me. You'll do what I say because that's what I made you for."

"Release them, and I'll go with you," I repeated, clamping down on the fear she might be speaking the truth.

Everything that happened. Was every single thing a result of her influence? Was I nothing more than a clueless pawn?

"Kill them," Carmen commanded.

"What!" I screamed, but the demonspawn surged.

I flung my magic out, an astral shield blooming to life around my friends just as the first talons sliced toward them.

The demonspawn howled in anger, but I sprinted forward.

Whipping out two potions, I threw them without aiming and slid through my shield before crashing into Rynac.

The bright flash burned my eyes, and the demonspawn shrieked.

My hand went to the dagger concealed in my boot, needing to sever their bonds so they could run away.

I cut through Rynac's first, and then turned to Indra, but my shield was already failing under the assault.

How had they recovered so fast, and where had Carmen gone?

Rynac tore off his blindfold and wobbled to his feet as I hacked through Indra's bindings.

"Run. The nephilim will protect you," I said, as the angel-born descended on the swarming mass of demonspawn.

We knew Carmen would attack, but I had hoped she would do so after I'd freed the siblings.

Astrid landed next to us, tossing weapons at the enforcers as I whipped out my conduit.

I poured more solar magic into the runed band before it could attack my shield.

Kaelan and Nathaniel launched themselves at the demonspawn, attempting to cut a path through them.

But as soon as we cut one down, two more would take its place as we inched closer to our escape route.

Where were they all coming from?

I channeled more power into the shield. Where in all the hells were the Inquisitors and the UMC?

With my magic activated, they should have located me by now.

Danika, update.

"*The UMC squad is a block away,*" she said.

I swore, could we hold out for that long?

Any sign of Carmen?

"*No.*"

Had she run?

I hurled another vial of ooze at the demonspawn snapping at Indra's back.

My fingers grazed over the lone enhancement potion, but I couldn't waste it on demonspawn.

If I wanted to capture Carmen, I needed to save it.

With a wave of magic, Astrid knocked back the two demonspawn that blocked our path. As if second nature, the angel-born formed a circle around us.

Rynac and Indra fought at my side, attacking a demonspawn who slipped through.

They were wearing us down.

Had Carmen known that I wouldn't come alone? Would I have to watch the demonspawn kill each of my friends before they took me?

They pressed harder until we had no room to fight.

I doubted the nephilim could even escape by flying with the enemy right on top of us.

Back-to-back, we faced the swarming horde, bleeding and panting for breath as we waited for the demonspawn to descend on us.

But to our surprise, they moved no closer.

I swallowed hard, surveying the sea of black eyes.

We would never make it out alive. There were too many.

"An impressive display," Carmen's voice said in my mind.

I whirled around, feeling her eyes on me, but only more demonspawn crawled onto the roof. How had she amassed such a force?

"But consorting with nephilim?"

"What do you want?" I shouted.

"You, of course," Carmen said. *"And I know you want to join me. Why else would you have come tonight?"*

"To save my friends."

"What will you sacrifice to save them? I have an endless supply of demonspawn. How long will your friends survive?"

I gulped, looking at my friends. Gold and red blood splattered across them, mixed with the black demon ichor.

Could they hold out until backup arrived?

"If I go with you willingly, will you call off your demonspawn?" I asked, ignoring the looks from the others.

They knew this was the plan.

Sure, it was the worst-case scenario, but what choice did we have?

Carmen appeared in the sea of demonspawn.

A wide grin spread across her face. "Yes."

"Do I have your word?"

"Yes, you have my word." She held out a hand.

Why did that feel too easy? I couldn't trust her. She wanted to wield my power to tear the veil, but what alternative did I have but to obey?

I would sacrifice my life to save theirs. I'd use every last ounce of my energy to protect them, to stop Carmen and her master.

It was my duty, even if it severed my magic and shattered my soul.

Rynac and Indra shifted away without a word as I stepped forward, but the gaze of the nephilim burned my skin.

The demonspawn parted, forming a path straight to Carmen.

Danika, I called out, holding the image of my fox in my mind. She didn't answer.

A twisting black portal formed behind Carmen as she beckoned me closer. I glanced over my shoulder.

My friends remained firm, waiting for an attack, but the demonspawn retreated, slipping into the long shadows cast by the full moon.

"Come," Carmen said, pulling my focus back to her.

Halfway between my friends and Carmen, I paused.

Moonlight cascaded over me, whispering for me to stop.

To look.

Something was wrong.

Deep in my bones, I knew something was amiss.

"Your attachment to your supposed friends weakens you. It blinds you from the future you should have. Don't let them hold you back."

She was half right. I forced myself to take another step.

Hesitation would only put them in danger again. I wanted this. Planned for it.

So why did it all feel wrong?

Shouts echoed behind me, and I spun around.

Relief washed over me as soldiers and enforcers appeared, many in civilian clothes. They filled the roof and perches surrounding us, their guns raised.

The breath rushed out of me. The moon reflected on their pitch-black eyes, and they trained their weapons on my friends.

"No!" I screamed as the first muzzle flashed.

Magic surged within me without hesitation. Flames wreathed my hand, and I crafted an astral shield around my friends.

Gunfire filled the air. My shield shuddered with every bullet that hit it. I lost sight of my companions, but my spell held.

Even when my arms shook, I continued pouring magic into it.

"That's enough!" Carmen snarled.

A claw wrapped around my throat.

Another dug into my arm, pulling me back against a hard body. The hulking demonspawn dragged me backward.

The more I struggled, the tighter its grip became, yet I had to maintain the shield.

Magic rippled through the air as more soldiers and enforcers descended into the area. And wolves. The additional forces tore into the thralls.

I ripped a potion from my belt, about to smash at my feet, when the demonspawn's claw raked up my arm.

A sharp gasp escaped me, and the vial slipped free, clattering to the ground.

Bright red blood poured from my wound.

The solar magic drained out, the rune damaged.

My focus slipped, causing my astral shield to weaken.

The demonspawn dragged me away with little resistance.

My eyes followed the long trail of blood I left behind as my legs struggled to hold me up.

The black portal loomed ahead of me, devouring all the light that touched it.

A figure launched into the air. Their wings flared a moment before they dove right for me.

The hand around my throat constricted, and I gasped for breath.

My magic sputtered and died.

The astral shield shattered as I clawed at the demonspawn's arm.

And then darkness engulfed me.

CHAPTER FORTY-EIGHT

Sharp pain snapped me back to consciousness. I swore my head was splitting in two as I rolled to my side and shoved off the cold, hard floor.

Sulfur and iron filled my nose, thick enough to taste. I choked, and every cough sent new shockwaves of agony through my body.

"And here I thought you were going to miss the entire party." An icy voice echoed around me, and I winced at the sound.

Carmen.

My memories crashed back into me: Indra and Rynac. The rooftop. The explosion.

Goddess above, had the others survived?

Ow. Why does thinking hurt?

My vision swam as I tried to get my bearings.

Blood, dust, and unidentified grime coated me. My left arm throbbed, and I flexed my hand.

The sight of the marred arm should've made me nauseous, but I was too numb.

A faint spell lingered over my wound, presumably to stop me from bleeding out, but the large pool of blood beneath it suggested it was ineffective.

Is that why my head is spinning?

Somewhere in the back of my mind, alarm bells sounded. Under all the blood, I knew that the inked rune had suffered damage.

Without it, I couldn't contain the solar magic so I could cast lunar spells. And that meant I couldn't channel my powers to trigger the tracking spells nor boost my connection to the moon-blessed.

But I feared that would be the least of my concerns.

Just hold on.

I attempted to reassure myself, but I wasn't very convincing.

The tracking spell had been my best bet. I'd known it might fail, but I had assumed there would be time for a Plan B.

I had to trust the nephilim.

And if my spell shattering injured them?

"You lied, Carmen," I rasped.

I squinted past the light that shone down on me. I'd foolishly trusted her word and now my friends' lives hung in the balance.

A shimmer of gold caught my eye. My stomach dropped.

Ensnared once more in spell array, this one inked in angel blood.

The latent power within it shivered across my skin. I sat in the center of a golden circle, positioned at the topmost point of the star.

A sacrifice circle.

Upon activation, the array would feed on the energies contained within the circle: Me.

Fucking hell. Could this day get any worse?

My head throbbed in response. I swiped the hair out of my face, my fingers coming away warm and sticky.

"Lied?" she said with mock offense. "I agreed to call off my demon-spawn. You never mentioned my thralls."

I squinted, trying to make out my surroundings.

Demonspawn swarmed the area, hundreds of hungry eyes fixed on me. Past them were bare concrete walls and a high ceiling.

Was I in another warehouse? Was I even still in Arkirith?

"You don't seem to understand how important you are, Nyssa," Carmen said as she paced at the edge of the spell array. "A lunar witch worthy of wielding her powers."

"So worthy that you are going to kill me?"

"Kill you?" she said in mock horror before it morphed into a smile. "No, I won't kill you. Not yet."

"This is you livening up the place?" I said, waving to the spell array.

"It's a test."

"And what are we testing?" I asked, knowing she wanted me to.

"How powerful you are, how much potential you have. This is all for your own good, and I'm going to help you achieve what you've always dreamed of."

The manic edge to her voice chilled me to the bone.

"This is your chance to seize the power you deserve to wield, to reject the box the witches would shove you in. That persistent drive within you has kept you going, even when everyone else wants you to give up. But I won't give up on you, and if that means I must force your hand, then so be it. You are the key, and tonight I will prove it."

"Key to what?" I asked, needing to hear it for myself.

"To breach the veil," she said, grinning with far too many teeth. "To form a portal strong enough for my master to enter this realm and claim it as their own."

Ice coursed through me. This wasn't about a tear, but opening a gateway for a demon lord.

I couldn't breathe. Couldn't think.

Why did Selene offer me a second chance at life if my fate was to start the next Great War? Why didn't she let me drown?

The vivid image of the vision flickered through my mind.

The roaring flames, the seething eyes brimming with malice. No wonder they wished to destroy me.

When I accompanied Carmen, I'd clung to the hope that the nephilim would arrive in time.

Now I hoped they wouldn't. That this spell would consume me.

My death to stop countless others. It was a worthy sacrifice.

Even if I survived, I'd be hunted for the rest of my life as the last lunar witch.

If Carmen knew about what I was, her demon lord would, too. I'd never be safe.

"But I'm getting ahead of myself," Carmen said, cutting through my spiraling thoughts. "This test is to create a powerful portal, capable of holding for days. Today, we summon enough demons to ravage this city."

When the warlock approached, Carmen stepped away. But I wasn't finished with her.

"I'll never help you. I will fight you every step of the way."

"That's a lot of talk for someone trapped within my spell array," she said, arching an eyebrow at me. "This is just a test, Nyssa. You were always brilliant at your exams through university."

"How are you so familiar with me?"

"My spies have been monitoring you for years. From the moment of your awakening, in fact. You've always had great potential, but I feared your parents would squander it. Lucky the Alchemy Guild offered you membership in Arkirith."

"That was you?" Was everything in my life a lie? Was everything a part of her game?

"I possess a greater understanding of your thoughts and emotions, far surpassing your own."

Carmen barked out a laugh, and I flinched.

"Every step along the way, each one exactly as I predicted. Why else did I take the altered? I knew my little lunar witch would do anything to retrieve them."

The demonspawn parted as Carmen turned.

My last ounce of hope fled as Rynac and Indra stared back at me. Bound, gagged, and coated in blood, they looked exactly as they had on the rooftop.

"How could you . . ." The words choked out of me.

My head swam. Was I nothing but a puppet?

"You said you'd let them go."

"I released the two enforcers from the rooftop. You never ensured the ones I let go were your friends. Good thing, too, as they are far too valuable."

Carmen scraped her nails down Rynac's cheek, leaving behind a trickle of blood. He tried to jerk away, but she seized his chin.

Her other fingers twisted into a gnarled, black claw.

She tilted Rynac's head back and pressed her razor-sharp talon against his throat.

"I knew you'd come for them, and I know you'll obey me to save them. Isn't that right, Nyssa?"

Heart lodged in my throat, I couldn't tear my eyes from Rynac.

Despite his swollen eye and split lip, determination shone in his gaze as he refused to cower.

He faced his death head-on. And it would be my fault.

I did this to them. My friendship has done this. I hurt those I love and care for. I poison everything I touch.

No, those were not my thoughts.

It wasn't my fault bad people wanted to hurt me and targeted my friends. I wasn't to blame.

The voice resembled mine, but I sensed the poison laced into those words. The taint of magic.

My gaze hardened as it narrowed on Carmen, but she only smiled.

"That little fox of yours did a valiant job of shielding you, so thank you for removing that necklace of yours and leaving that creature behind. It'll make this far easier."

Her words hit me like a physical blow. Everything I had done played right into her hand. I couldn't even trust my thoughts anymore.

"I am still with you," Danika whispered in my mind, her words so quiet I could barely hear them over my own thoughts. *"They haven't detected me yet, but if I shield your mind, the dark witch might notice."*

I sent a sense of acknowledgement through the bond as I kept my gaze on Carmen.

She was gloating about fooling the UMC, but I only half listened. The delay allowed the others more time to find me.

"I've disrupted some runes, but they might notice."

I'll buy you as much time as I can, I thought back.

My temples throbbed as I reached out with my awareness, spreading myself thin as I tested the wards. They had weakened but still held.

"Prove your worth to me, Nyssa," Carmen said, her red eyes burning with passion. "I can give you everything you desire. You'll never have to fear the Inquisitors again. We'll protect you and safeguard all those you care for. We'll never reject you for embracing your true self."

My resolve hardened with each word. While Carmen might understand parts of me, she would never see or understand what lay inside my heart.

"I've seen what's in your heart, Nyssa. That desire to help others drives you forward, and together we can do just that. We can protect this realm from needless deaths."

"Needless deaths? You want to destroy Arkirith and all my friends."

"Those who choose to fight always risk their lives, and civilians caught in the crossfire are beyond anyone's control. The city won't be destroyed, but it will grab the world leaders' attention."

I looked over the spell array. I'd never seen anything so complicated.

My time was running out and my choices few.

Once I'd desired what Carmen offered, but never like this. Was that what had corrupted her and made her bargain with a demon lord? I tucked those thoughts away for later.

If I survived.

I couldn't talk my way out of this, and I had zero doubts she'd use Indra and Rynac against me.

My only hope was the nephilim, but I needed to channel magic to empower the binding spell.

"The choice is yours," Carmen said. "Join me and I can help you reach your dreams. Refuse, and more will suffer. If you accept, you'll prevent avoidable deaths."

I kept my face a mask as fear clogged my throat.

No matter what I decided, people were going to die. But what choice did I have?

Resist and risk more casualties or accept and hope to save lives.

"What do I have to do?" I asked, furrowing my brow as I nodded at the array.

Carmen assessed me for a long moment.

Then she chuckled, her smile growing wider. "Lunar essence willingly given. Offer your magic to the spell array. We'll manage the rest."

"What if I fail?" I whispered.

My shoulders curled in, playing the part that Carmen expected.

A witch who had failed for years.

A defeated child, desperate for approval.

"You are stronger than you think, Nyssa."

No threats or coercion.

I swallowed hard. She believed I wanted this.

"Do I have your word that you will give me everything you promised?"

"You have my word."

My skin crawled at the lust that filled her voice and burned in her crimson eyes.

"Do you agree?"

"One last thing, and I will agree," I said. "Free Indra and Rynac first, and give me your word they will remain unharmed."

Carmen cocked her head, assessing me.

I let out a shaky breath, willing her to believe me. "You said you would safeguard those I care for."

"If you assume your friends will be able to lead the soldiers here to stop this, you are sorely wrong."

"No matter what, the portal will be opened," I said, my gaze unwavering. "And I do want to draw the UMC here, but only to keep the fighting contained and protect innocents within the city."

I willed her to hear the truth in my words, while ignoring the heavy stone that sank in my stomach.

UMC soldiers and enforcers would lay down their lives to protect the city. All I could hope was to give them an advantage.

"Very well, I give you my word."

She snapped some orders and thralls appeared, hauling my friends upright. They tried to resist, pulling against the thralls, their protests were muffled by their gags.

I turned away, fixing my attention onto the spell array, and schooling my features.

My heart constricted as I willed them to leave.

Follow them, I whispered to Danika.

"But the runes—"

Please, make sure they make it out and that they understand.

Danika was silent for a moment before I sensed her acceptance.

Carmen's intense gaze bore into me, pressing against my skin. I fought the temptation to meet her eyes.

"Whenever you're ready," she said with an exaggerated bow.

I nodded, lifting my arms. Invoking my magic, I let it gather in my hands drip by drip.

Danika?

"Almost to the ward."

Walk through it, then channel everything you have through the bond.

I pushed my magic into the array in a steady, controlled flow, trying to drag this out.

Teasing out a thread, I guided it into my bond with Danika and the moon-blessed mark.

The back of my neck prickled.

The angel-blood rune throbbed against my heart, a steady pulse of irritation, like it knew I'd been ignoring it.

I sent a tentative trickle of magic into it, then shoved more power through.

Even through layers of concrete, I felt the snap of contact when I reached Danika.

In my mind, I watched her melt out of the shadows behind my friends, silent and sure.

A wide door opened, and moonlight spilled through, framing Indra and Rynac as they crossed into the forest beyond.

And then Danika vanished.

I doubled over as something inside me tore free, leaving a raw, empty ache where she should have been.

Chapter Forty-Nine

"**S**teady now," Carmen barked. The golden runes around me lit up like stars in the sky. They hungered for my energy, gobbling up the silver light the moment it touched them.

I siphoned off more magic and funneled it into my bond with the moon-blessed.

Find me. Please, find me.

Every fiber of my being shuddered. My skin crawled, and I tore my eyes away from the runes.

Even with the deep cowl covering his head, I felt the warlock's gaze bore into me. He lifted his arms, revealing black, gnarled fingers.

A guttural chant clawed through the air, the words raking across my mind. I wanted to cover my ears, but I couldn't move.

Power poured into the array, summoning a wind that battered me.

Dark magic coiled through the runes, charging the sacrifice circle beneath me.

I needed to fight back, but my magic slipped through my fingers as I tried to control it. The array had latched onto my energy and ripped it from my grasp.

"Did you think I wouldn't notice?" Carmen snarled over the roaring wind.

I fought with everything I had, clawing back my magic and infusing it into the bond.

Let it be enough.

Sinister tendrils of smoke and shadows rose around me. Before I could even lift my arms, they pierced my body.

I screamed, scrambling for magic to shield myself.

The tendrils latched onto my power, dragging it from me and channeling it into the array.

They would strip every last drop from me.

No . . .

A whisper echoed amidst the screams in my mind.

No!

I refused to allow my power to open a portal to hell. To damage the veil and reverse what my ancestors had sacrificed their lives for.

I had to stop this. Had to hold on. But there was only one solution.

Destroy the spell array.

All the magic powering it had to be released.

If I was somewhere underneath the city—the backlash from breaking a spell with this amount of power . . . it would be cataclysmic.

I hissed out a breath through clenched teeth, gripping the flow of magic even as it was being torn from me.

Power thrummed above my heart, and a fortifying strength wrapped around me. I squeezed, attempting to stop the drain and wrestle control back.

My shaking fingers dropped to my belt, but my potions were gone.

Good thing I had backup.

I pulled the single vial from my cleavage—Nathaniel's suggestion. I'd laugh about that later if I lived through this.

The warlock screamed, but there was nothing he could do as I swallowed the empowerment potion.

Power rushed through me. I had to act fast before the array stole it.

My solar magic surged, now fueled by rage, and flooded my body, burning away the dark magic.

I staggered as the tendrils shattered, releasing me from their hold. But it wouldn't last long. I had to get out of the sacrifice circle to keep them from stealing my power again.

It was like wading through thick mud, but I pressed forward.

Blood dripped down my arm as the wound reopened. I probed the solar rune, but it was too damaged. The smallest distortion could alter a rune and its intended effect.

Not only was pushing magic into a flawed rune dangerous, but often fatal.

Damaged rune.

I blinked, scanning the array. The golden design and its runes flickered as I fought. There. A rune for stability. Another rune there to modulate the flow of power.

I'd have to start with them before I grew more desperate and just guessed.

The warlock snarled, and the pressure around me increased until I struggled to breathe. But I ignored him.

Magic wouldn't contain me.

The harder I fought, the harder he would have to push his own magic. I wouldn't give up without a fight.

We'd find out who was stronger.

I lifted my injured arm, letting the blood drip and pool into my other hand, then tossed it at the first rune.

A bright flash half blinded me, but I blinked away the white spots to find the rune obliterated.

The latent magic in my blood had distorted it.

The ground beneath me shifted, and the entire room wobbled from side to side.

No, that wasn't right. It was the magic. Destabilized, it could destroy the surrounding reality.

Great.

With heavy steps, I worked my way to the next rune. I did my best to ignore that the room tilted at a forty-five-degree angle, knowing it wasn't real.

I cradled my wounded arm against my stomach to contain the flow of blood, but every now and then white flared as it splattered a rune.

The floor undulated beneath me in a very un-concrete like way as I tossed another handful of blood over the modulation rune.

This time, I averted my gaze before I was blinded.

Another rune destroyed.

The magic shifted, no longer flowing smoothly, but going where it pleased. The glow of the runes ebbed and flowed.

I was almost there.

Potent magic surged like an angry storm through the spell array, and my head swam. Or was that from the blood loss?

I lurched forward as something seized my magic and yanked hard.

The warlock and Carmen stood together, their powers combining.

Dark energy gathered around as they chanted. Even with the array weakened, I was no match for both of them.

Someone yelled my name, willing me to hold on. But I wasn't strong enough.

An angry buzz filled my ears as my magic was ripped from my grasp. The force brought me to my knees.

In the center of the spell array, magic coalesced.

At first, it was just a flicker of darkness, barely noticeable, but then it spread, twisting and turning, gaining momentum and size with each passing moment.

The portal was forming.

I snarled.

This was not my destiny.

My magic would not be twisted into creating this portal.

Or let Carmen use me to start a new war.

I wrenched my power back, but at the smile on Carmen's face, I knew it was too late.

The air thrummed with potential, and even damaged, the array funneled power into the portal.

Bright flashes flared outside the spell array.

They'd found me.

Enforcers, nephilim, shifters, UMC soldiers. They all flooded into the room and faced the demonspawn who formed a protective barrier around the dark witch and warlock.

They had come for me. I wrapped the relief and warmth around my heart and gathered my strength.

I had to fight, or we were all doomed.

Sucking in a ragged breath, I closed my eyes, gathering what magic I had left within me.

Solar energies zipped through me, furious and demanding release.

Despite my diminished lunar powers, I could still sense the magic, like a mist floating around the spell array.

"Selene, offer me your guidance once more," I whispered. "Lend me your strength and your courage."

I didn't know if the Goddess had heard me, but this was my fate, and neither Goddess nor demon would control it.

It was mine and mine alone.

I envisioned the magic that saturated the air, then reached out with my will. I called to the power, compelling it to pool into my hands, to return to me.

At first, I didn't sense it, but then a warmth settled on my palm.

It quivered, waiting for my command.

I cast it out and wove it into an astral shield.

It snapped into place, a shimmering iridescent dome that covered the array. I pushed it, gritting my teeth as I willed it past the outer circle, so I could seize control of the array.

Carmen and the warlock reeled; their connection severed.

The spell was under my control now.

I channeled more power, strengthening the shield.

The demonspawn outside snarled, lunging at my barrier. I flinched at each attack, but I had to hold it.

Flames churned within me, begging to be wielded.

Soon.

I sealed off the astral shield spell, releasing my hold. Relief washed over me as it maintained itself.

But it hadn't stopped the gaping black hole, which grew larger.

Through it, I glimpsed a flickering land. Scorched black earth, void of life as hellfire rained from the sky.

Demons massed around the portal, waiting for it to fully form.

Taking a deep breath, I gathered the power still within me. I had to destroy this array, no matter what.

Exhaling, I pushed my magic out. Everything I had. Solar. Lunar. Every last drop.

Fire sizzled around me, chasing the glowing moonlight that rippled over my skin.

Gold and silver fought for control. I pushed harder.

This was who I was. The sun and the moon. Night and Day.

Both were part of me.

I couldn't pick and choose the parts of me I liked, while pretending the rest didn't exist.

They were all me.

They made me who I was today.

And I was done hiding it.

Something shifted deep within my chest.

Gold and silver fused around me.

Fire wreathed my body, but the silver light shone through.

Two sides of the same coin.

I gasped in air as if it was the first time I'd taken a full breath.

Power thrummed through my veins, a strength I'd never felt before.

A guttural growl cut through the air, and I fixed my gaze on the first demonspawn to crawl from the portal. More clawed and scrambled behind it, vying to climb through.

A sea of glowing red eyes burned behind them, each one salivating at the chance to enter our realm.

Raising my hands, I called to the array's magic.

Blood still dripped down my hand. Mixed with my power, it called to the demons like a beacon.

The stolen lunar power within the array heeded my summons, seeping into my body like the rising tide.

Higher and higher until I didn't think I could hold it any longer.

My arms shook, the surrounding air vibrated, as three more demonspawn appeared. I cast my magic out, summoning a massive moonbeam that washed over my body.

I pushed more and more energy into it. The light flared, and the demonspawn flinched away.

They circled me but didn't attack, even though the hunger in their black eyes lusted for my blood.

It was almost time.

I strengthened my shield, weaving fire between the strands of moonlight until it glowed as if stealing the light from the world around it. But it would hold. It had to.

Five demonspawn spread out in an arc around me, and I grinned. What better way to neutralize angel blood than with demon ichor?

"Secare."

With a flick of my hand, I shaped my power, crafting five deadly blades of magic and hurled them at the demonspawn.

Before they could recoil, my blades sliced through their thick necks like they were butter.

Black ichor sprayed from the stumps, and the world shuddered.

Calling my magic back to me, I reinforced the shield and wrapped the rest of the magic around myself.

It might not be enough, but a calm settled deep within me.

If that was my fate, so be it. This was my choice.

A sacrifice worth making.

Sulfur clogged the air. The runes fizzed and hissed as demon blood devoured the angel blood. I wrapped my magic tighter, like a cocoon of strength and solidarity, watching black ichor pour across the floor, dissolving every rune it touched.

The ground rippled beneath my feet as wild magic lashed out.

Through my shield, I sensed the others. I didn't know how I could, but I felt them with each beat of my heart.

Some were familiar, others unknown, but all of them were fighting with me. Many ached with new injuries; every wound throbbed as if it were my own.

My knees weakened. I infused power into my body, soothing the phantom wounds until their pain faded.

I drank in its strength, letting the ebb of the moon empower me.

The array faltered, and the world exploded.

Magic ripped through the air, lashing and tearing.

Wanting to devour and destroy. But I would not let it consume me. I had to hold the shield to contain this power.

Debris rained down, bouncing off my shield.

Chaotic magic blinded me, and I squeezed my eyes shut as fire and ice tore at my skin.

Shadow and light cut into me. The magic raged, a maelstrom of uncontained power.

Warmth trickled down my face, but I refused to release my spells.

My magic seared through me, but I held the shield in place.

My friends fought outside those walls. I had to protect them.

Each breath burned in my chest, as if the very air was aflame. I coughed, blood coating my mouth. Liquid poured from my nose and dripped from my eyes.

I couldn't hold on. This was going to tear me apart.

I screamed, but the power roared louder.

And then it was gone.

Like the final breath escaping the dying, my spells ceased to be.

Not a whisper of magic remained within me.

I crashed to my knees.

My ears rang, muting the screams of the dying.

Blood coated my tattered clothes, but I'd survived.

Blinking through the dusty haze, my heart stilled at the utter destruction around me.

The once sturdy walls had split and crumbled, while cracked slabs of the floor jutted up like broken teeth.

Fissures snaked across the ceiling, parts of it had collapsed and I could just make out the full moon glowing in the night sky.

Debris and bodies shifted as my allies emerged, battered and bruised but alive. Some aided the fallen, while the rest methodically ensured every last demonspawn and thrall was killed.

We'd done it.

The enemy dead. The array destroyed.

I swayed as the fighters' shouts mingled with the cries of pain and anguish.

Everything ached as if eternal fires scorched my insides, but my bones were frozen, and my flesh shredded.

The skin on my chest ignited. The angel rune infused my heart with strength and determination, refusing to let it stop beating.

Then the last of my energy flagged, and I slumped to the floor.

My body gave out until all I could do was wheeze in my next breath.

Magic flickered. Cool fingers caressed the back of my neck.

You're not finished yet.

No. This wasn't finished.

Power bloomed deep in my core, like the first glow of the crescent moon after the darkness of a new moon.

Magic flowed through my body. Silvery light rippled off my skin as I heaved myself off the ground and picked my way through the debris.

The power hummed around me, flowing over the bodies of the dead demonspawn and turning them to ash. Strength coursed through me as my gaze fixed on the crumpled form of the warlock.

Carmen was gone, but the warlock remained. He flinched as I loomed over him.

"You will never harm anyone, ever again," I said, power lacing my words.

With the last dregs of my magic, I shaped it. Silver bands wrapped around the warlock's wrists and ankles, and another covered his mouth.

"Justice awaits."

The final remnants of my energy slipped away, and I surrendered to the darkness.

Chapter Fifty

The world was dark, and my body wouldn't respond. *Was I dead?* No—death didn't come with this much screaming.

Shouts and cries crashed over me, each one a spike through my throbbing skull.

Why couldn't they all just leave me in the quiet?

A spear of light cut through the surrounding darkness, and I winced, squeezing my eyes shut.

Something wet dripped down my face, but I couldn't move to wipe it away. I coughed as dust clogged my lungs.

Waves of agonizing pain jolted through me. The tang of iron coated my tongue.

The voices grew louder. I wanted to sleep, yet a nagging sensation tugged at me. One by one, all the aches and pains of my battered body reawakened.

"Over here," a harsh voice called out, loud enough that my ears rang. "Arrest them and transport them to a secure location."

I opened my mouth to protest, but another cough wracked me.

Each breath was agony, like shards of glass shredding my lungs. I couldn't let them take me, not again.

"It's all right, Nyssa."

A familiar voice. I fought against the weight of my eyelids and found a battered and bleeding Rynac.

"They're taking the warlock away. The nephilim and other Inquisitors are pursuing Carmen. You're safe now. A healer is on the way."

His words faded.

Squeezing Rynac's hand, I let my eyes flutter closed.

Warm. Safe. Silvery moonlight cocooned me.

I didn't know how long I'd drifted.

Pain needled my mind, and with a groan, I returned to the waking world. A white ceiling greeted me. Where was I?

"Decided to join us?" a voice asked.

I squinted at the face until my brain dredged up the name.

"Matti?" Why was an enforcer healer here?

"You finally remembered me. That's an improvement."

"What are you talking about? The last thing I remember—"

Agony. Pain. Blood. Warlock.

I sat up too fast, and the world spun.

"Easy now," he said, grabbing my arms to keep me steady. "You've been in and out for five days."

"Nyssa!" a voice shouted somewhere outside the curtained walls.

Indra burst in, one arm in a sling, followed by Rynac.

"What have I told you about yelling in the medical wing?" Matti scolded. "Nyssa, if you need anything, put your call light on. You two behave. You've got fifteen minutes."

Indra just grinned at the healer; the bruises on her face had already turned yellow.

Rynac limped over, patting the bed before sitting down.

Danika! I lifted my blanket to find the fox curled up against my side.

I brushed a hand across her back, and a wave of relief washed over me, knowing she was unharmed.

She'd just depleted her magic by sharing it with me as I healed.

"How are you feeling?" Indra asked, wrapping her hand around mine and grounding me in the waking world.

"Like I fought a horde of golems. Ones that pummeled me inside and out," I said with a smile, but even that hurt. "What happened? What have I missed?"

"You mean besides how you single-handedly saved the city and captured the warlock?"

My ribs protested as I snorted, but then I sobered. "And Carmen?"

Both of them frowned.

"She escaped," Rynac said. "Most of UMC's forces are now either focused on finding her or investigating traitors among them. The number of thralls she created from within the UMC . . ."

He shook his head. How had Carmen twisted and corrupted so many from an organization meant to protect us?

"A few remained to eradicate the remaining demonspawn."

She was out there. After all of this, she escaped. Would she come for me again?

"They'll get her. Don't worry."

I gave them a weak smile. I wanted to explain everything to them, but my throat constricted, the pain still too fresh.

"Tell me what I missed."

"After you bargained for our freedom—" Indra said.

"Never do that again," Rynac interjected.

"—we emerged in a forest on the outskirts of the city. Danika appeared, and we followed her until we ran into the UMC squad and led them back to the entrance. Then it was chaos. They had an entire army of demonspawn. After the magical blast, we freed all the prisoners. They're resting and should make a full recovery."

"The captives we freed from that warehouse have all been discharged too," Rynac said. "Voren wants to take you out drinking as a thank you."

I huffed a weak laugh, more relieved that he didn't curse my name. "And the nephilim?"

"You don't have to worry about them anymore. They hightailed it after Carmen got away. Doubt they'll bother you again."

"Oh."

So they were gone. Their job was done, and they had moved on.

Why did that thought make my chest tight? Didn't I deserve a goodbye at least?

So much for that moon-blessed connection. Guess I was just a means to an end.

"They found me after we fled the Inquisitors," I said. "Without them, I might have been arrested."

"Oh," they said together.

"I can ask around," Rynac started, but I waved him off.

"It's fine. I'm sure they have more important work."

The words tasted bitter on my tongue. I was too exhausted to unpack *that* right now. Or ever.

"We should let you rest," he said, pushing himself off the bed.

"Wait." I grabbed onto their hands, panic rearing its ugly head.

Indra squeezed my hand. "We'll be back soon."

"I never got to thank you for coming for me—for saving me from the Inquisitors." My voice wobbled, and my traitorous eyes prickled.

How did I cram so many awful things into a few days?

The siblings wrapped me in a tight but gentle hug.

"We will always come for you," Rynac whispered. "And you rescued us."

"But I'm the reason she captured you."

"I'd say we're even," Indra smirked. Both placed a kiss on opposite cheeks, and I laughed.

Danika trotted along beside me as I ambled to the balcony. I'd finally convinced the healer on duty I was well enough to go for a walk.

Even without windows, I'd known the moon had risen, felt its tug, and longed to bathe in her embrace.

I hadn't admitted that the moonlight would aid my recovery, fearing they might check me for head trauma again.

Though my legs had protested, the moment I stepped out onto the moon-washed balcony, my fatigue faded.

Wrapping myself in a blanket, I settled into a chair with Danika curled up on my lap.

For the first time since waking, my mind was blissfully blank—at peace.

My eyes fluttered closed as I turned my face to the moon. Its glow infused me with strength, replenishing all that I had spent, and once again filling the gaping hole within my chest.

How had I lived my whole life without knowing a piece of me had been missing?

"You have visitors," Danika whispered.

Standing in the doorway was Ruby.

"I hope you don't mind the intrusion," she said with a grin.

For a long moment, I could only stare.

She almost appeared back to normal. The spark in her eyes was not as bright, but her smile diminished the pain lines etched onto her face.

I waved her over. "Of course not."

A second, older shifter followed, her pure-white hair twisted into a bun.

The deep creases on her face spoke of laughter and wisdom, but the twinkle in her silver gaze promised mischief.

"This is Nan. She's returned to our pack after we lost our healer and oversaw my recovery."

I nodded to Nan, though my smile faltered. "I apologize for not visiting again."

Ruby brushed it away. "You've been dealing with more important matters."

I winced; guilt still gnawed at me.

"Stop that," Ruby scolded. "The entire pack knows about how you battled the warlock. Word spreads quickly, but your secret is safe with us."

"I also wanted to tell you how sorry I am for what happened. I never—"

"Nyssa," Ruby said with a sad smile. "I am not angry with you, if that's what you're afraid of. None of that was within your control. I don't blame you for what occurred. Please don't let that weigh on you."

I attempted to protest that I deserved all the blame, but Ruby shot me a stern look. "Still, I'm sorry for it. How is your magic?"

"You mean after that dark witch clawed it out of me and forced it into you?" Ruby seethed.

She reined herself in when she noticed my wide-eyed expression.

"Sorry, I might not be angry at you, but I am spiteful toward *them*."

"I attempted to return your power," I said, with a shake of my head.

"Lucky it didn't work, otherwise you might not have been strong enough to save the captives or stop the demonic ritual."

Ruby squeezed my hand, warmth glowing in her eyes.

"I'm thankful my magic aided you, that I contributed to taking them down. Besides, you returned it in the end."

"What do you mean?"

"I oversaw all the shifters who had their lunar energies drained," Nan said. "When they woke up, they all had something missing—not just their magic, but a piece of their soul that connected to it. We had no way of healing that, but when you destroyed the spell array that was fueled by the stolen powers, it returned to its rightful place. Ruby and all those harmed by the dark witch and warlock have recovered."

Relief washed through me as a knot in my chest eased. Danika nuzzled my hand as if to reassure me.

"We also have an offer," Ruby said as I blinked away the tears.

An offer?

I looked between the two shifters, but their faces were unreadable.

"Another alchemy contract?" I guessed.

"Better." Ruby grinned. "We'd like to work alongside you, forming a partnership of sorts. Not just for your alchemy potions, but research too. We have a space in our den just for you, and access to all our resources and supplies."

"Our pack would also like to extend a formal invitation for you to train your magic with us," Nan added. "There are very few outside of our pack who could teach you how to harness your lunar powers, and as you have done a service to us, we wish to repay you."

"I—I really don't know what to say."

Accepting an outsider was one thing, but sharing their knowledge? Unheard of.

Nan patted my arm. "Think about it. Right now, you should regain your strength. We'll guard your secrets and be there for you whenever you require assistance or support. Our race and the moon-blessed are one under the same Goddess."

Rubbing a hand across my face, I let out a dry laugh. "I feel like everyone knows what moon-blessed are except me."

"Or perhaps our aligned energies have drawn us together," Nan said with a gentle smile.

"Let's go with that," I chuckled. "I would love to take you up on both offers. It's more than I could ever ask for."

Nan, Ruby, and I kept talking until the healer appeared and herded me back into bed.

I never thought that after my life was torn apart, I would feel this anchored, this sure of the future I wanted.

For so long, uncertainty had been my only constant.

I'd almost forgotten that it was possible to look ahead and feel pure, unashamed excitement about what lay in my future.

Chapter Fifty-One

After four endless days, the MEA healers finally set me free. Rynac and Indra escorted me home, hovering until they ushered me into my apartment and ordered me to rest.

I didn't even try to resist.

My phone rang, and I brightened, sure the siblings were already checking up on me.

Then I saw the caller ID.

My brother.

The excitement knotted into something else.

"Hello Tobin," I answered with my customer service voice.

"Hi. How have you been?" he asked tentatively.

"Good." Which, to my surprise, was true. "Just a little tired."

"And . . . how are *things*?"

"Better. I believe I've got a permanent solution."

"Really? Nyssa, that's wonderful! I'm sorry for ever doubting you. All I ever wanted was to protect you."

"I know. We all make mistakes, even you, Tobin," I said, grinning.

His warm chuckle wrapped itself around me like one of his hugs.

"But you've always been there, doing everything you could to keep me safe. I love you, even when you annoy the hell out of me."

"I love you too, little sister. You'll have to share all the details when we visit."

"Visit?" My stomach dropped.

"Yeah, Dad wants us to come visit you before the summer solstice. He wants to see how you're doing. You know how he worries about his little girl in the big city."

"Ah, yes. Of course. That'll be great." Could I sound any less convincing?

"I'll call you again soon when we have set dates."

"Sounds wonderful," I said, internally screaming.

In a few months, my family would visit. Somehow, I had to figure out how to explain what I was and what had happened to me.

"Nyssa, take care of yourself."

"I will."

It wasn't like I meant to become involved with a dark witch, warlock, and demonspawn, or planned to thwart their attempt to harm the city.

Hanging up, I pushed those complications to the back burner. I think I'd earned a break from solving problems for at least a few days.

Grabbing *The Lunar Codex*, I glance over at Danika curled up on the couch.

"Want to get some moonlight?" I asked.

She was up in an instant, racing ahead as I clambered up the stairs.

By the time I reached the roof, my legs trembled, but the reassuring glow of the moon over my skin melted away the fatigue.

My chest throbbed in response to the pulse of magic within the codex, weaker than before, but that was to be expected.

It'd take time to regain strength after expending so much power.

The UMC healer had warned me not to test my magic for some time, fearing permanent damage.

But I knew the truth. It would be stronger than ever. I'd felt Selene's touch that night, her purpose had flowed through me.

I'd find my place soon enough.

Leaning against the railing, I looked out over Arkirith. The lights twinkled back as if welcoming me home.

Home. I guess this was my home now.

So much had happened in a few months, but I couldn't imagine living anywhere else. And after almost sacrificing everything to protect the city, I think it owed me.

Then again, it had already given me plenty.

Danika. *The Lunar Codex.* Awakening my magic. Divine Coffee. Rynac, Indra, and all my friends.

Never could I have imagined the chaotic transformation that would upend my world.

Now, I wanted to embrace this new life.

Shuffling over to my little setup, I eased down onto the pile of cushions.

I was thankful nothing was missing up here after the Inquisitors had ransacked my place.

Pulling open the codex, I wanted to learn more about my magic and what I was.

But as I opened it, a note fell out, written in Astrid's unmistakable script. My heart skipped a beat.

MAY SELENE LIGHT YOUR PATH AS YOU TAKE YOUR PLACE IN THE WORLD. ALWAYS REACH FOR THE STARS. SEARCH YOUR HEART, FOR IT KNOWS THE TRUTH. MAY YOU SHINE AS BRIGHT AS THE MAGIC WITHIN YOU.

The faint shimmer of Astrid's magic lingered on the paper, and I ached, missing the fleeting bond we had shared. I tucked it away.

It sounded too much like a goodbye.

I sighed, my gaze lifting to the moon overhead.

What path did Selene wish for me? What path did I want to walk?

I closed my eyes, brushing against the magic locked away in my core.

A soft breeze washed over me, whispering everything my heart knew. I smiled up at the moon, saying a silent thank you.

My fingers trailed over the mark of Selene on the back of my neck.

"I am Nyssa Thornheart," I whispered to the moon. "I'm your moon-blessed, your lunar witch. And I willingly devote myself to you. Thank you for this second chance."

CHAPTER FIFTY-TWO

"Nyssa, there's a customer asking after you," Zola called.

"I'll be right out," I said, dusting the flour off my hands.

Business had been booming of late. During my recovery, there was an enormous demand for my baking.

Now that I was back, I had extra orders to fill, many of them placed by enforcers and shifters, and a few delivered to the fairies of the park.

Despite attempts to keep it quiet, news had spread of my involvement in rescuing the missing people and defeating the warlock two weeks ago.

Beylin and Zola had created a fundraiser, auctioning off my cookies to raise money for those taken by the warlock. Now I had a ton of baking to do, but for a fantastic cause.

"Don't over bake those," I called over my shoulder to the ovens. "No one likes dry brownies."

The oven doors clacked in response, and I was sure if they'd had eyes, they would've rolled them at me.

As I headed into the front-of-house, the rich aroma of coffee and the idle chatter of customers surrounded me. I really had missed it here.

"Who was looking—" I started, but my words fell away.

I took in the profile of the lone customer waiting, two boxes of cookies sitting on the counter in front of him. He had been looking over the cafe, the sharp line of his jaw silhouetted by the afternoon sun streaming through the windows.

He turned at the sound of my voice. Too many emotions jumbled through my head as Kaelan's bright green gaze landed on me.

A faint smile tugged at the corner of his mouth.

I attempted to brush more of the flour off my apron, conscious of how I appeared even as annoyance rose within me.

"What are you doing here?" I asked, more harshly than I had intended.

Guess I was more pissed off than I realized.

"I wanted to see you," he said. "And I hoped being in public and buying cookies would appease your anger at our disappearance."

Behind him, the two other nephilim sat at a table. Astrid waved while Nathaniel offered me a mock salute.

It was a relief to see them, but my annoyance hadn't subsided yet.

"Go on then," I said, crossing my arms.

"I can't explain everything here," he said. "We got into a lot of trouble with our superiors for, well, everything. They seized all our phones, but I wanted to give you this in person."

Kaelan held out my necklace, and I scooped it up.

"They confiscated it, but I struck some deals to retrieve it. I'm sorry I almost lost it after you entrusted it to me."

"Thank you," I said, looping it around my neck, the warmth of the stone a reassuring presence against my skin. "I'm sorry for the trouble you went through because of me."

Kaelan shrugged. "It's nothing, but we must return to our base in Orillian."

"Oh."

The small flicker of hope guttered in my chest. Orillian was on the east coast, a five-hour flight away.

"When do you leave?"

"We're heading to the airport now. I wanted to stop by and . . . well, the necklace."

"Right, well, thanks for returning it," I said, summoning my customer service smile. "I should get back to work. Have a safe flight."

"Wait," he said before I could turn away. "The Order will be out this way to deal with . . . you know."

I winced. Though I hadn't seen the gigantic crater that had been Carmen's lair, I'd caused it.

"It wasn't your fault," Kaelan whispered.

"I kind of think it was," I huffed with a humorless laugh.

His mouth twisted as if trying to hold back what he really wanted to say. "I know you don't want to join the Order, but when I'm back, I'd be more than happy to train with you. Or we could just hang out?"

I frowned. Was he nervous?

"You can say no, I'll understand. I just wanted to—"

"Sure," I said, cutting off his rambling. "I'd like that."

"Great." Kaelan flashed me a grin, his eyes brightening. "Until then."

He gathered up the cookies and joined the other angel-born as they headed out of Divine.

"Don't tell me you're warming up to the nephilim," Voren said, resting an arm on my shoulder as we watched them disappear out of view.

"Stranger things have happened," I said with a smirk.

My grin lingered as I headed back to the kitchen, the necklace a reassuring weight against my chest.

Even as I began portioning out my next batch of cookies, the nephilim occupied a decent portion of my thoughts.

How had everything changed so rapidly?

My fingers brushed over the smooth stone, and a tingle of the magic within buzzed over my skin.

The stench of sulfur and iron assaulted me; screams rent the air as shadows shifted and I flinched, hunting for the threat.

"Nyssa?" Danika's concerned voice cut through everything.

Gasping for air, I scanned the kitchen, my heart pounding.

Empty. Nothing was here.

The lights above pulsed as if Divine wanted to reassure me.

I'm okay. Just . . . spooked myself.

"You went through something traumatic—"

It will take time, I know.

How many times had I been told that over the past few weeks?

I'm fine, I reassured, but the lie sounded weak even to my own ears.

Potent magic pulsed again, my own responding in kind, and it was an effort not to shudder.

There were no shadows here, and yet I couldn't shake the feeling of eyes watching me.

Waiting.

***

Nyssa's adventure is far from over. A connection has been forged, *and more danger is to come.* Will *Nyssa and Danika be ready for the next threat?*

Find out in **Forged In Moonlight.** *Grab a copy today!*

FROM THE AUTHOR

Thank you so much for reading!

If you enjoyed this book, please consider leaving a review to help more readers discover it.

Do you want to know exactly what happened on Rynac and Voren's date?

To grab your bonus scene, **head to sfhenne.com/book1bonus**

This will also add you to my newsletter where you can get a deeper insight into this world, be the first to read new stories, and learn more about this series and when the next book will be out.

Thank you to my fantastic beta and ARC readers! Your feedback has made this novel shine and I couldn't have done it without you.

A big hug and thank you to my author BBF's who are always there to encourage and support me when I need it. Laura, Jay, Poppy, Konstance, and Marsha, I love you guys.

And last, but not least, thank you to my family for all of their support and understanding. Thanks for putting up with me.